LENNY MARKS GETS AWAY WITH MURDER

LENNY MARKS GETS AWAY WITH MURDER

KERRYN MAYNE

ST. MARTIN'S PRESS
NEW YORK

First published in the United States by St. Martin's Press,
an imprint of St. Martin's Publishing Group

LENNY MARKS GETS AWAY WITH MURDER Copyright © 2023 by Kerryn Mayne.
All rights reserved. Printed in the United States of America. For information, address
St. Martin's Publishing Group, 120 Broadway, New York, NY 10271.

www.stmartins.com

The Library of Congress Cataloging-in-Publication data is available upon request.

ISBN 978-1-250-34010-8 (hardcover)
ISBN 978-1-250-34011-5 (ebook)

Our books may be purchased in bulk for promotional, educational, or business use.
Please contact your local bookseller or the Macmillan Corporate and Premium Sales
Department at 1-800-221-7945, extension 5442, or by email at
MacmillanSpecialMarkets@macmillan.com.

Originally published in Australia in 2023 by Bantam

First U.S. Edition: 2024

For my mum, Heather,
who surrounded us with books

LENNY MARKS GETS AWAY WITH MURDER

CHAPTER 1

Monday, May 16, 2022

Lenny Marks seldom found herself unprepared. Lessons for her grade five students were religiously compiled a fortnight in advance, her tax return would be ready to submit no later than the fifteenth of July every year and her home fire escape plan was reviewed and updated each summer. Lenny knew the location of both of Selby South Primary School's defibrillators and exactly how to use them, she serviced her bicycle regularly to keep it in prime shape and carried a bottle opener on her set of keys despite never—as yet—needing it. She found tremendous peace in this level of organization, which was as close to happiness as Lenny Marks ever planned to be. Happiness, she knew, was unstable and quite unreliable. And Lenny was neither of those things. Instead she aimed for the contentment of a routine, which had served her quite well up to and into her thirty-seventh year.

And still, despite knowing exactly what her Monday morning should contain, Lenny now found herself under the unexpected and interrogating gaze of Mrs. Finlay, office administration. The clock had barely ticked over 8 A.M. and Lenny had only just turned her teapot the requisite three times—the way her grandmother had taught her, despite it apparently not making a jot of difference to the taste—when Mrs. Finlay bustled in to disturb the good order of things.

"So, is it a secret husband?" Mrs. Finlay asked, eyes alarmingly wide and voice predictably loud.

"Is what?" Lenny asked.

"Well, it's addressed to Helena Winters. And I didn't know who that was. A mistake, I thought, and was going to send it back *return to sender*. But Lora said, 'That's no mistake, that's Lenny Marks.'"

Lenny read the front of the envelope: *Helena Winters*. A name from long ago and of a girl she thought she'd left well and truly behind.

She didn't reply, which failed to slow Mrs. Finlay. Lenny cast her eyes around, hoping the other occupants of the staff room were not listening. It was fairly clear they were. Or at least Kirra Reid, grade four, was. Kirra dallied over the instant hot water tap a few moments too long. It was instant hot water after all, and there was no need to wait for it to boil; it wasn't a lengthy task. Deidre Heffernan, grade two, on the other hand, was poring over the form guide—as per usual—and had not even registered there were other people in the same space as her.

"And I thought to myself, I never knew Lenny was married. How interesting. Isn't it?"

"Isn't what?"

"That you've been married."

"I haven't," Lenny replied, lowering her voice. Lenny deplored other people knowing her business and felt anxiety growing at the thought of being the subject of office scuttlebutt.

"So why the different name then? I've racked my brain all weekend trying to figure it out."

Lenny hesitated, hoping she had a quick-witted, reasonable answer that didn't invite more questions. She didn't and quick-wittedness had never been her thing. Perhaps she should've claimed a secret husband she didn't have. Mrs. Finlay, not one to be deterred, changed tack.

"*And* it's from the Parole Board, just when I thought I had you all figured out. I said to Lora, 'She's an enigma that one, isn't she?'"

Lenny ran her fingers over the smoothness of the envelope. *Adult Parole Board Victoria* was emblazoned proudly in the top right corner, as if this was a regular and not at all concerning place from which to receive mail. It was clear, even to Lenny, who often found social nuances hard to decipher, what Mrs. Finlay was up to. She was meddling, hoping Lenny would spill all after a few pointed questions. But little did Mrs. Finlay know, Lenny had nothing to disclose. The letter was unexpected and she didn't intend to indulge Mrs. Finlay's nosiness with speculation about what it may contain. And she was absolutely not going to open it, not in front of Mrs. Finlay and possibly not at all. Lenny's curiosity didn't push her to explore the unknown; she was more than happy to retreat to what she knew and forget what she didn't.

She was good at forgetting, most of the time. Thoughts of Fergus Sullivan, for example, were normally pushed to the furthest corners of her memory. Now his image was disturbingly front and center. It made no sense whatsoever. It had been over twenty years since she'd seen her stepfather and surely she would be the least likely person to need to know anything about him. But what else could possibly be in that envelope?

Fergus Sullivan.

You did this.

When she did think of Fergus, which was as little as possible, her skin turned hot with the memory of the stifling garden shed, the last place she'd seen him. *You did this.* Three words, three syllables, a mere eighteen points on a Scrabble board. And yet infuriatingly unforgettable.

"I love true crime, you know, I listen to all the podcasts. When

I'm out on my after-dinner walks, I pop the headphones on and off I go, thinking maybe I'll solve this one."

Mrs. Finlay was particularly hard to tune out; her voice had a pitch and rasp that made it impossible to ignore. Lenny was usually able to distance and calm herself by rearranging words, and yet Mrs. Finlay kept breaking through and interrupting her anagrams.

Mrs. Finlay: rainfly, family, flimsy, snarly, mails, fail, liar

The letters would move around in a manner that was as involuntary as sneezing. She'd done it ever since she could remember and it was the easiest way to calm her thoughts or shut them off.

"My Frank says to me, 'Jeannie, you'll end up *on* one of those podcasts the way you block your ears up like that. Anyone could sneak up behind you.' And I just laugh, he's such a fuddy-duddy, but wouldn't that be ironic? Woman murdered listening to story about murder."

Mrs. Finlay guffawed in the way of someone who had never had anything bad happen to them, and therefore thought horrific crimes were fascinating.

"Did you get my work order, Jeannie?" Kirra asked from across the table, cutting off Mrs. Finlay, whose open mouth indicated she was poised and ready to carry on her cross-examination.

Mrs. Finlay turned to Kirra, and Lenny remembered to breathe. She was thankful for the reprieve, although it was incredibly poor manners of Kirra to interrupt.

"What's that, Mrs. Reid?"

"I put one in for the sink last week, the one in here's not draining properly. And it's still not. Hopefully the work order I put in hasn't got lost? Like the last one?"

"Oh." Mrs. Finlay hesitated. "Of course not. It's just hard to get a plumber in. Tradesmen can be incredibly unreliable, you know."

"Yes, they can. Unreliability is a particularly annoying trait," Kirra said. Mrs. Finlay checked her watch and Kirra took the opportunity to shoot Lenny a wink. Lenny wasn't sure what the wink implied, but she wasn't a fan of them in general. They always seemed so unnatural and a little slimy.

"Anyway, ladies, I must go, I've got other mail to attend to." Mrs. Finlay stood up and Lenny realized the downside of not ever disclosing her home address—even on official paperwork—was the opportunity it presented for exactly this sort of prying.

Lenny held the envelope, moving her thumb over the printed name in the clear window, just in case it wiped it away. Unsurprisingly, it didn't. Lenny pulled her satchel around from where it hung on the back of her chair and drove the letter deep inside. There was the unlikely, but faint, chance it might just disappear, Narnia-style, out the other side and no longer be her problem.

You did this.

By 8:15 the staff room was a hive of activity and the urge to leave was overwhelming. Lenny told herself that as soon as her tea was done, she could escape. She had the same internal negotiation most school mornings and was usually able to convince herself to stay put. At some point she assumed it would seem easier and perhaps she'd even initiate the conversations.

But this morning was different. Thoughts of Fergus were looming and hard to ignore, her shins felt sharp with anxiety and she couldn't even distract herself with her anagrams.

Fergus Sullivan: frailness, slavering, gainless, argues, evil

"Lenny, are you with us this morning?" Yvonne Gillespie asked. Lenny hadn't noticed her come in. Gregory Schwartz was in the staff room now too; his arrival time was always haphazard, a trait Lenny found disconcerting. He had a habit of slurping his morning cereal and Lenny preferred to be packed up and off to her classroom before he poured his cornflakes.

"Good morning, Yvonne," Lenny said, hoping Yvonne wouldn't regale her with one of her weekend monologues. It was always hard to slip out once she started. Not to mention, Yvonne's stories were notoriously boring.

Yvonne was also Lenny's number one suspect for tea theft. On more than one occasion, despite clearly Dymo-labeling her belongings so their ownership could never be mistaken, Lenny had found her tin of tea leaves a few scoops short. She hadn't mentioned her suspicions, not wanting to appear confrontational.

Thankfully Yvonne didn't start on a weekend story, giving Lenny the opportunity to depart. She tipped the remains of her tea into the sink, noticing it was indeed backed up, as Kirra had pointed out, and then put her things away in her drawer—which was also clearly labeled with her name. Perhaps Yvonne needed to get her glasses prescription checked. Or else she was really just a thief.

She heard Greg splashing milk into his bowl, and Trudi Kerr, music and arts, walked in with her normal Monday chirpiness. Lenny was at her limit for polite interactions and pleasantries and knew it was time to go. No point pushing herself; she had made significant progress in the past few weeks and was quite complimentary in her self-evaluations.

Lenny hadn't found it easy to make friends, but Fay, her foster mum, had been insistent that she try.

After Fay had caught her in a rare emotional outburst over Easter, Lenny had been cornered into one of those revealing conversations that she prided herself on avoiding. She was never quite right in the school holidays. Even fifteen years into teaching, she still couldn't get used to the times when she didn't have the bell to structure her day. She would always ensure there were a couple of house projects on the go, but even then she could never shake the feeling of being lost during the term breaks.

So she told Fay she was lonely. She meant it at the time, although it felt clunky and unnatural to say, even to her foster mum whom she was almost always honest with. It had never occurred to her before that particular moment that she was *lonely*. Although she knew the only text messages she got were scams or appointment reminders, and even they were few and far between of late. Lenny didn't have friends, she had acquaintances. Like the man who delivered her chicken pad thai each Saturday night, or Ned at the grocery store. She saw her colleagues daily, but didn't know a thing about them outside the school perimeter and was likely to avoid them if she saw them on the other side of the fence.

Of course she regretted her outburst as soon as the words were out of her mouth. Fay, true to form, insisted she take action, even delivering an ultimatum: make some friends (*it's time to get a life, Lenny-girl*) or go and speak to a psychologist (*it's time to get some help*). It really just made her shins ache.

It was not the first time this had come up with Fay. There had been cause to discuss this very topic at various life intervals: high school, university, then over the years while teaching. And Lenny had, in fact, had friends along the way—of sorts. Like Caroline Gordon, who taught at Selby South for eight of the years Lenny had. Together they shared quiet lunchtimes and polite, impersonal conversations, never asking each other "what are you up to tonight?" (because it was never much). Occasionally they'd meet up at the library for a game of Scrabble. It was a pleasant companionship she found with Caroline, who was in her fifties when Lenny met her. But two years ago, Caroline had moved back to New South Wales to support her elderly mother. They promised they'd keep in touch although it was never the sort of friendship that would survive outside of a shared workplace. They hadn't found cause to visit one another when they lived three suburbs apart, so it was extremely unlikely they would with a state border in between.

Caroline's departure was the start of a staff turnover at Selby

South. Two teachers retired, another moved and one went to a private college closer to Melbourne—the thought of the bustling traffic and towering buildings made Lenny shudder. This heralded the arrival of a new band of colleagues at the start of the school year, including Kirra and the prep teachers.

Once she'd wiped her tears and digested her outburst, Lenny realized perhaps she really was lonely. And saying it out loud, intentionally or not, meant that now Fay would push her. The challenge was set and Lenny was an outwardly reluctant, inwardly hopeful participant in Fay's plan. Perhaps she could, once and for all, get a life.

Choosing two of the new teachers, Amy Cleary and Ashleigh Burton, as her friendship targets had been a matter of simple deduction. She removed the too-old: Trudi Kerr and Deidre Heffernan; and the intolerable: Gregory Schwartz. She didn't consider Yvonne Gillespie for obvious reasons (her thievery) and Lora Pham, as principal, was too intimidating. There was Kirra Reid, but she wasn't quite sure what to make of her—a not unusual problem for Lenny Marks. And besides, it was hard not to covet friendship with the young, effortlessly personable prep leaders, Amy and Ashleigh. They wore bright colors and sparkly earrings and oozed confidence.

She gauged her progress with Amy and Ashleigh as significant, having been asked to cover their yard duty on no less than three occasions. She felt an out-of-school-hours invite was imminent; perhaps they'd even exchange phone numbers.

This was equal parts thrilling and terrifying. It was one thing to have someone's phone number, but what on earth would she do with it? Amy and Ashleigh were as tight-knit as Monica and Rachel, and Lenny hoped to soon be their Phoebe.

"How was your weekend, Lenny?" Trudi Kerr asked as Lenny swung her satchel over her shoulder. It somehow felt weightier now it held the letter, which she knew was ridiculous.

"Fine. It was fine," Lenny said briskly as she turned to leave. She didn't believe in redundant goodbyes, she would see these people at different points during the day and there was no obvious need for her to say hello and goodbye on each of those occasions.

She was disappointed not to have seen either Ashleigh or Amy as yet, although this was not entirely unexpected. They both had a tendency to arrive so close to the morning bell they'd have to dash from their respective cars to their classrooms. That sort of on-edge existence was something Lenny would never be comfortable with, but they managed to make it look spontaneous in a good way. She would have to catch up with them at first recess.

Lenny hurried out of the staff room and toward her classroom, looking forward to the morning bell, twenty-three sets of grade five eyes and the comfort of her preplanned morning maths lesson.

CHAPTER 2

Every weekday at 4 P.M., and never before, Lenny ensured her blackboard was clean and her classroom was straightened before heading home. She would unlock her mint green Polygon Zenith and ride the twenty-one minutes to her Tree House—which was not actually in a tree as the name may suggest. Lenny still felt a thrill when the wind buffeted her ears and threw her hair behind her as she rode. It felt like flying and she looked into cars as she whisked past them, feeling sorry for the occupants, who might not know how cathartic it was to be uncontained. Even on the days when the rain stung her bare skin like darts being hurled, she still revelled in it.

Two afternoons a week—always Mondays and Thursdays unless there was a public holiday—she would ride out of her way to the little cluster of shops set well back from the main shopping strip of Belgrave to purchase her groceries. She was a regular customer at McKnight's General Store; however, her patronage was less about loyalty and more due to the shop's proximity (hardly out of her way), lack of noise (they played no "background" music) and age (Lenny struggled to feel at ease with the modern lines and minimalist features of many new buildings).

Ned at McKnight's was one of the few people outside of work she counted as an acquaintance. Calling him a friend would've been far too ambitious, but regardless, she always enjoyed the repartee with Ned, son of *the* Mr. McKnight whose family name was proudly emblazoned over the entrance. She found herself looking forward to her twice-weekly visits and the possibility of seeing Ned's bespectacled, black-stubbled face appearing from behind the deli counter or arrangement of thirty percent off Weet-Bix boxes. He had been too brash for her liking when she first met him; he'd turned heads exclaiming over a Sunnydale High School patch sewn onto her satchel. Eyes wide, he'd asked her whether she thought Faith or Buffy was the better Slayer. She explained, with minimal detail to disguise her lack of knowledge, why she thought it was Faith. They'd been on first-name terms ever since. She never explained to him that Fay bought her an eclectic range of TV-show-inspired sew-on patches and she'd liked the colors on the Sunnydale High one the best, and that was the sole basis of using it on her bag. She wasn't much of a fan until that conversation with Ned. After it, though, she'd made sure to become well accustomed with Buffy and her gang of misfits so she could hold her own in any future conversations. Lenny refused to analyze her desire to impress Ned with her Slayer familiarity.

McKnight's General Store was a quaint Dandenongs institution. The green and cream gabled roofline sat comfortably between the community library and a residence that would have been more suitably placed in the English countryside. The front of the store was always, assuredly, set up in the same manner. A row of newspaper and magazine covers lined the footpath, encased in little metal cages to keep them proudly upright. A red postbox was conveniently placed by the door and a mix of woven baskets hung from a rope under the awnings. Lenny couldn't recall ever seeing one of the baskets replaced, let alone sold, and was of the mind they were more a fixture of the store than inventory. A shingle hung above the door announcing they'd been in business since 1955. She guessed the decorating hadn't been updated since, although the window-panes always sparkled and the stock was never dusty or neglected.

She propped her bicycle next to the store and diligently locked it. She wouldn't be long but there was no accounting for the opportunism of thieves. The local paper informed her there had been an increase in thefts that went, so they reported, hand in hand with a surge in cannabis availability. Lenny had no desire to add to these statistics by providing a would-be thief, and a drug-addicted one no less, the easy pinch of her primary mode of transport.

The doorbell jingled as she entered and she was greeted by a giant smile from Ned, who was standing behind McKnight's lone register. There were no customers with him and he looked actually quite delighted by her arrival—or perhaps she'd imagined that.

"Lennnnnnny, you'll never guess what I just got," Ned crowed as he bustled toward her. He was loud and she noticed heads turned as he boomed across the small grocery store. She blushed involuntarily at the attention he was drawing but met him halfway in any case, hoping as she gained proximity to him that he would drop a few decibels. He did not.

"Would I be able to guess?" she asked.

"No, never. Look." He pulled an oversized smartphone from his pocket and tapped away on it madly with his thumbs. He found what he was scrolling for and proudly faced the screen toward her.

"Coming from the States so I don't have it yet but whaddya reckon?"

A lady with a half-filled shopping basket brushed against Lenny's arm and she prickled at the unexpected touch. She backed up against the diced tomato tins to avoid any further contact from inconsiderate shoppers with little spatial awareness.

"Mr. Pointy," Ned said, barely containing his glee. "The *actual* one, touched by *the* Sarah Michelle Gellar. Given to Buffy by Kendra in season two, episode twenty-one. *That* one."

His screen displayed the listing, with a bright green "successful bidder" banner above it and a slideshow of photographs of Mr. Pointy, the infamous stake used by Buffy to dispatch many a vampire. It also revealed the cost and although she never would have asked, she couldn't help reeling at the hefty price tag.

He noticed. "It's an investment, you know. This stuff is priceless."

It was his money and his business what he spent it on; she had no intention of dampening his spirits or dispensing financial advice.

"What a find! There will be some disappointed fans who missed out on that one."

"I know, I've already posted that I got it and there's some haters out there. *And* someone has already offered me double for it." He considered the possibility. "I just hope it doesn't get lost in the post."

"Or seized at customs as a weapon."

He obviously hadn't thought of this. "Would they do that?"

"Oh, no," she hurried to reassure him, "it's clearly not a weapon. It's memorabilia."

She wondered why she had rained on his parade. Despite knowing importation of weapons was frowned upon by Australia's Border Force, a television prop would hardly be considered a risk to national security. Why some things rolled out of her mouth in the fashion they did she was never quite sure. It happened often in the company of Ned; something about him did manage to make her a tad discombobulated.

Discombobulated: combustible, bombilated, modulate, adieu, edit

"You'll have to bring it in and show me when you get it," she said, hoping to move on from her inconsiderate comment.

"Oh, no *way* it's coming in here. But you should come by and see it. I've wanted to show you my collection for ages. My girlfriend is mightily unimpressed. I don't think she realized the gravity of my deep-seated geekiness until she saw all my stuff."

Lenny hadn't known Ned had a girlfriend, not that it was the sort of conversation she would ever have thought appropriate to broach. She couldn't help but feel a little crestfallen. She had no right to be disappointed and yet it felt exactly like that.

Crestfallen: cleanser, reflects, careens, falters, fester, secret

"Oh, yes. Maybe we can do that. At some point. But I should really get going. Do you know if eggplants are on special? I need one."

It was a poor attempt at redirecting the conversation, but it did the job. She most certainly did not need an eggplant—nor did she know where to start to cook one—but they were in her line of sight, and therefore the first thing to come out of her mouth.

"Oh, nah, they're not. But the olives are and I know how much you love the lime-infused kalamatas."

With a careful balance of groceries between the front handlebars and the rear rack, Lenny cycled home.

She analyzed her conversation with Ned as she pedalled, chastising herself for her inability to just have a *normal* exchange with someone. Her social ineptitude never failed to disappoint her, no matter how old she got. At thirty-seven she should have been used to her own quirks. The analysis that followed almost any conversation was exhausting. She would rehash something again and again until she'd dissected it like a year nine science project. If she kept putting her proverbial foot in it, she would have to find an alternative place to purchase her weekly supplies, even though the thought made her queasy. On the most recent of her rare trips into the Belgrave Hills IGA, they'd used the intercom so frequently and at such a volume she'd thought someone was yelling at her down an aisle. She abandoned her trolley and left through a fire exit, which triggered an alarm. She didn't look back and knew she wouldn't return.

Arriving home never failed to delight Lenny. The descent down her driveway was almost a meditative experience. Not that she involved herself with nonsense such as meditation. It was a place where Lenny felt completely and totally at home, which was entirely fitting given that was exactly what it was.

Her house had already been christened the Tree House by its previous owners. Lenny found this misleading because it wasn't in a tree, nor did it resemble the child-size tree house that might spring to mind at mention of the name. It was, however, surrounded by mammoth mountain ash and sat high on its sloping block, perhaps giving some the idea it was just another tree rising from the ground. This was not Lenny's impression; it looked like a full-size house to her, but she liked the hand-painted sign beside the door and felt there was no harm in the house retaining its name. It was her favorite place in the whole wide world, not that she'd explored very much of the whole wide world. Lenny brought her shopping inside and double-locked the door behind her. She would check it at least eight more times before she went to bed.

Shoes off at the door and slippers on; they were exactly where she'd left them that morning. In fact, nothing had moved in the house: it was gratifyingly the same. She unpacked the groceries and tipped the kalamata olives directly into the bin. She put the container on the sink to wash for the recycling. Weeks ago, Ned had raved about them and she'd been so infected by his enthusiasm, she'd bought some. She'd positively hated them, despite telling him otherwise. She'd made two more obligatory purchases of them since and both lots ended up in the same final resting place. It was a small price to pay to avoid a conversation to explain why she'd lied in the first place.

The house was very much Lenny, which was to say it was homely and thoughtful but not inspired by any home and garden sort of magazine. She was not inclined to decorate and bought things as and when she needed them. She didn't have throw pillows, because her couch came with perfectly comfortable cushions of its own. She'd chosen her rugs because the hardwood floorboards were cold in winter, not because she'd seen them on a season of *The Block*. Which she didn't watch in any case, as the competitiveness caused her angst. Everything in the Tree House belonged somewhere, and if it wasn't needed it was no longer kept. Her bookshelf held books: no trinkets, knickknacks or photo frames. Errol was the exception Lenny made to discarding items of no practical use. He'd accompanied her to each house she traveled through in her childhood: Mum's, her grandmother's and Fay's. Although he was a teddy, he wasn't the sort children were allowed to play with. And now he sat on Lenny's bookshelf, keeping watch as he'd always done.

He'd seen a lot, that bear; he knew what she knew and he was good at keeping secrets.

Lenny patted Errol's tufty head and noticed one of her *Hobbit*s was farther back than the others; she pulled it into alignment, running her fingers over their spines. She owned thirty-six copies, of varying editions, and considered each and every one of them necessary. On this occasion they were arranged by publication date, so their heights were haphazard. Previously it was by height, and before that in colors, which was quite pleasing to the eye.

The house was quiet, which she fixed quickly with a few clicks of the remote; *Friends* lit up the screen. Lenny didn't watch the news, limiting her intake of the happenings of the world to the *Herald Sun* in the staff room and the local newspaper she picked up for free at McKnight's each Thursday. It was how she knew about the spate of thefts, which was useful information, but generally the news was more depressing than anything else. Sometimes she didn't even bother with the *Herald Sun* at work because if she didn't read it by lunchtime, Mrs. Finlay would have defaced it by scrawling all over the puzzle pages. Given it was a shared paper, Lenny found this the epitome of rudeness. Mrs. Finlay, it appeared, gave it considerably less thought and happily slurped her instant coffee while filling in the crossword to the best of her ability (not very able at all).

Friends was Lenny's favorite company. Except Ross, who could sometimes grate on her with his neuroses. She sat on the couch, letting the canned laughter fill her lounge room. Her conversation with Ned started to fade to a dull yet still embarrassing thud and the letter Mrs. Finlay had given her was now just a hazy rectangle of little importance. She really should open that letter, but nothing would change between now and tomorrow.

She'd read it the next day with fresh eyes.

It was probably addressed to the wrong person. Except Helena Winters wasn't a common name. And maybe it *was* about Fergus; perhaps it would reveal where he and her mum had gone. She attempted to re-create Tammy Winters's face in her mind, but struggled to define the features. Would she recognize her mother now? Tammy certainly wouldn't recognize her, because Lenny was not eleven years old anymore. They might have walked past each other and been none the wiser.

Maybe, if they were reunited, they could laugh about those sorts of possibilities. Maybe. She rubbed her right thigh, the one where a silvery scar ran in a long straight line. Sometimes it tingled, although she was quite sure that was her imagination. Fergus had been furious at her that day, and rightly so. She'd caused quite a fuss. *His* face, unlike her mum's, was easy to conjure. Reddened, nostrils flaring and spit showering from his mouth as he yelled as if she'd injured herself on purpose. Lenny had always been clumsy and really should have been more careful.

Tonight was not the time to read that letter.

Lenny only needed approximately fifteen minutes to prepare her dinner in its entirety, food being another aspect of life she refused to complicate. She could follow a recipe, or at least believed she could, given she was able to construct a pergola from the ground up. Surely the assembly of a bouillabaisse or fresh gnocchi wasn't any more complicated. But she just didn't see the point. It was an exercise in futility. A meal, regardless of how lavishly prepared, would not last the better part of fifteen minutes. Whereas her pergola was still standing and worthy of the weeks of planning, marking out and bicycle trips to Bunnings.

Monday and Wednesday were pasta (one packet of cheese and spinach ravioli would be enough for two separate dinners), Tuesday was always a toasted sandwich (cheese and tomato, cheese and ham or occasionally cheese and baked beans), Thursday was quiche (McKnight's sold them in four-packs) and Fridays were soup—tinned of course; she had no reason to think she could outdo the Heinz recipes. Sundays were lasagne, which she bought conveniently frozen in a box from McKnight's, although often she was so full from her fortnightly lunch at Fay's she didn't even bother to turn the oven on. That left Saturday as her night off cooking. Although calling her dinner preparation "cooking" was a bit of a stretch. It was more just a night off reheating, but she did enjoy having chicken pad thai from Joey's Nice Thai in Belgrave delivered right to her door. For years the same man had delivered her food and their interactions were practically set in stone. She would have the correct money ready to hand him, they would have an almost identical conversation on each occasion and he would always end it with "stay out of trouble" on his way back to his car. She was affronted the first time he said it, as if he thought she was up to no good, but grew to understand he was not implying impropriety on her part. Which was lucky, because she enjoyed their pad thai and had no interest in riding her bike in the dark to collect it. Joey (she assumed the delivery man himself was Joey, although never asked) was one of her out-of-work acquaintances, much like Ned. Whether Joey considered her one or not was never addressed and she'd never ascertained where he stood on the matter of who was the best Slayer.

Lenny's existence was many things: simple, predictable and uneventful. It had taken considerable effort and time to get to this point and she was not planning on disrupting the perfectly good order of things.

Routine: inert, ruin, rut

Contented: contend, endnote, conned

She ate her ravioli at the dining table. She always set out her cutlery, placemat and glass as she had done ever since her early teens when she'd gone to live with Fay and Robert Marks. This was one of the house rules at the Markses' home and was instilled in each new arrival right from the start. From where she sat she could keep watching Rachel, who was trying to cover up that she'd bought furniture from Pottery Barn and fooled Phoebe for the most part. They were easy dinner company; she never needed to cook for them or make polite chit-chat.

At 8 P.M., the dishes sat draining on the side of the sink. As dishes go, there were very few, certainly not enough to run the dishwasher, despite there being a top-of-the-line Smeg in her kitchen. After some internet research, she'd installed it herself. It was hardly worth getting a plumber in for such a straightforward job. However, since then, the most use she got out of it was the cleaning cycle she ran once a month to ensure it was in good working order. She wiped down the table, packed the placemat away and sat again;

this time opening up the Scrabble box and laying out the two tile racks and board as per usual. She always played with Monica because of all the Friends Monica would be the toughest challenger.

She would never dishonor her system by favoring her own tiles over Monica's; she systematically played the best possible moves, even if it would thwart the next turn. She knew she could play online, but she didn't like the idea of not being able to touch the tiles. Their smooth, cool corners were comforting.

Monica drew the highest tile and started the game.

Gluier: fourteen points

Lenny played her first word quickly.

Enamor: twenty-two points

And on they went: Lenny shifting from one chair to another to face the tiles she was playing; Monica appearing occasionally on the screen with a quip or nagging about cleaning something. Lenny absorbed it all as she moved the tiles on their racks.

The light was long gone from the sky outside her windows. The Tree House was on a street where no streetlights were installed, as was the norm in the Dandenong Ranges. The moon glimmering caught the tops of the trees and Lenny could see them dancing outside her lounge-room windows. The sound of their leaves scratching and rustling as they rocked backward and forward was a comforting soundtrack to her game.

Her hand drifted to the scar on her leg. She pressed into it, as if there was a chance it would still hurt all these years later. Of course it didn't, but it was her forever reminder of how clumsy she had been. But there was a sense of panic with it now, as if she'd got it out of order somehow. Why was Fergus so mad at her for injuring herself? Or was he mad *before* she hurt herself? And she'd wanted to get to her mum: to get help, or to help her. One or the other. But which was it? So much blood and the handle wouldn't turn. Lenny was trapped, and her leg hurt.

The credits music rolled, louder than the show itself had been, which snapped Lenny from her thoughts. She was still in her Tree House and drew in a deep breath. She reached for the comfort of her Scrabble bag and dug her hand into the cool tiles. The loud second hand on the clock in the kitchen ticked comfortingly. She was okay.

CHAPTER 3

Thursday, May 19

The letter reappeared on Thursday, falling from Lenny's bag as she pulled out her water bottle while the students concentrated on their current topic, prominent Australian citizens. It would appear the letter was not happy at being disregarded. It wanted to be found and it wanted to be read.

Adult Parole Board Victoria.

She pushed it back into her bag; it was inappropriate to be poring over personal correspondence in work time. She would open it as soon as she got home that evening and it would no doubt be something mundane and generic. A survey perhaps: *are you satisfied with our parolees?* Which was a yes from Lenny as they'd caused her no problems whatsoever.

As the bell announced lunchtime she dismissed her students, giving the stragglers the hurry-up to get out in the fresh air. It was especially cold and she'd insisted they wear their parkas; even Tom Campbell, who was only ever in a pair of shorts and a t-shirt. He'd dragged his feet and protested, but eventually zipped himself into his navy-blue jacket. There was no doubt he'd strip it off once he was out of her eyeline but at least she'd tried.

Lenny preferred to eat at her desk, but Fay suggested one of the easiest ways of naturally socializing would be spending breaks in the staff room. That way she was already speaking to people she had something in common with—teaching, she presumed Fay meant—and there was a time limit. She could literally be saved by the bell. Lenny created a mental list of topics for just these situations: weather, Aussie Rules football and the current exhibition at the National Gallery. She hadn't been, nor would she, but knew it to be van Gogh and could offer a few insights into post-impressionism or the loss of his ear. He had, in fact, died at thirty-seven, the same age she was now. Surely that was a fun bit of trivia to spark a conversation while she waited for her minestrone to heat through.

When she walked in she was glad to see the prep teachers. Amy was dominating the conversation, as was often the case, and Lenny wondered if she'd ever feel comfortable being that forthright in a group. Probably not. Amy had the attention of the staff seated around the table and Lenny subtly tuned in while remaining focused on the poster in front of her. "Cover your food and clean after using!" Lenny always felt the use of the exclamation mark to be excessive.

Lenny surmised the topic of conversation from hearing a few words: "trivia," "boyfriend" and then a shrill "*so* much fun!" Perhaps Amy was the creator of the microwave sign, as she seemed to use exclamation marks at the end of most of her sentences.

Within Lenny the desire to turn around battled with the need to somehow disguise herself as part of the linoleum floor. It was coming, she knew it, and now she was about to be invited to the place where Amy was planning on having *so much fun*. This was great, she would have plenty to tell Fay, and yet she was hoping for a little more time to prepare herself.

"At seven? Or should we meet a little earlier?" Trudi Kerr asked.

The voices grew hushed, but with her back to them she couldn't tell why.

"I'll message you the details," Amy said quietly.

"And are you guys eating there though?"

"Trudi," Amy said, her tone flattened. "Talk later."

Lenny caught sight of Amy's reflection in the microwave glass. Her eyebrows were raised and her head was on an angle. For a flash, she thought maybe Amy was keeping Trudi quiet because of *her*. It made Lenny spin around, just to check if she'd accurately read the room, something she did not often do well. She saw Lora Pham, school principal, in the doorway, and was relieved. Amy's quietening of the conversation now made sense.

Lenny always found Ms. Pham kind, if a little abrupt and refreshingly authoritarian. But Amy wouldn't want her boss to hear about her plans. It would be hard to relax and have *so much fun* with the head of your school in the room.

"Greg, Sarah Taylor's mum is on the phone about her skinned knees from PE yesterday." Ms. Pham's voice was clipped, disgruntled. "She wondered why she didn't get an injury email. This of course would make more sense to me if I had received an injury report for it."

Greg appeared a little uneasy over his chicken schnitzel roll, the crunchy bread of which had left a dusting of crumbs across his polo shirt, resting on the shelf his stomach provided.

"Ah, yes, she did have a little trip. Nothing major. Didn't I send that to you?"

"No, Greg. It must've got lost on its way via carrier pigeon, perhaps?"

"Sorry, Lora," he said, cheeks reddened.

"I'll apologize to Mrs. Taylor, but sort it out by the end of the day. Thanks."

Ms. Pham didn't wait for Greg to acknowledge this before she was gone from the doorway. Lenny would've hated such a confrontation, and yet Greg resumed eating his sandwich, apparently unperturbed. A splodge of mayonnaise dropped from the end of his roll onto the table; he ran his index finger through the blob and licked it. Lenny winced.

The microwave chimed its attention-grabbing beep of completion and Lenny took her soup to the table, finding a place next to Kirra. Ideally she'd have had a chair empty on either side, but the size of the staff room didn't always allow for this.

The table discussion didn't resume; instead the staff members nibbled at their various lunches and made mundane, idle chit-chat with each other.

"What about you, Lenny?" Kirra asked. "Are you coming tonight?"

"What's happening tonight?" Lenny replied, remembering to play it cool.

"Oh, I hadn't gotten around to talking to Lenny about it yet," Amy said. "And I've left it a bit late notice now, you probably have plans."

"On a school night? Surely not," Kirra replied. "Trivia at the Pint and Pickle tonight. Amy's new boyfriend is hosting."

"Lenny doesn't come out past dark," Ashleigh said with a giggle. This was largely true and Lenny noticed others nodding around the table in agreement.

No wonder Amy wasn't keen to invite her in front of everyone. She would've preferred to ask her quietly so Lenny didn't feel obliged to join in. Kirra really could be like a bull at a gate. But Lenny didn't want to give Amy and Ashleigh the idea this was a big deal. It wasn't, she could convince herself of that.

"Of course I do. Monica and I go out all the time. It's a wonder we don't come across any of you when we do," Lenny said. She was pleased her voice held so confidently.

"Where do you go?" Ashleigh asked, eyebrows raised, resting her chin on her hand. She fixed a stern gaze on Lenny, one she couldn't quite decipher.

"Oh, all over," Lenny started, her mouth feeling very dry. Lies did this to her. "The cinema, sometimes. And, ah, the bars."

Ashleigh blinked long and slow and looked back to Amy. Lenny took a large gulp from her water bottle, hoping to restore some moisture to her mouth.

Ashleigh was almost interchangeable with Amy. They were both in their twenties, accessorized infuriatingly effortlessly and knew how to use eyeliner and lipstick without looking like concubines. Lenny was keenly aware of this as she didn't know how to use either. Lenny wondered if any of the prep students would notice if Ashleigh and Amy changed classrooms. They were the sort of women Lenny found herself intimidated by despite them not directly doing anything to her. The Amys and Ashleighs of the world always either overlooked her completely or shot curious glances at her as if she'd stepped out of the TARDIS. She was glad, the more she got to know them, that Amy and Ashleigh *weren't* that type of person, although it didn't completely dissipate her nerves around them. Lenny feared she had been the judgmental one all these years, and not the other way around. She really needed to give people a chance.

"'The bars'?" Ashleigh said. "Just in general? Or somewhere more specific?"

"I didn't realize you were such a night owl, Lenny," Amy added, a smile spreading across her face. "You'll have to take us with you sometime, show us how it's done. You *and* Monica, of course."

Lenny noticed the other teachers were listening with a schadenfreude sort of intrigue. She knew it would take Amy and Ashleigh some time to warm to her. After keeping her distance from them since they'd started there at the beginning of the year, she was now attempting to get closer to them, which was no doubt confusing. At some point, they would forget about Monica, Lenny would take them up on their offer to associate outside of work and all would be fine.

Perhaps Lenny could tell them Monica's work as a chef meant she kept odd hours and was not often available in the evenings.

"Of course," Lenny replied.

"And how about tonight? Will you join us?" Kirra asked.

"There will be other trivia nights, so don't worry about it if you can't," Amy said, waving her hand around in front of her. "Next time, maybe?"

"I can," Lenny said.

"You can what?" Ashleigh asked.

"I can come."

"Oh. Great," Amy said. Ashleigh nudged Amy's arm and they looked at each other.

"You're so good with general knowledge," Kirra said. "I think our team will be in with a chance."

"A chance?"

"To win," Kirra clarified.

"What do we win?" Lenny asked.

"A venue voucher. Which would be perfect for you, Lenny, with the amount you like to hit the town," Ashleigh said.

Lenny heard Kirra inhale deeply and looked at her but couldn't discern her expression. It occurred to Lenny, maybe Kirra didn't want her to go. Maybe Kirra saw how well Lenny got along with Amy and Ashleigh and felt threatened.

Ashleigh and Amy, almost in tandem, rose from the table.

"Seven, then. Dress to impress and I'll see you all there," Amy announced and the two left the room, moving like synchronized swimmers.

Lenny sipped her soup and thought about the turn of events of this day. She didn't go out on weeknights and she *did not* go to pubs. She also had her Thursday night quiche defrosting in her fridge.

It was only later when she was back in her classroom that Lenny realized that, in the merriment of making plans, she had completely disregarded the signed instruction to clean the microwave after use.

CHAPTER 4

Dress to impress. Those three words made Lenny's shins ache. She had no idea what that dress code meant nor did she have anything she thought would fall into the impressive category. She mulled it over the entire ride home, taking all the joy out of the trip.

Impressive: permissive, empress, privies, misers, remiss, prim

Lenny's wardrobe was limited to four colors: black, charcoal, gray and navy blue. She used to only count it as three colors but the distinction between black and charcoal, and charcoal and gray, when they were lined up together, was evident. She was of the mind bright colors were for attention seekers, which she decidedly was not. Her only concession to this was shoes: in those she added burgundy, tan and camel to the color palette; a rainbow in comparison.

Lenny stood in her underwear in front of her wardrobe hoping an outfit would assemble itself for her. Style was not her strength. This didn't bother her ninety-eight percent of the time. She was currently within the other two percent.

Lenny slipped on a pair of black slacks, sized herself up in the mirror, then rolled them straight back off again. They were identical to the pair she'd worn to work and she didn't want to give the impression she'd made no effort. Although, if she made too much effort it may very well look like she was not accustomed to leaving the house, which she had just made clear she did frequently. She tried a pair of navy cords, then black jeans, before trying some gray culottes. The culottes still had the tag attached. They'd been an ambitious purchase—who needed pant legs to be so wide?—and she was almost certain she'd never wear them; even still she couldn't bring herself to put them in the charity bin. Lenny threw them aside and focused on her top half; the gray rollneck sweater she'd worn to work was comfortable and still clean. She could wear that or the matching black one she'd bought with it (a buy one, get one fifty percent off sale). However, it might be warm in the pub and she needed layers to allow for this. She realized there was no way of estimating the climate inside the venue as she tried on three black tops with different-shaped sleeves, none of which she felt comfortable enough to leave the house in. Next she tried a gray top she hadn't worn in a while but the cleavage made her uneasy; she wasn't going out to be preyed upon. Her navy-blue jersey tee seemed *too* casual and she was worried she'd look like she didn't care at all.

Dress to impress.

She was agitated and wanted to stamp her feet, fling the clothes about the room and throw a tantrum. But she didn't because she'd just have to tidy it up again.

Eschewing the entirety of her wardrobe, she wrapped herself in her dressing gown and retired to the lounge, wondering why she'd agreed to go out.

She switched the television on. Just one episode. It would reset her mood and she could get on with getting dressed. She was up to "The One Where Chandler Crosses the Line," which was fortuitous; Chandler always cheered her up. He was her second favorite character behind Gunther, who she'd always felt was underappreciated. Lenny could hear the voices reciting their lines but her eye was caught by a spider's web in the top right corner of the largest windowpane. It was a wonderful spot for a web. The view was magnificent and the late afternoon light made it look like a work of art. It was quite relaxing to gaze at, and she promptly fell asleep.

At 6:45 P.M., Lenny awoke, groggy and annoyed.

She was going to be late—the pinnacle of rudeness. She considered not showing up at all, but didn't have Amy's phone number to tell her she wouldn't make it. She didn't want to let her down. Lateness was rude, but unreliability was outright bad manners. She hadn't even eaten. Maybe the pub did food; surely they would, but she didn't have time to check it on the internet and the oven wasn't preheated for her quiche. She was in a spin as she returned to her wardrobe and the pile of clothes on her bed.

She picked up the same black slacks and gray sweater she'd worn that day and pulled them back on. Throwing her Kathmandu puffer jacket on over her outfit, she ran a hand through her bob and considered herself for a moment in the mirror. She looked matronly, which would have to do; it had always done in the past.

Matronly: normal, moral, only, torn

As she raced out the door she was aware she looked exactly the same as when the final bell had rung at 3:10 P.M.

She convinced herself it didn't matter, but knew Amy and Ashleigh would look sparkly and she wished she could sometimes be just a little sparkly too.

Lenny locked her front door, mounted her bicycle and pedalled into the night.

Entering the Pint and Pickle was a horrendous assault on the senses. Especially the smell, a heady mix of beer, underarms and musty carpet that must have absorbed all manner of transgressions since it was laid, which was certainly not recently. The music—unrecognizable to her ears—was far louder than background music should be, but also, admittedly, relatively inoffensive in its actual content. It was the din of others talking that really caused her head to spin. Her ears thrummed with shrieking, laughing and chatting.

From the safety of the front door Lenny scanned the crowd, seeking a familiar face, all the while feeling unable to cool down after her rapid bike ride while wearing her insulated Kathmandu jacket. She wasn't ready to remove it yet and considered, before anyone spotted her, just backing out the door and feigning some sort of short-term medical emergency that rendered her unable to come out that evening. A six-hour tummy bug perhaps, or a considerately timed migraine. But before she was able to beat her retreat she was swept farther into the venue by a group of people behind her who shared none of her hesitations.

She made her way to the bar, which was reassuringly sturdy. The venue was bustling and she hadn't spotted any familiar faces from Selby South Primary School. For her avid avoidance of her colleagues during the school day, she was now desperate to catch a glimpse of one of them so she'd know she was in the right place.

"What can I get you?"

The barkeeper tapped his fingers on the bar, apparently expecting a quick answer for what was a very legitimate question. The man's hair was long on one side and shaved on the other; it was an unusual look and she wondered how he'd come up with it. She couldn't imagine the ladies at her local Just Cuts would have suggested it.

He pushed two menus toward her with an indifferent glance.

"I might just need a moment," she said, pulling the menu toward her.

"Take your time," he said, moving to the next customer.

Lenny had no issue with drinking, even though it was something she seldom did, and it usually brought her grandmother to mind. A wineglass had always been Zanny's favorite accessory, as common-place as wearing a watch would've been.

The "per glass" section of the drinks menu was extensive and the barman was back so it was time for a snap decision.

Just pick one, Lenny, you don't even have to drink it.

The man beside her shuffled and leaned over the bar, money in hand, ready to place his order.

"Could you just choose a white wine for me, please?" she asked the bartender, hoping he wouldn't mind.

He nodded and turned away from her, busying himself with the bar fridge and a wineglass.

She contemplated the room, still not seeing anyone she recognized. They'd said the Pint and Pickle, hadn't they? She had no way of confirming this now, not being in possession of any of her colleagues' phone numbers. It was something she'd purposefully avoided for years. If they needed her and she was at work, she was available to them. If she was not, then she didn't need to be dealing with primary school matters. In hindsight, it would've been the perfect opportunity to exchange phone numbers with Amy.

"Lenny, you made it," Amy squealed, a few octaves above her normal pitch as she careened into view.

"Yes. I did," she replied, relief flooding through her aching shins.

"We're over there." Amy pointed into the throng. "I'm just getting more wine, before it starts." Her voice was again higher and chirpier than usual.

Lenny took a long sip of her wine and realized it was an excellent choice. Not that she could take much credit for it.

It was polite to wait for Amy, she decided, and her eyes darted around the room before resting on the long green trail of the (probably plastic) devil's ivy up the wall. She was happy to have company to battle through the crowded venue.

Turning back to the bar, she found Amy was gone. Lenny looked around frantically for a moment, wondering how Amy had slipped away so easily, then caught sight of her to the side of the projection screen at the front of the room, talking to a person bent behind a lectern.

Glad to have the wineglass to occupy her hands, Lenny tried to dismiss her reservations and headed into the crowd. She was relieved to catch sight of the back of Kirra's head as she squeezed herself past chairs that were so close to the neighboring ones it was definitely a fire hazard. With this in mind, Lenny checked the room to see where her nearest exit was and happily found a reassuring green sign lit up above a black door not far from the Selby South contingent. It was always helpful to have knowledge of emergency exits.

Kirra's thick, dark hair sat cleverly bundled atop her head, a single chopstick piercing the center. She wore a brightly patterned shift dress, which reminded Lenny of a cushion cover she'd once seen in the Adairs window display.

She took in the other occupants of the long table: Ashleigh Burton, prep two, was there of course; Gregory Schwartz, physical education; Yvonne Gillespie, grade three; Harrison Dyer, grade six; Demet Osman, grade one; Trudi Kerr, music and arts and, surprisingly, Lora Pham, school principal. She must have missed the subtleties Lenny picked up on in the staff room. Lenny hoped it didn't put a dampener on Amy and Ashleigh's night.

Ashleigh was hard to miss in a neon pink top that looked to have been borrowed from the school crossing guard. The color made Lenny feel self-conscious. She pulled at the hem of her jacket, wondering if she could just slip inside and disappear into the duck-down lining.

Kirra waved animatedly, beckoning her over. "I saved you a seat," she said, patting the empty chair beside her. It relieved Lenny of deciding, but gave her little wiggle room to try to sit closer to the prep teachers. She was now at the far end of the table and would be unlikely to hear any of their conversation. It felt like school bus seating all over again, where she was always relegated to the not-cool spots at the front.

A heated discussion was underway concerning the name of the team. She was offered a couple of quick "hellos" but nothing quite so warm as Kirra's welcome. Ashleigh didn't acknowledge her, which confirmed her thoughts about being positioned at the far end of the table.

"Quivia Newton John," Demet offered.

"No, I've heard that too many times. What about 'Quiz in my Face'?" Harrison said.

Ashleigh giggled. "Oh my God, no way. I think we should be 'Teacher's Pet.'"

"Of course she does," Kirra said, although no one but Lenny heard her.

"My Drinking Team has a Trivia Problem?" Yvonne threw out.

"Oh, that's *fun*!" Ashleigh replied.

Lenny sipped her wine, hoping no one would try to include her in the conversation. She had no names she wanted to add to the mix and didn't want to have to make one up on the spot. The room seemed to be increasing in warmth and she felt her underarms needle with sweat. She drank more wine and realized how quickly she was running out. Her eyes flitted back to the bar and her prospects of getting more. There was such a small amount of liquid in the bulbous glass; had she known, she would've got two and saved a trip. She unzipped her jacket and hung it on the back of her chair. It felt like removing a life vest, but she didn't want to risk passing out by overheating.

"How did they get you here?" Lora Pham asked. She was seated directly to Lenny's right.

"I was invited," Lenny replied quickly.

"I just wouldn't have thought this was your thing," Lora continued, waving her hands around, indicating either the pub, or the people, or the trivia night; Lenny wasn't exactly sure. Nor was she sure what Ms. Pham believed might be her "thing." She wondered what any of her colleagues thought of her. Some of them had known her for years, but they'd be hard-pressed to pinpoint anything they actually knew about Lenny other than the obvious: her name, job title and her mode of transport.

"Actually, I'm surprised to see *you* here, Ms. Pham," Lenny said.

"Lora, please—we're not at school now. Trivia and wine are some of my favorite things. Much more than children and their delightful parents." Lora swilled from her glass; this casual side was not a version of Lora that Lenny often saw. The last time was the staff "strategy" pizza night which was almost entirely deficient of strategies and appeared to have been a ruse for pizza and drinks on the school premises.

Amy swanned back to the table and leaned in, announcing with a tiny hand clap, "It's about to start." She sat between Gregory and Ashleigh and took charge of the pen and answer sheet.

A voice boomed from speakers. "Welcome to your weekly dose of brain strain, trivia lovers! Get ready for some heavy lifting!"

Lenny pivoted in her seat to get a look at the source of the voice and the boyfriend Amy was so eager for them to meet.

"I'm your trivia host extraordinaire, your host with the most, the meeple of the people . . . but you can just call me Ned. First round starting in five so get yourselves sorted."

Lenny watched as Ned McKnight flicked the switch on his mike and put it down on the lectern at the front of the venue.

Ned was Amy's boyfriend. *Ned McKnight*. She downed the rest of her glass in one long gulp and struggled to place the unusual feeling that had come over her.

CHAPTER 5

Three wines in and not yet a bite to eat, Lenny realized she was possibly drunk. She wondered if anyone else at the table could guess because she was fairly sure she was keeping it together rather well. She'd been able to answer questions the others couldn't, winning her grateful smiles from Amy as she scrawled down Lenny's replies.

What's the capital of Laos? Vientiane.

What is tonitrophobia? Fear of thunder.

Australia's fourth prime minister? George Reid.

She decided to get herself some food at the end of round two but when she went to see the half-shaved barman, he told her the kitchen had already closed. There were packets of crisps or bowls of peanuts. She didn't want either so ordered herself a fourth wine instead. She even felt so confident that she attempted to order her wine by name, enunciating each syllable of "pinot grigio" carefully.

Ned had been introduced to Amy's workmates when he collected the first round of score sheets. Amy fawned over him in a way that made Lenny think of a small dog lifting its leg on the way down a new street. To the point where, Lenny was fairly sure, Ned was blushing—visible even in the low light of the venue. They made a nice-looking couple: Amy long, slim and bright like a lighthouse, and Ned a slightly less hirsute version of Aragorn. Which she meant entirely as a compliment.

As she waited at the bar for her fourth—and she was positive it would be her final—wine, Ned sidled up beside her. He threw his burly arm around her shoulder and pulled her in to him. It was much more casual than he'd ever acted toward her while in McKnight's and she should have found his overfamiliarity and uninvited contact alarming, but somehow did not. He smelled like tomato sauce.

"It's so nice to see you here," he said. His arm was warm and heavy around her.

Lenny did not know what to make of such a comment. Was it that Ned was happy to see her at the pub, or was he just happy for more trivia participants? Obviously, if he didn't attract a crowd to his events then the establishment would surely discontinue them. Or was he indicating that he, Ned McKnight, was happy to see *her*, Lenny Marks? She was unable to clarify as Amy squeezed her tiny frame between them. Her near-translucent blouse showed the outline of her bra. Lenny wondered if she should let her know her underwear was on display, but didn't want to embarrass her. Fay always said to avoid personal comments, unless it was about something readily fixable.

"Babe, this is so much fun. Everyone is loving it. I just wish you had more music questions—I'm terrible at general knowledge and stuff," Amy said. She poked a finger into Ned's chest and leaned in to kiss him, but she landed it awkwardly on his stubbled cheek. This appeared to be a sign of Amy's increasing intoxication, not that Lenny was any better. Lenny looked away, feeling like she was interrupting a private moment despite being there first.

Unlike Ned's proximity, Lenny found Amy's closeness overwhelming. She took up space in an entirely different way and was near enough that when she tossed her blond locks over her shoulder, Lenny was whipped with her sea salt–scented hair. Lenny stepped backward, ready to return to the safety of the table, and collided with a man trying to wrangle three beers away from the bar. They sloshed over her back and she felt the cold liquid seep through her thick sweater.

She turned, inexplicably expecting to be faced with Fergus, but of course she was not.

"Sorry!" Lenny said to the stranger, her heart thundering in her throat.

She tried to step away from whatever tirade he was about to unleash, but she was off balance and lost her footing. Ned reached out to grab her, forcing Amy to jump sidewards. Amy shrieked, splashing her red wine out of its glass and onto her top, making the curve of her bra appear even more pronounced. The red ballooned across the delicate white fabric and gave the unfortunate appearance of Amy having been shot in the chest.

"Lenny! *Jesus*, be careful!" Amy snapped.

Lenny breathed out heavily and purposefully through her mouth. She knew this feeling; it wasn't new to her but it always took her by surprise. Cold sweat, aching shins, vomit rising, all in the space of seconds.

The stranger had been quick to steady himself and was relatively untroubled. "Saved them, it's all good."

"I'll replace them," Lenny said through clenched teeth and ears that felt like she'd thrust earplugs deep within.

"Nah, hardly spilled 'em at all. Sorry 'bout your jumper."

She almost cried with relief. Amy, however, was proving to be far less magnanimous. She looked wordlessly from her top to Lenny, and back again. Lenny picked up some napkins from the bar but Amy shooed her away. "*No!* They're black, they'll mark it. Just leave it alone!"

"I think it's good, it's like a designer pattern," Ned said, and winked at Lenny.

Amy tilted her head to one side and pouted, making it clear she expected far more sympathy from Ned. Ashleigh appeared, as if she knew Amy needed her.

"Oh no, your new top," Ashleigh cooed, delivering the compassion Amy had been hoping for. "Seriously, Lenny, why can't you be more careful?"

The two women spun around and sped off toward the bathrooms, not giving Ned or Lenny a backward glance.

"I'm sorry, I didn't mean . . ." Lenny said and turned back to Ned. Her high-necked pullover now felt like a coir doormat and she tugged at the collar. She wanted to go back to the table, collect her bag and jacket and bolt into the night.

"It's a splash of wine, not hydrochloric acid. She'll be fine," Ned said.

"I've wrecked her night."

"No you haven't. Please, don't let this ruin yours."

Lenny exhaled deeply and took another considered breath in. The panic made the wine fuzz dissipate almost immediately. She wanted it back, the nice warm feeling of levity. But the heady smell of spirits and the clink of glasses had unbalanced her. Ned didn't rush away; instead he kept his body squared in front of her. His presence was calming, which was incredible in such a crowded room.

"Plus, you have to stay," he was saying. "There might be a *Buffy* question or two next round. I reckon there's an easy couple of points for you there."

Lenny nodded and tried to force herself to smile, even slightly. The most she could manage was unclenching her forehead.

"Take a minute, this place can get loud. So many people, it's not really my thing either. But if I don't get out occasionally my parents may worry I'm a serial killer or a werewolf. Or worse, a board gamer."

She managed to smile, but thought there was a real chance she was about to cry in front of lovely Ned McKnight. And how would that look, crying over such a small thing? She couldn't explain to him that it wasn't so simple to her.

"Thank you," she murmured without shifting her eyes from the space between their feet. "I'll be fine, you can go."

Ned didn't move. "If I ever get stuck when I'm out, I run lines," he told her.

She shook her head, not sure what he was talking about.

"They chill me out. Songs lines, you know, lyrics. But I'm not going to tell you which song is my go-to in case you think less of me." He smiled. Warm. Genuine. "Okay, okay, you've convinced me," he said. "It's 'She's Like the Wind.'"

"Is it a poem?" she asked.

"Patrick Swayze. *Dirty Dancing*. Baby and Johnny? It's a classic."

"I've never watched it," she said.

"You have no idea what you've been missing."

She wanted to tell him how she shuffled letters around to calm her racing mind.

"You're up, mate." A man in an overly tight shirt tapped Ned on the shoulder.

"No worries, almost done here," Ned said and turned back to Lenny. "You okay?" he asked.

"Of course I am. I don't need lines, or anything silly like that. I'm perfectly fine, thank you," she said, forcing a smile and turning away from him, instantly regretting how rude and dismissive she sounded. She needed another wine, that would help.

Ned motored back through the room to his podium, flicked his mike back on and addressed the crowd.

"Last round, my friends! Time to put your thinking caps on—we're doing film and television," he said to the room, while looking right at her.

* * *

The final scores weren't announced until well after ten, which meant it was an incredibly late night by Lenny's standards. They lost, but not dismally, coming in third.

Amy mustered a brave face and told the Quizzards (the name they'd eventually settled on) they couldn't have won or the other teams would think the competition was rigged because Ned was her *boyfriend*.

Lenny fumbled for her satchel, realizing her affected motor skills were a definite sign she may be inebriated. The alcohol was giving her a dull, numbed feeling, which she actually felt quite good about. But she also knew it was time to get home and pulled on her jacket before disappearing through the dispersing crowd. She wasn't going to trouble herself with pointless goodbyes, only to see her trivia team in less than twelve hours. Also, if she was honest with herself, she wanted to avoid Ned. Or more specifically Ned with Amy. Every time Amy mentioned her *boyfriend* it reminded Lenny of a grade three student with a show-and-tell. Lenny put it down to the wine making her less tolerant than usual.

Kirra was not so easy to evade and found Lenny at the bike stand just outside the pub. "Please let me drop you home, it doesn't seem safe to ride," Kirra insisted as Lenny made a third attempt to unfasten her bike lock.

"I ride everywhere. It won't take me long."

Despite being undoubtedly more drunk than she'd been in recent memory, Lenny had no intention of leaving her bike behind and she didn't like anyone to know where she lived. It was why her mail either went to the school or to her post office box at Mc-Knight's. The Tree House was her private place and she was not letting anyone near it, even Kirra, who was apparently very well meaning.

"I don't feel right about this. My husband will be here any second. We can fit your bike in the back if you don't want to leave it?"

Kirra's insistence, coupled with her own inability to unfasten the bike lock, only increased Lenny's agitation.

On the fifth attempt at getting the dial on the lock to spin in the exact manner required to release its determined grasp, Lenny succeeded. She stuffed the bike lock inside her satchel, and felt *the* envelope in there. Hastily, she closed the bag, lest it jump out and accost her. It had proved to be very persistent so far.

"Lenny . . ."

"Just leave me alone!" she snapped. "I don't need your help."

Lenny saw hurt flash across Kirra's face. She hadn't meant to be so blunt with her and wanted to apologize, but more pressing was the need to ride away as quickly as possible.

"Just be careful. I'll see you tomorrow," Kirra said.

Lenny threw her leg over her bike and headed in the direction of home. She was too ashamed of herself to look back.

CHAPTER 6

Lenny rode quickly past the meandering pub patrons. The rush of cold air on her face was sobering. She was struggling to maintain her usual easy balance and worried she would do herself or someone staggering home some damage, and she wasn't entirely sure if drinking and driving rules applied to her bicycle. Erring on the side of caution, she resolved to walk. A couple in front of her were holding hands and blocking more of the footpath than required. She felt especially annoyed by this display of intimacy and changed her route home to avoid having to watch them any longer.

She turned down a side street and walked briskly, taking two more turns before allowing herself to slow down. Her feet felt firm on the ground and the rhythmic crunch was soothing. She appreciated the companionship of her bike beside her; the ticking noise the pedals made as they completed a full rotation was satisfying, reminding her of a trundle wheel, clicking over as each meter was traveled. The moon was almost full, casting a magical glow over the trees and streets as she passed. In this light Belgrave felt like it could be the Shire in Middle Earth—except for the power lines and bitumen, of course. Had she happened across Bilbo Baggins, he wouldn't have seemed at all out of place. She kept tight to the side of the road, in case a car appeared unexpectedly while her reflexes were compromised. The streets looked different in the dark, but Lenny knew her way home.

The most direct route was across the green wedge reserve, but even in her state, she knew that being a woman alone in a park at night was a risky move.

With this in mind she kept to the streets, which added almost ten minutes, but given the late hour it seemed irrelevant. She decided as she walked to eschew her morning workout and give herself a sleep-in; she *had* enjoyed the evening and there was no need to punish herself. This was almost an entirely new feeling for Lenny and she toyed with how it felt. The odd social occasion she had attended in the past, she had tolerated at best. But to enjoy it—was this the start of a new phase for Lenny Marks? Perhaps she didn't have to decline each and every invite she received. She could even seek them out. And this was despite progress with Amy and Ashleigh being less than perfect. Perhaps they weren't quite the people she'd taken them for in the first place. The way Amy had lashed out at her so readily, over an accidental spill, wasn't in keeping with the carefree persona she projected.

She pulled out her phone and reset her usual 5:45 A.M. alarm to a slovenly 7 A.M. She didn't want to give herself time to reconsider. Lenny pushed the phone back into her satchel and realized putting her oily bike lock in there had been a silly thing to do. She pulled it out and along with it came the letter, its reflective whiteness in the moonlight bidding her to pick it up. It was relentless. Lenny considered leaving it where it dropped, to be crushed into the gravel and hopefully into oblivion. But Lenny knew she wouldn't leave it there. It had found her once and she had no doubt it would find her again. She picked it up like it was contaminated medical waste.

A fallen tree offered a place to sit and Lenny pulled the Zenith off the road and leaned it against the weathered trunk. She sat down, feeling condensation wet the back of her pants.

She wanted to open the envelope, she realized. *She had to.*

Attached to this envelope was a feeling, like a part of a game, or a Choose Your Own Adventure book where certain things had to happen or the game couldn't be advanced. This was one of those things, she was sure of it. Although it could very well be the sort of game that would have her trying to undo everything and yelling "Jumanji!" into the air.

She wiped the moisture from her hands and tore it open.

The formalities slowed her down. She scanned the letter, hoping to take in the contents without having to concentrate on every word. The wine and the darkness were affecting her eyesight and the words were not as still as she'd like them to be.

"The Adult Parole Board invites you to make a written submission expressing your views about the application for parole of Mr. Fergus Sullivan. Submissions made by victims will be considered by the board and may influence any conditions placed upon a parole order. Please be advised that the final determination is based on a range of factors and a submission expressing your support or opposition is just one of these considerations."

Lenny read to the end before folding the letter back into thirds and then twice more. The smaller she could make it, surely the less weight it could carry.

Parole: pearl, opal, rope

Submission: missions, nimbi, ibis, bus

Victim: victim, victim, victim

It *was* for her.

She was the correct Helena Winters.

The letter had reached its intended destination.

CHAPTER 7

June 13, 1991
Fergus

Tammy Winters married Fergus Sullivan on a Thursday in June 1991, when the leaves had abandoned the trees and the sky was a constant uninspired gray. Lenny's job was to hold the rings and she clutched them to her chest like they were liable to grow legs and streak away from her. She didn't want to stuff this up.

They were in an old building, next to a lovely park where a woman holding a camera took them for photos standing under one of the naked-branched trees. Lenny had been into Melbourne only once before that day and it was an exciting adventure for a wide-eyed six-year-old.

Fergus clutched Tammy's hand and, when the camera lady told him, he knelt down beside Lenny, pulling her in close and encouraging her to smile. And when she smiled, she meant it. She couldn't recall her dad, and Fergus had told her that's what she could call him, if she wanted to. And she wanted to.

He was tall and safe and made her mum smile in a way Lenny couldn't otherwise remember. Even when they watched funny movies together and Tammy laughed—she was still happier than that.

Lenny was wearing a rainbow dress she'd picked herself. Her mum took her shopping and let her choose whatever she wanted to wear for the wedding. This one was the brightest and most beautiful and she'd loved it the moment she saw it. She felt like a ballerina in it, the skirt billowing around her knees. She couldn't help but keep spinning in it to watch the colors come to life around her.

It was exactly what she was doing when she tripped over someone's bag and plowed into the back of Fergus's legs. He was sipping his drink and the unexpected knock meant beer ran down his chin and onto his white shirt.

He spun around and she saw a different Fergus, like he'd been wearing a mask for months and it slipped off, for just that moment.

He leaned down to her and gripped the top of her arm, squeezing tight enough to make her eyes water.

"Everyone's had enough of your showing off today. Cut it out and watch where you're fucking going," he snapped, his voice a low rumble delivered only to her ears.

Before she could react, or realize what had happened, he turned back to his friends and rejoined their conversation. His mask was back on and his laughter boomed, as if nothing had just happened.

She looked for her mum but she was sitting with people Lenny didn't know well and she was too scared to tell her what Fergus had said in case she didn't believe her.

Lenny retreated to her seat and tucked her dress in under her legs, trying to make it less obvious, less bright. She didn't want to be the rainbow anymore. Nothing in the room looked different and yet it felt like everything had changed.

The spot on her arm where Fergus had grabbed her smarted for the rest of the night. A silent reminder of her mistake.

CHAPTER 8

Friday, May 20, 2022

The alarm clock sliced through Lenny's fug of sleep at precisely 7 A.M., an inconsiderate blast of sound that didn't give her the opportunity to ease into wakefulness. She woke with a jolt and no memory of turning on her alarm or setting it for seven. She wondered what her previous night's self had been thinking. Or not thinking.

She realized she was on her couch and fully dressed, minus her shoes. The lights were still on and she could feel the dry, gluggy furriness in her mouth of unbrushed teeth.

Worst of all, she couldn't recall getting home, let alone going to sleep.

An overwhelming feeling of disgrace seized her and she raced to the bathroom to empty the contents of her stomach. Which, given she'd not eaten since the afternoon before, were limited.

Irrational thoughts clambered for attention as she tried to recall what she may, or may not, have said to her colleagues. She was usually so measured and controlled, but what if she'd commented inappropriately on Greg's rotund midriff, or Yvonne's terrible overbite? She remembered calling Ms. Pham by her first name; she'd have to apologize first thing. And she hoped Amy and Ashleigh would still want to be her friends.

She tried to count how many wines she'd drunk and recalled splitting a bottle with Ms. Pham and Kirra in the last round. It meant the large glasses could be filled much more generously.

The thoughts skittered through her mind and she kneeled back over the toilet. The tiles were cold even through the fabric of her pants. Lenny couldn't remember the last time she'd thrown up, and certainly not from drinking too much. She was almost forty years old; this was completely unacceptable. Her face felt like someone was standing over her with a heater, the sort they have for patios and footpath dining areas that leave your front smoldering while your back freezes. The nausea subsided and she lay down, pressing her cheek against the cool bathroom floor, recalling her final conversation with Kirra. She'd been unforgivably rude. It sent her leaning over the bowl one more time to retch and heave.

Lenny walked into her bedroom and peeled off yesterday's clothes. She would just have time to shower and get to school, but wondered how she would face her colleagues. For the briefest moment she considered calling in sick, but taking an unplanned day off unnerved her more than turning up hungover and embarrassed.

The other choice was quitting her job, which was only an option if Ms. Pham didn't dismiss her for her woeful behavior first. And if she resigned, she'd have to give notice. There was no instant fix readily available.

Disgrace: cadger, caged, ideas

The sleepy face that rose to meet her when she sat on her bed to peel her socks off was a complete surprise.

But when she took a moment—which she did—she knew exactly how this had happened, and how she came to be staring into such mesmerizing brown eyes.

CHAPTER 9

Thursday, May 19
11:10 P.M.
(The night before)

Lenny looked around her; Fergus wasn't there, just the giant trees, her bike and the bothersome letter. All covered by a pleasant haze of wine. Even still she rubbed her arm, as if Fergus had only just let go of her, but it was not sore. Of course it wasn't. That was thirty-odd years ago.

The whimper came from the yard directly behind her.

Leaving her bike where it lay, she moved toward the house and found the palings easy to spy between. The fence was rudimentary, made of rough treated pine and not neatly capped or evenly leveled along the top. It was clearly made for privacy, not presentation.

The yard she peered into was darker than the street, caught in a dark pocket hidden from the moon by the towering trees. Her eyes slowly adjusted. She heard the same sound again and it drew her eye to a kennel attached to the garage. The resting head of a Rott-weiler lay at the mouth of the small structure, its body ensconced inside. The dog was as black as tar and she wasn't surprised he was hard to see. A light illuminated the front window of the house and cast shadows over the yard, which was not at all welcoming. It was a landscape of stark contrasts: sparse, overgrown patches of grass and barren, muddy pockmarks. A verandah of dubious structural integrity was roofed with sheets of waved Laserlite and held months (years, probably) of lichen and whatever debris the surrounding trees deposited. She cleared her gutters and checked the roof for leaf litter regularly; it was a fire hazard not to and showed the disregard the occupants of this house held for basic fire safety measures.

Large plastic garbage bags were stacked as if they'd been tossed out the front door and ignored forthwith. She could make out three cheap plastic chairs, a weather-warped tallboy with peeling laminate, a microwave with a smashed door, building supplies and a smattering of aluminum beer cans in various states strewn throughout. If the state of a house was a reflection of its occupants, Lenny summed them up pretty quickly.

The dog's head shot up and it looked around frantically. Lenny was sure she hadn't made a sound. Maybe he sensed her there, a stranger on the other side of the fence. His job was probably to guard the house from interlopers, which she would likely be considered, although her purpose was not untoward.

The sound of the front door made her take a step backward, glad to be in dark clothing—unintentional camouflage. She didn't want to be caught peering through someone's fence.

"What the fuck's wrong with you?!" A man's voice pierced the night, the malice of the words reverberating in the quietness of the street, the tone and pitch bringing Fergus's face hurtling into her mind. He felt so close in that moment she thought she smelled his beer-soaked breath across her face. She pressed her eyes closed; Fergus was not there. But a new panic arose, and Lenny felt her throat constrict. She'd been spotted. Her first thought was to run, but she would have to stop for her bike and that would slow her down. She didn't want to leave it behind. Perhaps she could apologize profusely and hope he'd just consider her a slightly drunk oddball wandering the streets.

She'd done nothing wrong, but that didn't make her any less anxious.

A canine yelp made her realize the man wasn't addressing her; it was his pet he had taken issue with. She was grateful, but only for the briefest of moments as guilt overwhelmed her for not being brave enough to step in. Lenny felt her skin prickle and turn cold, the hairs on her arms becoming individual antennas. She forced herself to step back to the fence and see what was happening. Holding her breath, she pushed her eye back to the gap between the pickets, and caught sight of the man's boot colliding with the wall of the kennel. It shook so violently Lenny was surprised it didn't fall apart.

"Just shut up!" the man roared.

The dog scurried from its confines. She watched as it raced toward the fence, which was also directly at her, only to be thrown backward as if hitting an invisible force field. It was then she noticed the chain attached to its neck, tethering it to the garage wall, keeping it prisoner and within reach of the baseball-capped man with his angry voice and heavy boots. He staggered toward the Rottweiler and let fly again with his left foot, this time directly at the poor creature with deliberate force. Lenny was sure a yelp slipped from her lips and she clamped her hand down over her mouth to stop any other cowardly noises from giving her away. She closed her eyes and hoped it would end soon, imagining herself in the warmth of her house. Her mind deposited her inside the base of her wardrobe where she could close the door and feel safe. And hidden. When Fergus was angry and storming around the house or yelling at her mum she would go there. Or if Lenny was lonely, or just wanted time alone, she would tuck herself in that small space, beneath her clothes and beside her shoes, and find comfort there. She hadn't thought of that hiding place for years and years. How was it that the first mention of Fergus had her reverting to her childhood self?

Wardrobe: arbored, broader, bared, robed, bear

She heard more yelps, more whimpering, and she hated herself for doing nothing. But her feet felt like they were in wet cement. She pressed her forehead against one of the rough palings and waited until it quietened down on the other side. The door of the house slammed and the dog fell silent. The night air that had seemed so refreshing now hung thick with savagery. She felt sick.

Lenny prised her eyes open and scanned the yard to find the dog. Thankfully, he was walking around but, heeding his owner's brutal warning, moving very quietly.

Silenced: declines, denies, sliced, need

There was never a doubt in her mind she would take the dog. Leaving it there to endure a lifetime of pointless hardship was more than she could bear. Reporting its owner to the RSPCA seemed desperately inadequate and she gave no consideration to calling the police. If she was going to do something, she'd do it properly. Or as Robert Marks would have said, "A job half done is as good as none." She missed him and his one-liners.

Bilbo may as well have been right beside her as she stalked through the darkness to liberate the downtrodden animal. There was only one life to save, not the thirteen as Bilbo had done, but the pressure felt just as intense as if she were right there in Mirkwood.

It had been a long time since Lenny Marks had attempted to act outside the law.

She could only hope this time it worked out better.

CHAPTER 10

Friday, May 20

That bleary, hungover morning, as she sat on her bed, the Rottweiler's brown eyes told her he was a thankful and agreeable accomplice to her midnight larceny. He had come willingly and with little fuss.

As for Lenny, she had no regrets.

But now she had issues of a more logistic nature. She had nothing to feed him. Lenny surveyed her refrigerator but didn't consider a defrosted quiche to be a wise thing to give an animal, even one at risk of going hungry. She'd pick up dog food at McKnight's on her way home—she didn't have time to get there and back before the morning bell. It was already past 8 A.M. and the lateness of the morning was troubling her more than her hangover or thievery. Although one of those two things was making her eyes water and head throb, as if her brain were trying to set sail from her skull. Perhaps her class would be happy with some quiet reading this morning; she might even turn the lights down low. She wondered if they were too young to realize napping at her desk during quiet time was unprofessional.

She readied herself in record time, all the while being watched by the new arrival.

On her kitchen counter she found the dog's collar and tag

which, presumably, she'd removed the night before to disguise her crime. Clearly, she was no diabolical criminal genius, having left it plain as day in the middle of the bench. She studied the round name tag dangling from the collar and wondered about the intelligence of a person who would look at any living thing and decide to call it "Beast." It wasn't clever and validated her conclusion that his owner was a thug.

She would give a preferable moniker some thought over the course of the day. For now, it was well beyond her capabilities to consider anything other than swallowing two Panadol and getting to work on time.

The dog formerly known as Beast followed her to the front door—perhaps sensing she was leaving. This was a time when it would be incredibly handy if Monica did exist as a housemate; she would be able to sort out Lenny's mess while she was at work.

Lenny put a plastic container full of water on the kitchen floor and then laid some sheets of newspaper in various spots in the lounge room and in the bathroom. Her head whirled as she bent down to open the sheets, arranging them in large enough areas for the dog to aim at.

She had no idea what he would do to occupy his time while she was gone. It was a potential disaster in the making, she was well aware. But there was nowhere safe to leave him outside that wouldn't risk him getting loose and wandering on roads or being picked up by the council ranger. Or worse, being found by the baseball-capped thug and dragged home.

With a wave of inspiration, shortly thereafter followed by a wave of nausea, she remembered the rubber ball she used to massage her plantar fasciitis. She retrieved it from the hallway cupboard and placed it a respectable distance in front of the dog, motioning to it with her hand. It may have smelled like feet so she couldn't really blame him for not hurrying over.

"Go on, all yours," she told him, but he made no move to pick it up.

She checked her watch and realized she was going to be late.

Before leaving, Lenny switched on Netflix and selected *Friends*, hoping they would at least keep him company during the day. Maybe he would even enjoy it. She hoped so.

She scratched the top of his head and hurried out the front door. He watched her go with something like indifference.

Indifference: redefine, decree, fenced, fiend, friend

The lock clicked into place behind her and the fresh morning air filled her nostrils, which was refreshing, but didn't take the edge off the need to vomit again. Something about leaving the house that morning made her think of Fergus. He was becoming all too frequent a visitor for her at the moment and she was struggling to push him to the hidden recesses of her mind, the places where she had kept him at bay for years. She rubbed at her thigh. There'd been a lot of blood that day and she'd waited so long for her mum to let her out of the shed it had started to congeal. It had felt like hours—and may have been—before someone finally came to let her out, but not her mum this time. A kind face and a scratchy, static voice—like a radio—accompanying him. The last day she saw her family. That was a bad day.

Lenny heaved again, this time over the *Boronia megastigma*, but there was nothing left for her to throw up.

Kirra tracked Lenny down at lunch, despite her attempts to avoid anyone other than the twenty-three grade five pupils she couldn't. Not that she did a very good job of hiding, given she was in her classroom, which was—presumably—the first place someone would look for her. She'd not gone into the staff room before class that morning, nor for morning recess or lunch. Yvonne would be having a field day with her unsupervised tea leaves. Lenny was of the mind that if she could hide from her colleagues for the day, then by the other side of the weekend they'd have forgotten. She was at her desk eating a dry cracker—which was all she could stomach—when Kirra interrupted her.

Lenny was unable to stop herself from apologizing profusely. Kirra cut her off almost immediately, waving her hand, her loose black waves swaying around her shoulders.

"You were fine, honestly. I was being pushy. I should be apologizing," Kirra said.

"Oh, please don't, you will make me feel worse."

"You're a grown woman and you got home just fine. Obviously. You just hear stories, you know, and I didn't want to be the friend who let you walk into the darkness when I could get you home." Kirra's nails were painted a glossy peach color and she drummed them on the table in front of her. Lenny wished she could pull off nail polish. The few times she'd tried it, she ended up feeling like a child who'd raided their mother's makeup drawer.

Kirra made herself comfortable on one of the classroom chairs and Lenny remained behind her desk. She was fidgeting with a pencil sharpener, twisting an unfortunate No. 2 pencil into it and watching the wood shavings collect in a small pile.

"I appreciate your efforts to keep me safe. But it is really important I apologize properly. I shouldn't have raised my voice. I'm afraid I drank more than I should've."

"Like you're meant to when you go to the pub. Did you have a good night?" Kirra asked.

"Yes, I did," Lenny said. And she wasn't lying.

"Ned seems nice, doesn't he? Although he and Amy make an odd pair."

"They're two very nice people who seem happy together,"

Lenny said, not wanting to be a rumormonger but quietly glad Kirra thought they weren't well suited.

"You're right, I shouldn't indulge in gossip, but my goodness she was territorial last night. She could turn very quickly into a bunny boiler."

"A bunny boiler?"

"*Fatal Attraction*?" Kirra said. "Never mind. It's not for me to say. You're right. But honestly, I think my kids are more mature than Ashleigh and Amy sometimes."

"They mean well," Lenny said.

"Do they? Amy was so condescending to you."

"I did ruin her top," Lenny replied.

The pencil continued twisting as she recalled Amy's hostility. She really did owe her a sober apology.

"Anyway. Last night was the first time I've seen you outside the schoolyard; I was starting to think you slept under your desk." Kirra snorted.

Lenny looked down to her feet and the small space under her desk. "I don't think I'd fit."

Kirra laughed again; her teeth were brilliant white and so straight, like she'd stepped out of a Colgate commercial.

"Did I make a fool of myself?" Lenny asked.

"Don't worry about what those women think of you. Really. It's not worth it," Kirra said reassuringly. "And *no*, you didn't. I think Amy was annoyed with you for getting more TV and film questions right than her."

"Did I?"

"Yes, you smashed it. I'd have you on my trivia team any day of the week."

Another recollection came careening back into her mind. The moment when she'd grabbed the pen from Amy's hand to scrawl

an answer to a question about *M*A*S*H*, a well-loved and religiously watched show in the Marks house. She knew the answer
was "Hot Lips," but she couldn't get Amy to understand what she
was mouthing across the table. She couldn't say it any louder lest
the team at the next table stole their answer. Lenny cringed and felt
her face sear with heat at the memory.

"I'm sorry, I didn't mean to take over."

"You got us to third place, don't apologize."

"I'm sorry," Lenny said automatically, looking at the rapidly di-
minishing pencil rather than at Kirra. She put the pencil and sharpener down and tried to still her hands.

"Lenny. You don't have to try and fit in with Amy and Ashleigh,
you know," Kirra said.

"Have they said something to you?"

"No . . . I meant that you should just be yourself."

"I can only be myself," Lenny replied, wondering where Kirra
was steering the conversation.

"I know. And that's enough. I just don't particularly like the
way they talk to you."

"It's just the way friends joke around, I think," Lenny said. "Although I'm not very good at the friends stuff, so I'm only guessing."

Lenny felt embarrassed. It had been silly of her to make such a
mess of it the night before. Of course she'd pay for the dry-cleaning
and maybe they would all end up laughing about it. She wondered
if Amy or Ashleigh liked Scrabble.

The thought of mending things with Amy before the weekend
was an instant mood-lifter. Her hopes of friendship weren't dashed
yet. She needed to wind up this conversation so she could track
Amy down and offer her an olive branch.

Forgiveness: sovereigns, governess, versions, envier

"Sorry, what were you saying?" Lenny asked, realizing she'd
zoned out and not wanting to be rude.

"Just that if you were up for it I'd love you to come to Darcy's sixth birthday. We'll be overrun with kids, but I thought you might come along and be my friend for the day?"

"When is this?"

"Tomorrow," Kirra said.

The invitation hung between them like a plastic bag caught in the wind. Lenny couldn't accept because she was thinking she might ask Amy and Ashleigh if they'd like a game of Scrabble over the weekend. She wondered what time the Ferny Creek library was open so they could go there.

"I can't. I have plans," Lenny said, mind scrambling for the right words and deciding to keep it simple. "With my housemate. Monica."

"Oh, of course. Your dance card is already filled," Kirra said.

Lenny was unfamiliar with the expression and Kirra must have registered her confusion.

"You're booked up," Kirra said. "Sorry, one of those sayings my mum uses. Maybe you and I can do something soon. A movie? Or a coffee even?"

Lenny nodded. She knew when most people said "soon" it rarely evolved into fully fleshed-out plans. She assumed this was just such an invitation and therefore safe to accept.

"I'd like that," Lenny said.

Kirra got up to go and Lenny stayed seated, unsure of what was polite in the circumstances. She hoped the bell would ring and save her the decision.

"Have a good weekend, Lenny," Kirra said as she disappeared out into the hall.

Only as she heard Kirra's disappearing footsteps did Lenny realize Kirra had called her a friend.

CHAPTER 11

Lenny couldn't find Amy at afternoon recess, so she placed an envelope containing eight dollars in change on her desk. On it she wrote: *Sorry again. Kind regards, Lenny Marks*. During her last class of the day, she wondered if she'd explained the purpose of the money well enough. Eight dollars seemed more than ample given three items could be dropped off at McKnight's for dry-cleaning for twelve dollars, but now she worried Amy might think she was suggesting that the eight dollars was reasonable compensation for the top itself.

After her students left for the day, Lenny went straight back to prep one, but she knew by the darkness of the classroom that she'd missed Amy well and truly. She didn't even check the car park for Amy's little red car, knowing it would be a long shot to find her within the school grounds after the final bell on any day of the week, let alone a Friday. As Lenny hadn't exchanged mobile numbers with Ashleigh or Amy, she found herself with no way of making weekend plans, or explaining the loose change.

Despite it being outside her usual Monday and Thursday schedule, Lenny made her way to McKnight's, where she found herself overwhelmed with choice in the pet food section. She had no idea what variety of food would be to the dog's taste or what his specific dietary requirements were. She selected three different brands—the ones with the happiest-looking dogs on the labels—and picked two flavors of each, to give him options. She would hope for the best and that there were no stomach upsets.

"I didn't know you had a dog," Ned said, attempting to fit all Lenny's items into her shopping bag.

"I don't know why that would be something you'd know," she said, wanting to remain cagey about her pet's origins.

"Oh—well, because you shop here all the time and I've never seen you get pet food before," he replied. "You're not cheating on me, are you? And shopping somewhere else?"

"Certainly not," she said, uncomfortable at Ned's line of questioning. "I just haven't had him for long."

He laughed. "It's all good, Lenny, I'm just messing with you."

She wished it was Deb on the register today. She always liked seeing Ned, but she was tired, wanted to get home and was incredibly paranoid about being arrested for theft.

"What's his name?"

"Whose name?" she asked.

"The dog's?"

"Oh, of course. Yes."

Lenny mulled over the question while she pretended to be deciding between spearmint or peppermint Mentos from a stand next to the register. Of course she would have a name for her dog if it were a dog she legitimately owned and had not stolen from someone the previous night.

"Malcolm." She said the first name that sprung to mind.

Malcolm: local, coal, calm

"Ah, nice. People names for pets are the best," Ned said. "A friend of mine has a Norwegian Forest cat called Barry."

Lenny smiled, glad her choice of name found favor with Ned, although uncomfortable with it at the same time.

Malcolm. She hadn't heard that name for so long.

"What a small world, hey, that you know Amy," Ned said.

Lenny disagreed with this sentiment. "It's not a very large sub-urb, and taking into account the majority of people here are families or elderly, the possibility that two people in a similar age bracket would meet is not altogether unlikely."

Ned nodded. "You make a good point."

"Apparently, after a certain age single people seeking compan-ionship will couple up with almost any other person they find to be basically satisfactory. It's human nature to form monogamous bonds," Lenny continued.

"Well, hang on, I'm not sure that's quite what it is." He looked mildly unimpressed. " 'Basically satisfactory'? "

Shut up, Lenny.

"I don't mean it in a bad way. Just the older we get, the less fussy we tend to be."

"I'm not sure that's any better," Ned replied, tapping at the reg-ister and finalizing her purchases.

Lenny felt as if they were treading into delicate territory. They'd never discussed anything more personal than *Buffy the Vampire Slayer* or *The Lord of the Rings* previously, which she hardly con-sidered intimate.

A slightly stooped lady, who looked somewhere around the ninety-year-old mark, started emptying her basket onto the conveyer belt. With dismay, Lenny noticed the cardigan the elderly customer was wearing was one she also owned. The groceries were paid for and Lenny realized she was the only one who could walk away to conclude the conversation. She wanted to clarify what she'd said, worried it sounded derogatory; she'd stepped on enough toes in the last twenty-four hours. Although she was not sure Ned would want to discuss his personal business within earshot of another customer.

She hesitated, leaning in to say more, but then losing her nerve.

Having been previously delayed by customers who were unable to keep their discussions within the time it took to ring up their groceries, she knew how frustrating it was to be stuck in the queue. She needed to rectify things quickly and move on.

"Amy is a good friend of mine and I'm sure you've chosen well," Lenny said.

"Thanks. I think?"

Lenny gathered her shopping bags.

"Hello there, Ned," the elderly lady said, signaling the end of Lenny and Ned's conversation.

"I'm very sorry for the delay," Lenny said to the elderly woman, taking the receipt Ned held out and making for the exit.

"See you soon, Lenny," she heard Ned call as she powered out the door.

As she secured her groceries onto the front and back of her bike, Lenny considered that if she kept it up with the verbal diarrhea, she'd not only have to find a new job but a new place to shop as well.

CHAPTER 12

May 30, 1997
Malcolm

Lenny was up to "A Warm Welcome," again. She loved that Bilbo's plan to free the dwarves from the wood-elves' caverns worked, even though some of them were not in a great state by the time they tumbled out of their respective barrels. The sound of Lenny's own voice reading those tried and trusted words comforted her in the cramped wardrobe space. It wasn't home, but it was her favorite place in her grandmother's house so far. She heard footsteps padding through the bedroom. Zanny was probably looking for her, yet Lenny made no attempt to disclose her location.

A rush of fresh air stirred the pages as the door beside her creaked open.

"Helena, I've been looking for you. What are you doing?" her grandmother said, sighing with relief.

"Reading," she replied.

"Oh, I can see that, darling. But why here?" Zanny motioned to the wardrobe and the clothes hanging above her. Admittedly, it was a tight fit even for a slight girl.

She'd been living with her grandmother for four days. It felt as unfamiliar to her as the house of any stranger would be. As if it were a temporary room at a school camp. And just as she had when her school took them to Portsea in grade six, she longed to go home. She reminded herself this was someone she was *meant* to know, someone she was related to, in fact. It just didn't feel very much like that. She wanted her mum to come back. Even Fergus, if that meant she got to go home. If they were to come back, Lenny would be on her best behavior. Surely after some time and space, they'd forgive her and return.

Because her mum loved her, she was almost entirely sure of this.

Zanny's bracelets chimed the length of her arm as she leaned against the doorframe. Lenny had taken the quilt from her bed and wrapped herself in it before wedging herself in the wardrobe. She was barely able to shut the door, such was the tightness of her hiding place.

"Darling, you have the whole house to go where you please. You're folded up in here like a garden chair."

Lenny noticed the wineglass in Zanny's hand. It had been obscured behind her dressing gown sleeve, the turquoise peacock feathers flowing down it as if they were falling from her shoulder. It meant Missy wasn't home. Drinking in the morning wasn't allowed when Missy was home.

"Then I choose here," Lenny said, meaning no impudence with her reply.

Zanny propped the bangle arm purposefully on her hip. The other hand, still clutching the wineglass, jutted out, giving Lenny the impression her grandmother was a sad, colorful teapot.

"Well, why don't you come out and read it to me?" Zanny suggested. "I love Tolkien. I started your mother on it, you know."

Lenny didn't know. There was a lot she didn't know. But she had no interest in reading out loud to anyone other than Malcolm. She wanted to be left alone, yet didn't want to appear rude by saying so.

"What about a game? I've got Scrabble?" Zanny suggested.

"I don't know how to play it."

"Well, I'm quite the aficionado. I'll teach you."

Lenny shook her head. "No, thank you. Maybe another time. We like it in here."

Zanny's eyes cast around the wardrobe, the teapot hands falling by her sides.

She sat down in front of Lenny, her knees folding beneath her and the wine sloshing dangerously close to the rim of her glass as she did so.

"Who is *we*?" Zanny asked.

Lenny looked around the wardrobe.

"Malcolm," Lenny said.

"Oh, darling . . ."

Lenny cut her off. "I know no one else is here. *Not really*. But it makes me happy to think he is."

Malcolm was as perfect as a friend could be, even if he was imaginary. He would go wherever she went and never made her feel awkward or out of place. And she was happy reading to him in the bottom of the wardrobe, just as she'd always done.

"Okay then, you keep reading. To Malcolm," Zanny said, her voice dropping to barely more than a whisper. Lenny supposed it was the wine making her act peculiarly. She was glad drinking didn't have the same effect on her grandmother as it did on Fergus.

Zanny shut the wardrobe door and Lenny's torchlight glowed in the small space, illuminating the pages she wanted to read and making her feel as if she were back home.

What she didn't want to tell Zanny was that Malcolm wasn't even there in her mind now. He'd always been easy to conjure, her most faithful friend, but since leaving home she just couldn't find him anymore. Like he'd been left behind in the confusion. And she wasn't ready to let him go yet.

She'd left far too many things behind in such a short time to lose her only friend as well.

CHAPTER 13

Friday, May 20, 2022

The dense garden was well established by the time Lenny bought the Tree House. It had been one of its immediate appeals. Retaining walls held the garden beds in place and made the front yard multi-tiered, in the style of terraced rice paddies. The plants were devotedly tended to by Lenny through all seasons. The grassed areas were dutifully kept trim with the old petrol-powered Victa left behind by the previous owners, who'd moved to a retirement "lifestyle" village.

Ten years earlier, when the househunting had commenced in earnest, Lenny had seen numerous properties within riding distance of Selby South Primary, and they were all out of her price range. The Tree House came on the market as if it were meant to be—which was a notion Lenny did not actually give any merit to. Serendipitous timing and fate were made-up explanations for coincidences. Some things just happened, regardless of the insubstantial links one could make between them.

Insubstantial: abstains, blatant, instant, bails, taunt, stab

Prior to the Tree House, Lenny had rented a unit in Ferntree Gully—and hated it. Fay would've always made her welcome, but once she was gainfully employed it seemed distinctly non-adult-like to live with her mum. And it left more room for the children who needed Fay more than she did by then. Besides that, it was too far on her bike to Selby South Primary from Fay's. So she patiently saved her deposit and tolerated the electro-trance music her closest neighbors played far too frequently. The real estate agent who had already showed Lenny through several other properties—which all went for well above their asking prices—notified her of the Tree House's availability and took her through it that same afternoon. Lenny couldn't believe her eyes the first time she saw her future home. It was a remarkably quaint, modest house in need of some maintenance. To Lenny Marks, who dreamed in other worlds, it had an air of the Last Homely House from Rivendell and she was lovestruck. Lenny offered the asking price without any attempt at negotiation. She should have been wary that the unexpectedly reasonable price likely meant restumping, a termite infestation or rot in the kitchen. But she was too busy signing over her deposit to pay any mind whatsoever to such trivialities. And Fay had personally vouched for the real estate agent. That was enough for Lenny.

In the years she had lived there, Lenny had learned the faces of her neighbors, but beyond a courteous hello in passing she didn't interact with them. To be on *too* good terms with the neighbors would be almost as constricting as not being on good terms at all. The exception was the house directly to her left. She knew Maureen Simcock, of 19 Callistemon Court, by name, despite never having cause to use it. Lenny mowed Ms. Simcock's lawn. It was not neighborly spirit that sent Lenny and her Victa through the fence and across her neighbor's yard once a month (fortnightly in spring). Instead, it was a necessity, given the risk of bushfires in their area. Also, the unkempt grass was—quite simply—an eyesore and Lenny could see it clearly from her lounge room windows.

Luckily, their dividing fence was a token effort to delineate their respective blocks and proved no obstacle. Lenny was able to mow in glorious straight lines from one yard right through to the other.

Once the lawn was under control, Lenny started noticing other garden maintenance issues next door. She grew tired of watching the agapanthus lining Maureen's driveway go to seed. Dispatching their wilted, browned heads took little time and she swiftly filled her neighbor's green bin with them. Personally, Lenny would've ripped the agapanthus right out of the ground; she held a particular dislike for them. The natural progression was to maintain Maureen's hydrangeas (they would only thrive if pruned back seasonally) and the leptospermum (which appeared to double in size monthly). The first couple of times she trespassed on Maureen's property with pruning shears in hand she returned home and waited for the police to turn up with an intervention order prohibiting her from ever crossing the boundary again. Instead the opposite happened: a handwritten note arrived in her letterbox, thanking her for her gardening efforts and inviting Lenny for tea with "Ms. Maureen Simcock." These were the sort of overly friendly terms Lenny worked hard to avoid. She needed no thanks or payment of any kind, only to know that she wasn't in line for a stern talking-to about her overzealous mowing. It was lovely Maureen took the time to appreciate her efforts, but she didn't think she had the wherewithal for tea with a stranger and returned the note with her own message on the back: "Ms. Simcock, thank you for the kind offer, there is no need for you to trouble yourself. I shall continue to mow your lawn. Lenny Marks."

It wasn't the only time Maureen reached out to her, but Lenny deflected any further invitations as politely as she could. On occasion, she noticed Maureen watching her, the wraparound verandah of number nineteen providing Maureen with a variety of views and seating positions from which to observe her property. But if Lenny felt Maureen was on her way down to speak to her, she would politely wave and ensure she finished up promptly. Deadheading her plants was one thing, unbidden conversation an entirely other beast.

Today Lenny noticed the hydrangeas were not in need of her services and the agapanthus nodded their vivid purple flowers to welcome her home.

Lenny walked in her front door and called to Malcolm—she would stick with the name, even though she bristled to say it out loud. She pictured him bounding to the door like Dino would greet Fred in *The Flintstones*, but this was not the case. Presumably such things would take time, if they occurred at all. He wasn't a cartoon. But the house was so quiet she wondered if he'd managed to get out. Or perhaps even decided to leave and find his way back to his original home, because sometimes familiarity was easier than change. The thought made her charge through the house, searching each room to locate him. She wanted him to be there. She *needed* him to be there.

Eventually she found him, hunkered in the laundry between the washing machine and the laundry trough. Lenny would not have previously imagined a fifty-odd-kilogram Rottweiler could fit in such a small cavity, so it was among the last places she looked. When she approached him, he cowered, and she immediately drew back to reassess. She wondered if he thought she was a kidnapper and planning on doing him harm. She was of the impression that dogs were good judges of personality. Surely he knew he was in a safe place. Although she *had* kidnapped him, so maybe he was just waiting to see whether she was a good kidnapper or a bad one. She left him where he was and returned to the kitchen to prepare his food in the hope he might be lured from his self-imposed purgatory.

Netflix was frozen on the menu screen asking *Are you still watching?* She used the remote to register her response and let "The

One with the Candy Hearts" play. She hoped Malcolm wasn't in hiding because of her choice of viewing; that would make living together quite difficult. Although she understood everyone had different tastes. With that in mind she switched to season one of *Buffy*, just in case. Maybe that was enough of *Friends* for one day.

Lenny filled one of her large pasta bowls with dry food, guessing at Malcolm's approximate weight in order to follow the instructions for how much she should give him. She added an extra scoop given he'd not eaten all day. She was impressed he hadn't destroyed her couch or anything else in her absence. He was, so far, a very polite house guest, even managing to keep his toilet trips almost within the confines of the newspaper.

Lenny put the bowl down in front of the laundry door and gave Malcolm his space.

"Country lamb, apparently. Sorry if it's not your favorite," she said to the black nose protruding from behind her laundry hamper. "It looked better on the label, it always does."

After cleaning up the soiled newspaper and putting it in her outdoor bin, she made herself a pot of tea—English breakfast, despite the time of day—and sat on the couch. The day was catching up with her; she felt exhausted. Whether it was due to her overindulgence in wine, her criminal act, the conversation with Ned or her now-shaky standing with Amy and Ashleigh, she felt overwhelmed. Not to mention how the thoughts of Fergus were weighing her down after she'd managed to keep them at bay for so long.

Lenny sipped her tea and checked newspaper headlines on her phone. She saw nothing of interest before typing "Belgrave," "Theft" and "Rottweiler" in the search engine to see if the police were onto her. She wasn't really sure what she'd do if they were; perhaps she and Malcolm would have to go into hiding.

There were no headlines addressing overnight dog thefts in the area and her relief was palpable. The only crime articles she found for Belgrave were regarding the increase in burglaries relating to the "scourge of weed" in the Hills. This was hopefully diverting the attention of the police from her antics, or at the least their prime suspect would be a drug-addled drifter. With the knowledge she was unlikely to be subject to a police raid in the next few hours, she put her phone down, drank her tea, pulled the throw rug over herself and settled in for a nap.

Lenny dreamed: a blurry collection of thoughts, people, places. As if she was walking along a clifftop and struggling to keep her feet steady, the dream threatened to drop her into a fully fledged memory at any second. But she didn't drop, not quite. She stayed on the rocky ledge and watched as the images formed like rockpools at her feet. A boy whose face she couldn't see, books read by torchlight, ripped pages from *The Hobbit*. She wondered why the dark smelled like potting mix. That particular odor didn't bother her on its own, but now it conjured up the last time she saw her mum and Fergus. It had never sat well with her that they left while she was in the shed. Even after what she'd done, surely her own mum would understand, if only she'd had the chance to properly explain. Instead, they waited until she was locked away and left her.

Nightmares: streaming, rightens, nastier, shaming, garish, remain

When she woke from her nap it was 9 P.M. and she found Malcolm on her left foot. He had curled himself tightly at the end of the couch and was now snoring quietly. How he'd done this without stirring her was either testament to his stealth or evidence of her exhaustion. It was the second night she'd spent on her couch, although this time she remembered how and why she'd ended up there. It was rare she didn't make it to her bed and there were even fewer times she recalled not performing her nightly rituals: double-checking all the doors were locked, laying out the following day's outfit and brushing her teeth, before checking the doors once more. Unlike the previous night, she made the conscious choice to stay put.

CHAPTER 14

Saturday, May 21

In the first light of Saturday morning and with no hangover hampering her thoughts, she studied Malcolm. He was a handsome, broad dog, with a decent case of halitosis and fur caked with the remnants of many nights spent outdoors. Potentially, he also harbored a number of fleas given the way he was inclined to dig his teeth into his rump. She really should give him a wash, although she worried that might be pushing the friendship. Either way, she would appreciate him smelling less like he'd climbed out of a dumpster.

Lenny considered her impending weekend. She would wash Malcolm, but otherwise Saturday was looking pretty quiet. It was her Fay weekend, which meant lunch on Sunday in Ringwood. Lenny was frustrated she didn't have more to report on her progress with *getting a life*. There was little point lying; Fay was too astute to buy into Lenny's half-cooked stories. And they were always half-cooked. She wasn't particularly good at lying and would usually resort to talking about someone familiar. And that meant someone from a TV show or book.

These stories were intended to make her sound less alone, but had caused her some issues along the way. Pretending to visit her three friends who lived in a lighthouse with their widowed father was readily discovered as a lie. Lenny hadn't realized the *Round the Twist* books were also a TV show, seen by most of her school. She didn't want to tell anyone that her mum and Fergus had a massive fight about the cost of sending her on the end-of-term excursion to Gumbuya Park. The lie came easier than the truth. And then she'd come unstuck again at university when she pretended to have a boyfriend. Dawson was too identifiable a name to use and she should've been more creative, but had been caught on the hop. One of the girls sneered and asked her if Pacey and Joey were her friends as well. Lenny felt herself turn so incredibly red she probably could've lit up a small village. She took the next three days off. Worst of all, she didn't even like *Dawson's Creek*; she'd just grabbed at an available name.

Admittedly, it had been easier to talk to people at university. It wasn't as cliquey as high school and there were enough faces on campus for her not to stand out or have to hide. She even managed to off-load her virginity while she studied for her degree. But they were uni friends, whom she saw regularly because they needed to be at the same location. And once the degrees were handed out, Lenny didn't keep in contact and neither did they.

As for Monica, she had become Lenny's housemate as an excuse to decline an invitation to a hens' night some years earlier. After that, Monica gave Lenny a way to circumvent social occasions of all sorts, from the staff Christmas events to Tupperware parties to wine-tasting tours. Having just rewatched *Friends*, season four, "Monica" had rolled freely off her tongue. Had Lenny possessed a better imagination, she could have mixed character names with the personalities of others and come up with someone unique, but she was inclined to keep it simple, lest she forget the story she'd created. And she did actually see Monica every day. So it wasn't really that much of a stretch.

Pretending there were people in her life seemed to quell the concerns of others. She'd noticed many times that being alone was akin to having a medical condition, especially once she was over thirty. Well-meaning people wanted to offer solutions or anecdotes on a regular basis.

Have you tried internet dating?

My sister thought she'd be alone forever and now she's married with three kids. You just never know when it will happen.

You just haven't met the right person yet.

You're still young, don't worry.

She *wasn't* worrying, not in the least. She was actually happy being alone. Not to mention, people put too much stock in being happy. Happiness was immeasurable and moveable. That sort of instability was fraught with hazard. Lenny was a functioning, contributing member of the community who abided by the rules—with a recent exception—and was not a burden on anyone. That, in her books, was a definite marker of success. And she only answered to herself—well, and Fay, if she was completely honest—so if she wanted to sleep on the couch in her clothes with a stolen dog she could do just that.

But that morning she felt a flicker of disappointment that she hadn't accepted Kirra's offer. She'd declined everything for so long it was her default setting. While it was likely Darcy's birthday may have involved people jostling her, sticky-handed children and possibly even obligatory party games, it now seemed sad to have declined something that might have been moderately enjoyable for the sake of an imaginary housemate who was available at any time.

Malcolm climbed off the couch and padded to the door. It was hard to let him out with the fences in the state they were. They contained him somewhat but they certainly weren't dog-proof and if he wanted to leave her, he could. She unlocked the door and let him out, standing on the patio to watch him find a spot to relieve himself. She didn't want him to wander too far. She would have to make a secure space for Malcolm in the yard, which she decided was now top priority on her to-do list.

There was no time to give energy to her disappointment at turning Kirra down. She would likely have had to cancel going to Darcy's birthday anyway, due to her pressing jobs around the house. So it actually worked out for the best.

Malcolm padded back inside and Lenny closed the door against the frigid outdoor air.

Yes, she was content on her own. She had almost completely convinced herself of this.

CHAPTER 15

Sunday, May 22

Fay opened her front door to Lenny with a fervor that was entirely over the top. Her foster mother had a way of smiling with her whole face that made her eyes close to slivers. She was one of the few people who could touch Lenny without making her recoil like a threatened turtle. Fay wrapped Lenny in her arms, trapping her against her chest and radiating scents of fresh powder, both baking and talcum. Fay used the latter so liberally after showers she would leave white footprints from bathroom to bedroom.

"So good to see you, my Lenny-girl. Get in here, I need help with the melting moments." Fay released her and all but pushed her through the door.

Her foster mother didn't need help with the melting moments; she was a much better cook on her own, but she always had a job or two for Lenny to do when she came. Lenny was happy to help, even if the tasks felt a little inconsequential.

Two little girls sat on the rug in the front room; the television wasn't on and they were playing with the My Little Pony collection, which seemed to have expanded every time Lenny saw it. The girls weren't familiar to Lenny and this was neither off-putting nor unusual. Visits with Fay usually gave rise to a new face or two (once there were five) and as they were generally aged twelve or under, it caused her little angst.

Lenny stopped to introduce herself. She got down on the far end of the lounge room rug and stayed a respectable distance from them. No one liked to be crowded upon meeting a new person, she knew all too well.

"I'm Lenny, how do you do?" she said.

The elder of the two girls moved position, shuffling in front of her sister and performing her duty as a safety barrier. She was a tiny mountain of courage wrapped in a *Frozen* jumper, with pink leggings that were too short for her long legs.

"I'm Skye and that's Paige. She doesn't like strangers."

"And rightly so. Neither do I," said Lenny.

"She's no stranger, Paige, that's Lenny. I've told you about her. The schoolteacher with the bicycle," Fay announced. "She was just like you once. I think she even played with a couple of those very ponies."

Lenny did not think this was the case at all; she'd been twelve when she arrived and a bit past toys, but she wouldn't correct Fay.

"And I never left," Lenny said. "Or at least not for a long time."

Lenny noticed Skye slip a cushion from the couch and prop it up in front of her. *Good Vibes Only* was emblazoned across it; Fay was not opposed to that sort of homeware. Lenny always thought that particular cushion imposed undue pressure on anyone who came across it. Sometimes one had only mediocre vibes, which should also be acceptable.

"Ten minutes until lunch," Fay said, shuffling off toward the kitchen.

"Did you bring your bike with you?" Skye asked.

"No, not today. I caught the bus."

"We don't know how to ride a bike," Skye said.

"Well, it's very practical. It doesn't need petrol and it gets you places quickly," Lenny said. "And I have always thought it's quite a fun way to get around."

Paige's eyes emerged from behind the cushion.

"We're too little for bikes," Skye said, with some authority. Lenny presumed an adult somewhere, at some time, had told her this.

"Well, I'm not so sure about that. How old are you?"

"I'm six and she's four and half," said Skye, indicating Paige.

"Well, I'm thirty-seven," Lenny said. "But I imagine six and four are very good ages to learn how to ride a bike."

"Four and a half." Paige spoke quietly, only raising enough of her head from around the cushion to correct Lenny before disappearing again.

"That cushion talks, did you know that, Skye?" Lenny said.

Skye giggled, a glorious sound.

"It wasn't the cushion, it was me." Paige peered out even further.

"Oh, that's a relief. I was worried the couch would start talking to me," Lenny said, and both girls erupted into a spray of laughter.

"But I do know there are some bikes around here somewhere. Maybe we can find them. I've always thought riding a bike is a bit like flying."

"Are they magic?" Skye asked.

"Oh, not quite magic," Lenny said, and she noticed Skye's smile dipped, which she didn't like. Lenny most certainly didn't believe in magic, but she supposed when you were very little it wasn't so bad an idea. Like Santa or the Easter bunny. "Or should I say, a different sort of magic from Elsa."

"Really?" Skye's eyes lit up again and Paige let her cushion barrier fall to the floor.

"Fay's bikes make you feel like you're flying. And so they are a little bit magic."

The girls exchanged smiles.

"Should we try after lunch?" Lenny suggested and both girls nodded enthusiastically.

"I'm going to wash my hands so I can help Fay," Lenny said. "Can you set the table, please?"

Skye and Paige skittered off to the dining room to put out the plates. Lenny knew that would have been one of the first things Fay had shown the girls. Dinners, as well as Sunday lunch, were formal dining table affairs in the Marks house.

"Do you still have those bikes in the shed?" Lenny asked, watching Fay's glasses fog as she pulled a shepherd's pie from the oven. It smelled delicious: crispy potato, gravy and memories. She would cover hers in tomato sauce and Fay would scold her for it; they'd had the same conversation for years.

"The magic ones?" Fay chortled. "Of course I do, but they'll need the tires pumped up."

She removed her glasses and rubbed the lenses on her t-shirt. Fay loved a loud character t-shirt and this one was no exception. Lenny recalled the stares they sometimes got at the supermarket, or at school pick-ups when Fay was wearing one of her Disney or Japanese anime tees. It was a stark contrast to Lenny's attempts to shroud herself in gray or black cloaks of invisibility. Today's offering was baby Groot in a flowerpot with *Grootings, earthlings* emblazoned above it. The t-shirt itself was an eye-watering shade of green, more suited to a fern than a woman. Lenny was always surprised they were available in adult sizes.

"Do you mind if I show the girls how to ride after lunch?"

Fay grinned. "I was counting on it."

Fay's husband, Robert, had died when Lenny was seventeen, just when she had become comfortable calling him Dad. It was the departure of yet another family member, although this time she was sure he hadn't been involved in the plans. Fay's uncharacteristic silence in the days that followed also signaled she had not been warned her husband was going. He was old in Lenny's eyes, because she was a teenager and he an adult. But he was not old enough, not to leave forever.

Forever: fever, ever, over

After lunch, Lenny, Paige and Skye were excused from dishes duty to locate the bikes in Robert's garage. The garage would always be Robert's, even though he hadn't set foot in it for almost two decades. If it were appropriate to sprinkle his ashes there they would have, although he'd have hated the mess. Lenny was still surprised not to find him inside every time she lifted the roller door. She expected to see him hunched over the workbench, the bare bulb strung from one of the cross beams above him, bathing him in a tungsten glow. She missed him even though he'd been out of her life now for longer than he had been in it.

She had always been fond of being called Lenny. It was the plainness of it that appealed to her; she could have been anyone. When Fergus called her Helena, he'd managed to make it sound like darts being thrown. It was as if he knew she preferred Lenny and so refused to use it. But from the moment she'd arrived at the Markses' home, Robert called her Lenny-girl and it was an instant comfort. When they enrolled her at Menzies High, she'd asked to simply be Lenny from then on.

The bikes were not hard to locate. Robert had always kept his shed in good order and it still remained largely organized. Only now, everything was covered in a layer of dust and the odd spider was in residence. As Fay had anticipated, the bikes had flat tires. Lenny made short work of them with the pump, and sized each girl up against the bicycles to raise or lower the seats as required.

The bikes were newer than the one Lenny had learned to ride on. That one had long ago been sent out with the hard rubbish.

It was such a simple thing, a kid on a bike, but before Fay and Robert she'd never been shown how to ride. A few years later, when it was time to learn to drive, Robert took her to get her learner's permit. He had been so confident she'd pass the test he'd been waiting for her in the passenger seat so she could drive them home. He was relatively unflappable, which was lucky because she wasn't a natural in the driver's seat. When Robert died, she'd completely given it up; she didn't have the courage or resolve without him around. And in any case, she preferred being on two wheels.

Riding the bike was the first thing to bond her to Robert and it had made her feel at home. Effortlessly gliding down a hill, wind pounding her ears, feeling like she was flying. It gave her no time to consider anything but what was directly in front of her; riding was a balm for a broken girl. Maybe Robert knew it was exactly what she needed, or maybe he just didn't know what else to do with her.

Lenny hoped it could be the same for Paige and Skye, even though she wasn't aware of what they were trying to forget. But they wouldn't be with Fay if there was nothing. She was glad they'd found her foster mum, however temporary it may be. It gave them at least a few days—maybe longer—full of Fay's routines, big love and being safely cuddled up under a quilt smelling of fabric softener in a way Lenny could never replicate, even with the same box of Omo.

"I'm scared," Paige said as Lenny helped her mount the blue BMX.

"Well, you don't have to do this," Lenny told her.

Paige considered the reprieve.

"Or," Lenny said, "I'll just stay with you the whole time. And maybe that will make it less scary?"

Paige's eyes were automatically drawn to her sister; nothing without her approval.

Skye nodded.

Go on, she's okay, she was saying, even though her mouth didn't move.

The dynamic between the two was warm but it pained Lenny; their dependence on each other was almost guaranteed to set one or the other up for failure. As Lenny knew, being so attached to anyone could never end well.

A tiny voice reached her ears. "I'd like to try now, please."

Paige's initial nerves were short-lived. She quickly managed to coordinate her movements to balance and pedal. She was a natural, but Lenny hung on to the handlebars until Paige was ready for her to let go. She wouldn't let either girl down.

The sisters squealed and yahooed at each other as they circled the driveway, each building up speed along with their confidence. Lenny felt a quiet happiness brimming as she watched them. It was the joy of childhood; they could be so easily damaged, but so quick to forget. It was okay to live with almost-truths some of the time.

"Will they stay long?" Lenny asked when Fay brought out the melting moments with steaming cups of tea. The cookies were still oven warm and dissolved into a burst of sugar on her tongue.

"I don't know. I can never predict how long the kids will be with me, so I've given up trying," Fay replied, sliding the tray onto the cast-iron bistro setting under the large oak on her front lawn. The tree was a magnificent centerpiece but the quantity of acorns it dropped was incredible. Lenny remembered mowing the front lawn and acorns ricocheting from the mower blades like bullets, causing many a bruise and once a broken front window. Lenny had hidden when that happened, terrified she would be in all sorts of trouble for causing the damage. Robert found her at the bottom of the wardrobe. He didn't try to coax her out; instead he sat outside the door and said, "You know, broken things are good. It means they have a story or two. We don't mind things being broken around here, Lenny-girl." Then he waited for her to come out, humming to himself and not mad in the slightest.

Fay sat on one of the chairs and pulled her cardigan tight around herself.

"I'll get going soon, before it's dark," Lenny said.

"I've packed you some leftovers. And extra biscuits for the bus."

"Thank you."

The women watched the girls in silence for a moment, Fay topping up both their cups.

"I know about the parole hearing," Fay said. "For Fergus."

Lenny didn't reply and shuffled her feet. His name was like touching a battery to the tip of her tongue.

"Are you going to write something?"

"No, I don't think so."

"You should consider it—it may make a difference. And it might be a good way for you to move forward."

Lenny watched as the girls cheered each other on, hoping Fay would stop talking.

"There's nothing to move forward from."

"Helena, this is why I keep telling you it's time to speak to someone." Fay's usually confident voice wavered just slightly and Lenny turned to her.

"What he did once he and Mum left doesn't matter. It can't fix the past."

Fay's brow creased, her face a landscape of lines. She looked weary, which was unusual for the indefatigable Fay Marks.

"Lenny, you can't just ignore this," she replied. "I've let you do that for far too long."

"We will talk about this another time." Lenny knew she sounded petulant and didn't care.

"When?" Fay asked. "The hearing is soon. I'm writing something."

"Good for you." Lenny regretted her tone immediately. Fay shot her a look, but when she didn't reprimand Lenny, it was clear she was more worried than mad.

Parole hearing: orangerie, orphanage, helping, reaping, roaring

She wanted to stop thinking about it. It was making her feel like she was holding her breath, and she realized she had been doing just that. She let her lungs fill to capacity and then released the air.

Oak tree: retake, karo, toke, eke, rat

Melting moment: mignonette, longtime, mention, entoil

Breathing: hearting, earthing, brighten, gather, garnet, triage

"Stop doing that," Fay interrupted her.

"Stop doing what?" she snapped.

"You're rearranging letters, I can tell. You've done it every time I've tried to have a serious conversation with you since you were a teenager."

Teenager: generate, greaten, negater, agent

Anagram: ragman, garam, agma, mag, man, mar

Her brain scrambled to refocus.

"Lenny-girl," Fay said, louder now, "I just want you to be happy."

"What makes you think I'm not?"

Lenny stood; she needed to convince Fay it was all okay, *that she was okay*, and then she could end the conversation and leave.

"Years of being your mother makes me think you're not."

"I'm doing it, Fay, I'm doing what you asked me to. I have friends, I am speaking to people."

"But are you enjoying it?" Fay asked.

Lenny paused. That wasn't part of it. It wasn't in Fay's original ultimatum. She recalled the conversation clearly, although she may have simplified the meaning over time. Fay never specifically said, "I want you to enjoy meeting people and be happy." She just told her she needed to get out more and meet people. *Get a life, Lenny Marks.* Lenny didn't want to lie to Fay but she did want a quick way out of this conversation. She'd looked forward to reporting back on Ashleigh and Amy and the trivia night, but now she just felt uncomfortable and deceitful.

"Yes. I should've done it years ago."

Fay gave a single hearty snort of laughter. "Who are you trying to convince here—you or me?"

"I'm fine, Fay," Lenny said, trying to regain her equilibrium. "Mum, really. I am."

"Don't pull the mum card on me. Fine and happy are not the same thing."

"Then *I'm happy*," Lenny said, but it was stiff, even to her own ears.

"Sit back down—you're not to leave in a mood," Fay ordered. Lenny did as she was told but in childish protest sat on one of the concrete steps that formed part of the path to the front door.

"I'm not trying to make this difficult, but I won't be around forever and I want to know you have people in your life," Fay said, and she stuck her little finger in her tea, fishing out a bit of leaf. "There are stories about people who die at home and no one knows to go looking for them. They get eaten by their cats or slowly decompose into the floorboards."

"I don't have a cat," Lenny replied.

"Well, don't get one."

"Speaking of which, I adopted a dog this week. And went out to a pub with work friends."

Fay looked genuinely surprised. "Are you making that up?"

"No, not at all."

"Could you have mentioned that an hour ago?"

"I could've. I probably should've."

"Well, that's great, Lenny-girl. It really is."

"And work is good. And . . ." She petered off. "I think Amy and Ashleigh and I will do something next weekend. They're the prep teachers I told you about."

Lenny wished for the ability to sound more convincing, but wasn't sure if she'd even persuaded herself into believing she had actually made some friends.

"Did you see us, Fay?" Skye asked as she raced to the table, her eyes bright, her arms flapping as if she were about to take off. It was glorious unbridled happiness. Lenny felt a tingle of warmth at the brightness of the girl's smile. It was a work of art, a smile so genuine. And it was one she had helped bring to life.

"Yes, love, I did. You're a natural," Fay said, holding out the plate of biscuits to the beaming child.

Lenny didn't realize Paige had also come closer, she was such a quiet child. The first thing she was aware of was Paige's tiny arms, clad in her red waterproof parka, wrapping around her neck in an attempt to cuddle her. "Thanks for helping me fly," Paige whispered.

Lenny's entire body seized with the unexpected touch. She knew, somewhere deep within herself, that it was *just a child* and she was *not* a threat. But her reaction was uncontrollable. She sprung to her feet, sending Paige sprawling onto the grass. The noise Lenny made was almost primal, her movements jerking and reflexive as she retreated toward the house. Her breathing quickened, her heart thumped, the small, soft, well-meaning hands burning like scorch marks on her skin.

You did this.

Paige cried out as she tumbled backward onto the lawn and Skye was by her side in seconds. The two sisters clung to each other on the grass while Fay surveyed the scene. She had seen this reaction from Lenny before.

Lenny hunkered down behind the balustrade along the verandah and sobbed into her hands like a lost child. She hadn't wanted to scare the girls and she couldn't bear to look up and see their small upset faces. They'd trusted someone, and she'd let them down. Worse, she'd scared them.

Scared: raced, sear, read, arc, scar

Maybe Fay was right. There was something very wrong with Lenny, and she wasn't sure it was repairable.

CHAPTER 16

Fay herded the girls inside and sat beside Lenny on the cold concrete of the front porch. The tears stopped and Lenny pressed her face against the smooth wood of the railings she'd helped Robert paint many years ago. The paint was weathered now and chipped in places, but the rails were solid and comforting. She wanted to close her eyes and fall asleep; the emotional outburst had sapped her energy.

"The girls are fine," Fay said, taking Lenny's hand in her own. Lenny attempted to pull it away, but Fay held firm.

"I didn't know she was there. She surprised me."

"I know."

"It hasn't happened for so long."

"But it still happens. This is why you have to speak to someone," Fay said.

"You said I didn't have to," Lenny replied.

"No, that's not what I said. You're remembering this how you want to and not how it was."

"I don't want to . . ." Lenny began.

"I *know* you don't. But that doesn't mean you shouldn't. You can't avoid people forever. You're missing out on some of the most beautiful moments in life."

"But what if it's like it was before?"

"Before? Do you mean when you were thirteen?"

"Yes," Lenny replied.

"Oh, Len, I think things have changed a bit in two decades. It won't be like that. She didn't understand you. We shouldn't have taken you to that silly woman. I think she pulled her psychology degree out of a cereal box."

After Zanny died, she'd been taken to a place that didn't feel anything like a home, but not quite like a hospital either. They'd clearly run out of family members to take her in. Lenny believed she was fine, but every day someone would ask her more questions, query how she felt, give her ideas of how to cope. There were other teenagers that lived there, but they didn't seem like people she wanted to talk to. So she kept to herself, which was her usual way by then. The new, strange house was like starting over again, and she didn't think she could stand it. She shared a room and had very little time to herself; there wasn't even space in the wardrobe for her to hide.

She was upset Zanny was gone, of course she was. By that point, she'd grown accustomed to life at her grandmother's. Regular Scrabble bouts, records being played a little too loud (until Missy turned them down so Lenny could sleep), Zanny's unpredictable moods that kept her in bed sometimes for days at a time, and Missy's cheerfulness that filled in the places Zanny could not. Sometimes her grandmother would have friends over. Always groups of women whose high-pitched chatter would send Lenny into the depths of her wardrobe. Occasionally, the gathering would pile outside, into the cold, and stare at the moon. Lenny would watch from the safety of the indoors as they threw their arms wildly about or hugged each other.

Finally, she was taken to the Marks and she was back to being brand-new and lost all over again. If someone had explained things to her, it had long since vanished from her mind. Almost everything before living with her foster parents seemed to carry discomfort with it and was best avoided.

Fay and Robert drove her to twice-weekly sessions with a psychologist, a woman with untamed hair and stiff blouses. After a number of appointments, Lenny overheard a discussion not meant for her ears. She was supposed to be in the waiting room, but had found the intensity of the other people there overwhelming and retreated down the hallway, finding refuge in a quiet corner. From behind a potted fiddle-leaf fig, she heard Fay, Robert, her psychologist and an unknown man talking about her. The words went over her head, but the concept was not incomprehensible. Intensive treatment. Traumatic disorder. Diagnosis. *Inpatient*.

Lenny found herself hot with fury. The psychologist had lied to her. She'd told Lenny the conversations were confidential, and here she was telling everyone there was something wrong with her. The thought of going to hospital was terrifying. What if they found out what she'd done? They'd never let her out. She'd be deemed dangerous and not allowed to stay in the Markses' nice family home.

Still tucked behind the plant in the corridor of the psychologist's office, Lenny resolved to do better at making everyone think she was as happy and balanced and as *normal* as every other thirteen-year-old. If she persuaded them of this, she'd stay safely installed with Fay and Robert. She knew how powerful lies could be, especially from someone as unassuming as her.

Lenny went back to the rowdiness of the waiting room and pretended she'd never left. But if she had stayed and kept listening, she would've heard an indignant Fay Marks tell them they were all mad themselves. That Lenny was staying with her and she was special in a way none of them understood. She told them in no uncertain terms that Lenny had more tenacity and resilience than they had in their *over-educated arses* and Lenny *is a Marks now, and we stick together.* Robert tried to rein in his wife, but it only resulted in her becoming more incensed. Lenny never heard a word of it. All she knew was a very tense and irate Fay collected her from the waiting room a few minutes later and Lenny blamed herself for causing her foster mother's foul mood.

"I'm worried about you," Fay said now, beside her on the porch. Despite holding Lenny's hand, she was keeping some distance between them.

"Fay, you don't need to worry about me. I just didn't know she was there." Lenny took her hand back. "I am fine." She forced a smile.

Fay wasn't convinced, but sighed in resignation.

"I've got a card of someone you can ring and make an appointment with. It's important to me, Lenny-girl."

"I'll take the card, but I won't make any promises."

"Just think about it. And maybe I can come over soon and meet this new dog of yours? What's his name?"

"Malcolm," Lenny replied.

Fay sucked air in quickly enough to make Lenny turn her head. "*Malcolm?*"

"Yes. He was a rescue dog . . . of sorts. So I got to name him." Lenny felt dangerously close to revealing too much about his origins. "And yes, you should come and meet him sometime."

Fay said nothing, instead scanning Lenny's face, looking for an answer to a question she didn't seem able to ask.

"Well, then, come say goodbye to these girls. You'd better shake your tail feather if you don't want to catch the bus in the dark. You know I don't like that."

Fay held the door open and waited for Lenny to collect herself and do as she was told.

CHAPTER 17

Monday, May 23

Lenny yawned, quietly considering a staff room poster on occupational hazards. Who would've thought lifting things above head height would require such detailed instructions and warnings. She mindlessly turned her pot of tea the requisite three times as she read.

She'd completed her run that morning and was disappointed it took three minutes and twenty-seven seconds longer than usual to finish the six kilometers. It surprised her how quickly her fitness could dip and how heavy her legs had felt on the hills she usually managed to power up with only mild exertion. And it wasn't just the extra time weighing on her—she couldn't stop thinking about the terror on Paige's face. Lenny didn't often react that way anymore, which she knew was due to her avoidance of physical contact more than resolution of any underlying issue. Fay probably had a point when she said Lenny needed to do something more than just add to her phone contact list. Which, thus far, had been an abject failure.

Lenny didn't realize Ms. Pham was in the room until she heard her voice beside her.

"Can you pop by my office before you head to your classroom?" Ms. Pham asked, with no warmth whatsoever. This was not the same tone as "Lora" from Thursday night.

The weekend had evidently not served the purpose of diffusing her misdemeanors.

Lenny immediately assumed a worst-case scenario that involved packing up her desk and being escorted off the premises by hulking security guards. This was despite the school not having security guards, hulking or otherwise. Either Lora knew about her larceny or she was about to be fired for insubordination.

Insubordination: insinuator, ruination, disunion, tornado

With a desperately dry mouth and no stomach for her tea, she decided to face her fate immediately. She remained hopeful she'd be granted the leniency to finish the day and farewell her class. She'd grown fond of her band of students, as she did every year. Once they accepted her teaching style and she adapted to the different characters and range of personalities, the days ran as smoothly as her Stihl chainsaw.

She tentatively poked her head around Ms. Pham's door only to find her on the phone. The principal beckoned her in with her free hand and Lenny skulked to one of the chairs usually reserved for mischievous students. She felt a dampness forming in her armpits and dryness tickling the back of her throat. She tried not to listen in and focused on the series of motivational prints hanging the length of the wall.

RESILIENCE. PERSEVERANCE. COURAGE.

The posters were a little too prescriptive to be considered inspirational, and she recalled ones of a similar standard on her own year twelve coordinator's wall back when Lenny had her mandatory career guidance meeting with her.

Mrs. Hudson was meant to help her decide on university preferences or alternative pathways, but when Lenny announced her choice was primary school education, Mrs. Hudson had actually laughed out loud.

"But you hardly say anything," Mrs. Hudson said, incredulous.

"I speak when I need to," Lenny responded.

"But you don't seem to like people."

"And neither do you," Lenny replied, because this was a well-known school fact.

Mrs. Hudson pursed her lips and put her pen down on her desk so she could knead her hands together. "You've got some spunk, Lenny."

"I don't know what that means."

"But you'll need more than that," said Mrs. Hudson, not stopping to explain or even acknowledge Lenny had said something. "What do I know, though? You might make it."

Lenny almost thanked her for the semi-compliment, but realized Mrs. Hudson didn't need her to participate in this conversation to keep it moving.

As she'd only taken Lenny for one semester of social studies, Mrs. Hudson would be unlikely to have any idea about her strengths and weaknesses. This was a common mistake; Lenny was often misjudged and underestimated. Academically she could've considered a wide range of university courses. She wasn't quite up there for medicine or law, nor did they interest her. But Mrs. Hudson didn't know she'd just motivated Lenny in the most powerful way possible. She'd challenged her to fail. And she wouldn't.

Put that on a motivational poster, Lenny thought to herself.

"Good luck—I think you'll need it," Mrs. Hudson had said in parting, dismissing Lenny from the meeting as the next student rapped at the door. Fifteen minutes hardly seemed like sufficient time to resolve one's future, but that was all Menzies High School allowed.

As soon as Ms. Pham put the phone down, Lenny cleared her throat and launched her campaign to stay employed. Begging wasn't beyond her. "If you give me one more chance, I won't let you down."

The principal considered this. "A chance at what?"

"I presume you would like me to vacate my position?"

"God, no. What are you on about?" Ms. Pham said, leaning back in her chair.

"My poor behavior last week. I am awfully sorry, it won't happen again."

"Do you mean at the pub?"

Lenny's cheeks radiated.

"That was the most relaxed I've ever seen you. You should have wine more often; I liked that side of you. The only thing that annoyed me was your recollection of general knowledge—I'm terrible at it. In one ear, out the other. I still couldn't tell you the capital of Laos and it's been less than a week."

The relief was so profound, Lenny was barely able to talk.

"I can stay?" she managed.

"Stay? You have to stay or I'm the one who gets stuck with hiring someone new. And let me tell you, I've never felt so old as when I filled the prep spots last year. You know Amy and Ashleigh were both born in the nineties. *The nineties*, Lenny. I could have children their age. I *don't*, but I could."

"You didn't mind me calling you Lora?"

"I've been called much worse. And it *is* my name, after all. You are allowed to use it."

"What about the dog?"

"What dog?" Lora asked.

Lenny realized she'd said too much. No one knew about Malcolm, much less the way she'd acquired him. A change of subject was required.

"What was it you wanted to see me about?" Lenny asked.

"Parent–teacher interviews are on Thursday."

"Yes, I know, I've got them all booked in."

"I just want to make sure we don't have a repeat of last year."

Lenny felt her cheeks reignite. She remembered last year's interviews all too well. Liam Backman's parents had earned an indelible spot in Selby South Primary parent–teacher history.

It was never easy suggesting to a parent their child was not ready to go up a year level and Mr. and Mrs. Backman were the extreme example of how that meeting could go awry. They were none too pleased, to say the least, that their son had failed to demonstrate even a basic understanding of the syllabus. Were he to be progressed to grade six, he'd only fall further behind. This had been communicated to them at various points throughout the year, yet they had remained uninterested in Liam's schooling, which was reflected in his aptitude. Not having taken Lenny's comments about Liam repeating the year well, the Backmans became further incensed when she suggested their son be assessed by a psychologist for his apparent sociopathic tendencies. The final nail was asking if either of Liam's parents had achieved a grade five level of reading, writing or maths. Her questions were well intentioned: she needed to know if they had the capacity to help Liam at home, or if she should apply for a school-funded aide. But her delivery had been off, as it so often was.

The meeting came to an abrupt end when Mr. Backman picked up a chair and threw it through the window, resulting in the police being called.

"I know it wasn't your fault *entirely*. But I just need you to be mindful that parents can be very sensitive and sometimes don't want to be faced with too much truth."

"I don't want to lie to them. If they ask me questions, I feel I should answer honestly."

"And you should. But perhaps we could omit some things if they sound less . . . favorable. Any sort of psychological diagnosis perhaps. Certainly no mention of sociopaths. Or psychopaths, or any of the paths, I'd say, in general."

"I really did think the behavior Liam displayed was in keeping with the Hare psychopathy checklist," Lenny said.

Lora took a deep breath, and for the first time Lenny realized that the woman in charge of the school didn't look to be much older than she was. She was perhaps only early forties, although she had the deportment of someone older. She oozed a gentle, but definite, level of intimidation. Her eyebrows were immaculately groomed and moved further than Lenny thought eyebrows could. She found herself watching them to see where they'd go next. It was almost like making eye contact without the discomfort.

"I know you were trying to help Liam. But let's just keep to the schoolwork and the positives," Lora said.

Lenny nodded. She was embarrassed to have to be pulled aside and reminded of what constituted appropriate conversation. Over the years she thought she'd gotten better at avoiding these uncomfortable situations; had Mr. Backman not caused damage to school property, no one would've been any the wiser. But she did have a genuine concern about Liam's future because she knew all too well the struggle to fit within the confines of societal expectations. She'd even checked her own traits and tendencies against the checklist— just in case—and felt fairly comfortable she was *not* a sociopath.

"Perhaps I could remove the chairs from my classroom, to limit the objects that could be thrown?" Lenny suggested.

"Uh, no. I think that's over the top."

"I will do my best to not be controversial," Lenny said, chastened.

"You'll be fine. I just need you to be aware of what you're saying and who you're saying it to."

Lenny was always, almost painfully, aware of the words coming out of her mouth. But Lora was not taking her job away and so Lenny needed to accept her advice and get out of her office before she changed her mind.

"Yes, of course. Thank you for bringing this to my attention," Lenny said.

Lora smiled. "Lenny, you're a real asset to the team here. And you cause me no trouble, which I very much appreciate."

"Thank you," she mumbled, not liking to accept a compliment too readily in case she seemed arrogant.

Lora said nothing; it was apparent their meeting was over. Lenny stood to leave.

"Vientiane," Lenny said.

"Sorry, what was that?"

"Vientiane. The capital of Laos. You'd forgotten it," Lenny said.

"Good, I'll try and remember." Lora smiled shrewdly.

"Thank you," Lenny said awkwardly, as she hurried out the door.

CHAPTER 18

At McKnight's that afternoon, Lenny looked for Ned purely to avoid him. However, after finding he wasn't there and the avoidance was unnecessary, she was rather disappointed. Debra was stationed at the checkout and nodded at Lenny in an automatic way that suggested she'd been told to greet all the customers on arrival.

Lenny returned the gesture and picked up a basket.

Twenty minutes later, she wrestled a ten-kilo bag of dog food onto the handlebars of her bike and wondered if it would be safe to rest it there for the journey home. She had panniers attached to her rear bike rack for just this purpose, but was reluctant to put the heavy bag on one side and affect her balance. It was also starting to rain. The rain didn't bother her, but it did tend to make drivers a little less wary of bike riders; they were busy keeping their tires on the wet roads.

"You know we do home delivery?" Ned said from behind her.

His voice had a thrilling quality to it. Gravelly, earthy, almost roguish.

"Not necessary, thank you. I can get home," Lenny replied tersely.

"But why would you when I'm here to drop it on your doorstep?"

"I am more than capable of managing my groceries," she told him, her words sharper than she intended.

"I'm sure you are. But I'd like to help," Ned said.

She paused, balancing the awkward bag, and looked over to where he leaned comfortably against the shop wall. He sounded a little smug, as if watching the battle between the dog food and gravity was entertainment. "And it's raining."

Lenny had known it would be an issue when she'd picked up the oversize bag in the store. She should've purchased the smaller bag, but the difference in price made no sense. The company that manufactured the food counted on people buying the smaller, more convenient size for this very reason. Meanwhile they laughed all the way to the bank.

"I appreciate your offer, but I can manage."

"Everyone needs help sometimes, you know."

The word "help" made her bristle; she was *not* a damsel in distress.

Apparently unwilling to take no for an answer, and forgoing the retail mantra of "the customer is always right," Ned lifted her two canvas shopping bags off the footpath. She'd already determined they'd go either side of the bike to keep her upright. She reached for them, to take them back, but in doing so her grip on Malcolm's food slipped and the bag dropped to the ground with a thud. She stood back to reassess her options.

"Come on, I'll take you, the bike *and* the groceries. My van's right there. It's a free service."

"You think I'd just get in a van with you?"

"I'm not a stranger," Ned said.

"You're not far from it."

Ned put both his hands on his chest and feigned sadness. "I'm wounded. You're my favorite customer. Just don't tell Mrs. Hearst."

"I don't know Mrs. Hearst so I am unlikely to tell her anything," Lenny replied, lifting the hefty bag and draping it over the rear bike rack. Its new position was not ideal either; it drooped down toward the spokes and looked likely to interfere with the rotation of the rear wheel. She would just have to push the bike home while she balanced it, like leading a heavily laden donkey. An entirely frustrating situation. There was sure to be an online bulk-purchasing solution she could explore once she got home.

Ned laughed and lifted the dog-food bag from her bike. "You crack me up. Come on, I'm going your way anyway."

"And how would you know which way was *my way*?" she huffed.

He didn't answer, only smiled at her and walked toward the McKnight's delivery van at the end of the parallel parking at the front of the store. She often saw the van parked there and hadn't realized it was Ned's. It was a Holden panel van sprayed a brilliant blue, with white trims along the panels. The paint was so polished it was gleaming. The rain balled into neat drops as it lightly spattered the blue. Lenny had always assumed the van was more of a front-of-shop sculpture than a working vehicle.

"Does this run?"

"Of course she does. What do you think, it's just for show?"

"Well, yes," Lenny replied.

"Cordelia is not just a trophy car, she's reliable as they come. We've spent a lot of hours together, Cordy and I."

Ned unlocked the car and put her bags in the back. He affectionately rubbed Cordelia, as if she were a cat getting a belly scratch. He opened the passenger door and waved his hand with a flourish.

"Madam," he said.

"I don't know that I'm comfortable with this," Lenny said.

"Sorry, *mademoiselle*?"

"No, I meant the van."

"I know what you meant."

Ned was not perturbed by Lenny's hesitation and took the

handlebars of her Zenith, wheeling it to the rear of his van. She wasn't sure why she didn't protest further; had she wanted to *actually* leave under her own steam she could have. But something drew her to the husky man and his glossy van. Ned loaded her bike into Cordelia and gently closed the rear door. As he did, Lenny caught sight of her reflection in the sheen of the side panel. She looked at her bike-helmet-tousled bob, damp with the rain, and stiff black v-neck knit. She wondered what Ned must see when he looked at her and was suddenly not happy with being perceived as matronly. Not by Ned. Not when he was often in the presence of vibrant, young, self-assured Amy. Amy, who was colorful and unabashedly so. Lenny was annoyed at herself for drawing comparisons with her colleague, and then embarrassed when she realized the reason why her mind might wander in such a direction.

Lenny decided to ignore the rabbit hole of thoughts she'd fallen down and just pretend it was a completely platonic home-delivery service Ned offered every customer, their bike and their large bag of pet food.

She clambered into the front seat of Cordelia and Ned roared the engine to life, the van shaking them both as he started to reverse.

"You're wondering about the name, aren't you?" Ned asked as he rattled them into third gear.

"I understand the reference."

"Yes, but you're probably thinking, 'Why didn't he name her after one of the more lovable characters?' Right? Willow, Tara, Buffy herself?"

"Cordelia was misunderstood and ended up being very valuable to the vampire slaying outfit. I imagine your van is of similar assistance to you, and McKnight's, and therefore the name was apt?"

"Well . . . yeah. You've pretty much nailed it. She was a bit of a bitch at the start, caused me all sorts of problems, but we have grown very close, old Cordelia and I. So just what you said really, except you have a much better way with words."

"You really love that show."

"Yeah, it's silly, I know. I'm a grown man—but what's the harm, hey? I feel like I've justified it to my old man about a thousand times," Ned said.

"Like me and *Friends*."

"Your friends give you a hard time?" he asked.

"No. I meant the TV show. *Friends*."

"You're into that?"

"Yes. It makes me feel . . . comfortable. Happy, I guess. I like the familiar."

"You don't have to explain it to me, I understand. Watching my shows is like meditating—I tune in, brain switches off. I get it, you get it, just maybe my dad expects more or something. Like I should be watching *Landline* or David Attenborough docos."

"He doesn't approve?" Lenny asked.

"Yes and no. It keeps me out of trouble, sure, but I think it embarrasses him for people to know I dress up as Angel and head to Comic Con." He laughed. "Which, to be honest, I haven't done for some time, but I wouldn't rule it out in the future. Although I'm not really in David Boreanaz shape anymore. Or probably never was. Might be better off going as Gimli from *Lord of the Rings* now I'm a little more portly."

Ned patted his stomach and laughed. Lenny was not sure she wanted to agree with his self-deprecation and was tempted to say something complimentary, but she worried it would sound flirtatious. And given Amy was her friend, she wouldn't want to imply this was the sort of line she would cross.

"You're too tall for a dwarf," Lenny told him. "Maybe one of the orcs?"

Ned laughed. "I didn't know that's how you felt about me. An orc?!"

"Oh, no, not that you look like one. Just because they come in all shapes and sizes."

"That is true," he said, nodding along. "And they are some staunch bastards, those orcs. Maybe you're onto something."

She didn't want to carry on talking about what character he should role-play, in case it appeared she'd studied him in detail.

"Why the trivia nights? It seems you have enough work commitments with the store?" she asked, changing the subject as tactfully as she knew how.

"Well, I'm not planning on being a checkout chick forever," he told her as he negotiated a roundabout.

"But your dad owns the store," she said. "Wouldn't you end up running it?"

"If he gets his way, yes, I would. But he works his tail off and I don't want to do that 'til the end of my days. He's sixty-eight—he shouldn't be working at all really, but he still clocks up more hours than I do. I'm exhausted just thinking about it."

"So you'll run pub trivia nights? That doesn't seem like a highly lucrative alternative."

She cursed herself. Talking about money was incredibly rude and Fay would be horrified.

Ned laughed. "No, no. The trivia is for a mate of mine who's helping me out with the Grand Plan."

"The grand plan?" she echoed.

"The *Grand Plan*," he repeated, waggling his eyebrows and chortling in a way she'd come to think of as very Ned-like. "The idea is much bigger. I run the trivia nights as a trade-off with a mate who is going to print the pilot version of my game. He's a graphic designer and has access to all the printing equipment. Plus, it's kinda fun. Who'd have thought hosting trivia would be the thing to make me popular with the ladies!"

She didn't think Ned would need much help attracting women, but refrained from making any such comment. "Your game?" she said instead.

"Yes. Are you into games?"

"How do you mean? Like tennis?" she asked.

"No, no. Does this look like the physique of an athlete? Board games. Strategy, worker placement, you know?"

"Oh, yes, sort of. I play Scrabble."

"Ah, I see. A classic."

"I play almost every day."

"Online?"

"No, with my housemate. Monica." She hesitated. She didn't want to lie to Ned, but he knew Amy and it was easier to maintain the same story. Also, saying she avoided online and in-person challengers sounded quite isolated. Even a bit sad.

"Ah, cool. I reckon I could've picked that about you. It makes sense why you're so wordy."

Lenny wouldn't have called herself wordy—in fact, far from it. She did, however, have an extensive vocabulary and a love of words. In the past it had ruffled people who assumed she was talking down to them. This was not the case at all; she just liked the way some words rolled off her tongue more than others, like *peculiar* or *imperturbable*.

"I'm sorry," she said.

"No, it's a good thing. I mean you're good with the words. Words are good." He laughed.

"I agree, thank you." Lenny found herself smiling and relaxing in his easy company. She noticed her grip on her satchel had loosened and she had even managed to lean back into Cordelia's bench seat.

Compliment: compel, notice, topic, plot

Ned chortled again and she felt a tingle of satisfaction at being able to make him laugh, and not apparently at her own expense.

"So basically, it's my mate's trivia business. I do the Pint and Pickle night for him and he'll do a print run of my game for free."

"Well, it's not free then. It's quid pro quo, isn't it?"

"Is it?" he asked.

"You're performing a service for him, so it's just an exchange of services rather than you paying a fee. Quid pro quo."

"See, good with words. You're one out of the box, Lenny."

"Out of the box?"

"You're a good one."

She blushed and realized they'd got closer to her house than she'd intended. She'd meant to tell him to pull over far enough from Callistemon Court that he wouldn't be able to figure out where she lived. Instead she'd been caught up in talking and just kept directing him toward the Tree House.

"Just pull in here, thank you," she said quickly, pointing to a bus stop that provided a gravel shoulder on the road.

Ned slowed down and pulled over.

"Which house?" he asked, even though there were none either side of the bus stop.

"I'd prefer to just get out here."

"I'm not just gonna leave you stranded."

"I'm hardly stranded," she replied. "I'm almost home."

"Well, then, let's just go the whole hog and I'll drop you all the way there," he replied.

"Ah, no. Really, it's fine," she said, in a tone she hoped conveyed it wasn't open to debate.

"What sort of bloke just dumps you on the side of the road?" he asked. "In the rain?"

She sighed, knowing there were plenty of men out there who

would, like Fergus for instance. He probably wouldn't even have slowed down to let her out.

"Besides, I'd love to meet Malcolm," he said.

When Lenny wasn't forthcoming with any further directions, Ned put the car in park and turned toward her.

"Let me be a gentleman and at least carry your groceries?" he offered.

She looked at Ned. She'd known him for years, albeit in a relationship where she was a customer and he the service provider. He'd never given her any cause for concern and here she was acting like she lived in witness protection. She wondered if he had spent the past couple of years establishing common interests just so he could deliver her groceries one afternoon and murder her. Surely that was the storyline of at least one episode of *Law & Order: SVU*. Which she didn't watch because she didn't want to think about such things. Besides, that sort of victim selection would be time-consuming if he was thinking about becoming a serial killer.

Stop being ridiculous, Lenny.

"The next right and it's number twenty-one," she said quickly, before she could change her mind.

Ned doffed his imaginary chauffeur's cap, which she found incredibly endearing.

Endearing: endanger, neared, daring

"Yes, ma'am," he said, firing Cordelia back up.

Her palms prickled with sweat. She tried to wipe them discreetly on the black fabric of her pants.

Ned coasted into her driveway and Lenny scooted to the edge of her seat, ready to prise the door open and make as quick a getaway as she could. Being in Ned's presence was alarmingly easy and she didn't want to let her guard down any further.

If he noticed her agitation, he put on a good show of appearing oblivious to it as he lifted her bicycle out of the van and lugged

Malcolm's food under his free arm to the front door. Lenny carried the other bags and took her time fossicking for her house keys, hoping to delay any need to invite Ned in.

"Your house is really cool," he said, taking in the roofline and letting his eyes sweep the multi-tiered garden.

"Thank you, I like it."

"Wow, I bet. I'd want to keep this place to myself as well."

Lenny opened her front door. Malcolm, still not at Dino Flintstone level, was nowhere to be seen. She dropped her shopping just inside the front door and pulled it almost closed before turning back to Ned.

It was likely the polite thing to do, to invite him in. But then again, she'd never invited the man from Joey's Nice Thai in and he performed a similar service on a much more frequent basis.

"I just remembered," she announced. "Monica. She's my housemate. She's asleep. She is working tonight and this is when she sleeps."

"Oh, right. Sorry, listen to my booming big voice. I hope I haven't woken her."

"I'm sure she's fine. But maybe you can meet Malcolm another day? He might be sleeping too. Who wouldn't want an afternoon nap?" she said, attempting humor, but knowing it sounded clunky.

"Of course, yeah. Saturday?"

She looked over her shoulder, hoping Malcolm didn't appear and delay Ned's departure.

"Saturday?" she asked.

"Yeah. What about Saturday? We can get out for a walk with Malcolm and my little old lady?" Ned said.

"With your mother?"

Ned laughed. "No, Mum's really opposed to being on a lead. I meant my other old lady. Rosie, my dog."

Lenny let out a genuine laugh as she realized her mistake. "Oh, I'm so glad you meant your dog."

"You have a brilliant laugh," he said, sending the capillaries in her cheeks into overdrive. She focused on the thick rim of his glasses, avoiding his eyes.

Ned placed the dog food just inside the front door, his arm brushing hers as he did.

"I'll meet you here about ten, then? We can take them down to the old rail trail; there's a good off-lead area just up from there."

"That sounds lovely," Lenny said.

Ned jumped in his van and backed it up the driveway. Minutes later, long after Cordelia had shuttled Ned out of sight, Lenny realized she was still standing in her doorway, smiling ear to ear.

Anticipate: captain, panic, nice

Lenny put her groceries away and eased onto her couch. Ned had saved her time by dropping her home and she wanted to watch some TV before even thinking about dinner. She flicked on *Friends*. Malcolm snored lightly at her feet as Phoebe went about delivering her brother's triplets. Malcolm had shown himself to be adept at falling asleep wherever he pleased. She was just glad he was out of the laundry and had accepted her as more savior than tormentor.

They were just finding out baby Chandler was actually a girl when her phone started ringing. She sat forward to see if the caller's name showed, but the screen said *Private number*. She didn't answer as a matter of principle. If someone wished to speak with her, they could at least have the courtesy to display their number. It rang out and a chime followed to announce a voicemail.

She paused the show while she listened to the message, not wanting to miss any good bits, even though she had seen it before.

"Hello, Helena, my name is Wendy Dalton and I'm from the Victim Support Unit. I want to speak to you about the upcoming parole hearing for Mr. Sullivan and hope you can get back to me. I know this may be a difficult time, so please call me at your convenience so we can discuss what's best for you."

Lenny hung up the phone and put it back on the coffee table.

She pressed play on the remote, but her skin itched. How did Wendy Dalton know so much about her, when she knew nothing at all of her? Wendy's voice was so cheerful and spirited, saying things she expected her to understand, as if Lenny were part of a game no one had bothered explaining the rules for.

Difficult time: filicide, fitful, muffle, tedium, clued, left

Fergus had only been present for a tiny portion of Lenny's life, but he had certainly left an indelible impression. And she'd shelved that period of her life in a box, sealed tight. She had no intention of reopening it.

What she did wonder, though, was if Fergus had ended up in jail, which he evidently had, then why hadn't her mother ever sought her out? She wasn't impossible to find. Her mum could've tracked her down if she'd wanted to.

Clearly Lenny's actions were so reprehensible even her mother couldn't comprehend what she'd done. Lenny wished she'd had the chance to explain it to Tammy.

I did it for you, Mum.

Lenny deleted Wendy's voicemail, then thumbed through the missed calls and deleted the line in red.

Private number 6:13 P.M.

She would not be returning that call.

CHAPTER 19

Thursday, May 26

Twice yearly Lenny was forced to speak with more adults in the course of one evening than she did over the rest of the entire year. She had twenty-three students, and the majority of their parents came in pairs. The parent–teacher interviews were enough to send her looking for a career change. The eye contact, the questions, the need to be tactful yet honest were grueling. She would never understand why a written report card wasn't sufficient.

Lenny was ready for the onslaught of parents in eight-minute increments. She prepared two adult-size seats on the other side of her desk, along with printouts of the reports the parents had already received. She would heed Ms. Pham's advice and keep any potentially window-breaking comments to herself. To that end, she would avoid speaking about Troy Cole's constant scratching that had to be worms. Surely his parents had noticed and would treat them at some point. But it wasn't for her to say. Ms. Pham had been explicit in her instructions: she was to make no diagnoses, which Lenny took to mean in any medical field. Happily, she had no students falling behind Liam Backman–style. They were all meeting at least minimum requirements. This, she felt, was a positive reflection of her proficiency as a teacher and as a result she expected no controversy to arise with any parents. But human nature was forever unpredictable so she wouldn't be confident of this until the interviews were done.

After her first few meetings, she was running on time and took her scheduled break. After visiting the loo and refilling her water bottle, she was surprised to find Haillie Thompson's parents already in her classroom, four minutes ahead of schedule. They were inspecting the book reviews aligned neatly on the corkboards at the rear of the room. Haillie's efforts had been average. She'd done the minimum in discussing Brian's journey and his growth throughout *Hatchet,* appearing to have spent the bulk of her time on the stencilled borders. Which were lovely, even if they didn't relate to the theme.

Lenny made a beeline for the safety of her desk and sat down in her chair. Haillie's parents looked over and she gestured, inviting them to take the seats in front of her. They came straight over and Haillie's father held out his hand, which happened with seventy percent of fathers who came along. For some reason, the women were usually content with just a "hello."

Lenny remembered Lora telling her to be on her best behavior. Seeing no other way forward, she averted her gaze and quickly took Mr. Thompson's hand, giving it two firm pumps and hastily dropping it. She hoped Mrs. Thompson didn't follow suit and thankfully she didn't. Lenny eyed her hand sanitizer, but knew how impolite that would look. Instead she shuffled her papers, bringing Haillie's report to the top.

Only then did she look properly at the two faces in front of her. Mr. and Mrs. Thompson.

Kurt Thompson.

Of high school.

It was Kurt Thompson who had started a rumor in high school that she would perform oral sex in return for cigarettes, instigating the nickname "Longbeach Lenny." He made sure the moniker was used regularly so it didn't peter out into extinction.

Kurt was not stuck in any sort of high school awkwardness; he was a proficient footballer, popular among the female students and even the teaching staff. Prior to this rumor, Lenny had harbored a secret crush on Kurt Thompson. Or at least what she thought was a crush, having never previously had one and having no proper friends to ask. Until her unfortunate luck, and free period, meant she caught Kurt at Frying Fin's fish and chippery with his hand up the school shirt of Rose Hopkins. And they'd seen her. She was just there to get two potato cakes and a Corn Jack and was certainly not interested in whether or not Kurt was cheating on his girlfriend. Sure, she liked him, but she would've been terrified had he wanted to pull any such move on her. It was better left to Rose, who seemed quite at ease with it. By the time Lenny returned to school, Kurt's infidelity had been announced to Sophie Jackson who, as his actual girlfriend, *was* interested in whose school shirts he was putting his hands up. Kurt and Rose held Lenny entirely accountable for the exposure of their affair despite her never saying a word.

It was more than likely they'd been seen by multiple people. Frying Fin's was a highly frequented lunch outlet for the student body of Menzies High and Kurt and Rose weren't particularly discreet about their liaison. Lenny didn't rebut their accusations though, hoping they'd forget all about it. But they didn't. Kurt denounced her publicly and frequently in an effort to deflect from his own actions. And possibly because he gleaned some sort of enjoyment from it.

Lenny's crush evaporated rapidly, not that Kurt would have noticed.

She certainly wasn't prepared to see him in her classroom.

The silence stretched too long and Kurt Thompson and his wife were waiting for her to make a start. Suddenly, Lenny was at a loss as to how to begin and pictured herself picking up one of the small chairs and throwing it out the window just to shift everyone's focus.

Diversion: derision, visioned, roved, drove, void, rid

Maybe he didn't realize who she was—she now used a different surname. Despite living with the Markses through most of high school, she'd only started using Fay and Robert's surname when she reached university. It was bittersweet to stop using Winters. She'd kept it thinking it made it easier for her mum to find her. But as the years passed, it seemed more important to be a proper part of a family again. And changing to Marks did just that.

Now she thought about it, Lenny wasn't at all surprised that Kurt didn't recognize her. He had probably tormented too many people to remember them all. She would barely have registered as a blip in his high school life.

Talk, Lenny, talk.

"I'm Lenny Marks, I'm Haillie's grade five teacher," she said, although presumably Mr. and Mrs. Thompson knew this already. Lenny noted Mrs. Thompson was neither Sophie Jackson nor Rose Hopkins.

"I'm Stella and this is my husband, Kurt." Stella beamed, sitting up straight, as if her deportment would reflect directly on her daughter's academic performance.

Lenny saw no sign of recognition on Kurt's face. Quite the opposite, he looked rather uninterested. Lenny tried to stay focused and complimented Haillie's use of stencils, about which Mrs. Thompson seemed thrilled. Lenny was tempted to ask what the motivation behind the unusual spelling of their daughter's name was, but thought this could be misconstrued, which would surely place it in Ms. Pham's list of things to omit.

"I feel like she's really found her feet this year. She has made a lot more effort with her homework—I think, anyway. I don't have to nag her about it," Stella said, laughing awkwardly.

Lenny didn't return her laugh and neither did Kurt, his lack of interest remaining steady. He'd even taken the time to check his messages, which caused Stella to swat his phone and whisper, "*Put it away.*"

"Haillie gets all her work done to the required standard," Lenny said. "She is very popular."

"Oh, yes, so many friends. The whole class came to her birthday. It was *exhausting*. Sometimes I wish she was one of those quiet sort of kids."

Lenny said nothing, knowing being the quiet kid wasn't an easier path.

"But of course I wouldn't change her one bit. Would we, Kurt?" Stella patted Kurt's leg. He looked at his wife as if he were unsure where he was.

"You went to Menzies High, didn't you?" Kurt said, instead of replying to his wife.

Lenny paused, hoping Stella would intervene and cut her husband short, but she did no such thing. Instead they both looked to Lenny, waiting for her answer.

"*Yes*, Lenny Winters. Right? I've been trying to place you this whole time," he continued.

She could tell the redness was spreading from her nose to her ears, and her tongue felt like a lump of sourdough bread in her mouth. Lenny sipped from her water bottle, swallowing deliberately and hoping she didn't choke. Although if she did, at least she'd be excused from the situation.

"I don't use that name anymore," she managed. "Thank you both for coming. Haillie is a pleasure to teach, a really lovely student."

"I can't believe it took me so long to remember you. You're exactly the same. Do you remember me from school? I think we were the same year and all," Kurt said, verging on excitement, as if they were close friends who had fallen out of touch.

"No, not really," she lied and stood, hoping this would signal the end of the meeting. She would even shake their hands if that helped them leave faster.

"What a small world," Kurt continued.

"Yes, I suppose it is," Lenny agreed, although she hated the saying. It wasn't out of the question to run into someone you knew in high school, which was only twenty-five minutes away. Perhaps if they'd found her teaching in Reykjavik that would actually be considered a coincidence.

Stella seemed to have a better sense of Lenny's urgency than her husband and politely thanked Lenny for her time, bringing the meeting to its excruciating close.

It was incredible how she could go from an almost forty-year-old grade five teacher to an ostracized teenager in seconds. Calling her Longbeach Lenny had obviously been just a joke to Kurt and his mates, but for an already reclusive adolescent, the impact on Lenny had been resounding.

"Come on, we have Jaxon's teacher next," Stella said to her husband, who was still meandering somewhere down memory lane. "We have a preppie as well," she explained to Lenny. "So, off to Miss Cleary's room next."

Lenny nodded and forced a smile as they left the room.

Despite another break not yet being scheduled, Lenny made a quick dash out the rear door of her classroom, down the steps and into the dark of the courtyard.

When Lenny arrived at Fay and Robert's she had been barely an outline of a thirteen-year-old girl. The mere fact she was in yet another new home had made her conclude, once and for all, that she was the problem. If family members could walk away without a backward glance, then a non-relative could oust her at any given moment. It meant she buried any thoughts of it not being fair as deep as she could. Fair or not didn't come into play; this was a matter of survival.

There would be no complaining from Helena Winters; she would be on her best behavior and she wouldn't make the mistake of assuming her position was permanent ever again.

It took time, but Fay and Robert slowly gained ground with her, prising her from the shadows and into everyday life. They had setbacks, one of which was midway through high school when Kurt Thompson decided he would make Lenny's life miserable. It threatened to break her completely, because teenagers could be relentlessly cruel. There were times when Kurt would simply hold a cigarette out to her with a group of his friends looking on, causing them all to erupt in maniacal laughter. She refused to give them the satisfaction of crying or storming off. But her reaction was irrelevant to them; the pleasure they derived from teasing her seemed to be all they needed to keep the joke in a horrible perpetual cycle.

Deep down, Lenny knew she deserved it; she was paying a penance and they could call her any name they wanted—it still wouldn't fix what she'd done.

CHAPTER 20

Kirra found Lenny in the dark, quiet courtyard and her tone implied she'd been looking for her for some time. Lenny could have sworn she'd only walked out of her classroom two minutes ago.

"Jamie Tran's parents wandered into my classroom looking for you. I've sent them to the music room first to see Trudi and then they'll come back," Kirra said, assessing her. "But only if you can go back. Are you okay?"

Lenny looked at Kirra and wished she hadn't asked that question. It was the one she found hardest to answer. *No, I'm not okay,* she was tempted to say, but Kirra couldn't fix this.

Kirra sat quietly beside her and Lenny resisted the urge to move, grateful for the unobtrusive company.

Their moment was broken by a voice drifting over the brick partition they were hidden behind. A voice, connected to a man, speaking to his wife; presumably neither party was aware Kirra and Lenny were only meters away.

"I don't even know where the nickname came from," Kurt said. "Something about her giving blowies for smokes, I think."

"Longbeach Lenny? She doesn't seem like the type to do that sort of thing. It's all a bit weird," Stella replied.

"*She* was weird."

"She still seems a bit that way . . . I guess. But Haillie loves her."

"She was really smart. I know that. But I hardly remember her saying anything at all. That just then was the most I've ever heard her talk and I was at high school with her for years."

Kurt and Stella's voices drifted away. Lenny wondered if Kurt was honestly unable to recall that he was the instigator and enforcer of her high school nickname. Or if he wanted to play the oblivious, innocent schoolboy and fool his wife into thinking she'd married the nice guy. It was infuriating. Of course, Lenny would say nothing; she didn't even have to bite her tongue—the muteness of high school returned to her in an instant. She hated being so pathetic.

"Can I do anything?" Kirra asked.

She wanted to tell Kirra it felt like she was knee-deep in mud and needed someone to pull her out. But Kirra had her own parent interviews to run, two kids waiting at home and no doubt more than enough on her list of things to do. She didn't need to be covered in mud trying to help her colleague out. The only thing either of them needed was for Lenny to toughen up and return to her classroom so they could both finish their respective interviews.

Push it down, Lenny.

"No. I'll head back up, thanks for checking on me," Lenny said, although she made no attempt to move. Her body was tired and the effort seemed enormous. She hoped Kirra would go on without her.

"Was he that big of a dickhead in high school?" Kirra asked, the words forming a visible cloud of breath.

Dickhead: chided, hacked, aided, ached, idea, hide

Lenny paused and let a smile flit across her lips.

"At least that big," she replied.

"Some people grow up, some people don't," Kirra said.

"I am all right," Lenny told her, aware of how unconvincing she sounded.

"You don't have to be."

"But I don't know what else to be," Lenny said, surprising herself with her honesty.

Kirra reached for her hand, then pulled back before making contact, perhaps sensing that was one step too far.

"It's my birthday today," Lenny said, not realizing she was going to share this information before it was out of her mouth.

Kirra almost jumped to her feet. "Why didn't you say?"

"I've never celebrated it. It's in the same week my mum..." Lenny hesitated. "The same week I went to live with my grandmother." She rubbed her thigh, hoping the pressure would stop the throbbing of her scar. It didn't. Two days before her eleventh birthday, her mum and Fergus had abandoned her forever while she wasn't looking.

Kirra was, unusually for her, at a loss for words.

"I'd better go back in," Lenny finally said. She stood and peered over the brick wall behind her to make sure Kurt and Stella weren't lingering.

"And can you not mention this to Lora? She's expecting me to refrain from doing anything odd tonight," Lenny said, starting back up the steps. "Which evidently I have trouble avoiding."

"I won't mention it," Kirra said. "And happy birthday, Lenny Marks."

CHAPTER 21

Saturday, May 28

Saturday arrived quickly and Lenny hadn't canceled her walk with Ned. She had purposefully avoided McKnight's on Thursday, which meant she didn't see him. And as she didn't have his phone number, she was unable to do anything other than go through with their plans.

After the parent–teacher interviews and her birthday, the remainder of the week was relatively unremarkable. She'd exercised, eaten her usual rota of meals and stolen no further dogs. Malcolm spent less and less time in the laundry, which was reassuring. He was either getting used to her or suffering from the canine form of Stockholm syndrome.

She'd avoided two more phone calls from Wendy Dalton, who left voicemail messages that Lenny deleted immediately.

That morning, she ate a doughnut for breakfast: jam-filled, strawberry-iced with a light dusting of sprinkles. Half a dozen had been left on her desk the day before and there was no point wasting them; breakfast was as good a time as any to eat one. There were no more or fewer calories in a doughnut whether it be eaten at 7 A.M. or 3 P.M.

The card the doughnuts had come with was perched on her

bookshelf, on the rung above her *Hobbit* editions. It read: *Dear Lenny, Happy Birthday, with love from Kirra, Hugh, Cody and Darcy. PS I know you don't like cake, but we hope you like doughnuts xx.*

It was true, she didn't like cake, most recently declining the Coles supermarket sponge the staff had shared for Deidre's fiftieth in February. It was overloaded with cream and looked unappetizing. Lenny was surprised Kirra paid so much attention to what she did and didn't like. The card itself was rudimentary and homemade, depicting a green woman with short hair, on a pink bike with a number of balloons attached at various intervals. Lenny assumed it was an illustration of her and decided it was a good likeness, given she'd not met either Cody or Darcy (the picture didn't specify who drew it).

Lenny couldn't recall anyone making her a birthday card before. Each birthday, Fay bought her something useful and thoughtful. A leaf blower for the garden last year, and a nice new quilt cover and pillowcase set the year before. But Fay was somewhat obligated, given the child–parent relationship. Kirra was not, and Lenny was overcome by the gesture.

As 10 A.M. drew nearer, waiting for Ned to arrive felt like slowly being suffocated. There was a host of concerns filling her head like a bad song on the radio. Everything from saying something stupid to Ned (which was almost a given), to Amy thinking she was trying to steal her boyfriend. And then there was the added complication of the chance of Malcolm being spotted. Lenny gnawed at her thumbnail, workshopping possible and acceptable reasons she could use to turn Ned away when he arrived.

Her excuses were all a little weak and not without flaws. If she told him Malcolm was under the weather, Ned might insist on taking him to the vet. He knew she didn't have a car and was the sort of person who was inclined to help. That wouldn't do at all. It was a small suburb—and not a small world after all—and the vet might recognize Malcolm, and her crime would be uncovered. She wouldn't be allowed to take him home and the vet might make a citizen's arrest, or call the police. And Ned would be there for all of it. There would be no way to keep it from Amy, which would affect her position at Selby South. A thief should not be in charge of multiple small, impressionable minds.

Walking without Malcolm wasn't an option either. It would negate the very reason they were meeting and might give the impression she'd lured Ned into a date-like situation. Even though he'd initiated the date. Which was definitely not a date.

With the start of a tension headache simmering behind her eyes, Lenny decided the only immediate remedy was an episode of *Friends* on the couch, where hopefully the answer would spring to mind.

The answer did not come to her, but a knock at the door did—interrupting "The One Where Rachel Smokes." She found Ned beaming with an excited corgi by his side, and any idea of derailing their plans flew immediately out the door.

"Good morning," he said, his voice its usual thundering volume. She presumed he knew she wasn't hearing impaired.

"Hello, Ned, I won't be a moment," she said, still not wanting to invite him in. She closed the door again in order to get herself and Malcolm sorted.

Malcolm lifted his head lazily. The night she'd stolen him, she'd guided him home with the rope he'd been tethered to, and then threw it away in case it reminded him of his former conditions. She'd bought a lead since, but not yet tried it out. Lenny hoped Malcolm would be amenable to letting her walk him. Surely they were friends now.

He didn't seem bothered when Lenny hooked him to the lead and he obediently followed her to the door. It was a good start.

It was only as she went to leave the house that she found her nervousness about being spotted by the dog's former owner had been almost entirely replaced by a different feeling. Something that wasn't altogether unusual when she was in the presence of Ned McKnight: a buzzing energy, making her feel delightfully electrified.

Electrified: reflected, lifted, fire, free

Lucky it wasn't a date.

Ned made conversation easy. She wondered if this was a skill he'd learned from years of customer service, or if he was just naturally gifted in this manner. It did help that they had things in common: *Buffy*, *Lord of the Rings*, sensible haircuts, dogs and McKnight's General Store. That wasn't much, but it was more than she had in common with most people.

Amy was perhaps their most obvious common ground, although she was yet to be broached by either party. Lenny wondered if Amy knew about their morning walk. Of course they weren't doing anything untoward. They were just two people exercising their pets. Hardly a hand-holding, romance-inducing start of anything. Ned was in a relationship and Lenny respected those boundaries. Although having never been in a romantic relationship, she wasn't exactly sure what the protocol would be in such a situation. Maybe he was meant to avoid women in general on a one-on-one basis.

"Rosie as in the flower?" Lenny asked, finding she fell into step with Ned quite easily. Even Malcolm, after excitedly greeting Rosie in an overly intimate manner, had been walking comfortably beside Lenny.

"No, it's short for Rosie Cotton," Ned replied.

"Oh, of course," she said.

"Do you know what it's from?"

"It's Samwise Gamgee's love interest," she replied quickly.

Ned laughed. "I knew you'd get it."

"Do most not?" she asked.

"Hit-and-miss. Amy didn't, turns out she hasn't seen any of the movies. I've told her I will get her started on *The Fellowship of the Ring*. It's what we're doing tonight."

"That sounds nice," Lenny said. She imagined sitting side by side with Ned in the Tree House, the fire lit and the first installment of Frodo's epic adventure starting in front of them; it wasn't even slightly unpleasant to think about.

"Well, you should've seen the look she gave me when I told her it was over three and a half hours long. I'm hoping once she gets into it she won't even notice." Ned grimaced. "I don't know if it's her ideal way to spend a Saturday night."

"Would she prefer a different movie, do you think?" Lenny asked.

"No, I think she'd rather be out, but to be honest I'm a bit over nights out. We've spent the last few weekends at one place or another. Last weekend she had a house party at hers and they were still going when I went to bed at 3 A.M. I was working Sunday and I'm too old to rock up completely hungover."

"Not pleasant at all," Lenny said, recalling the morning after the trivia night. It made her stomach heave just thinking of it.

Malcolm stopped abruptly to sniff at something, his tail wagging furiously as he did so. She gave him a moment with whatever he'd found before gently nudging him back onto the track.

Another thought occurred to her: if Amy had held a party, why hadn't she invited Lenny? Perhaps there was a limit on numbers?

Lenny recalled a time, in high school, when she actually received a birthday party invite from Elliot McShea. Elliot was turning sixteen and she invited *everyone*, and so finally Lenny made the guest list. And Lenny went, more than anything just to prove she could, but she was overwhelmed by the noise, the dimness (why didn't they just turn on the lights?) and the free-flowing alcohol, which reminded her far too much of her stepfather. There was all sorts of intimate coupling going on in Elliot's house, and a distinct lack of parental supervision. She left early, not waiting for Robert to pick her up, but instead walking home and crawling into bed. Even once she was lying on her comfortable pillow in the quiet Marks house, it still felt like the music was pounding in her head.

"There's a few years between us," Ned continued. "But sometimes it feels like a chasm."

"Like the Plains of Rohan," Lenny added, not wanting to suggest anything negative about Amy and Ned's relationship.

"I mean, Ames is great. Fun to be around. And oh my God, she's gorgeous. It's just, we're different, you know." Ned paused and Lenny wasn't sure where the conversation was heading. If he was seeking advice, he was barking up the wrong tree. Her knowledge of coupledom could be grouped with what she knew about flying a plane or doing French braids; she knew these things could happen but had no idea how.

"And she's so intent on getting photos for her socials, which I have no real problem with, except it seems a bit . . . false? Like she needs people to see us together or something?"

Lenny was out of her depth and tried to think of a neutral answer. Ned may have been correct, but agreeing might sound like she knew something he didn't. And she couldn't say he was wrong, because perhaps Amy did have ulterior motives. Ned McKnight and Amy Cleary were not exactly a classic match. But then, neither were Ross and Rachel at the start. Who was she to judge?

"I mean, tell me I'm crazy?" Ned sighed.

"Oh, no, I'm sure you're not," replied Lenny, although she wasn't sure that was the right answer.

"And listen to me, don't I seem vain? I have been told many times I'm batting above my average with her."

"What is that based on?" Lenny asked. "Baseball?"

"Ha, no, based on looks. I'm hardly a centerfold."

"Surely a better criterion for compatibility would be personality? I'd definitely dismiss those comments—that's an incredibly superficial way of seeing things."

"You're not wrong," he agreed.

She worried he was about to ask her what she thought of Amy, or what she thought of him, or worse, what she thought of the two of them together. She needed to get him onto a less controversial topic.

"What's your game called?" she asked.

"Ah . . . good question, I don't have a name yet. I've got a couple I'm playing with, trying to see what fits. What rolls off the tongue, you know?"

"Try them on me," she suggested.

"Only if you give me your honest opinion."

"I can do that."

"Dark Riders of Tethys," he said.

"What's the other one?"

"Man Versus Asteroid."

"The second one is terrible, you shouldn't consider it at all."

"Wow, brutal."

"I'm sorry," Lenny said.

"No, I appreciate the input."

"The other one is better. I assume it's based in or around Saturn?"

"Not many people know Tethys is a moon of Saturn," Ned said, impressed.

"I teach children about the solar system, I should know these things."

"True that."

"Titan may be the more obvious choice, if you want to go with something easily recognizable as a moon of Saturn?"

"Yeah, yeah, good point."

"And the dark riders, could that be confused with the Ringwraiths in *Lord of the Rings*? If you're looking for something that stands alone, perhaps marauders? Bandits, even?"

"Bandits of Titan," he said, toying with the words. "Don't mind it."

"But please, I have no idea what your game is about and your choice may be more suitable."

"Yeah, maybe. It's a space opera board game," he said proudly. "I don't want it to take itself too seriously. It's meant to be fun."

"I'm really not sure I know what a space opera game would consist of," she replied.

He laughed. "I don't think anyone does. But I'd love you to help me test it out. I'm ironing out some of the final hiccups in it and need some wily opponents."

"I don't know if I'd be considered wily, but I'd be honored to try your game."

"Awesome," he said. "Ames seems to glaze over a bit when I mention it. Also not her thing."

Lenny realized they were right back where they had been earlier and let his comment play out into silence. She noticed Malcolm happily walking in time with her, keeping close to her side as if she'd taught him to do so. He didn't seem to mind the lead, or the outing, at all.

"Right then, enough about me. Tell me something about yourself, Lenny Marks."

"You have to be much more specific than that," she said.

"Okay," he said, appearing to mentally toss around options. "Any siblings?"

"No," she replied.

"Favorite time of the year?"

"In what way?"

"You know, are you Christmas-mad or are you an Easter fiend? Maybe you are a Halloween diehard?"

"No. Not at all," she said firmly. "I like the school terms. I like the workdays."

"That is not how I feel about going to work," Ned said. "Yet another reason I shouldn't work at McKnight's forever."

"Oh, but you need to stay."

"Why?" he asked.

"I like seeing you there."

"You can see me not-there though."

Lenny considered this and deemed it borderline flirtatious. She was concerned he was misinterpreting what she said. She preferred things to be familiar and Ned being in McKnight's was what she had come to expect and she liked it when things ran as they always had.

"So where did you grow up?" he asked her.

"Ringwood."

"Are your parents still there?"

"I don't know about my parents."

"You don't see them?"

"They don't see me."

"Oh, sorry, I feel like I've been a tad too nosy."

"Not at all," she replied. "I didn't know my father. My mum and stepfather left when I was eleven so I lived with my grandmother until she died. I have a foster mother in Ringwood, it's where I grew up. I had a foster father too, but he passed away some years ago."

"Wow, Lenny. That's intense."

"Oh, was it? I apologize for oversharing," she said.

"No, no. I mean, you've been through so much."

"No. Not really. I always had somewhere to live. And that's more than some people have."

"That's a good way to look at it."

"There's no other way to look at it," she replied.

The track funneled them out into a reserve where a number of people were doing various Saturday morning activities: walking dogs, walking prams, walking prams and dogs, exercising in groups, watching kids flying along at breakneck speeds on scooters. Lenny preferred the seclusion of the track, but Ned continued unperturbed.

"How's Malcolm with a ball?" he asked.

"I have no idea."

From his jacket pocket Ned produced a rubber ball with bite marks all over it. It looked like a rogue mouse had gotten at a shiny red apple.

"Wanna give it a go?"

"No, best not," she said. "He's not used to being off the lead."

Nor was he used to being on a lead, but she felt it was safer to keep him nearby.

Ned shrugged. "I'm gonna let Rosie have a run around. She's like a crack addict when the ball comes out—there's never enough."

He unclipped the excited corgi and she raced ahead of him, bounding across the grass, every paw off the ground, so she looked more like a stumpy-legged gazelle than a dog.

Lenny spotted an unoccupied park bench and decided they'd take a break.

She perched on the bench and Malcolm leaned into her legs. The sun finally emerged and it was a lovely feeling on her skin. Only then did she notice the information board beside them, next to the map of the reserve and its extensive walking paths. The entire right panel of the board was reserved for community notices and there she saw Malcolm staring back at her.

STOLEN.

DOG.

Lenny's eyes flicked left and right, thinking maybe the notice had just been posted and the poster of the sign was in the area, watching for people reading and looking guiltily around. Although nothing yelled "guilty" quite like having the stolen dog attached to a lead and sitting right beside you.

She was a terrible criminal. There may as well have been a neon sign above her head pointing at her and Malcolm.

She got up and not at all surreptitiously tore the poster from the board and shoved it in her jacket pocket. Realizing how that might appear to anyone nearby, she ripped two more posters off, just so it looked like she was either a bit batty or cleaning up the noticeboard.

"Excuse me," a voice behind her said.

Lenny jumped, sure it was the police, who would drag her off in handcuffs in front of Ned. Malcolm would be sent to the pound, where they would euthanise him because he was an unregistered dog and a notorious breed. Or worse, he would be returned to his chained prison, where his beatings would resume and he would forever remember Lenny as the person who could not keep him safe. She'd let Malcolm down.

Tears were threatening to spill.

Criminal: manic, calm

"Excuse me, I can't see the map. If you could just shift a bit, sorry." The voice was attached to a pleasant-looking woman clad in Lycra pants, leg warmers and a puffy purple North Face coat, who did not look at all like a police officer. She was trying to peer around Lenny at the map.

"Apologies," Lenny said and hurried away from the board.

She tugged Malcolm and started to power walk back to the track that would lead her home. As her feet took her on autopilot toward the quiet of the less crowded area she stopped. Ned. She couldn't just disappear like a bad magic trick. Plus Cordelia was at the Tree House; he'd have to come back eventually.

Lenny was furious at herself; she was so cocky thinking she could just go out with someone else's dog and someone else's boyfriend and smugly enjoy her morning. How arrogant to think Ned would see her as anything other than a customer of McKnight's or a lonely woman with a dog. She squeezed her eyes shut and chastised herself for not just accepting the status quo.

The anger she was directing at herself grew as she led Malcolm back to Ned and told him it was best they go. He didn't ask why; perhaps she conveyed a suitable level of desperation. She wasn't brilliant at being subtle.

Their walk back to the Tree House was not the easygoing stroll they'd enjoyed on the outward-bound trip. She kept looking over her shoulder, concerned the man who so unpoetically named his dog "Beast" would come charging up behind them at any given moment. She didn't want Ned to feel compelled to defend her honor and she didn't like confrontations. They could end very badly.

"Something wrong?" Ned asked as they neared her house. He was out of breath.

"Ah, no. I just thought I saw some parents from school and wanted to avoid them."

"Oh, cool then. I thought I'd said something wrong. Amy's all funny when she sees the kids outside of school too."

They'd put considerable distance between themselves and the park and Lenny felt the tight grip of panic slowly unwinding. She attempted to focus on her conversation with Ned.

"Is she? Well, I'm glad it's not just me."

"Can I ask you something?"

"Yes," Lenny replied.

"Has this got anything to do with why we left the park in such a hurry?" He produced a scrunched-up wad of paper from his pocket and smoothed it out. A poster. *The* poster.

She patted her own jacket, thinking the poster must have fallen out, but felt it firmly installed within her deep pocket.

"They were all over the park," Ned said, left eyebrow askew.

For the first time she looked him directly in the eye. And he looked back at her, a hint of something dancing in his expression. Mischief? Solidarity? Intrigue? She wasn't sure. But she found meeting his eye unusually comfortable. Those tiny circles held a spray of colors—brown, green, blue and gray—as if they were mini universes struggling to be contained.

"Well, he is a rescue dog," she said finally.

"I won't tell anyone. I don't think you'd have him if you didn't have a good reason. You don't seem like some sort of professional dog-napper," he said.

"I guess I am though."

He thought for a moment and shrugged. "I guess you are."

CHAPTER 22

Monday, May 30

Lenny spent her Monday avoiding Amy, the complete opposite of what she'd made a point of doing over the past weeks. She didn't want to be asked about her weekend and to have to omit her outing with Ned. Because, apart from seeing him—and the brief dash from what she was sure was impending arrest and imprisonment—nothing else of excitement had happened over her days off. And given her thorough enjoyment of the time spent with Ned, she was worried it would spill from her if the opportunity arose. It wasn't out of the question Amy herself could have been there and they may have had just as pleasant a time. But she hadn't been there, and she might not approve. And if Ned hadn't mentioned it to Amy, then it certainly wasn't Lenny's place to do so. It was seeming very likely that her perfectly innocent outing with Ned was going to either damage her blossoming friendship with Amy or her ability to shop at McKnight's.

Before Ned left her house on Saturday, he'd said "Same time next week?" in such a casual manner that Lenny forgot to decline. It was nice to think she could spend time with Ned without being at the mercy of whoever was waiting behind her in the queue at McKnight's.

But Saturday afternoon and Sunday had given Lenny plenty of time to think on it, which was to say she'd completely overanalyzed it. And Lenny realized someone looking in on her actions would think she had something to hide. Otherwise, why not just tell Amy about her lovely stroll with her boyfriend on Saturday morning?

Lenny Marks was not a sexually inexperienced thirty-seven-year-old. Although she thought of having sex in the same light as other once-in-a-lifetime sort of things. For instance, bungee jumping or visiting the Pyramids; tick it off the list and move on. Not that either of those things were on her list. The bulk of Lenny's experience came from nights alone reaching a level of satisfaction she hadn't realized was possible when she parted with her virginity under Damon Hughes in her first year of university. Once she'd worked out the mechanics of bringing herself to orgasm, it became a regular occurrence. It required no polite conversation or trimming of her pubic hair and, as an added bonus, she always slept better.

Although polite conversation had proved a little too subtle for Damon, now she came to think of it. As the credits rolled on *The Scorpion King*, Lenny had finally had to work up the courage to let Damon know she wasn't at his apartment to watch a movie. The two of them had done something akin to flirting during their tutorials for most of the year, despite Damon seeming to be as socially uneasy as Lenny herself. He was as good a candidate as anyone. She had no qualms about her motive when she arrived at Damon's apartment with a bottle of lukewarm chardonnay in a Woolworths chiller bag. She'd even purchased condoms in anticipation, given it was a dual responsibility to be prepared. Damon was grateful for her advances, if a little surprised, and in a heady blur of clammy, tangled limbs she quickly dispatched with her virginity. It appeared to be his first time too, but it seemed too personal to ask and she didn't want him to think she was suggesting he didn't perform well.

Lenny had nothing to compare it to; all she could say was it served its purpose and was satisfactory. To say it was satisfying would have been a bit too close to a lie.

Damon was asleep—or appeared to be—when she dressed, took the remains of her chardonnay and disappeared from his apartment. It certainly wasn't love; it was barely even lust. They were in the same tutorials for the rest of the year, but neither of them broached the subject.

A brown cardboard package caught Lenny's eye as she freewheeled to her front door. She wasn't expecting anything. Fay was one of the few people with her address and would surely just hand something over at their fortnightly lunches rather than post it.

It was right to assume there had been a mistake: the parcel was addressed to Maureen Simcock. The Tree House was clearly identified as number twenty-one. Likewise, nineteen was properly marked with the correct numbers. The failure of the postman, or postwoman, to perform the most basic function of their job now made it Lenny's responsibility and this annoyed her.

She parked and chained her bike in her carport. There were no groceries to get inside that afternoon; she'd skipped McKnight's to avoid Ned. Avoidance would suffice for now and she'd make do with whatever her freezer and pantry held.

Package under her arm, she marched past the hydrangeas and up the wooden stairs to the porch. Lenny had left misdelivered mail there before, approaching stealthily to drop and run. When she'd first moved to the Tree House, Lenny had noticed two women of similar age lived next door. She'd not seen the other lady there in years and assumed she'd moved out. As far as she was aware, Maureen had been on her own for quite some time.

Quietly, Lenny placed the box beside the doormat, in front of the door painted a lurid shade of violet. She took note that the vine covering the verandah was in dire need of pruning. It was risky to bring her pruning shears this close to the house, but it wasn't going to cut itself back. She turned to leave, only then noticing the woman sitting beneath the blanket of vine-cast shadows.

"Hello there," said the woman, who Lenny knew to be Maureen despite not having been properly introduced.

"I have a parcel for you. I mean, I'm not the delivery person. I'm your neighbor, I—"

"I know who you are, Helena. Thank you for bringing it over."

"It's correctly labeled, so no fault at all of the consignor," Lenny continued. "I think our delivery person could do with paying a little more attention."

Maureen laughed, a bell ringing out into the afternoon sky. The laughter faded and neither woman spoke. Lenny found her feet were not trying to move her on as quickly as they usually did.

"And it's Lenny. I mean, it is Helena, but I prefer Lenny."

"Lenny. Of course. Won't you join me? I'm having tea."

"Oh, I have to . . ." Lenny trailed off.

Have to what?

Instead of finishing her sentence with whatever hollow excuse she could muster, she nodded. She imagined Fay gasping with relief, or perhaps needing one of her small glasses of sherry to recover from the shock of seeing Lenny not racing off. She imagined Fay would be quite pleased. Only once she was seated opposite Maureen did she notice the elderly woman was sitting in a wheelchair.

"Oh, so that's why you stay up here," Lenny said.

"What's that?"

"You're in a wheelchair."

The woman's laugh chimed again and this time Lenny joined in, although she wasn't sure she understood the joke.

"No, I stay up here because I know you don't want company,

plus you move a bit fast for me. I'm very glad to finally have you up here. You've been a wonderful neighbor."

Lenny blushed. A compliment, even from a stranger, was hard to take.

On the table between them sat a delicately painted teapot and two cups, as if Maureen was expecting company. Maureen turned her pot three times before pouring.

What are the chances?

"Of what?" Maureen asked.

Lenny didn't realize she'd spoken out loud.

"My grandmother. She used to do the same thing," Lenny said.

"Did she? It is a bit of an old wives' tale, I think. Doesn't make a lick of difference, but I like doing it."

"Me too," Lenny said.

Maureen leaned back in her chair, holding her cup with both hands and seemingly enjoying the silence.

"Milk's there if you want it," Maureen said.

Lenny tipped some milk from the red ceramic jug into her cup and leaned back too, all the while studying the woman across from her. Maureen's hands were splashed with constellations of paint flecks. The nails were embedded with crescents of ink, or paint, or something that wasn't meant to be there, but looked as natural on Maureen as someone else wearing earrings or a scarf. Maureen's hair was plaited loosely and draped over her shoulder. The plaited segments were woven with just a few strands of black, a remnant of what had once been among the gray. Her face, devoid of makeup, held barely contained stories.

The elderly woman didn't attempt to fill the space with chatter or inanities, so neither did Lenny. It was peaceful where they sat, the afternoon not yet lapsed into the chill of evening and the wind barely strong enough to lift the leaves. The finely detailed floral teacup Lenny held warmed her hands, and the overall effect was quite soporific.

Lenny drained her cup and stood to leave, not wanting to over-stay her welcome.

"Thank you for the tea."

"Come back anytime," Maureen said, smiling sincerely.

It had been an unintentional and unexpected visit. But the light-ness Lenny felt as she walked back up Maureen's driveway was lovely. Being in Maureen's presence was like an episode of *Friends*: familiar, easy. She knew by that feeling alone, she'd go back.

It was only when she arrived home that she thought to wonder how Maureen had known to call her Helena. She hadn't used that name on anything for years.

CHAPTER 23

May 26, 1997
Zanny

Lenny waited with her red suitcase, which was formerly her mother's, who was formerly the person she'd lived with. It had been almost two hours and no one had explained where Zanny was or when she'd be back. They simply told her that Zanny had been *caught up*. Lenny was both physically and mentally bruised, and to add insult to the abandonment, Susannah Winters (Lenny couldn't recall why, but she'd always just been Zanny to her) had not been home to greet her. Instead, Missy was there, explaining at the front door that she lived with Susannah and would make them all tea while they waited. Missy served Lenny and the social worker—Charmaine, or Cheryl, or maybe even Sheila; she'd not committed the name to memory—cups of tea. There had been too many different people and names in the past two days for her to remember them all. And of course Zanny had come too, although she had been distracted and unpredictable, laughing one moment and tears rolling down her cheeks the next. Lenny wasn't sure what to make of her, but tried to be on her best behavior despite her concerns.

Missy was very accommodating and Lenny was quite sure she was lovely, laying out malt-o-milk biscuits on a dainty turquoise platter and making polite conversation, which Lenny participated in only when it was rude not to.

Neither Sheila nor Missy seemed perturbed that Zanny was not there to meet her granddaughter, who was now to live with her because home was, according to Sheila, "no longer a possibility." And in fairness, it would appear unwise to allow her to live by herself now Fergus and her mum had gone who-knew-where. She only wished she'd taken more from the house as keepsakes, but she'd been so busy listing the necessities for the social workers, she forgot to request such things. Clothes, underwear, shoes, *The Hobbit*, her schoolbooks. She remembered to ask for Errol, that silly old bear. He wasn't her favorite by any stretch, but it was important he was out of the house and with her. She didn't want anyone digging too deep into what Errol knew.

Errol knew far too much.

Lenny could only hope the other important stuff would still be there when her mum came back.

Two days earlier, after she'd waited for what felt like hours, someone had finally let her out of the shed. The man who opened the door was surprised to see her. Perhaps he'd anticipated nothing more than a lawnmower and old pots in the garden shed. And likewise, she was startled to see him; it had only ever previously been her mum. He spoke into his crackling radio in hushed—almost panicked—tones before crouching down in front of her. He approached Lenny as if she were a timid cat, and perhaps that wasn't far from the truth. The man wasn't in a uniform, but assured her he was a policeman. He showed her a small card that hung around his neck. The photo depicted a man with less-gray hair than the one in front of her. But he had the same kind eyes.

"Hello there. What are you doing in here?" the policeman had said.

"Counting," she told him and indicated the seed packets. Broad beans were easier to count than some of the others, especially in the dim light.

His brow crinkled and Lenny worried she'd said the wrong thing.

"I'm sorry. We didn't know you were here. Are you hurt?"

Lenny realized the mess she must look to this man.

"My leg, I've hurt it," she replied, not wanting to imply any wrongdoing on Fergus's part, because she'd caused enough trouble in the preceding days. Her mum would want her to keep family business to herself.

Her leg ached and so did her neck. But they were minor compared to wondering why Tammy hadn't been the one to open the door.

"Can I see my mum?"

He hesitated a fraction too long. "That's not possible right now."

"Did she leave without me?"

The man was disturbed by people behind him and turned to them, speaking in hushed tones and not giving Lenny an answer.

Lenny stepped out from behind him.

"Can I go inside now?" she asked.

Their collective response was a little too quick and much too firm. "No."

Lenny knew she was in trouble. They must all know what she'd done and she was incredibly ashamed of herself. After that there was a steady stream of people and she wondered what the right thing to say was. Telling them Fergus had caused the cut on her leg would lead to questions about her picking up the knife in the first place. And then it seemed like a slippery slope to the actual truth.

Two days and too many questions later, Lenny was let out of hospital and sent to Zanny's.

Her grandmother's couch was a decadent velour, over which Lenny rubbed her hand forward and backward, watching the dark plum turn to shimmering mauve. It was the first time in a long time Lenny had been in her grandmother's house and it felt as unfamiliar to her as a total stranger's.

She needed to be on her best behavior so Zanny didn't leave her as well.

Her teacup clattered and threatened to slip and she jolted and gripped it with both hands. The two women stopped conversing to look at her. The china appeared so thin and delicate Lenny wondered at the decision to—even temporarily—entrust it to someone so young. She was uncomfortably aware of the first impression it would make should her grandmother arrive home and find one of her beautiful floral cups shattered to pieces. A broken cup and a broken girl would be too much today.

This day, of all the days, surely Zanny could've made it on time. Sheila resumed her conversation with Missy, as if they were old friends. Lenny would later find out it was not unusual for her grandmother to run late or eschew schedules. Evidently, this pivotal day in Lenny's life was not so important to anyone else. She sipped her tea, the first she'd ever tried, and it was bitter and hot, but she managed to swallow it politely.

In the car on the way to Zanny's, Sheila (who may actually be Shirley), had turned to Lenny and said, "I wish I'd got to live with my grandmother." It was a silly thing to say, because Lenny's grandmother was not the storybook version of a grandmother that perhaps Shirley's was. In truth, Lenny didn't know Zanny well enough to be relieved or happy to be there. Zanny's visits had all but ceased after the day Fergus threw her out in a tirade of angry words. Lenny wished Shirley would just be honest and say there was nowhere else for her to go.

Lenny finished her drink, not particularly enjoying it, and put her empty teacup down on the coffee table. She unzipped the front panel of the suitcase and pulled out her book.

"What's that you've got?" Missy asked.

Lenny looked down at *The Hobbit*. It was falling apart and the spine was more sticky tape than not. But the cover remained smooth. Lenny ran her hand over it, still disappointed she hadn't managed to find all the pages.

"It's a book."

"Oh yes, I see that, love. What are you reading?"

"*The Hobbit*."

"That seems a big read for someone so young," Missy commented.

"No, it's not very big at all." Lenny held up the book, to show the thickness of its spine.

"We'll have to get you a new copy, that one's all tatty," Missy said, smiling.

Lenny gripped the book, worried Missy would take it from her. She didn't want a replacement. "It was Mum's. She might want it back, so I need to keep it."

Missy looked to Shirley and they exchanged tight smiles. Lenny worried she'd said the wrong thing. Already. She'd have to be more careful.

When Susannah finally arrived she swept through the door like a puff of confetti, all color and movement, and she walked as smoothly as if she were wearing roller skates under her long skirt. She was so glorious a presence that Lenny forgave her lateness immediately.

Zanny swooped down and embraced Lenny so enthusiastically she almost needed to push her away. But she resisted the urge, desperately hoping Zanny would like her enough to keep her. The air around her grandmother smelled distinctive, thick with coconut and wine.

The three adults removed themselves from the room and Lenny's earshot, setting her up with extra biscuits, as if she could be so easily distracted. In a fleeting moment of hope, Lenny wondered if Zanny was late because she had been collecting something to celebrate this day, not just Lenny's arrival, but her twelfth birthday. Lenny repositioned herself to hear the conversation, just in case. She was not a fan of surprises and preferred to be prepared.

"The decision was made by the time I got there. Apparently I was not needed," Zanny said. Her voice, in both tone and pitch, traveled further than most, making it easy for Lenny's prying ears. "It was like a cattle call. Horrible."

"I would've thought they'd want to hear from you anyway. It affects you," said Missy quietly. "And *her*."

"I know, but it seems—at least for now—everyone is staying put.

Helena's here and staying here. No one is going anywhere. Not until the next meeting, or hearing or whatever they call them." Zanny sounded resigned, exhausted.

They didn't want Lenny there, this was abundantly clear. But where else could she go?

Lenny willed herself to focus on the passage she was up to: Gandalf defending his choice of Bilbo to the dwarves. He was such a small and unlikely hero, they were right to doubt him. The words became difficult to read as her eyes blurred with tears.

As hard as she tried to block them out, snippets of the conversation kept finding their way to her ears.

"A complete waste of space," Zanny hissed. "I'm sorry, I know, it's family. I shouldn't have said that."

Did they mean her? Who else could it be?

Missy's voice reassured her. "It doesn't matter, we're all very emotional right now."

"She should be with her mother," Zanny said.

The others murmured in agreement before Shirley reminded them Lenny was in the next room and to perhaps *keep it down*.

Lenny knew better than to make a scene. It was best to pretend she hadn't heard a thing. Little wet blooms formed over Tolkien's words as her tears fell in noiseless drops.

CHAPTER 24

Thursday, June 2, 2022

After four days of avoiding Amy, Lenny knew it was time to make a choice about whether she should continue to socialize with Ned. She devoted an exceptional amount of thought to this and finally settled her uncertainty with an online quiz, "Your Best Friend's Boyfriend: have you crossed the line?"

Starting it, she'd been confident she'd not done anything untoward, but by the end, *That's Life!* was unequivocal that she fell in category C: "check yourself before you wreck yourself (and your friendship)."

As tempted as she was to redo the quiz and answer differently to skew the result, she resisted. The decision was made and now, standing behind a woman with a pink-cheeked baby strapped to her chest in the line at McKnight's, it was time to tell Ned.

He looked over and shot her a smile. The genuine kind, with eyebrows raised and a slight toss of the head. It was, she was quite sure, a smile for her and not the one he used for every customer who walked through the door.

She chastised herself; she was—and could only be—just a customer. Nothing more.

It wasn't only the quiz that had brought her to this conclusion;

it would be reckless to put all her faith in *That's Life!* or "Dr. Beth," who gave no further background to her qualifications, or even a surname. She may not have even been a doctor. Lenny had tried to apply some common sense to the situation as well. She saw Ned in very limited time frames, whereas Amy was around five days a week (with the exception of school holidays). And Amy came with the added bonus of Ashleigh, so it was really two friends for the effort of one. If Lenny saw Ned more frequently than within the confines of McKnight's and Amy took umbrage at this, it could affect Lenny's standing among the staff and students at Selby South. She didn't want to move her work location any more than she wanted to find a new place to shop.

"Lenny, how goes it?" Ned asked, pulling her shopping basket down the conveyor belt toward him.

"I'm well, thank you," she said in an effort to sound detached. She didn't want to blindside Ned by appearing to be friendlier than necessary.

"So Mr. Pointy arrived, and it's more awesome in real life than I imagined," he said, scanning her tins of soup and other items through the register.

There was no one behind her in the line and she decided it was best to get her point heard before an impatient shopper delayed the speech she'd rehearsed.

"Ned, I am no longer able to see you outside McKnight's. This is a personal decision I've come to and I won't be swayed."

"Everything all right?" Ned asked, his scanning of groceries slowing down significantly as he processed her words. She couldn't look up and meet his gaze, instead focusing on the loose corner of a specials poster affixed to the side of the register.

"Yes. But I have no intention of doing the wrong thing either accidentally or on purpose and I don't want to be put in that position. By taking steps now to ensure neither of us has to make any difficult decisions later, I think I am doing the right thing by both of us before any damage is done to the relationship."

"Our relationship?" Ned asked.

"No, mine and Amy's," Lenny said. "Or yours and Amy's."

"What about us?"

"There is no *us*, Ned. I'm being very careful to make sure of that."

Ned didn't reply and she heard nothing from the register. It made her glance up, and Ned was giving her a look she couldn't quite interpret.

"I'm sorry if you think I was doing something improper," Ned said. "I just thought . . ."

Lenny nervously fidgeted with the corner of the poster, pushing it back into place, although the tape had lost its adhesiveness.

"Thought what?"

"I thought we were friends, is all."

"Well, I'm glad to have put it straight then. I didn't want any sort of confusion."

Ned exhaled audibly. She was not sure this was going as she'd planned; it wasn't giving her any sort of relief or a sense she'd put things right. It felt much more like losing something.

"Fair enough," Ned said finally.

A man with two girls in school uniform—not Selby South—got into line behind her and unloaded his basket onto the belt.

She'd done what she came to do, and she couldn't fix it now. Even though it really seemed more of a mistake than a relief.

Lenny tapped her card on the EFTPOS machine, picked up her shopping bags and left. She wouldn't turn back and say goodbye in case it belied her certainty.

Goodbye: boogey, goody, body, bye

CHAPTER 25

Saturday, June 18

Monica took the lead on their score averages, which still felt like losing to Lenny, even though she played both hands. Lenny scooped up handfuls of tiles and put them back in the bag.

The past few weeks had rolled by as they always did, routinely and without drama. Which suited her just fine. Although she had thought she might have been on the receiving end of an invite from Amy or Ashleigh by now. She had assumed there would be some sort of reward for doing the right thing about Ned, but it was yet to materialize. She wouldn't overthink it, not yet.

Everything seemed exactly like it had always been and Lenny couldn't quite work out why she wasn't satisfied with that anymore.

Malcolm shuffled around, wanting to go out.

Lenny got up and opened the door. She'd finished a secure and quite attractive fence so Malcolm could go outside without having to be watched like a hawk. The fence allowed him to wander between her yard and Maureen's, Maureen having suggested this at one of their front porch visits, which were becoming a semi-regular occurrence. With Lenny gone throughout the day, Malcolm kept company with Maureen and all parties seemed pleased by the arrangement.

Now she noticed Callistemon Court had become quite congested: cars were nose to tail around the part of the court she could see and were even partially blocking her driveway. Music rang out through the otherwise quiet night and laughter and voices filled the air. Lenny wandered down into her yard and saw it was Maureen's house causing the traffic; her balcony was full of light and activity. Paper lanterns were strung from the verandah to the trees, looking like a diorama of planets. The noise from next door sounded happy and Lenny recognized a Jimi Hendrix song playing, which brought her grandmother to mind. Zanny's record collection was extensive and used frequently. Even though she could play a CD, which would have been easier (and probably sounded clearer), Zanny insisted on using her turntable as it was the way the artist had intended.

Lenny noticed Malcolm standing amid the small crowd. She and Malcolm couldn't have been more different; the things she hid from, he seemed to gravitate to. She left him to enjoy himself and carried an armful of wood inside for the fire. It was her night for Thai, but too early to order yet, so she went back to the dining table to see if she could gain on Monica's thriving average.

Halfway through the game, with Lenny twenty-six points in the lead, a knock sounded at the door.

Lenny considered ignoring it because she wasn't expecting anyone. There was, however, a chance the knock would precipitate a burglary. The ruse of a clever thief would be to check if anyone was home with a knock on the door. In that case, she'd be wise to answer it in case she caused them to think she wasn't home.

The knock sounded a second time, more impatient. Presumably the lights and television being on made it fairly obvious someone was inside.

Lenny answered the door to find Maureen.

"Helena, you'd think you'd walked down Mount Dandenong itself to get to your door."

"You can walk?" Lenny said, eyeing the stick Maureen leaned on heavily. The crossing between properties was not smooth terrain.

"It's quite the miracle, isn't it?" Maureen laughed. "I *can* walk, but I usually need some help. So you must come with me."

Maureen nodded her head toward her house with a smile. It was as if there was a conversation Lenny was forgetting, so certain did Maureen seem that Lenny would follow her. But had Lenny accepted an invite she'd have mulled it over tirelessly, so she knew this was the first she'd heard of it.

"Why?" Lenny asked.

"The Moon Goddess waits for no one," Maureen said, throwing her hands skyward. Lenny sensed that Maureen was a good two—or three—drinks in.

"The winter solstice, it's tonight, isn't it?" Lenny said, the sudden recollection like she'd just been prodded.

"Ah, good girl. You remembered."

"Remembered?" Lenny asked. Maureen's hand flew to her mouth, as if she'd said too much. Her eyes sparkled and she somehow seemed younger, brighter.

"Actually, it's on Tuesday, but we felt the Goddess wouldn't mind us picking a more socially convenient evening."

Lenny was already pulling on her coat and locking her door, anticipation nipping at her heels like a new puppy. She knew she wanted to follow Maureen into the moon garden next door.

Malcolm found Lenny within seconds of her arrival at Maureen's and she gently patted his head, thankful for his calming bulk leaning into her.

The low evening light was punctuated by the lanterns, which lit up faces in unexpected and enchanting ways. The pool of guests was entirely female and dressed in a cosmos of colors and textures: plum cheesecloth, yellow scarves, rainbows of drapey, flowy skirts and pewter earrings that scraped collarbones. Lenny took it all in from within the security of her sensible gray buttoned coat, black slacks and flat-soled Diana Ferraris. Sandalwood and citronella invaded her nostrils and she realized she was standing beside sticks of it, burning into the night; warding off the mosquitoes, she guessed, although perhaps these women used it for a more esoteric reason.

Esoteric: secret, soiree, rise

The smell took her somewhere else—a fleeting and distinctive feeling of being at Zanny's, which she quickly dismissed. She wasn't fond of sentimentality.

"Are you witches?" she asked Maureen.

Maureen studied her warmly and expectantly and Lenny looked to her feet, feeling childish for asking the question. "I'm sorry, that was rude. I just . . ."

"No, not at all, it just reminded me of something a young girl said to me a long time ago." Maureen reached over and squeezed Lenny's forearm. The touch did not make her bristle. "We are *not* witches, we're far worse: we're artists."

Maureen laughed heartily before continuing. "Tonight, Helena, we thank the moon and welcome the return of longer days. But it's really just a good excuse to get us all together. You don't have to stay if you're not comfortable, but these women are all friends. You're welcome here."

And Lenny felt it; it was okay to be there. Malcolm helped, and so did the proximity of her own house. An easy getaway made her relax somewhat.

"Maureen, this must be the woman from next door?" said a

heavy-set lady with a wreath of daisies sitting on her close-cropped hair.

"Yes, this is Helena," Maureen told the woman.

"Helena, I am Heather. It is so lovely to finally meet you."

Finally?

Lenny managed a smile and realized Maureen was right: she did feel welcome here.

"It's Lenny now."

"Oh, yes, Lenny." Heather nodded. "Do you mind?" Heather asked, but didn't wait for an answer before pulling Lenny's hand into her own. The woman held her hand longer than Lenny thought she could stand, clutching it firmly and closing her eyes. Then her eyes sprung open and her mouth moved as if she was about to announce something, but didn't. Heather dropped Lenny's hand, pulling her own hands to her chest quickly as if they'd been touched to a flame. Lenny didn't feel burned but she did feel something, like a bolt of light reverberating through her bones. Each vertebra springing suddenly to attention, the spaces between her ribs feeling stretched, her toes curling in her Diana Ferraris, an involuntary shudder rising through her.

"You have a blockage. You need to do something about that," Heather said, as if this should make perfect sense. "I've moved a little something, but there's more to do."

Lenny looked to Maureen and back to Heather, hoping one of them would reassure her they were joking. Neither did. Maureen looked engrossed and Heather seemed determined. Lenny couldn't help thinking of a backed-up sink, which she really didn't like to compare herself to.

"You should come and see me. When you're ready, of course. Maureen knows where to find me," Heather said, nodding sagely. "You need to trust yourself—you have very good intuition. Oh, and you must stop ignoring the past. She doesn't like it."

"Who is *she*?" Lenny asked.

"Your younger self."

Lenny couldn't think of a polite way to respond. She was quite sure her younger self and her current self were the same person and perhaps it was Heather who was not quite right.

Heather touched Lenny's biceps reassuringly, and this time she couldn't help but flinch at the contact. The moment was gone. Without any further ado, Heather wandered off, her head swaying to the music (Joan Baez now), as if this was all just normal business for her.

Maureen motioned for Lenny to follow her and together they walked inside to the lounge. Maureen eased herself into her wheelchair and Lenny sat down beside her. It was nice to sit, the couch was comfortable and the velour fabric felt lovely under her fingertips.

"Are you feeling unwell?" Lenny asked.

"No, I'm fine. I just tire quickly." Maureen smiled calmly.

"What's wrong with you?" Lenny asked.

Maureen laughed. "Plenty!"

"Oh . . . I'm sorry. No, please don't answer, I didn't mean to say that." Lenny was ready to run into the shadows. No wonder she didn't get invited places often.

"You can ask, it's fine. It's MS. and some days are better than others. But it's wearing me down, bit by bit."

"I'm sorry."

Maureen leaned forward and put a hand on Lenny's knee. "Don't be—we can't live forever. As for Heather, she's very good at what she does, but a little intense when you first meet her."

"What is it that she does?"

"She's a healer. She's been doing Meliae healing for a long time and I think she just did a sneaky bit of it on you then, did you feel it? She's a devil for doing that." Maureen paused. "You mustn't worry, she means no harm. And she's very good—she's helped me no end over the years."

Healing made Lenny think of velvet drapery, tarot cards and two-dollar-shop magic balls—the set-up of a charlatan trying to coax money from vulnerable people. It sounded like absolute nonsense to her. That aside, it was hard to dismiss the way she'd felt while Heather was clutching her hand.

A drink was thrust into Lenny's hand; it was cold and refreshing and burned all the way down. The women chattered constantly: to each other, to the sky, to Malcolm, to her. She didn't have to think up conversation, nor did she have time to mull over what to say. They just pulled her in and made her one of them. She managed to feel relaxed—or at least as close to it as she could remember being in a social setting. It wasn't lost on Lenny that the drinks did help settle her nerves.

It was late and the moon was high in the sky when the women started peeling off their shoes and dropping them on the well-trodden boards of Maureen's deck. A pile of heels, laces, zips and buckles. Their laughter rang out like a riot of kookaburras as they descended the stairs into Maureen's backyard, where thick-cut logs were arranged in a circle on the grass.

Lenny struggled to look away from the women assembled on the lawn. They were a whirling, dancing, laughing mess of color and light.

"They'll tell stories, dance, maybe sing, stare into the sky; it's good for the soul. You're welcome to go down there," Maureen said, finding Lenny and Malcolm side by side. They were the only ones left behind; the rest of the party was now beneath them.

"It's not really my thing," Lenny said. "Do you want me to help you down there though?"

"No, I'll stay with you."

Lenny was grateful for her company. "Why do they do it?"

"Nothing like putting bare feet on dirt, you know. It's liberating to be so close to the earth. Like a tonic for happiness. More potent than Preeti's punch," Maureen said, tinkling the ice in her glass, the liquid swirling, the vibrant orange reminding Lenny of SES overalls.

"Is that the be all and end all?" Lenny asked.

"What?"

"Happiness."

"No. Not at all. It's decidedly overrated," Maureen said.

It was refreshing to hear this spoken out loud.

"But you've got to aim for something," Maureen added. "And these women, they weren't always so free. Most of them had to fight for it, so they know its value."

"I'm fine as I am," Lenny said.

"I didn't say you weren't."

"Everyone else seems to think they get a say in it."

"Maybe they care about you?"

"Maybe. But things are good as they are," Lenny replied, realizing how defensive she sounded.

"Are they really?"

They both looked at the heads bobbing below them. Some of the women were whirling or swaying or just gazing skyward. They looked beautiful, free, *happy*. Lenny could go down there and spin in circles but it wouldn't be the same. She'd be wondering the whole time what the other women thought of her; she'd feel out of place and she would have hair in her eyes and dirt on her feet and her toes would get cold and all those things would bother her. Lenny took that as a sign she'd probably reached her social threshold for the night. These women were easy to be around, but that didn't change Lenny's own unrest.

"Thank you for inviting me over, but I should really go home," Lenny said, nudging Malcolm to follow her and moving quickly before Maureen could convince her to stay.

With Malcolm in tow she walked home, feeling like Alice being spat out of the rabbit hole and back into normality. Or Lenny's normal at least, where no one spoke to the moon or used their energy force field to heal people. Or whatever it was that Heather purported to do.

Blockage: backlog, lockage, cable, globe, able

As Lenny considered all she'd just encountered, she caught a glimpse of something moving in her front yard. It was too far from the front light to be clearly visible and her eyes took a moment to adapt to the darkness. The figure moved again; it was far too tall to be a fox. It was a person, she was quite sure. Lenny straightened up a little so she looked bigger and not easy to attack, just in case it was a prowler.

Fergus swam into her thoughts, a sobering slap.

Had he been released? Was that what Wendy Dalton had been calling to tell her? She'd deleted the last two messages and disabled her voicemail; maybe that had been a mistake.

"Who's there?" she said, mustering some faux confidence.

The figure moved again and her night vision was good enough to make out someone too small to be Fergus. It was a child, a young girl.

Her stomach unwound and she felt her shoulders drop, although the adrenalin surge continued to make her heart beat just a little too quickly.

Lenny thought perhaps Malcolm would scare the girl off. So she let him into the Tree House before turning back to the bushes in her front garden. She couldn't see the girl now; she wasn't standing beside the grevillea where she'd been just a second earlier. Lenny listened but heard nothing other than the noise from Maureen's.

Tentatively, she stepped out of the light and moved through the bushes, speaking quietly as she did so.

"Hello, are you there? Don't be afraid of me," she said, although it did cross her mind that she was seeing things. Perhaps she'd overdone it with Preeti's punch.

Lenny saw no one and received no reply. She now doubted she'd actually seen anyone. Surely if someone had been there she would've heard them run away, or found them hunkered down in the lilly pilly. It must have been a fox.

She went to her front door and opened it. Malcolm was waiting patiently for her inside and the warmth called her in. Still, she checked over her shoulder just in case. But there was no one there.

Once inside, she locked the door carefully behind her, making sure both locks were firmly in place. The fire had dipped, but not died, and she stoked it back to life and stood at her window, watching the dark silhouettes of the bohemian women next door moving about in wild abandon.

Sisters: resist, stress, rites, rises, rests, stirs

Lenny felt restless. Despite being more than ready for sleep, she felt edgy with unexpended energy.

She went to her *Hobbit*s; they would help her to settle.

They were in height order, which seemed silly now. Far too trite. She wanted them in order of purchase. Some of her thirty-six copies were almost identical editions, but Lenny knew when each had come into her possession. It had been almost a year since she'd added to the collection. They usually came to her organically: spied at the second-hand bookshop in Belgrave or gifted to her by Fay. Lenny would have to keep her eye out for another one. Methodically, she pulled them off the shelves and lined them back up, beginning with her earliest copy, the one that had started it all. The sticky tape keeping it together reminded her of Fergus ripping it from her hands. She'd been busy reading and had not heard him call her name. She hadn't meant to ignore him; she would never dare to do that. He'd taken the book and ripped it straight down the spine, sending pages scattering. She'd cried, which had made him madder and he'd sent her out to the shed. To *think about what she'd done*. She never managed to find all the pages, but had stuck it back together as best she could.

Lenny rested her hand on it and felt comfort in its tattered state.

She finished lining up the books and ran her finger over their spines. Neat and ordered. That was Lenny's happiness. She didn't need complications. She just wanted the comfort of her life the way it always was, or at least the way it had been for as long as she could remember.

Her body felt heavy with tiredness now and her eyes were starting to close involuntarily. She walked into her room, but instead of sinking into bed, she took her quilt and a pillow and dragged them into her wardrobe. There, on the opposite wall to her neatly laid-out shoes, she curled up, pulled the quilt over herself and, feeling very much eleven years old all over again, fell asleep.

At eleven, Lenny still had her family: Tammy, her mum, and stepdad Fergus. Even Zanny, although she saw her rarely. At eleven, her best friend was imaginary and they colluded like no other friends could. At eleven, she was on the cusp of becoming a teenager, but felt desperately unwilling to let herself be taken by it. Unlike girls her age at school, Lenny had no desire to grow up and deal with the tyrannies of adult life she watched her mother grapple with. While the other girls were busy talking about makeup and *Girlfriend* magazine, Lenny was happy to construct Lego forts and cut Barbie's hair with Malcolm, the friend who only she could see, and who would never force her to grow up, because he couldn't either. She remembered sleeping many a night on the carpeted floor in her wardrobe, inhaling the scent of the polished leather of her school shoes and listening to her mother playing music downstairs. It would play from the old Panasonic stereo in the kitchen and Lenny could always gauge the mood of the house by whether or not Tammy was singing along.

Half-asleep, adult Lenny held her quilt tight, another sound ringing in her ears and forcing her back to the wardrobe of her girlhood. It was as clear as if it were in the Tree House with her. A clunk as an empty bottle hit the side of the bin, a door slamming and the sound of the television turning on. It was always the late news, the volume going up, higher than the music, obscuring the Mamas & the Papas singing about summer days in faraway places. Muffled voices next, louder and angrier. Sometimes she could make out the words, but she didn't ever want to. It was always the same: Fergus was always right, don't question him, don't talk back, just hope he falls asleep soon. Lenny's small fingers would grip the well-thumbed pages of her book, their dark-inked words a welcome comfort to her. She and Malcolm didn't always read the words, they just needed them there, waiting with them. Were they waiting? Or were they hiding? She couldn't remember. The feeling of a small, smooth-skinned hand in hers, incredibly vivid for an imaginary friend, filtered through.

In the bottom of the wardrobe, Lenny shuddered in her sleep.

CHAPTER 26

Sunday, June 19

When Lenny woke up, she didn't know where she was. The sullen-colored array of clothes hanging overhead helped her orient herself as she stretched out, feeling every one of her years after sleeping on the hard floor. She knew from the trivia-night experience that her dry mouth and headache were probably a hangover, but she wasn't about to admit this and so dragged herself up and dressed to take Malcolm out for a walk.

Crossing her front garden, she stopped to check behind the bushes, just in case. But there was no sign anyone had been there and Lenny shrugged off her silliness. Clearly the punch had been stronger than she thought. And whatever it was Heather had said she did, it now sounded even more ludicrous in the bright, cool morning light. It seemed more than likely Heather needed a mental health assessment.

Her feet and Malcolm's paws fell into step, crunching across the fallen leaves and loose gravel of the path. If she'd been paying more attention to her surroundings she might've noticed the man before he noticed her.

"Hey! You!" the man shouted, shattering her reverie.

Her immediate thought was that she'd dropped something and

the man was pointing it out to her, but one look at his reddened, incensed face suggested this was not the case.

"That's my dog, you thieving fucking bitch!"

He was obviously not interested in discussing whether there was an issue of mistaken identity.

Lenny looked around, hoping someone was nearby to help, but of course no one was; solitude was one of the reasons she took that particular trail.

She found no words, only the urge to run.

"Come here, boy," the man demanded of Malcolm as he approached.

Malcolm's lead was held firmly in her hand; she couldn't very well deny knowing him at this point in time, nor did she want to.

Confrontation: coronation, nonaction, fraction, traction, infarct, cannot

Brushing her hand over the top of Malcolm's head, Lenny felt his skin tense and a low growl emanated from him, as if he'd turned to thunder. She hoped to convey through the tips of her fingers that they were in this together.

The man stopped in front of them, feet planted in a wide stance, arms at his sides, fingers curled into fists and knuckles pulled white and taut. Surely he was aware this dog did not want to be with him.

"Beast. Get here. *Now*." The man stepped forward, closing the distance.

The growl intensified.

Lenny felt her muscles contract and wondered if she would be able to move if she tried. She considered the best route for escape: forward and past him or turning her back to him. Neither was ideal. Nor was leading him directly to the Tree House.

If only she'd never left home.

"Jase," said another voice, farther away and far less confident.

She tried to imprint a description of Jase on her mind. Average height, slim build, brown goatee, skin tinged gray; lack of nutrition or proper cleansing, she would surmise. Baseball cap pushed down over tufty brown hair that looked coarse and unwilling to cooperate. The cap was emblazoned with a Holden logo and a solid, greasy stain lined the rim where it met his forehead. Jase wore a zipped-up black parachute jacket that looked neither clean nor warm. He was alarmingly small for someone so intimidating. Malcolm on his hind legs would be nearly as tall as him, and twice as powerful. But she didn't want Malcolm to fight him. It would be a convenient moment for a large eucalypt branch to fall on him. Not to kill him necessarily, but just to pin him down long enough for them to get a safe distance away.

"Mate, it's my dog," Jase called back to the second man, who wore a hooded jumper and beanie, much more suitable for the current clime. This other man was looking nervously over his shoulder as if expecting someone.

"We've gotta go," Hoodie said to Jase. He was, inexplicably, carrying a watering can and a green reusable Woolies bag.

"Not without Beast," Jase replied.

Hoodie rolled his eyes. "How do you even know it's him?" he snapped.

"Look at him, mate."

"*Jase*, let's go."

Lenny prayed Hoodie's pleas would be enough to convince Jase to leave without Malcolm.

"She stole m' fuckin' dog."

Jase leaned forward and grabbed Lenny's hand. She could feel the calluses on his palm graze her skin as he tried to prise the lead from her fingers.

"Let go," he hissed through clenched teeth, his pungent breath reaching Lenny's nostrils.

She *had* stolen his dog, but it wasn't a straightforward case of right and wrong, nor was she prepared to simply hand Malcolm over.

"Come on, mate, we don't want to be caught out here," Hoodie insisted.

Caught?

"Gonna say something, bitch? What's wrong with you? That's *my dog*." Jase sprayed spit over her face as he spoke. She dropped her eyes. Malcolm's thunder continued and Jase grabbed his collar and fumbled to undo the clip of his lead.

"Stupid dog," he hissed.

Lenny wanted to yell, hit, push, fight but none of these things came to her. Was she really going to let this violent, unwashed man take her best friend? She needed to do something. *Anything.*

From Fergus she'd learned that the quieter she could be, the more likely the tirade would finish and he'd move on. She was such a *coward.*

Voices reached them from down the track. More than one person, maybe even a group, chattering as they headed directly toward them. People. An audience. And for whatever reason, these two men didn't want to be seen out here.

Hoodie gave up and started walking off into the scrub. Jase dropped his hand from Malcolm's collar and looked about; Hoodie was now just a flash of movement in the trees.

Lenny took her opportunity. Without uttering a word, she picked up one weighted foot and gave Malcolm a nudge with her knee. Her feet—as unsure as a newborn giraffe's—started taking them toward the voices, barely managing to walk but making progress all the same. Malcolm didn't falter; he stayed with her, his flank brushing reassuringly against her thigh. A group of five walkers appeared ahead. They were her oasis, her ticket out of there. She was Bilbo, slipping out of the caves, past the elves and into the daylight.

Just keep walking.

Her feet rose and fell, faster and faster until they neared a bend. One of the walkers gave her a smile and a nod, which she returned. They could have no idea how brilliant their timing was. She didn't dare look behind her, but felt Jase and Hoodie wouldn't have the mettle to follow her with an audience. As they rounded the bend, she realized she was jogging despite never making the conscious effort to change her stride.

They ran, taking a haphazard route through the trees to avoid being followed. The shrubbery was thick and jagged and smacked her shins and snagged in her hair and jacket. Malcolm followed unquestioningly.

She knew they couldn't go home yet. It didn't matter that they'd lost sight of the men; Lenny didn't want to risk exposing the Tree House. No amount of checking and rechecking the door locks would help if Jase and Hoodie knew where they lived.

A tree root tripped Lenny and she fell forward, putting her hands out just in time to stop her face from colliding with the damp ground. She was panting and sweating and then, from nowhere, she was laughing into the quiet of the forest as Malcolm patiently watched her, breathing heavily and waiting for her to compose herself. She listened for the telltale sound of feet or voices, anything that would signal they were being followed. But she couldn't hear over the thrum of her heart. She waited a few minutes longer, until it was just the forest she could hear.

She'd kept them safe for now. She couldn't fail someone else. Not again.

Her mind clicked and whirred with familiar yet distant memories of things she thought she'd blocked out. Jase's tense face and hot breath reminded her of Fergus. Despite not having seen her stepfather for over two decades, he loomed as big as ever. If she made things difficult—by running, answering back or defending herself—he'd grow bigger and angrier and *he'd still win*. Lenny was useless and small; she couldn't stand up for Malcolm, let alone herself.

Lenny's stomach lurched and the memory of trying to defeat Fergus solidified around the edges. She rubbed the scar on her thigh and reminded herself to breathe.

You did this.

CHAPTER 27

It was just past midday when Lenny and Malcolm reached the familiar frontage of McKnight's, the baskets swinging happily in the wind, as if they were hammocks for Lilliputians. The chalkboard-black of Malcolm's coat seemed the opposite of camouflage and she was worried they wouldn't make it home without being spotted. She could only hope Jase and Hoodie weren't adept at surveillance. She was loath to underestimate them.

Underestimate: determinate, interested, remediates, terminated

McKnight's hadn't been her destination on purpose, but it was where they'd ended up. She felt relief at the sight of the store and Cordelia parked out the front.

Ned would help. He was fond of Malcolm and already knew of his dubious origins.

Lenny tied Malcolm's lead to the bike rack beside the store, checked for suspicious characters and raced inside. She asked for Ned as soon as she walked in, not wanting to leave Malcolm alone for too long.

"He's not here," Deb said from the front counter, a spark of interest igniting behind her wire-rimmed spectacles. She was inclined to gossip, Lenny could tell.

"But Cordelia is out the front," she said.

"Who?"

"His van," Lenny clarified, annoyed at Deb's vagueness.

"It's the delivery van, love."

"Do you know when he will be back?" she asked. "Will it be today?"

"No, he's over at the Montrose store. Mr. McKnight put him in charge there."

As if the very mention of his name had summoned him, Mr. McKnight appeared.

"She's looking for *Ned*, not you, Ed," Deb said, emitting a grunting laugh as she spoke. Lenny must have missed the joke.

She had a particular opinion of people who named their children after themselves; it suggested a lack of creativity and a sense of grandiosity. It would also make sorting the mail difficult.

"He's not here, darl," Ed said.

"I told her that," said Deb.

"He's managing the Montrose store, I needed him in charge over there."

"I told her that too," Deb piped up.

"But he doesn't want to run a grocery store," Lenny said, without pausing to consider that perhaps Ned didn't want Ed to know this.

"I think he's played board games in the spare room for long enough, little lady."

Deb and Ed laughed as if they were sharing an uproarious joke, although Deb's guffaw morphed into a hearty smoker's cough that petered out into sputtering. Lenny drew back, making a mental note not to purchase any of the items from the register point of sale.

"But he loves it," Lenny said.

"If we could all do what we loved I'd be sailing a yacht on the barrier reef with an esky full of Crownies. Life isn't that simple though, is it?" Ed said.

Deb rasped another laugh.

No, she supposed it was not. Nor was it her place to meddle in an arrangement between father and son. And yet Ned's father stomping all over his son's ambitions was intolerable. She wanted to push over the boxes of Coco Pops that stood tall beside her (thirty percent off this week); she wanted to throw one of the half-price tins of spaghetti at Ed and tell him to stop being an oppressive bully. An outburst of some form felt dangerously close to the surface.

But then Lenny remembered she'd removed herself from Ned's life. Perhaps this was exactly the arrangement he wanted. Maybe he'd given up on the game-making himself and asked his father for the promotion. But why would he? His face lit up with pure joy when he described the characters he'd created. Giving up would be like being lobotomized.

Lenny turned on her heel and headed for the door, stopping just short of the exit. She was so sick of being spineless.

"It is that simple, actually," she said timidly, her voice so low she wondered if anyone else heard her.

"What's that, love?" Ed asked.

Her feet urged her out the door, but she didn't move.

Say it, Lenny.

"It is. That. Simple. If you want to be on a yacht, do it. You're the only one stopping yourself. Ned is not culpable for *your* lack of ambition."

Ed looked surprised more than anything and she didn't give him time to respond.

She turned to Deb, anger bubbling now. "And cover your mouth when you cough."

Then she was gone, hurrying out the door and back to her dog before anything beyond her control was released.

* * *

Lenny and Malcolm returned home unscathed and undetected. She was so relieved to be back at the Tree House she didn't think she'd ever leave again.

The adrenaline was draining rapidly and she dove onto the couch, curling her knees into her body and pulling a blanket over herself. She would make a terrible action hero; one mild adventure scene was enough for her.

Lenny slept until it was almost dark. A solid, sweaty, dreamless sleep, as if she hadn't slept for a month. Malcolm's snuffling around the kitchen for food made her open her eyes, although she felt she could close them again and disappear straight back into sleep. The trees danced somberly out the window in front of her, back and forward beneath the gray, cloudless sky.

It wasn't just Malcolm who was hungry, she realized. And her mind was firing with thoughts of people past and present. The sleep hadn't served to erase anyone from her mind; in fact, of late she was getting increasingly bad at blocking out the excess noise. The volume dial appeared to no longer be in her control.

Lenny pulled a packet of Ritz crackers from the pantry, at the same time noticing a neglected bottle of port on the top shelf. It had been a Christmas gift from a student the year before. Presents were allowed, but certainly not alcohol, and Lenny had dutifully taken it to Ms. Pham to report the infraction. Lora insisted she keep it and, with a conspiratorial wink, said, "Merry Christmas." Lenny loathed bending rules almost as much as she disliked winking, but she didn't want to throw it in the bin at the school lest a student find it. So she brought it home, where it sat unopened at the top of the pantry.

She poured the thick plum liquid into an Ikea tumbler and took a large sip. It burned and warmed and made her promptly take another sip. The second went down better, and she topped up her tumbler, alternating between the Ritz crackers and generous gulps of port. She tasted cherries and it reminded her of thick slabs of Fay's Christmas fruitcake.

Lenny fed Malcolm and he wolfed his food hungrily. She longed for the simplicity he seemed to thrive on. It was 6:30 and she realized she'd missed her usual Thai order last night; she wondered if anyone had remarked on it. Presumably not. No one would notice Lenny Marks's absence in their life. She likened herself to the word on the tip of your tongue that you can't quite recall. It's there, only it won't come to mind and it is of no consequence if it doesn't. She was the reason you walked back into a room, thinking you'd forgotten something, only you didn't remember what it was because it had never been all that important. Lenny was a shadow.

What am I doing?

You can't ignore it forever.

Yes. I can.

You are not okay, Lenny.

She watched the trees move in their slow, lovely dance and sipped from her glass. The burning had become satisfying. Something caught her eye out in the shadows of her backyard. Beneath the trees, looking straight at her. Lenny stepped back from the glass, startled.

It was not a fox.

Lenny slipped out her door and walked past the end of the house and into the dark, tree-studded expanse of her yard. The smell of red-gum smoke hung in the air, circling in the sky from both her and Maureen's chimneys. Malcolm's face was in the window of her lounge room; he hadn't followed her—presumably one adventure was enough for the day.

"Do you need some help?" she asked, nearing the place where she'd spotted the movement but unable to see anyone there. Her voice sounded echoey, hollow, as if it belonged to someone else.

She should've armed herself, she realized; this whole situation could be incredibly dangerous and no one knew where she was. She could be the lead news story tomorrow: *Murdered Belgrave Teacher Didn't Stand A Chance.*

Then a small person moved forward just enough for her to be able to make her out. A shadow-girl.

"Do you live near here?" Lenny asked.

The girl shook her head, a red flower hovering near her cheek. What a silly question to begin with, Lenny thought; children are taught not to reveal their address to strangers. And Lenny was a stranger, even though it was her backyard.

"Are you lost?" Lenny said.

The girl stared straight at her and gave a slight nod.

Lenny wished she had her phone with her; she could've called the police to come and collect the child, whose mother would be (or should be) beside herself. The girl was lucky she'd come across a good-hearted person, one who held a current Working with Children check.

Lenny didn't often have to deal with children outside the school, where there was protocol for all sorts of things. But here, in her own backyard, she wasn't sure what the right thing to do was.

If she invited the girl into her home, it might look as if she was luring her into an unknown place. If she ran back for her phone, the girl may very well disappear. She could wait with the girl and hope someone would come along, but there was little chance of that.

Dash the perception, she thought, the girl should be inside and have her parents called as soon as possible. Unless they were the sort of parents who wouldn't come. Or had already left. Or perhaps weren't safe to be with. Regardless, she couldn't stay in Lenny's bushes all night.

"We should go in, I'll be able to call someone from there. Someone you feel safe with," Lenny said.

"I feel safe with you."

"Do I know you?" Lenny asked.

The girl nodded.

"Did I teach you?"

She shook her head.

"You're very familiar. Do you go to Selby South Primary?"

Lenny knew that face, the soft curve of her nose and the dappling of freckles across the bridge. Maybe she was in one of the other year levels. She looked younger than her grade fivers.

"I have to give you something," the girl said.

"Me?" asked Lenny.

The girl bobbed her head again. Her brown hair fell softly about her shoulders, much longer than Lenny's.

She didn't emerge from the bottlebrush, but held out something in her hand and Lenny stepped forward to take it. It was a piece of paper, but she couldn't make out what was on it in the dark.

Lenny turned toward the house to let more light fall on it; it seemed desperately important all of a sudden to know what it was. She hoped it was the contact details of this girl's parents or legal guardian, to have her reunited with them before they became too worried. But it didn't look like a phone number or an address.

It was silly standing out in the dark. Lenny would get her to come inside and make her a hot Milo to warm her up.

But the girl was gone.

Disappeared: apprised, paradise, appease, resided, appear, despair

Lenny checked behind the shrubbery, in case the girl had crouched down. She looked slowly at first and then frantically, branches whipping her face and arms as she dived into the bushes looking for any sign of the missing child.

Lenny's breath was a plume of whiteness in front of her face. The darkness was suffocating and she wished she could switch on a light and see where the girl was. People don't just disappear.

Although sometimes they did.

She raced inside, deciding she must call the police. Lenny was a teacher and had a duty of care to look after the child, even if it was outside of school hours. She grabbed her phone and dialed triple zero. The police would help, they'd set up lights and search for her. They might have already taken a missing person report from a frantic family and know exactly who she was.

"Ambulance, police or fire brigade?" the call taker asked.

"Police," Lenny said, her eyes scanning the paper the girl had handed her.

"At what address do you need police?"

The words stuck. The volume dial in her head was turned up.

"Hello, are you there? What's the address where you need police?"

Lenny looked at the paper and the unmistakable handwriting on it. It was the title page of *The Hobbit*, ripped from her copy long ago. She looked over to her shelves where the repaired copy sat first in line.

Her mother's handwriting swirled unnecessarily on both the T and the W of Tammy Winters. The blue pen was faded, but nonetheless clear. *Helena Winters* was written underneath Tammy's name in the same cursive. A gift from mother to daughter.

"Do you need the police?" The call taker's voice was insistent.

Lenny hung up the phone.

It was clear now who the girl was and why she wouldn't find her. Lenny also came to the conclusion she was rapidly losing her grip on reality.

Imploding: limping, doping, limpid, long

Reality: tearily, layer, teary, liar

Impossible: omissible, imposes, impel, spoil, loss

Heather's words rang loudly in her head: *Stop ignoring your past. She doesn't like it.*

The girl was her.

CHAPTER 28

Monday, June 20

Lenny attempted to keep Monday as uneventful as possible. She was concerned Jase and Hoodie might resurface and she rode to school at such a rapid pace that her legs burned and continued to do so throughout the morning classes.

Kirra came to see her after her students had disappeared to music with Trudi Kerr. Lenny was cleaning the board, zoned out on using the duster in neat horizontal lines, and didn't notice Kirra's arrival.

"It was my dad's birthday on the weekend," said Kirra, startling Lenny, who dropped the duster at her feet in a small puff of chalk. "Sorry, didn't mean to scare you."

"No problem. But I don't think I know your father," Lenny said.

"No, well, you wouldn't," Kirra said. "My mum cooked up a storm, so I thought maybe you'd like some leftovers?"

Lenny eyed the jute bag Kirra carried with her.

"Good for now, or for dinner maybe. Whatever you like." Kirra put it down on Lenny's desk, pulling out a couple of containers. "Samosas, onion bhajis and gulab jamun, which I would eat until I exploded or gave myself diabetes."

"Thank you," Lenny said, still not entirely sure. This interaction wasn't in keeping with their usual contact and now Lenny worried that her emotional outburst in the courtyard had changed something. She did not wish to be pitied.

"And this one is biryani. Most of it needs to go in the fridge."

"I do have food," Lenny said.

"Of course you do. But there was too much at home for just us. And the kids are picky and think they're too Aussie to touch some of the stuff my mum makes. If it's not for you, that's fine, but it makes me feel better than tossing it in the bin. You know? Oh, sorry, I'm waffling, my husband says I have a tendency to do that." Kirra sighed and piled the plastic containers back into the bag.

Lenny realized how rude she had sounded when Kirra was simply extending kindness toward her. Fay would be furious at Lenny's poor manners.

"Thank you, you're very kind to think of me."

Kirra smiled warmly and perched on the edge of Lenny's desk.

"I know you're very private. But if you want to bounce some stuff off me, I'm pretty good with that sort of thing. And trust me when I say it won't go beyond me. I can be an ear, or some company, or a distraction, or . . . there I go again." Kirra laughed, but looked toward her hands. Lenny knew she was making things awkward. How she wished Kirra hadn't overheard what Kurt had said about her.

But that wasn't Kirra's fault. And Lenny could do with a distraction.

"Do you play Scrabble?" Lenny asked.

Kirra's head shot up. "Not for a long time."

"Well, maybe you might like to play with me at some point?" Lenny felt childish as the words rolled out of her mouth. It was a throwback to primary school and asking Jessica Hennessy if she was meant to get a birthday invitation, as she was the only girl in grade four without one. Lenny hadn't been overlooked, as it turned out. Jessica explained her mother had measured the lounge room and there was only room for a set number of sleeping bags on the floor. Lenny's name had been crossed off the list, apparently purely at random. Jessica shrugged and ran off to play with the other girls. Lenny's cheeks burned; she knew it wasn't the truth, but what could she do?

"I would love that. Maybe Friday? If you don't already have plans? I can bring some snacks," Kirra said.

Lenny felt as if Mordor's fiery Mount Doom had just erupted in her stomach. Kirra expected it to be at Lenny's house, and *of course* it would be if Lenny was the one extending the invitation. The library wasn't open that late; she couldn't suggest going there. And Kirra was ready to lock in a date and time, not just a loose *let's do that soon.*

"Yes. Good. Let's aim for Friday," Lenny said, trying not to wince. "At my house." She would concoct a story by Thursday as to why she must cancel.

"Great. I love getting out, and my hubby is having a couple of mates around to play poker so this is perfect timing. Want me to take this to the staff room fridge?" Kirra asked, indicating the bag.

"No, that's fine, I am heading that way shortly."

"Okay. Great." Kirra clapped her hands together. "Bye then."

Kirra bounced out of the classroom and Lenny wondered at the mess she'd just made.

Cancelation: connect, locate, once, toil

Lenny picked up the bag of food and walked down the hallway. She would make her mid-morning tea and buy herself a chocolate bar from the staff room. She could do with the sugar hit.

Ashleigh and Amy were seated in the staff room when Lenny arrived. Their conversation sounded guarded so Lenny quietly went about her business, affording them their privacy, playing her recurring role of shadow-girl. Surely they'd notice her eventually. She was displeased to find the tea thief had been in her tin again. Eventually she would catch Yvonne out, but until then she couldn't accuse her without firm evidence.

From the box on the counter, Lenny picked a Cherry Ripe and made sure to put her dollar in the slot and jiggle it around so it was clear she'd paid. There'd been previous issues with the kitty coming up short and Lenny thought Yvonne could probably answer for that discrepancy too.

The prep teachers were still speaking in low but rapid tones. It was something about a netball club, she caught that much. It sounded like a discussion she could safely participate in, despite never donning a netball bib or skirt herself. She couldn't expect them to do all the work to include her. Lenny steeled herself and sat down next to Amy, her teapot thumping on the table.

Amy and Ashleigh both looked to her and then around the otherwise empty seats.

"Hi," Lenny said. "Um, seen any good movies lately?"

Amy appeared confused and raised a very neat eyebrow. Perhaps she'd forgotten watching *Lord of the Rings* with Ned, or just didn't want to discuss it.

"Not really," Amy said. "You?"

"Um, no, not really. Mainly I just watch *Friends*." Lenny took a bite of her Cherry Ripe.

"That's so old now," Ashleigh said. "But Jennifer Aniston is *stunning*. Timeless."

Amy nodded in agreement. "I've always been a big fan of Courteney Cox. But I can never remember her character's name. It's not Phoebe, is it?"

"Monica," Lenny said quickly, biting further into her chocolate.

"Oh, that's right. It's *Monica*," Ashleigh said, smiling knowingly.

"Like your housemate, Lenny," said Amy.

Lenny gulped; she couldn't exactly come clean now. It would seem so foolish.

"Ah, yes. Just like that. So what's the netball thing?" Lenny asked, hoping to divert attention from her faux housemate.

"It's their annual fundraiser. They do an auction and make money for the club, you know," Amy explained.

Lenny did not know; she'd never been to anything of the sort. Still, she was determined to prove Fay wrong, *she was fine*. She didn't need any help.

"Can I come?" Lenny asked boldly. "Unless I need to know how to play netball, because I don't."

Amy pursed her lips. "Oh, actually you've got to be a member of the footy or the netball club to come. Sorry," Amy added, although she looked distinctly *not sorry*.

"And I'm already her plus-one," Ashleigh said proudly, not one to be left out.

"Not Ned?" asked Lenny.

"Not his thing. And he's got an early start on Sunday, so I'd prefer not to have to worry about him all night."

Amy and Ashleigh exchanged a glance, and with it all manner of unsaid things.

"Fair enough," Lenny said, taking another bite. It was Jessica Hennessy all over again. But rules were rules; if she wasn't a member, she couldn't go. If they allowed one extra in, they'd have to do it for everyone. Plus, what would she wear? And who would she talk to? They were actually doing her a favor by not letting her go. She'd just wanted to do something other than sit at home with her made-up housemate, or talking to her imaginary self in the garden. Lenny wasn't quite sure what was happening to her and felt it best to ignore it. If she was busy, she presumed Young Helena would leave her be.

"I'm so jealous you can eat like that and not worry about staying in shape," Ashleigh said, motioning at Lenny's plus-size Cherry Ripe.

"And real dairy too," said Amy, nodding at Lenny's tea. "It's refreshing to see someone who just doesn't care about all that stuff."

"What stuff?" Lenny asked.

"Oh, just like, you don't worry about having lactose, or sugar, and I love that you don't care about what you look like," Ashleigh said. "I don't think I've had real dairy since high school."

Amy and Ashleigh laughed. Lenny joined in although she wasn't entirely sure what it was they were finding so amusing. It was nice to be part of the conversation even if it didn't ring completely true. She *did* care about her appearance; she just wasn't very good with that type of thing.

"Because we've said a heap of times, you'd be really pretty if you tried," Ashleigh said, nibbling on a cashew from the small plastic tub in front of her.

Lenny wasn't sure how to reply.

"No offense," said Ashleigh, popping another nut into her mouth.

"None taken," Lenny lied before standing up. Maybe she didn't mind telling Amy and Ashleigh fibs after all.

Offensive: envies, seven, sniff, veins, nose, offs

Her tea wasn't finished, but she was done. She didn't have the fortitude for socializing if this was how it made her feel. She wished to be back in her classroom talking to Kirra.

Lenny rode to McKnight's after work, as she did every Monday, but looked in the window before she entered the store. Deb was in deep and lively conversation with a customer at the counter and Lenny knew she could slip in unnoticed. But she didn't think she would be able to slip out in the same manner; she would have to face Deb and did not want to. Her surge of confidence had ebbed considerably since Saturday.

Instead, she rode to the service station on the roundabout at Burwood Highway. The fluorescent lights hummed and pulsed in the dimness of the late afternoon and their glare made her eyes hurt. She missed McKnight's.

And she missed Ned.

She picked up a liter of milk (the real dairy type) and a loaf of Wonder White before riding home. She didn't pack it well and the milk compressed the bread into an awkward sunken shape by the time she arrived at the Tree House. She had the food Kirra had given her and she would try that for dinner, despite not knowing half the dishes Kirra had listed.

The phone call caught her as she was bustling through the door, and she answered without consideration.

"Helena?"

"Who is this?" she asked.

"It's Wendy Dalton, from the Victim Support Unit. I am so glad I caught you. I was starting to think you were avoiding me."

"I am," said Lenny after a pause.

Laughter trilled down the phone line. "You wouldn't be the first!"

Wendy's upbeat reply made Lenny hold off pressing the disconnect button. There was something warm about her tone. It was nice to hear someone so pleased to speak with her.

"I'm sorry," Lenny replied.

"Don't be. It's fine, I don't take it personally. First and foremost, I wanted to make sure our correspondence reached you? We only had a work address for you."

"It reached me."

Lenny looked at the satchel she'd just hung on its hook next to the front door. The letter had remained there since she'd opened its can of worms.

"Have you given it some thought? Are there any questions I can help answer?" Wendy asked. "I'd be more than happy to talk you through the process."

Thoughts: oughts, tough, gusto, guts

Process: score, cross, ropes, cope

Lenny's questions weren't ones she believed Wendy could answer. *Where is my mum? Why couldn't you just leave me alone?*

"Helena, are you still there?"

"Yes I am and I prefer Lenny now. Why would they want to hear from me?" Lenny knew she sounded brusque.

"They want to know the impact of the impending release on you. What you think of it. How it sits with you, you know?"

"No, not really. Fergus and Mum abandoned me, a long time ago. Surely someone else would be better placed to speak of it. They had nothing to do with me after they left."

"Abandoned you? Honey, you . . ." Wendy paused. Lenny heard papers being shuffled. As if Wendy was considering what it was she was trying to say. Or perhaps she made so many phone calls she needed to clarify she was saying the right thing to the right person.

"Lenny, honey, do you remember what happened?" Wendy's tone was different now. Trepidation radiated from it, or perhaps something else. The way Wendy said "honey" didn't prickle Lenny like it sometimes did.

"What do you mean *what happened*? They left. My mother and Fergus left. Without me. What he did after that is not my concern."

More silence, more shuffling of paper.

"Do you think maybe we could meet up in person? I would love to be able to put a face to the name."

Lenny hesitated.

"I can come to you, whenever you like," Wendy said, more insistent now.

The letter had been enough of a disruption already.

"I would prefer not. You can let them know I'm not interested."

"And that's fine. Is there someone home with you at the moment?"

"No, there's not. And please stop addressing me as if I need to be handled delicately."

"It's the phone, I'm sure of it. I am much better at meetings in person. Are you sure I can't come and see you? Tonight, perhaps? Or tomorrow?"

Lenny considered this. Wendy's insistent calls. The letter. What it said. What it *actually* said.

Parole.

Prison.

Victim.

"Fergus did something bad, didn't he?" she asked.

"Yes. Yes he did." The reply was breathless.

"He hurt someone, didn't he?"

But she knew, even before Wendy spoke the words. He'd always had a temper, a propensity for violence.

The bottom of the wardrobe. The small hand in hers. The locked shed. It was all right there. Threatening an avalanche. Her mother's packed suitcase, sitting at the front door like a bright red beacon. Tammy hadn't put it there, Lenny had. Because she'd wanted them to leave; it wasn't safe to be in that house anymore. But it was meant to be Tammy leaving with *her* and not with Fergus. She wasn't meant to be left behind. And yet that suitcase sat in Lenny's hallway cupboard.

Which meant her mum left it behind, which made no sense. Things were not adding up anymore. They were scrambled, like an anagram she had to put back together.

"Yes, honey, he did," Wendy said. Pause. No more shuffling of paper. Just a deep exhalation as she mustered the words. "You. He hurt you."

Lenny felt defeated, as if her legs would give way at any moment. The power to hold the phone to her ear was gone and she let it fall, knowing how rude it was not to finish the conversation, but with no energy to care or capacity to pick it back up.

The need to disappear was intense and she actually considered how she could leave her life, which was an entirely different notion to wanting to end her life. She wanted to walk through the back of a Narnia-esque wardrobe and be transported somewhere different, better, anonymous. She wanted to be left alone and she desperately didn't want to remember what happened; the edges of memories were now appearing more and more rapidly. She knew no way to cease their advance. Like jigsaw pieces, the puzzle was coming together but it was ugly and hateful and she wished to remain ignorant of its existence.

Lenny went to her hall cupboard and pulled the red suitcase from the top shelf. She hadn't used it for years because she never went anywhere that required packing. It was dusty, but otherwise just a run-of-the-mill suitcase. The fabric was burned sienna, although she always recalled it being a vivid, vibrant, unmistakable red, like a matador's cape.

The tag hung from the handle, the sort with a leather flap so the name was concealed. She pulled it back and read the handwriting she knew was her mum's: *Tamara Sullivan*.

Her mum had taken this and she and Fergus had left Lenny behind. Hadn't they?

The day after Fergus's allergic reaction when he'd almost died. *Almost.*

How could her mother have left with that bag if Lenny had it? It wasn't possible.

So if her mother hadn't left, then where was she?

But Lenny knew.

She realized she had always known.

CHAPTER 29

The need for company was overwhelming—not to mention quite unusual. Lenny's first thought was Maureen and the soothing sense of being herself she experienced in her neighbor's presence. It was exactly what she needed.

Hopefully Maureen would tell her to put her bare feet on the earth or some other simple balm to soothe the speeding thoughts. It was nonsense, but it was all she could think of.

Lenny put on her jacket and hurried next door.

There was a chest-compressing sense of foreboding as soon as the striking purple door came into sight. Despite not having studied the minutiae of her neighbor's house, today she was sure something was different, as if the marrow had been sucked from it. Today it was *just* a house. And that seemed wrong. After knocking several times to no avail, Lenny was even more concerned.

Despite their now-cordial relationship, she and Maureen hadn't exchanged phone numbers. It was never Lenny's first thought; she didn't enjoy telephone calls and was always reluctant to abbreviate things to fit text message conventions. But it would be handy to have Maureen's number now. Instead she resorted to banging excessively on the front door (no answer) and then hammering on various windows (also no answer).

There was the possibility that Maureen was out, but there was no way of knowing if this was the case without a key or contact details, so Lenny was left trying door handles (all securely locked).

Perhaps Maureen was having an early night. Lenny couldn't smell the fire burning and there were no lights on inside. The curtains were drawn: thick and impenetrable eyelids. In two laps of the house she found no open windows or doors and no sign of her neighbor. She pressed her face up against the cold glass and watched as her breath made the window frost over, but she still couldn't make out any movement inside.

She stood for a moment on the deck that had held Maureen's solstice gathering. Would Maureen forgive her for breaking in because she *sensed* something was wrong? If Maureen arrived home to find Lenny stepping through broken glass, would she assume she lived next door to a felon? (Not entirely untrue, as Malcolm could attest.) She'd be arrested, shamefacedly paraded before the neighbors, and would never feel like she could be anonymous inside the Tree House ever again. Maureen would probably seek an intervention order, considering her vulnerable state and the violent ways of her neighbor. Lenny wouldn't be allowed home, or would wind up in jail. She was well aware she wouldn't survive being incarcerated.

Stop it, Lenny, you're being ridiculous.

Remember what Heather told you. Trust yourself.

With no further time for analysis Lenny took hold of a cement dragon, one of many statues lining the rear deck.

"Sorry, Smaug," she told the dragon as she wound her arm back and brought it crashing down on one of the windowpanes. It shattered spectacularly, a noise that was both earsplitting and satisfying.

But in a lesson learned a few seconds too late, she should've released Smaug earlier.

Her arm carried through the glass, her own momentum propelling her forward, and her biceps was sliced open, her thick jacket no barrier whatsoever. Blood dripped onto the merbau decking, but she'd worry about the cleanup later. A dull pain crept up her arm, throbbing into her shoulder, and she wondered if the lack of acute pain was from the cold or if she'd cut herself so deeply she'd bypassed the pain receptors.

Refocusing, she reached through the window, unlatched the door and stepped inside, feeling very much like an intruder.

"Maureen, it's Lenny. From next door. Lenny Marks at number twenty-one."

There was no harm in being specific. And she didn't want Maureen hiding away thinking it was a home invasion.

Lenny started down the hallway, taking tentative steps. The house was cold and the lack of light from the thick curtains made it hard to navigate. It smelled of dust and turpentine and Lenny sensed a sneeze coming, although it disappeared in the unsatisfying way sneezes sometimes do.

Her arm throbbed and she raised it above her head, hoping to stem the flow that was making her feel light-headed.

In the room at the end of the hall, Lenny found Maureen's bedroom. Her eyes struggled to adjust but when they did she made out the form of her neighbor lying on the floor beside her bed, her long hair unplaited and fanned out as if she were a sculpture. For the briefest of moments Lenny paused and took in how beautiful Maureen looked lying there.

But not for long. She called out again. Maureen didn't move when Lenny spoke and she didn't stir when she shook her—quite firmly—by the shoulders. Lenny slipped her hand into Maureen's; she was cold but not so much that Lenny thought she was gone from the world. Tears sprung to her eyes as she whispered desperately, "Wake up, please wake up!"

Lenny kept a firm hold of Maureen's hand while she spoke to the ambulance dispatcher. It had been a long time since she'd been physically attached to someone for so long, not to mention being the one to instigate it. She was grateful for the measured voice of the call taker at triple zero, although she wondered if her number had been recorded after hanging up the other night. They might deem her a hoax caller and send no one.

Lenny felt paralyzed, unable to make any sort of decision of her own accord. Instead, she followed the calm instructions of the woman on the phone, checking for a pulse, for breathing, for dangers in the immediate vicinity. She didn't move Maureen, but covered her with a thick blanket. She unlocked and left the front door open for the ambulance, stopping short in the entryway to the house. Or more specifically, to study a portrait that hung there. Her brain was not entirely sure how to translate what it was she was seeing and how it fit into the world she thought she understood.

"Lenny? Are you still with me?" The call taker jolted her back to the present. "I need you to return to the patient. Can you please go back to Maureen now?"

So she did, forgetting what she'd seen because it was confusing, and when things weren't altogether straightforward Lenny found it easier to disregard them and file them away with all the other not-so-easy-to-understand things in her life.

Lenny didn't know how to reassure Maureen; she wasn't good at that sort of thing. School was different; a skinned knee or a bloody nose was easily overcome. An ice pack, a Band-Aid or a pat on the back were all manageable with her first aid level-two certificate. But this was insurmountable. Maureen's skin felt like crepe fabric, more like a doll and not a woman at all. She was reassured to see Maureen's eyelids flicker at times, the twitch of the eyeball underneath suggesting she was trying to stay or at least that she wanted to.

In the absence of her own words, Lenny relied on the tried and trusted ones that had kept her company on many a long night. She knew them by heart, or at least near enough, and quietly recited the start of Bilbo's epic journey to Maureen as they waited.

CHAPTER 30

"Let's have a look at that arm, shall we?" the woman said to Lenny. An instruction, not a question. Three paramedics had arrived after an excruciating wait, and once inside their pace was frantic. The woman led her down the hall and into the light of the dining room. Something tore at Lenny as she walked away. Like she shouldn't be so easily removed; she needed to stay put, to help, to make it right again.

The presence of these people, their radios crackling and the nononsense way in which they moved about Maureen, was disarmingly like déjà vu. A policeman asking why she was there, speaking into his own radio. But then it was gone again.

The woman, whose name badge said *Julie*, but whose face was more of a Juliet or Julianne, was speaking, although Lenny struggled to hear her over the blood pumping in her ears. All she wanted to do was close her eyes.

"What's your name?" Julie said, possibly for the fifth or sixth time, as she pushed a blood pressure cuff onto Lenny's uninjured arm.

Julie wore clear, wraparound safety glasses that made her eyes look glazed and kept sliding down her nose. She used the back of her hand to push them into place.

"Lenny," the answer finally came.

"Lenny, I'm Julie. How did you get this cut on your arm?"

Lenny motioned toward the broken window with the almost numb hand attached to the aching arm. Julie looked up, repositioned her glasses again and nodded, perhaps satisfied that the injury could have in fact been caused by the broken pane. Smaug lay discarded amid the shimmering shards on the rag-knotted rug. His head was detached from his body; he hadn't dealt with the adventure well.

"Is she alive?" Lenny asked.

Julie smiled as she wrapped gauze tight around Lenny's upper arm.

"Can you hold this up while I take your blood pressure?" she asked, and Lenny raised her now bandaged arm. She felt as if someone was playing drums up close to her ears.

"Is Maureen okay?" Lenny asked again. Maybe Julie didn't hear her the first time.

Julie scrawled numbers—blood pressure, presumably—on the back of her blue rubber glove and then looked at Lenny.

"My colleagues in there are very good at what they do. She's in the best hands."

That's not what I asked, Lenny thought. But she knew not to ask again. She wasn't sure she even wanted to know the answer.

"We are going to take you to hospital, you need stitches."

"I've never had stitches before," she replied.

Or maybe she had. She thought of the silvery trail that ran down her thigh. Nothing seemed clear anymore.

"That's a pretty good track record for a thirty-something-year-old. But today, I'm afraid, we are breaking your streak."

Lenny liked Julie; she was diplomatic. Even mildly humorous.

A sturdy man with a ginger beard arrived in the dining room; he reminded Lenny of a later-series Chandler Bing.

"It was lucky you came across her when you did. We're taking her to hospital, she's responsive but unconscious. We just need some more details of your grandmother before we go," Chandler said.

"She's not my grandmother," Lenny said. "I'm just her neighbor."

"Oh, right. Sorry, it's just you said—" Chandler started but stopped himself, looking to Julie for prompting.

"I said what?" Lenny asked.

Chandler explained, "When we first got here you told us she was your Zanny? I just assumed you meant 'granny.'"

CHAPTER 31

March 31, 1999
Zanny

Despite not taking one of the six hundred and seventy-six days she lived there for granted, Lenny didn't last at Zanny's.

Zanny was in the house more than Missy—because Missy went to work and her grandmother did not—but it was Missy who made it feel like home. It was clear Missy didn't like Zanny's drinking any more than Lenny did. But even so, the cardboard box with the plastic nozzle stayed a firm fixture on the kitchen bench.

I may not be all right, Helena, but this certainly makes me feel I could be, Zanny told her once.

Zanny was the one who introduced her to Scrabble. It was where the two bonded, as much as they did. Over a square board and a bag of tiles, grandmother and granddaughter felt a little less like strangers. They always played on a Sunday afternoon, but there were many nights after dinner too. If Zanny was up to it, which meant not too drunk and not too distant, she would tap the top of the game box, bracelets jangling along her wrist, and make the same pun every time: "Are you game, Helena?"

Lenny was in year eight when it ended. A particularly fractious time for even the most confident of adolescents, entering teendom and not sure how to tackle it. Along with puberty and hormones, there was the added concern that she could be out on her own at a moment's notice.

Or worse, be in trouble because she'd not told the truth. She sensed love from Zanny and Missy, but still always felt like a guest.

Especially after last week, when Zanny and Missy had driven her to the Supreme Court in the city. It was overwhelming and hot and Lenny was in stiff clothes she didn't like. Well-meaning people spoke to her before she was ushered into the courtroom with unfamiliar faces everywhere except one. Fergus.

They explained to her why she was there and what she needed to do. Until that moment, she had harbored a fear that she was in more trouble than they could bear to tell her. But it was Fergus. What he'd done was unthinkable, and she wasn't sure she believed even he was capable of such things. But it made sense, because otherwise–where was her mum?

A man with a fancy pen and bad dandruff asked her questions in a not-very-polite way. She answered him, the whole time hoping that what she was saying sounded like the truth. Occasionally it was just that, but there were many things she couldn't say out loud. Lenny sensed the heat coming off Fergus that day: that if no one was around and there wasn't a big desk and a courtroom between them he would've been in her face, telling her she was useless and stupid. Or he would be destroying her things, or pinching her so hard on the back of the neck that she could never bear to be touched there by anyone ever again.

The days since going to court had been tense. Zanny drank more and Missy flitted about the house, attempting humor to lift the mood, but neither Lenny nor her grandmother was interested. Lenny spent a lot of time in the wardrobe, and despite not having to go to school (Missy and Zanny told her to forget about the rest of the term), she went anyway. The routine helped her cope; between nine and three-thirty she could forget.

It all ended the final day of school before Easter break. Lenny walked the four kilometers home to Zanny's, her heavy schoolbag laden with a new supply of library books to last the duration of the holidays. She never relied on Zanny to collect her, especially given it was the time of day by which a sizeable wine had usually been poured.

When she got back that afternoon, Lenny found the house extraordinarily quiet and Zanny nowhere to be found. It made her shins ache and told her something was not right.

It took some time but Lenny found her grandmother in the garage. The old Ford Fairmont XF—bought brand-new and always kept under cover—was running, the heat emanating from it making the space stifling. The garage door was a large counterweighted slab of metal that swung up, but only if you were able to turn the handle in exactly the right way, because it was old and weathered. Lenny never got the knack of it and didn't yet know about WD-40. She always used the side door. From there she could see Zanny in the driver's seat, head slumped forward toward her chest. Lenny knew something was seriously wrong; the garden hose was pushed through an opening at the top of the window. Lenny felt the hair in her nose stand to attention as the fumes fought with the small amount of clean air that had trailed in after her.

The scar on her thigh throbbed; *You need to save this one*, it said, even though it said nothing at all. She ripped the hose away and tried to open the car door but it was locked, the keys dangling in the ignition. Zanny's keyring with the bright yellow smiley face was out of reach and mockingly cheerful. The gap left by the hose was too small even for Lenny's little hands to fit through, and she tried with all her might to pull the window down lower. The smell grew from noxious to overwhelming and her head ached. She resented being so small and powerless. It was incredible how loud the car sounded inside the garage.

She ran out the side door and yelled toward the neighbors' houses, but she saw no one. She yelled again; she couldn't remember what. "Help!" or "Call an ambulance!" or maybe she screamed nothing at all. Because no one came.

In the shade of the garage sat a line of Zanny's pot plants. Each pot contained bulbs–daffodils, hyacinths, tulips–so half the year they had nothing at all to show for themselves. Lenny picked one up and took it back into the garage.

There she threw it as hard as her thirteen-year-old arms could manage at the back passenger window of the Fairmont. It cracked the window and exploded the pot, which became a mosaic of pieces on the concrete floor. She collected another pot and tried again. This one made much more of an impact, or maybe she'd mustered more strength on her second attempt. Potting mix flew over the roof of the car and the blue pot landed in a never-to-be-repaired state beside the rear tire. The hole it made in the window was small, but big enough to serve Lenny's purpose. She reached her arm through and plucked up the lock so she could open the door. The jagged glass caught her arm, making a line so long and perfect it was as if Lenny had used a red marker to draw down the length of her forearm. She crawled across the back seat, flicked up the lock to the driver's door then threw herself out of the car. She wanted to vomit; the sandwich and banana she'd eaten for lunch were gurgling dangerously in her stomach, but she kept them down.

She needed a moment in the fresh air. Lenny ran outside, breathed deeply and yelled once more in the hope someone would hear her. There was no one around and she raced back to her grandmother.

Zanny was heavy and Lenny knew there was no chance she could shift her by herself. Even so, she tried. The garage felt like it was collapsing in on her; her body felt slow, and dirt, grit and blood seemed to be everywhere. Her snot mingled with tears that she hadn't even realized were flowing.

Zanny was wearing one of her spectacular kaftans. A floaty material, patterned from seam to seam. Lenny found her eyes tracing the design, looking anywhere but directly at her grandmother's face.

Why did no one want to stay with her?

"Wake up, please, Zanny, wake up," she repeated, as many times as her dry and constricted throat could muster. Lenny climbed onto the seat and put her arms around Zanny, clinging to her, hoping somehow she could save her.

Light filled the garage as the door swung up on its rusted axis and a man's bulk appeared, backlit and anonymous. Someone had heard her.

Later she would wonder what could have been if that man hadn't lifted the door. She would think of this as she was taken to another place, a different strange room with an unfamiliar bed and people she needed to learn to please so they didn't leave. What if no one had found them? She could have just closed her eyes and at least she wouldn't have been anyone else's problem.

CHAPTER 32

Tuesday, June 21, 2022
12:45 A.M.

The tang of disinfectant was so thick she could taste it. It reminded her of the place they'd taken her twenty-something years ago after Zanny's neighbor had found her in the car, clinging to her grandmother. Her arm had been cut then too, but not like this. That time it was hardly more than a scratch. They'd used Dettol to clean it and didn't even bother with a Band-Aid. And then they told her she couldn't go back to Zanny's. Another home pulled out from under her. She wondered if she'd succeeded in saving Maureen, unlike Zanny, whom she had been too late to help.

The social worker at her bedside that long-ago afternoon was particularly concerned with what the paramedics had reported. Which was that when they'd arrived, Helena Winters had been sweeping potting mix from the garage floor and trying to plant bulbs. It was quite obvious, Lenny thought at the time, they should be replanted before being irrecoverable. Not to mention, she'd made the mess so it was her responsibility to clean it up. She couldn't have Missy arrive home and have to deal with it all. And she was no longer of use—the neighbors who'd arrived had carried Zanny out to the grass and were making phone calls and doing all sorts of frantic, important things.

She'd just wanted to make sure the plants were looked after, and this was met with something like suspicion from the social worker. Lenny didn't like her from the start.

But now, so many years later and despite not wanting to be there, Lenny appreciated the smell of the hospital-grade disinfectant. It was a comfort to know they would scrub, spray and scour a place that was awash with all manner of bodily fluids from various orifices. Shuffling to the edge of the bed, Lenny let her feet dangle over the side. She wanted to leave, but hadn't been given permission yet. And Lenny Marks was (almost) always a follower of the rules.

Permission: impression, remission, mission, inspires, promises

Once her arm had been stitched up by a tired-looking—and very young—doctor, a terse blond nurse with a crooked nose and a wispy fringe instructed Lenny to wait for a script for Panadeine Forte and a medical certificate for a day's absence from work. She was to attend her GP surgery in a few days and have the wound checked. Lenny never took anything stronger than Panadol and she didn't have a GP, but the nurse didn't take a breath before disappearing, so Lenny wasn't able to tell her not to bother with the script. Or the day off.

The emergency department was busy, and Lenny knew her arm, which was not life-threatening in the least, was not top priority. So she waited patiently, passing the time as best she could.

Defibrillator: airlifted, riflebird, airfield, biforate
Emergency: regency, emerge, renege, emery, germy

Last time she had been given no choice about when—or where—she was allowed to go. Surely now though, as an adult, she'd be the one making the decisions.

Dropping her feet to the ground, she checked both ways before stepping out of her curtained cubicle. Having been wheeled in, she wasn't sure of the layout or how to leave. It was claustrophobic and panic held her back. More than anything she needed to be home and see Malcolm and not be in this place that filled her nostrils with reminders.

Reminders: denies, reside, mind, sneer, mend, rise, rids

Her feet took her down the brightly lit hall, causing her to almost collide with a gurney being wheeled the other way.

"Sorry, love," the hospital porter said as he hurried by. It bolstered her confidence because he did not question her presence. It was hardly a thrilling jailbreak to anyone but her.

Jailbreak: bailer, bleak, rile, leak, liar

She eyed a green exit sign and headed for it.

The taxi dropped Lenny off at the top of Callistemon Court. Although in pain and incredibly tired she knew better than to trust a stranger with her personal particulars, even a stranger who kept his taxi immaculately clean and didn't harangue her with any attempts at polite conversation. Malcolm sniffed excitedly at her as she came in the door. She could only imagine the unfamiliar smells he'd detect on her clothes after being in the hospital. She dropped to the floor beside him and leaned her head into the scruff of his neck. The sweaty, earthy smell of his thick coat was reassuring.

With restless hands, Lenny went to her books and counted them. Still thirty-six. Counting them again, she removed them one by one and stacked them neatly beside her. The shelf was dusty; she wiped it clean with her hand and picked up the book on the top of the stack. The cover showed Smaug lying on top of the dwarves' gold and jewels. He was huge; how could anyone win against such a mighty foe? It was impossible.

Impossible: possible

How was it that every time she got close to someone, something bad happened? She was a human-size bad omen, as if she'd smashed every mirror, walked under every ladder and put new shoes on every table she'd ever seen. Lenny didn't really put stock in superstitions and yet her track record spoke for itself.

Robert, her mum, Zanny, and now Maureen.

She considered the book in her hand before throwing it across the room, then the next and the next and the next, until the pile grew shorter and Lenny pushed the rest of her *Hobbit*s over, letting them slide across the floor.

Errol eyed her curiously from the top shelf. One of his glossy button eyes had been missing for as long as she'd known him. For a teddy who was never allowed to be played with, he was remarkably worse for wear.

Lenny pulled Errol off the shelf and squeezed him, feeling for the hardness hidden beneath his stuffing and wondering what she'd do if it wasn't there anymore. The solid lump felt reassuring against her fingers, a concrete reminder of what she'd done to make them leave. There were so many times she found her memory to be unreliable, but by keeping a tangible link she could remind herself of the truth.

You did this.

Yes, I did.

She put Errol back, but left the *Hobbit*s where they'd fallen before slipping out the door and feeling the cold air pull her skin tight.

There was something next door she needed to see. And she did have concerns about leaving Maureen's house wide open to the elements. She'd caused the damage and would ensure she fixed it before a determined possum or wandering cat found its way inside.

From her carport she retrieved a long panel of MDF, big enough to cover the window. It wasn't waterproof, but it would do for the short term.

On the other side of the broken door, discarded medical wrappings lay on the ground as well as a pair of abandoned rubber gloves. The furniture was pushed back where the paramedics had made room to treat Maureen, bumping walls and skittering Maureen's trinkets as they went. A bull in a china shop came to mind.

Lenny moved through the space, trying to make as little sound as possible despite no one being home. Then she stopped in the entryway alcove, the purple door as garish from the inside as it was from the verandah. She wanted to check what it was she'd seen the previous night as she'd rushed to open the door for the paramedics.

The portrait that hung there was unmistakably of her. Despite the hair being a little longer and the painted version wearing earrings—which she never did—it *was* her. It was painted lovingly, an artwork that would have taken considerable thought and time to complete. It was an unsettling feeling not to have known the work existed and a little disturbing to think of how long Maureen must have studied her in order to create the likeness. Lenny wondered if Maureen intended her to see the portrait at some point; it was surely inevitable.

Lenny considered the painting; it felt invasive and yet she didn't feel anger. What she saw in the framed work that adorned Maureen's wall was a list of adjectives she'd never before thought to use to describe herself. It was beautiful. Was this how Maureen saw her? Lenny didn't think she'd ever looked more alive. The soft and careful coloring of her skin; the purposeful, direct stare of her eyes, which she'd always thought were just plain hazel, but here were alive with color, as if golden specks were woven into olive and eucalypt tones.

Standing in Maureen's hallway, she considered committing another theft. But if she stole the portrait, it would lose something. It just wouldn't feel the same if she did the wrong thing by it. She'd never thought of inanimate objects as having feelings before, but she just knew it was best left where it was. Lenny retreated back to the shattered glass pane, where she swept up as best she could in the predawn light. She picked up the rubber gloves and the packaging the medics had left behind and threw them away.

Once she was sure she'd righted the room as much as possible, she stepped back outside and affixed the wooden panel to the window. Lenny checked each corner was possum-proof and determined the temporary fix was sound.

"You saved her."

The voice was small and familiar and she knew who it was without looking.

"I hope so," Lenny replied to her younger self.

"No, not her. You saved Zanny."

"I'm sorry, but you're wrong." Lenny was matter-of-fact, spinning around to make her point clear. "Zanny died."

"No. I'm not. She didn't die that day. We got to her in time."

Lenny frowned. "Then why didn't I go back to live with her? That doesn't make any sense."

Young Helena shrugged. "I don't know."

"She didn't want me?"

Neither Helena spoke.

Lenny turned her back and rechecked the sheet of MDF covering the window.

"Go away. I don't want you here. You need to leave me alone."

"It's not up to you anymore."

"Go away," Lenny snapped. She put her head against the timber and counted to ten.

When she turned around Young Helena was gone. The verandah was empty and the darkness seemed especially black.

"Are you there?" she asked, but received no reply.

It seemed very lonely and Lenny looked back toward the Tree

House, not wanting to have to move through the dimly lit morning by herself. Her scar throbbed and her arm hurt, but the pressure in her head was all-encompassing. Lenny knew she was falling, she just didn't know what she'd land on.

CHAPTER 33

8:35 A.M.

Lenny found herself at school with no real memory of getting dressed or leaving her house. She hadn't slept but she couldn't account for the time between walking back from Maureen's and pedalling out of her driveway. She chained her bike in the allocated area, and as she clicked the lock into place the red suitcase flashed before her. A vivid and undeniable memory now as clear to her as the mint-green frame of her bicycle. *She* was the one who packed that case. *She* was the one who'd wanted to leave. Lenny had attempted to force her mother's hand, and it hadn't worked.

She hurried away from her bike and went straight to her classroom, bypassing the staff room and her morning tea ritual. Lenny kept her head down, watching the ground under her feet, but barely registering touching it.

The students filed in as they had done for the past few months; it was autopilot now, this particular part of the day, but she couldn't recall what she'd put together for them for the morning. Her words were unable to form sentences and they were jumbled when she tried to arrange them.

What is happening to me?

She considered she might be having a stroke; it would explain at least some of her sudden symptoms. Her arm was still throbbing; the effects of the Panadol she'd taken the previous evening had well and truly dissipated.

Maybe it's shock?

Forty-four eyes were trained on her. It should've been forty-six, except Amos Davies was absent. Inhaling deeply, she pushed a sentence out of her mouth as calmly as she could.

"Books out, everyone, ten minutes of self-guided reading time, thank you."

The successful production of this sentence made her conclude she wasn't having, nor had she had, a stroke.

They nodded and shuffled and produced their books from the piles on their desks. A couple of them wandered to the reading area to relax into one of the two overstuffed corduroy beanbags in the corner.

She reached into her satchel, deciding to do the thing she never did in class time—use her phone. She needed to check she wasn't suffering from shock. Lenny was in charge of a room full of pre-teens and it would be irresponsible to compromise their safety simply because of her strict stance on mobile phone use in the classroom.

Symptoms of shock comprised clamminess, anxiety, rapid heartbeat, nausea, dizziness or unconsciousness. She determined herself to be mildly anxious, but not unusually so. The other symptoms did not appear to be presenting themselves. It was probably not shock. Perhaps just overtiredness.

Her class were dutifully leafing through the pages of their books and she slid her own novel out of her bag to join in reading. It would help, she thought, to take her mind elsewhere. She found herself staring in disbelief at *The Hobbit*, and realized she had no recollection of packing it that morning.

The page Young Helena had handed her was sticky-taped in at

the front. It was smooth and straight and she was glad to have the page back in its rightful spot. But now she looked at it, she wondered if it had just been there all along. Maybe she'd retrieved this page way back when Fergus tried to destroy it. Maybe that was when she'd taped it back in. And surely that made more sense than her repressed memories manifesting an eleven-year-old girl in her garden.

Lenny was nine when she had first found the book in her wardrobe after school. That afternoon, when she'd folded herself into the corner and tucked her knees in under her school jumper, there it was leaning against the wall. Such a small, ordinary-looking book. Lenny never thought she'd find such a magical world in that dark space. And until then she hadn't realized her mum knew she hid there. Because it was, she realized, *hiding*. It was on the nights when the clinking of Fergus's bottles hitting the bin on the back porch was extra loud that she'd go there. Lenny would hear the clattering of bottles and know he'd only come inside when he'd drunk enough (which was always too much), or when he'd run out. And she knew better than to go downstairs on those nights. Even if she was hungry, or needed something, or just wanted to see her mum. She would stay quiet and stay small and use her torch to see the words so her bedroom light didn't signal she was in there. She hoped on those nights she could be as invisible as Malcolm. She'd read to him as quietly as she could because she found comfort in the noise, even if it was only the sound of her own voice reading about a wondrous, faraway place she wanted to be in more than anywhere else.

"Ms. Marks?" A small voice broke through her reverie.

She looked up. Twenty-two pupils were watching her, all from their respective seats. Zita's hand was raised.

"Yes, Zita?"

"We need to go to Japanese now."

Lenny looked at the clock above the chalkboard. Forty-five minutes had elapsed.

She was shocked at the time; she'd ignored her class for an entire session. Lenny scanned the room and caught sight of a new pupil sitting at Amos's vacant desk. The familiar face made her voice catch in her throat.

"Of course," she finally said. "You're all dismissed. Off you go."

The students snapped into action, not especially perturbed by their teacher's lack of concentration or ability to tell time.

The new girl didn't move. But of course she wouldn't. It was her again and she watched Lenny intently.

"Why are you here?" Lenny asked her younger self, her voice terse and stretched.

Frustratingly, the girl shrugged.

"You must know," Lenny countered.

"I think I've always been here. But now you've noticed."

"You're not real."

"If you're real, I *must* be real," Young Helena said.

"I don't want to remember you."

The girl looked sad, or maybe it was just Lenny who felt that way.

"You were trying to help them," said the girl.

"Help who?"

"You couldn't have known what he'd do. You were trying to keep him safe."

"Malcolm?" Lenny's voice choked on the name.

"Who's Malcolm?" Kirra's voice rang through the space from the doorway.

Lenny's eyes darted to Kirra and back to Amos's desk, which was empty. She understood the girl, *the actual girl*, wasn't there. But she'd seemed so real she could've walked over and put a hand on her.

There was no easy explanation for who she was talking to; her brain wasn't working fast enough. Kirra stepped into the room, wearing a warm but cautious smile.

"You okay?" she asked, her brow crinkled. The lines were like rungs on a small ladder climbing into her swathe of black hair.

"I was just talking to myself," Lenny said; no lies told there. "Can I help you with something?" She realized she sounded unwelcoming.

Kirra looked taken aback, or perhaps just unconvinced.

"I was wondering if you wanted a coffee in the courtyard with me? Sun is shining, thought it would be nice."

"I don't drink coffee."

"Well, you know, tea, coffee, Bonox." Kirra laughed. "Sorry, that's what my mother-in-law says."

"I think I just need a minute to myself, actually," Lenny said, not wanting to meet Kirra's eyes. "I don't suppose you have any Panadol?"

Lenny didn't want to worry anyone, but maybe she'd feel better if she could just get her headache to go away.

"Yeah I do," Kirra said. "Headache?"

She nodded, feeling unable to answer without sounding terse again. Lenny pressed the palms of her hands hard against her eyes, enjoying the depth of the black as she did so.

"I'll be right back," Kirra said and Lenny heard her footsteps disappear.

Once Kirra was gone she cast her eyes around the room, thinking Young Helena may have reappeared. Thankfully, she had not.

Lenny stood, deciding to set up for horticulture, which was the class after Japanese. The fresh air would do her the world of good.

Forgetting Kirra was coming back, Lenny made for the back steps and happily didn't encounter anyone else, real or imaginary, on the way.

* * *

The garden was lacking some of its usual magic that morning and none of Lenny's agitation eased when she stepped in through the gate. Her shins felt as if skewers were pierced along the length of them and the discomfort radiated throughout her body. Maybe she was getting the flu.

Lenny had helped construct the raised garden beds with heavy pine sleepers over the autumn school holidays the year before. Each year level got their own plot and grew whatever seasonal vegetables the students decided on. The kids loved the gardening and it was an easy lesson to teach.

She opened the shed and collected a bucket of garden tools and one of the containers of worm food. The door blew shut behind her and she stopped short, shuddering at the thought she was trapped in the small space. She heard the door click as if it had locked, but Lenny refused to panic. Not yet.

Placing the bucket down, she tried the handle. It barely turned; it *was* locked.

Entrapped: ardent, papered, trapped, depart, repeat, ranted, deter

Lenny took deep breaths and tried to apply logic to her situation, but the darkness, the stench of potting mix and the overwhelming feeling this had all happened before made her pulse quicken. She closed her eyes and hoped for the feeling to go away.

He was her stepfather—he was meant to look after her.

They were all meant to look after her.

She never saw him hit her mum. But she knew what he did when she was hiding upstairs. On the days Lenny got in the way or refused to run and hide, he would take her to the shed. His giant rough hand would squeeze tight on the back of her neck and march her outside. And he would hiss at her to keep quiet and remind her if she wasn't so bad *this wouldn't happen anymore*. And she'd tried, of course she tried to be as good as possible. To be as quiet, as compliant, as obedient and helpful as she could. But still, it happened. And it became apparent it was simply the fact she existed that incensed Fergus.

Sometimes she would be out there for hours. The hot days were hard, almost suffocating. And on the cold days her toes would feel as if they'd snap off if she moved them. It was dark and it was dirty and eventually she realized hiding a torch in one of the empty terracotta pots was a good idea.

What Lenny didn't want to admit was that being in the shed when he was like that was better. Being in the house was unthinkable, but in the dim flicker of light from her secret torch, sitting atop a bag of potting mix and hoping she didn't encounter any spiders, there was an odd sense of comfort. Once she was out there, she wouldn't see Fergus again until the tirade was over.

Then her mum would sneak out and open the door and tell Lenny it was *time to apologize now*. Tammy would keep her eyes downcast and somehow her whole being seemed a little bit less colorful. Fergus was erasing her mother. Bit by bit and piece by piece he was taking her away. Until she was gone.

CHAPTER 34

11:10 A.M.

"Ms. Marks? Why are you in the shed?" The voice was small, sweet, peppered with a lisp. Madeline Harvey.

Lifting her head, Lenny was surprised to see the majority of her class clustered in front of her, curious faces peering in from the doorframe, the kids at the back scrambling to get a better view of their teacher.

The concrete floor was cold and she couldn't be sure how long she'd sat there. She hadn't heard the door open, or her students arrive.

What time is it?

She checked her wrist for her watch but it wasn't there; she must have forgotten to put it on that morning, which was almost unprecedented. Her wounded arm throbbed incessantly.

"Yes, Madeline, I am just fine," she said, the words robotic and not at all effectual. "How did you unlock the door?"

"I didn't, we just opened it," Madeline said, blue eyes wide.

Lenny was positive it had been locked but there was no reason Madeline would lie. She was now entirely sure she was having a medical episode.

She stood quickly, dusting the dirt off her pants and inspecting the handle of the door. Maybe it was faulty on the inside; she'd put in a works order with Mrs. Finlay.

Expectant faces watched her. She was the teacher who was never short of things to do. She always followed a lesson plan rigorously. She was never not ready for them.

Her eyes roamed the baffled faces before her, searching for her younger self. She wasn't there and Lenny exhaled a breath she didn't know she'd been holding. Surely you couldn't be haunted by the ghost of someone who hadn't died. But she believed in ghosts as much as spirits, which was to say not in the least.

It was clear now she was probably in shock and she was proud of herself for being lucid enough to identify the problem. Maybe that meant she was coming out the other side of it. Otherwise her only recourse would be to march herself up to Ms. Pham's office and report herself unfit for work. But given her ability to rationalize, she thought this would be excessive. She did not want to sound crazy. Anyway, the most pressing thing was to get away from the shed. Although it was horticulture on the timetable, she didn't think her students would mind the disruption.

"Everyone, come with me," she announced and they stepped aside.

As she led them away from the shed, she hoped Fergus stayed behind with it.

She took them out the gate and down the gravel path. Her eyes scanned left and right and rested on the grass strip behind the basketball court. The row of school buildings perched above them and tentative beams of sunshine reached the spot she'd chosen.

"Shoes off, everyone," Lenny instructed.

The children chattered excitedly as they removed their school shoes. Buckles clinked, laces unfurled and socks dropped to the ground. Lenny stripped her own off too, unzipping her sensibly heeled ankle boots and throwing them on the grass beside her.

"What are we doing, Ms. Marks?" Etta asked.

"We are getting back to basics," she said, because she really wasn't all that sure herself. It wasn't something she thought she'd be including in the curriculum. Although it was outdoors and involved grass, so it was essentially horticulture.

What would Maureen tell them if she were here?

"We are connecting ourselves to the earth. It has a story to tell you—try and hear what it is."

They wandered aimlessly, unsure at first as their bare toes explored the cold grass. Her pupils were ten years old, just old enough to be self-conscious, and no one, least of all Lenny, was really sure what it was she hoped they would do.

Lenny pressed her feet into the soil, the grass feeling soft and wet between her toes.

She was trying to forget.

Freedom: deform, erode, free

She wanted the grass and earth to absorb her thoughts. So she started whirling. Slowly at first and then faster, picking up confidence as she gained speed, closing her eyes and loving the feeling of moving in an unusual manner.

She didn't have to open her eyes to know her class had joined in. Through her own feet she could feel the way the earth moved ever so slightly and the sound the grass made as it was trampled by the toes of children. They hadn't had to, and hopefully never would, deal with locked shed doors on hot days or listening to their own voices read *The Hobbit* to an imaginary friend to escape reality. They wouldn't be left behind.

The kids giggled, they snorted, they chuckled and they all joined in.

Lenny opened her eyes, gazed skyward, felt the levity of the moment and the sharp, salt tang of tears lapping at her top lip.

Eventually she stopped spinning and wiped her nose and tears on her sleeve. She smiled at the carefree faces around her before joining them in dancing to music that sounded only in their own heads.

"Lenny?" Trudi Kerr asked.

Lenny opened her eyes, although she couldn't recall the decision being made to close them. Her forehead rested against the smooth, cool laminex of the cupboard over the staff room sink. Her cup was in her hand and she was washing it mindlessly. She could see why Trudi had thought it necessary to interrupt her; she was being incredibly unprofessional. Lenny looked around and was pleased to find they were alone.

"Everything all right?" Trudi let her hand fall on Lenny's arm, directly onto the bandaged gash. Lenny wrested it away and cradled it in against her chest.

Ashleigh and Yvonne Gillespie stepped into the staff room and found themselves seats. They sat close to where she and Trudi stood, which made Lenny feel claustrophobic. She wanted to be alone, or at the very least to be left alone.

"I'm fine." Lenny spoke quietly but brusquely.

Trudi looked taken aback and Lenny felt the urge to tell her to toughen up.

"Sorry." Lenny shook her head, trying to shake herself into a more lucid state. "I'm just tired today."

Lenny continued scrubbing her cup in the sink with violent fervor, surprised she didn't erase the reclining cat painted on the side.

"Maybe you need to head home? Maybe you're coming down with something?"

"Oh, *bugger off*, Trudi," Lenny said, surprising herself as much as her colleague. Visibly displeased, Trudi backed off and Lenny knew she owed her an apology. Just not right now.

Lenny noticed Amy standing in the doorway and wondered

when she'd arrived. Ashleigh's head shot up like her best-friend radar had gone off and Amy made a beeline for her. Usually, Amy would be talking before she'd even entered the room, but today she radiated a different energy. Even Lenny in her sleep-deprived state could sense that. The prep teachers spoke in hushed tones. Lenny couldn't hear them, but sensed it was about her. And the uneasy realization came to mind that neither Ashleigh nor Amy were her friends. She wasn't sure if it was because they didn't like her or because people like Lenny didn't really have friends. But given she'd sought them out *and* made an effort, it was surprisingly hurtful to find it wasn't reciprocated. Lenny always assumed she didn't have friends by choice, that she chose to keep to herself. But perhaps this wasn't the case. Any remaining lightness from dancing barefoot with her students was gone. She was back to feeling like she was attached to an anchor.

Lenny ripped two squares of paper towel from the holder and wiped the dripping water from her cup.

Feeling heavy she sat, acutely aware of a silence falling over the prep teachers. She hadn't packed her lunch in the race to leave that morning and was going to have to make do with a pot of tea and snack-size packets of crackers from the tea club range. It was a pity Kirra didn't have an overflow of food today. That reminded her, Kirra had gone to get her some Panadol and she'd wandered off before getting it. No wonder she still had a headache.

The room was filling with more staff, but Amy remained uncharacteristically quiet, allowing Ashleigh to fill in the silence with an update on eyelash extensions. Had she really wanted to be friends with these women?

Lenny took the lid off her Harrods tin—a present from Fay from a trip years ago—and found her little scoop sliding around the bottom. It was otherwise empty, save for a few lonely curled tea leaves. Not enough for even a thimble-size cup of tea. And she knew this wasn't right because there had been more than enough when she'd looked the previous day. And it was suddenly and over-whelmingly more than she could stand.

Breaking: again, begin, break, brink, rage

The staff room hum she had hoped would be a balm to her rac-ing mind was now loud and grating. The way Gregory Schwartz was eating his reheated leftovers—shovel, chew, lips smacking, then snorting the mucus back up his nose prior to shoveling another spoonful of sausage casserole into his still-full mouth—was disgust-ing. Ashleigh's hyper-aspirated pronunciation as she explained to everybody why she was only having a green smoothie for lunch and the benefits of detoxing, despite no one asking, was exasperat-ing. And Yvonne Gillespie sipping her tea and trying to refrain from looking at Lenny and her empty tin was the final straw.

Yvonne dared to glance in Lenny's direction and she caught a glimmer of guilt, but no remorse. Lenny screwed the lid back on her tin, a tidal wave of something attempting to break forth from her as she met the eyes of the woman who held such a blatant disregard for other people's possessions.

Disregard: dreads, raised, dared, raged, dead

"That wasn't yours to take," Lenny said. Her words were an an-gry whisper, but Yvonne's change in expression indicated they had reached her perfectly well.

"I'm . . . sorry," Yvonne said. Lenny noticed for the first time that her eyes were unusually far apart and her face flatter than it should be, a human equivalent of a frog, or a snake perhaps. Some-thing reptilian and easy to dislike. "I'll replace it."

"Had you just asked, I'd have let you have some. But you don't ask, you never do. You just take and take and take until there's nothing left."

Ashleigh drew her hand to her mouth, overdramatic as always. Amy appeared thrilled to be seated center stage for the performance.

They were watching her fall down and she was powerless to stop herself from plummeting further. Lenny wasn't sure where she'd stop now that it had started. She was the anchor, free-falling through the deep, dark expanse of ocean.

"And then you just leave, like they all do. Everyone leaves me behind. With *nothing*."

"Um, Lenny, it's just a cup of tea. Use one of the bags over there," Amy said, dismissively.

Lenny's eyes shifted, focusing now on the disdainful face of prep one's selfish leader. Lenny knew Amy was goading her, but applying logic was beyond her.

"It's not the same. And it's hardly the point. It is the courteous thing to do, to respect another's belongings. A fundamental truth even the students understand," Lenny said and noticed Yvonne was, incredibly, sipping her tea.

Lenny was rooted to the spot. Her mind was saying *run, run, run* but her feet were glued down. It was all beyond her control.

"Ironic, really, given *you* have trouble keeping your hands to yourself," Amy said.

"That's not true—I always keep to myself."

"Yeah, just you and Monica, hey?"

Lenny sucked in air. Did they all know?

Imaginary: aiming, airing, grainy, angry, grim

"You think none of us watch *Friends*, Lenny? You think we don't know Monica is a character from TV?" Amy's face softened, giving her an unfamiliar expression. "And apparently you've always done it. A friend told me even back in high school you'd invent friends. I've been really worried about you."

The room was quiet. Lenny couldn't find words, her anger replaced with embarrassment. They were all looking at her and she wondered what they must think of her. She'd never be able to face these people again.

One glance at Amy was enough to see that her concern for Lenny was as fake as her blondness. Now that Lenny was the focus of everyone in the room, Amy returned to wearing a smug sneer.

"What's going on here?" Kirra's voice cut through the tense atmosphere in the staff room.

"Lenny's just found out that people taking your things isn't very nice. Tea, boyfriends, you know. Things like that," Amy said.

"What are you talking about?" Kirra asked, moving to stand near Lenny.

Amy crossed her arms over her electric-purple wraparound blouse and fixed her gaze on Lenny. She radiated the air of an aggrieved six-year-old. "I know about you and Ned."

Lenny's eyes scanned the room: the other teachers were looking to and fro like a tennis match was underway before them. Ned was her friend. She hadn't done anything wrong.

Say it out loud, Lenny. Tell her.

Instead she gulped, heavily, noisily. The sound and action of someone with something to hide.

Amy drew her hand to her mouth, stifling a sob. But it didn't appear she was genuinely upset. Or was she? Lenny found it hard to read people at the best of times, and this was not a good time.

"You're being ridiculous, Amy. Whatever problems you're having with Ned are not Lenny's fault," Kirra said.

Amy closed her eyes and sniffed a few times. It *sounded* like she was crying, but Lenny couldn't see tears. Ashleigh flew to her side.

"Kirra, Amy is really upset. You could be a bit more sympathetic." Ashleigh put an arm around her friend's back.

Lenny wondered if she could disappear quietly while the focus was on Kirra, although it seemed disloyal given Kirra had stepped in to help her.

"And I'm worried about Lenny too—did anyone else see her this morning?" Ashleigh continued. "Doing something strange out in the schoolyard with the kids? I feel *really* bad, but I have to tell Lora about it."

Ashleigh did not look like she felt bad about it at all and Amy made another exaggerated sobbing noise. Lenny's cheeks flushed, realizing how silly she'd been. Of course they'd been seen, an entire class barefoot and trampling the grass. Not that she'd been trying to hide; nor had they been doing the wrong thing. But if she'd known they were being watched by Ashleigh or Amy, who were evidently *not* her friends, she may have reconsidered.

Right now, in the suddenly cramped staff room of Selby South Primary School, there were too many eyes on her. Too many sets of ears listening. Belonging to people she'd seen day in and day out for years and who still had no idea who she was.

Lenny's feet unstuck and she made an ungainly lurch forward, like stepping onto an escalator she hadn't realized was stopped. Then she corrected herself and was off and moving, out the door and up the hall, almost colliding with Ms. Pham as she stepped out of her office.

"And here she is!" Lora said, finishing a sentence that Lenny was not privy to but clearly the subject of.

Lenny considered powering on, collecting her things, getting out the door, hopping on her bike, putting her feet on the pedals and not stopping until she saw the Tree House. For years she'd done the polite thing, doing as she was asked and trying to please people. Only she *always* said the wrong thing and she very rarely pleased anyone, least of all herself.

Breathless, she stopped.

"Everything okay?" Lora asked. She was flanked by a stranger, shorter and less stern-looking than the principal. Not a teacher, Lenny guessed.

No, she was not okay. And she was sick of being asked if she was.

The two women looked at Lenny, waiting for her to say something, and she wondered if the lava bubbling through her system would come spewing out all over them if she did. It would burn down the remainder of her career, her life and everything else.

"Lenny, this is Wendy Dalton. I don't think you two have met yet. She was hoping you could spare some of your lunchbreak for her," Lora said. She paused, waiting for a reply, but when none came she continued. "You can use my office for some privacy."

The visitor smiled at Lenny, not at all aware she'd just walked in on a fight about an empty tea canister, and also so much more than that. It wasn't her fault; she wasn't there to make it worse. But that was exactly what she did. Her presence told Lenny those things she remembered were actually what happened and not TV shows, or plots of books or things she'd imagined.

She *had* been left behind by everyone, again and again and again.

Her thigh throbbed, and she held her hand to it. She couldn't feel the long, fine lump of scar tissue under her clothing, but she knew it was there. Fergus did that. She wasn't sure how she'd ever forgotten. It wasn't her clumsiness, it was him. How had she ever forgotten that?

Think of the good, Lenny.

But the good thoughts weren't the strong ones. The ones with all the power were the ones that ripped you apart and left you bleeding and scared and locked in a shed at the back of a house while your stepfather took your mum from you forever. The bad memories were the ones that sent you to live with your grandmother because of Fergus Sullivan. And the bad memories were the ones that made your grandmother realize you reminded her of the daughter she couldn't save and so she couldn't be around you either.

Of course there was Fay. Bright, loving, animated. And Malcolm: warm, loyal, fur smooth and darker than the night sky, and darker than the thoughts that came and sent her to the bottom of her wardrobe. Darker than Fergus Sullivan's temper. They weren't enough to pull her up from this. She was at the bottom of a well and no one knew she was there.

"I told you to leave me alone," Lenny said to Wendy, the person who had torn through her ordered, content, oblivious existence with her phone calls.

He hurt you.

She heard the noise of rubber-soled shoes meeting linoleum and looked behind her. Her colleagues were there. They'd followed her from the staff room like hyenas circling, wanting more. Kirra's kind but uncertain face was at the front of them all.

Lenny wanted to say then all the things she'd never said. The things they didn't expect to come out of her mild-mannered, compliant mouth. She would tell Ashleigh and Amy they were vacuous wastes of space, Gregory that his ego was as inflated as his midriff and Trudi—well, Trudi was actually quite lovely and she shouldn't have snapped at her. She would tell Yvonne it wasn't the tea theft that bothered her; it was the righteous way she assumed things were hers, and her dumbstruck face at staff meetings.

But she didn't have the energy. So she just left.

Lenny made her way to the bike rack, undid her chain and started pedalling. She almost skittled Mrs. Finlay, who was engulfed in a cigarette cloud in the smokers' area of the car park, as she rode past. Her class would be waiting, she had responsibilities, but the decision was made. She needed the Tree House, she needed to be inside, to shut out the world and to hear nothing else. She was Bilbo longing for Bag End, desperately wanting the adventure to end so she could get home where it was safe.

CHAPTER 35

1:30 P.M.

Her house was more inviting than ever before. Lenny couldn't recall the trip home, only opening her door, collapsing into the sheets, pulling the quilt over herself and listening to her breathing in the cocoon she'd created.

When she finally slept it was a deep, dreamless sleep that lasted for hours.

She hoped sleep would erase everything. She needed it to. She switched everything off, each whirring cog in her brain, the muscles that remembered each step she'd ever taken and the pockets of time she glossed over every day so she could somehow manage to make it to tomorrow.

She felt it all close down on her as the dark took her, and she wondered if she would ever be back.

Or if she'd want to be.

CHAPTER 36

7:30 P.M.

The banging on the door was relentless.

In a house of these proportions, if anyone was home they'd have heard the knocking. If they hadn't opened the door, they didn't want to or they couldn't. Lenny was not sure which category she fell into. If she willed herself to move, perhaps she could, but she certainly did not want to.

The knocking again, and again, and again.

Maybe it was someone looking for her, checking on her. But no one cared; she was the girl who made up friends.

She closed her eyes, buried her head deep and refused to get up.

She didn't want to remember, but the memories came to her anyway. The inevitable avalanche was here and she'd failed to find adequate shelter.

He started out as a small bundle, wrapped in a gray knitted bunny rug, squirming in his mother's arms. *Her* mother's arms. Lenny waited all morning for the Ford Taurus to return home with her mum and baby brother.

It had been all she had thought of for weeks as her mother's stomach grew larger and her stepfather's temper grew shorter. He went from mad sometimes to angry all the time. Tammy was exhausted and it slowed her down. Zanny came to help, but Fergus didn't like her being there, despite pretending the exact opposite in front of her. He was good at keeping up appearances. Each time Zanny left, Lenny felt her stomach flip-flop and she knew the smiling Fergus would be gone and the other one, the real one, would replace him.

The baby would fix everything and make Fergus be nice to her. Her brother would be the glue that kept their little family together; Tammy told her that time and time again. Her mum wouldn't have to shut herself in the bathroom and cry into the hand towels with the neatly cross-stitched flowers on the edges. And Lenny wouldn't have to wait in the shed for Fergus to be too drunk to remember or care anymore. Sometimes she was in there so long she fell asleep, using a bag of potting mix as a pillow and letting salty tears mingle with the dirt on her hands and face. Lenny knew to stay quiet or it all just got worse.

They were unrealistic, hoping Fergus would change. But they had to be optimistic, because the alternative didn't bear thinking about. Hope propelled them forward. Even when the shed was blisteringly hot in the dense heat of summer, or when her mum was putting on makeup because she didn't want the other parents at school to notice what he'd done. Fergus wasn't the way he was from lack of children in his life to love. He was irreparably broken. He was a blizzard with no chance of sun.

By the time the Taurus pulled into the driveway with Fergus, her mum and her brother on board, Lenny was bursting out of her skin. The concrete path was scorching as she ran to the car, but her bare feet hardly registered it in her excitement.

"He's asleep, Helena, don't you dare wake him. You can meet him later," Fergus chided, stepping in front of her and blocking her view as he opened the car door. He always managed to make her name sound like he was cursing.

Fergus lifted the baby capsule out of the car. He made sure to cover it completely with a thin blue cloth before whisking the baby inside. She was desperate to catch sight of him, a toe, a hand, his little nose, or to see if he had wispy hair or none at all. Zanny squeezed Lenny's shoulders and pulled her close, but there was no consolation from the embrace.

"That's right, you know. You never wake a sleeping baby," Zanny said with an empty smile, as if she'd just caught a glimpse of something she'd never noticed before.

Later that night, when Lenny finally got to hold him, she breathed in the scent of the tiny human lying in her arms. His skin was loose and pink and hot, as if it didn't fit him properly just yet. His eyes were closed and his bottom lip sucked in, contentedly moving as if he was dreaming of milk. Such a simple existence. Lenny stroked his tiny hand; it was the softest thing she'd ever felt in her life. The five perfect fingers wrapped themselves around her own index finger and she held her breath, hoping he wouldn't let go. He was everything she wanted him to be, but so much more. And she knew it was up to her to guard him absolutely and completely.

She would keep her little brother safe.

She would protect Malcolm.

Imagining a small boy becoming a man was not so hard once Lenny put her mind to it. The cheeky grin that hung upside down on a monkey bar in a schoolyard could easily grow facial hair. The hand she held as she crossed the street to the milkbar to spend pocket money would be calloused and rough in its adult years. The boy whose tongue couldn't wrap around the words Granny or Susannah, and so settled on Zanny, would pronounce hundreds of different words without a second thought as a man. Little Malcolm, who drew dinosaur after dinosaur and was able to list them all by name, would grow into a man who would maybe be less imaginative, but no less clever.

She remembered the boy with the crooked smile and the freckle on his left earlobe and hated that she would never know him as an adult. But she hated even more that she'd trivialized his existence into being imaginary, because he deserved much more. He was worthy of being remembered for every one of his freckles and his dinosaur roars and his tight, warm cuddles. For his thick swathe of umber hair, which she would run her fingers through as he snored lightly on her lap while she read from *The Hobbit* at the bottom of the wardrobe. He knew his sister was there and so he could sleep soundly, even if his dad was thundering downstairs. Lenny would make it an adventure; they were in their Hobbit Hole and the dwarves were making a ruckus. It didn't matter if he didn't believe her, as long as he felt safe. She would doze sometimes too, waiting for her mum to come and tell them *it's fine now, you can come out.* Lenny had kept him safe, until she hadn't.

She'd failed him and she wasn't sure who she hated more, Fergus Sullivan or herself.

You did this.

CHAPTER 37

The knocking was back, with an impolite intensity and raucous tempo that sent Malcolm into a barking frenzy. She was allowed to be selfish; she didn't have to answer.

She didn't need anyone.

She would only let them down anyway.

Hoping to distance herself from the noise, Lenny crawled from the bed, pulling one of her blankets behind her, and headed for the wardrobe. Her eyelids had never been so heavy nor the need for sleep so pressing.

For so long she'd expected her mum would be back to claim her, that at some point Tammy would realize she couldn't live without her daughter and decide Lenny was more important than Fergus.

When Lenny had to leave Zanny's, her biggest worry was that Tammy wouldn't know where to come to pick her up. Lenny remembered asking Fay how Tammy would know where to find her. And she wondered why Fay hadn't just told her then, but knew perhaps that sort of omission was a kindness. Trying to protect the broken heart of a lonely girl waiting for her mother to return. Or maybe Fay did tell her. It had always felt like a grenade had been thrown into her head, leaving only partial memories and inaccurate truths, haphazardly spread about.

But now Lenny remembered it all. Her mum had never left that house.

Lenny remembered Fergus as being over six feet tall, a dizzying, basketball player–size giant, but the truth of it was, Fergus was probably much smaller than that. He was the biggest man she thought she'd ever met and she assumed for a long time all fathers were just like him. She'd never met hers, so she had little in the way of comparison.

On the Tuesday that changed everything, Lenny was waiting. She knew it was only a matter of time before Fergus and her mum came home. Fergus had been taken by ambulance to hospital after an allergic reaction the night before. Her mum had been out at the time, arriving home to be told what had happened and rushing back to her car and straight to the hospital. She rang later that night to assure Lenny that Fergus was fine and they'd release him when the doctor was happy he was stable. Her mum told her this as if it were *good news* and all Lenny could do was pretend it was. What else could she say? That she'd hoped he'd die?

Instead Lenny said, "I want us to go to Zanny's."

"Oh, darling, don't be worried. It shouldn't be much longer here."

"I'm not scared of being home alone, I'm scared of *him*."

The line fell quiet, just Tammy's considered breathing and Lenny's hopeful pause. They were words she'd never before spoken aloud.

"Darling, I'll be home soon and we can discuss it then," her mum said.

And when she'd said "I," Lenny thought that meant her mum would come home *without* Fergus. That he'd have to stay in hospital until he recovered, at least for the rest of the day. They'd have time to go; Lenny would convince her mum they had to escape. Then she would tell her mum what she'd done.

Lenny hadn't slept, instead mulling over everything. She'd been the one to call the ambulance the previous evening, exactly as she was meant to do: call triple zero in an emergency. *And she had.*

Fergus's swollen, blotchy face had scared her more than she thought it would. Between rasps, and clearly fearful of dying, he still managed to convey a terrifying level of anger toward her. She was in so much trouble.

During her sleepless night, she packed three bags, one for each of them. The basics for them all plus Errol shoved deep inside her bag. She would have only a short time to convince her mum it was time to leave the house for good. They would be okay, the three of them together, wherever they went; Zanny's, she hoped. Lenny picked up the phone and dialed her grandmother's house. A woman answered, with a gruff "hello" that wasn't her grandmother's voice. The croakiness made Lenny realize she'd woken her up, which made her panic and think she'd be in trouble, so she hung up the phone without saying a word. Lenny picked up the phone twice more, but she couldn't bring herself to press redial. It was late and it seemed like the sort of call her mum should make; Zanny might have questions she couldn't answer. And what if she came straight over? That could make things worse.

How she wished she had made that call.

The car pulled up just before 6 A.M. Lenny watched from the lounge room window as her mum stepped out of the driver's side. But instead of heading for the front door, she walked briskly to the passenger side and helped Fergus out. It jolted Lenny from tired and nervous to just plain terrified. Her shins radiated pain and there was a chance she'd vomit. Lenny froze, unable to decide what to do first: run and pretend she was asleep or hide and hope he didn't seek her out straight away.

As soon as her mum and stepfather stepped inside, Lenny realized her first mistake. Fergus—face still red and mottled—noticed the bags packed and waiting by the door. They were so out of place, and her mum's bright suitcase was like a red flag to a bull.

Fergus charged at Lenny; he was all but breathing fire.

"I know what you did," he snarled. His hands locked down on her arms and the harder she squirmed, the firmer his grip became.

"Fergus, stop, just leave her," Tammy pleaded, dropping her handbag and running to them. "What are you doing?"

"She tried to kill me, Tammy. I knew she wasn't right. She's a fucking psychopath." He pinned Lenny against the wall, his breath washing over her, hot and unbrushed.

"No, no, no. Helena, tell him that's not true," Tammy said. "We love you, Fergy, please, let her go. Helena, just say you're sorry. Please."

And there was Lenny's second mistake, thinking her mum would choose her.

Tammy tried to wedge herself between them, attempting to get Fergus to shift his focus, but he wouldn't. He let go of Lenny's right arm for the briefest of moments and struck out at Tammy, sending her sprawling. It wasn't so much the force of the blow as the shock; Tammy hadn't seen it coming. In the seconds Fergus released his grip to strike his wife, Lenny took her chance. She dropped her weight, slipped from his hands and raced into the kitchen. She knew she was no match for this version of Fergus, not without help. Lenny fumbled in the top drawer as he rounded the bench and grabbed her again, by the hair this time, sinking his fingers into the base of her ponytail and wrenching it back so she could only see ceiling. There was no telling what he was capable of in this state of mind, nor did she want to find out. If he'd seen her grab the knife, he made no attempt to take it from her and she held it firmly to the side of her leg, not sure she had the courage to use it.

Tammy was back on her feet, talking to Fergus. Using her low voice, the soft one that put Lenny and Malcolm to sleep when their eyes wouldn't close. The one Lenny heard in between the songs from the stereo downstairs on those nights when her mum tried to reason with her unreasonable husband.

Fergus let go of her hair and grabbed Lenny in a headlock. He dragged her slight frame, letting her feet only just make contact with the ground. She did not want to go into the shed today.

Not today, not today, not today.

If she was locked away, she was useless to her mum and Malcolm.

Lenny closed her eyes, imagining Bilbo's Sting, then gripped the knife with both hands and plunged it into Fergus's stomach. It was harder than she'd thought, pushing it into him from the angle he held her. She'd expected it to feel like slicing into a tomato. He growled and reeled back. Surprise was on her side for the first strike; he didn't see it coming and she pulled the knife from his stomach as he released his grip on her. She fell to the floor, narrowly avoiding falling onto the knife, which she'd kept hold of. She couldn't relinquish her grip on it, even now it was slick with Fergus's blood. She knew letting go would be the worst possible thing she could do.

Tammy's eyes darted between her daughter and her husband.

Surely her mum knew how urgently they needed to leave.

Pick me, Mum.

Fergus grabbed Lenny's hand, the one holding the knife. His

fingers were so big they enveloped it entirely. Her knuckles were crushed beneath his hand and he wrenched the knife from her pathetically inadequate grip. She saw on his face there was no coming back from this. A rapidly blooming red rose grew across the front of Fergus's t-shirt, centered where she'd struck him. But it wasn't enough.

He dragged her by the scruff of her windbreaker, the neckband cutting into the soft skin of her throat and making her short of breath. Had this been a chapter in one of her books she would be crying out in frustration at the main character, telling them not to stop until their enemy was felled. But now she had no weapon and, what's more, she was only eleven. This wasn't an even fight. She needed help.

Help me, Mum.

She didn't know if she spoke those words out loud or not.

With all the strength her lanky arms and legs could muster, she swung them wildly, hoping to loosen his grip. She grabbed the doorframe as they passed through it, but he prised her fingers off, yanking them back so forcefully she thought they would break. Unable to find anything else to grab hold of, she turned her attention to him, digging her fingers into the wound in his stomach, hoping to cause as much pain as she could. Fergus yelped and swung the knife toward her. He drove it into her thigh, although she didn't properly register what he'd done until much later. Of course, by then, it wasn't all her blood. Lenny couldn't remember making much noise as she fought; if she had been, she wouldn't have heard the tiny cry. It was so out of place it made them all stop in their tracks, even Fergus.

Malcolm.

He'd been in bed.

Until he wasn't.

Time froze: slowed, stilled then stopped. It was his tiny voice, yelling in pain as the knife in Fergus's hand struck him, a powerful but inadvertent blow. It was meant for her, she'd realize later and then quickly force herself to forget. Fergus was swinging for her and he never made it. How she wished it had been her.

Fergus dropped her and Lenny rushed to Malcolm, who'd fallen to his knees, confused and scared. Malcolm was staring straight at her, his sister, his keeper, the one who'd failed him. There was so much blood and it was spreading over his Spiderman pajamas in a beautiful, horrifying pattern. Lenny put her hands on his chest, where the blood bubbled. It did nothing to stem the flow.

Tammy was at his side, cupping his head in her hands; the child her mum wanted to save, the one she loved the most. Lenny didn't care; she loved him more too.

Tammy's muffled cries rose to a tormented grunt and then a wail as she pulled Malcolm onto her lap and cradled him as if he were still a tiny baby in his gray bunny rug. Fergus was still, and Lenny could tell he was horrified by what he'd done. This was *his boy*; this wasn't meant to happen. No one hurt his son.

"Run for help, Helena! Go. Fast," said her mum, her voice piercing.

Lenny heard her, but she was stuck. Transfixed by that soft head of hair in her mum's lap. Was this really happening? He should have been upstairs on his bed, making He-Man attack T-rex.

"Lenny!" her mum shouted.

This time she snapped out of her trance. Unfortunately, Fergus did too. His openmouthed horror refocused on Lenny, and when he looked at her it was all hate.

Lenny went for the phone, but Fergus stopped her short of the handset. He wrenched her backward with such force that her neck would ache for weeks.

"I need to help him!" Lenny yelled. Surely he wanted that too.

Gripping her harder than before, he took her outside. In a heady blur of flailing limbs, pain and her mother's anguished cries, he threw her onto the concrete shed floor.

"*You* did this," he snarled before he shut the door, followed by the telltale sound of the bolt sliding into place. His footsteps, despite being on grass, were heavy, determined, angry as he left. And all she could think was: *He's right, I did this.*

In the dull light of the shed, where Lenny was trapped while everything changed forever, his three words seared into her skin like a tattoo.

CHAPTER 38

The sound of shattering glass sent Malcolm from frenzied barking into absolute meltdown and Lenny realized he would slice his paws open if she didn't get up. As a secondary thought, she realized she should investigate the breaker of the glass; for all she knew it was a serial rapist.

A long, thin arm reached through the now shattered window-pane next to the front door. It was almost the exact way she'd managed to get inside Maureen's house just nights earlier, although Lenny had a push lock installed at the top of the door for extra security. It was something the person attached to the arm was unlikely to know, and she watched them fumble with the handle, trying to gain entry.

"What do you want?" she asked without approaching the door. Her voice was a husk of itself.

A face appeared in the small frame. Kirra.

"She's here, she's all right!" Kirra yelled to someone out of sight.

Fay's familiar face appeared next.

"Helena Marks, open this door right now!" she said, leaving Lenny very little choice than to do exactly that.

Lenny was barefoot, so she quickly donned a pair of shoes before crossing the floorboards glittering with glass.

The idea of letting two people inside was disconcerting, but Fay barreled her way in and wrapped Lenny in the embrace of a Venus flytrap before she could think about stepping out to greet them.

"My girl, we were *beside ourselves*." Fay spoke into the curve of Lenny's neck, her breath warm on her skin.

Lenny couldn't speak. She wanted to say so many things but didn't know where to start. She needed to know if it was all true.

Kirra appeared with the broom and only then did Lenny notice Ned standing there too, looking somewhat awkward. He took the broom from Kirra and started sweeping, apparently glad to have a purpose.

Three people. She'd never had so many people in the Tree House at one time.

"What are you all doing here?" Lenny asked.

"I was worried when you ran out. So I went to see Ned to find out if he knew where you live. Your address in the school records is McKnight's," Kirra said. "And when we came looking for you yesterday, there was no answer."

"So they rang me this morning—I'm recorded as your next of kin. And your next of kin needs to be supplied with a bloody house key, do you hear me?" Fay said, her tone firm. "We looked everywhere for you, but I knew you'd be in here. I'll get the window fixed. But what's going on, Lenny-girl, what's happened?"

Lenny wanted to ask about Malcolm and her mum, but the words caught in her throat.

"You need to let it out, you can't keep on like this," Fay insisted.

"But I'm fine. I'm fine. I'm fine." Lenny knew the words were hollow.

Fay leaned back, a hand on each of Lenny's shoulders.

"But you're not. You. Are. Not. And I've pretended for too long."

"Malcolm?" Lenny asked.

"He's fine," Ned replied, digging at a corner with the broom. "I've shut him in the bedroom."

"No. My brother," she said. "He was, wasn't he? I thought I dreamed him up. To be my friend. But he was real, wasn't he?"

Fay bit her lip, tears dropping onto her green Incredible Hulk t-shirt, making darker spots where they spattered. "Yes, my love. He was a very real little boy."

"And I *forgot* him," Lenny whispered. Snot and tears mingled and cascaded down her face.

"You did not forget him. No, not at all. You were just trying to survive. You were little too."

"Why didn't you tell me? About him and Mum and Zanny?"

"Oh, my love. We did, we tried. And then it was all too much. But we should've kept telling you. But seeing you like that was so painful, which was me being selfish."

Fay pulled Lenny back into her tremendous chest and walked her into the lounge, where they dropped into the couch like a koala and her joey.

"I should've taken better care of you," Fay whispered to her. "I'm so sorry."

Fay kept murmuring apologies until Lenny fell asleep.

She would sleep in deep, dark waves for the better part of a week.

CHAPTER 39

Tuesday, June 28

"How did I ever forget?" Lenny asked. "It just doesn't seem possible."

Fay and Lenny were on the couch. The television was on but Fay refused to watch back-to-back episodes of *Friends*, so they were watching *Dr. Phil*.

"About what, Len?" Fay asked. Given Lenny's question was out of the blue, it was fair she needed some context.

"About any of it. Mum, Zanny, Malcolm, Fergus?"

Fay's exaggerated exhalation made it clear she had a story to tell and she stroked Malcolm's head as she seemed to contemplate the best place to start. Her solemn face made an interesting contrast to her bright orange Dragon Ball Z t-shirt.

"I asked the same thing. And Robert and I were told—eventually— you were suffering from a dissociative disorder. An amnesia of sorts. Basically gaps in your memory where in order to cope, you removed yourself from the bad things that happened. And in some cases made up a more preferable version of events."

"And that psychologist, she wanted to send me away?"

"I didn't know you knew that. But yes, she did. She was a psychiatrist and she was insisting on intensive inpatient therapy, which

I wasn't comfortable with. You'd had so many terrible things happen in a short period of time, and I wanted you to know Robert and I were with you for the long haul. And that meant keeping you close."

"But you let me think my mum left me?"

"Not at first." Fay blew her nose before continuing. "There was a time we would remind you of what happened. And it was terrible, like you were reliving the whole ruddy day again. And in the end, it made it so much worse. So instead of telling you what really happened, we just let you believe the version you wanted to. It seemed kind at the time, but now I think we did the wrong thing. You were just so content, for such a long time. I let myself believe the truth didn't really matter."

Lenny felt the sting of being kept in the dark about something so important, but Fay had made an impossible decision. There was no easy route through any of this.

"It was another thing I never saw eye to eye with your psychiatrist about. She was mandated by social services—who I didn't think much of either, just quietly." Fay kneaded the top of Malcolm's head and his snoring turned into small whimpers of satisfaction. "She said the way through the dissociation was to keep reminding you of the truth. But *she* wasn't the one that had to do it. I recall her telling me how unhealthy it was that you thought Malcolm was an imaginary little boy. And you know, I agreed with that. But it made you so happy and those were some of the best days you had. Reading to him, talking to him, whatever you wanted to do. You and your pretend sidekick. And it petered out over time. You spoke to Rob and me more and Malcolm wasn't around as much and it all seemed—to me—like you were coming out the other side of it."

"I'm sorry," Lenny said. "For making it so difficult for you and Dad."

"Don't be. It's not for you to be sorry. You were thirteen years old. You didn't need a hospital, you needed a home: a family, to be loved as much as you could be, and I wanted to do that for you. All I could think of was electric shocks and straitjackets. I was horrified. Your entire life had been uprooted, twice. And on top of that, you were made to live it all over again in court because that disgusting man just wouldn't own up to what he'd done."

"Fergus said it was my fault?" said Lenny.

"Yes, love, he did. Hateful man. Blaming a child."

"What did he do to my mum?"

Fay stopped short; she used the back of her hand to wipe her eyes.

"I want to know." Lenny moved closer to Fay. "I need to know."

Her foster mum took a deep breath. "I was told that after Fergus locked you in the shed, he went back inside. Your little brother, Malcolm, wasn't able to be saved. And Fergus found Tammy on the phone. She'd called for the police and was giving them the address. They heard enough to know where she was, and she managed to tell them what he'd done. But they couldn't get to her in time. She was so brave."

Fay was sobbing, but Lenny couldn't let her finish yet.

"He killed her?" Lenny asked.

Through tears, Fay nodded. "She fought him, that was very clear to the detectives that came to the house. But"—Fay breathed deeply—"he still had the knife."

Both women sat quietly, the Rottweiler's heavy, rhythmic breathing the loudest thing in the room.

"And they didn't know you were there, Lenny-girl. You were in that shed for hours, and when they told me that, all I could think about was how scared you must have been."

Lenny couldn't remember being fearful. Instead the memories

were of the throbbing from the gash in her thigh and of Malcolm. His tousled hair and his tiny fingernails and the reassurance she felt when he would slip his hand inside hers. Now she could recall talking to him in the shed, as if he were right there beside her. Is that when she'd turned him imaginary? It had given her so much comfort to think of him nearby.

"How are they letting Fergus out? He should never get out of jail," said Lenny.

"It doesn't work like that though. It should be that way—and would be if I was in charge—I'd lock him up and throw away the key. But he was only found guilty of manslaughter for your brother. And even with the murder of your beautiful mum, he was only given a minimum of twenty-five years. And he's done that."

"It's not enough."

"I agree. And you know, I was told they were rapt with that sentence. Other murderers get much less. Despicable what people can do and still be allowed to walk around with the rest of us."

Yes it was.

You did this.

"What if it was my fault?" Lenny heard her voice and it was barely a whisper. Maybe she was as heartless as Fergus.

Fay spoke firmly. "It was *not your fault.* It's just a pity that allergic reaction didn't keep him in hospital for longer. Or kill him."

Lenny looked at Fay, wondering if it was time to tell her yet.

"Sorry, I shouldn't have said that. I just think of how different things could have been for you if it had. And you were the one who saved *his* life, calling the ambulance like you did."

"I shouldn't have called for help. I should've . . ." Lenny didn't know how to finish.

"But then you wouldn't be you, would you? You're not engineered the way he is. Not a bad bone in your body," Fay said.

Lenny couldn't tell her the truth; what a disappointment she would be to Fay.

"Zanny didn't die, did she? That day I found her?" She remembered what Young Helena had told her and it was starting to sound very much like the truth.

"No, you're right. You saved her life."

"Why couldn't I live with her then? After that? Was it because she didn't want me?"

"Oh, Lenny-girl, she *did*. Of course she did. You were her family. And she'd lost so much too. But after she did that . . . after you found her that day, it wasn't safe anymore. Even Susannah knew it. Her drinking and her mental health weren't great. You needed to heal, and so did she, and it didn't work in the same house."

"So she just let me live with strangers?"

Lenny knew this sounded callous; Fay and Robert were wonderful foster parents, but had Zanny known this? Did she care?

"She tried to visit, Len, but the visits never went very well. They confused you and upset her. In the end, she stayed in touch with me, but kept her distance. You were much more settled that way."

"Where is she now?" asked Lenny.

"I think you should go talk to Maureen—she'll be able to fill in some gaps," Fay said. She'd drained her tea and put her cup down on the coffee table.

"Maureen? My neighbor?"

"Yes, Lenny-girl."

Lenny thought then; cogs whirred, clicked into place. Faces became clear again. Zanny's face had never fully faded, but it was much crisper now. And the woman she lived with. Now her image came to Lenny like the haze lifting after a morning fog.

At one time she knew her as Missy. It was Maureen.

CHAPTER 40

Next door suddenly felt so much farther away, as if going there were like embarking on the inaugural space journey. But the questions were nipping at her heels so Lenny left Fay to her episode of *The Bold and the Beautiful* and went to see her neighbor.

"Maureen?" she yelled from the front door. "It's Lenny Marks."

"I'm down here, Lenny. Door's open," Maureen called back.

Lenny moved quickly past the portrait in the entryway, not wanting to make eye contact with herself. Even still, she caught it in her peripheral vision; she *hadn't* imagined it. The painting was as striking as she remembered.

When Lenny saw Maureen, relief washed over her. The color in her neighbor's face was back, her hair was twisted and scooped into a pile atop her head and she was seated on her couch, in front of a crackling winter fire. She was home where she belonged. Maureen looked tired, but welcoming. Lenny wondered again how she'd managed to forget this woman.

"I'm so glad to see you. I owe you a great deal. Come and sit." Maureen patted the empty space beside her. "Thank you, a million times thank you. I wasn't ready to go yet."

Lenny sat and realized what it was about the couch she'd found so mesmerizing. It was the one from Zanny's house. The plum velour was worn, but well cared for and still lovely to run her hand over.

"You knew my grandmother?" Lenny asked, before remembering her manners. "I'm sorry. I shouldn't start there. I mean, I want to know, but firstly, how are you?"

Maureen rubbed the back of Lenny's hand; her fingers were icy, not the same cold as they'd been when Lenny had found her on the floor, but not as warm as they should feel in close proximity to a fireplace.

"Poor circulation. Always had it," Maureen said, noticing Lenny's reaction and rubbing her hands together. "My fingers are fairly useless now, mostly numb. A right shame for a painter. I'm fine though, better than I was when you found me."

"What happened?" Lenny asked.

"Well, I'm almost eighty so they don't bother putting too much time and effort into us old, discontinued models. But it was blood-sugar related. I don't think I'd been quite looking after myself like I should have been."

"I'm glad you're home," said Lenny.

"Me too. Better food here. And company." She smiled.

"I should've been over earlier. Sorry."

"No need to apologize. You've done more than enough. And I've spoken to Fay, you've had a bit going on."

Lenny blushed at the thought of people having conversations about her.

"I did know your grandmother. Very well," Maureen said. "And I'm very happy to have a reason to talk about her."

"You loved her?" Lenny asked.

"Everyone who met Susannah loved her. But I *loved her*. In all ways but legally, she was my wife. We couldn't, of course, it wasn't allowed for us back then. Apparently you could marry an abusive man and that was much more acceptable than being in love with another woman." Maureen patted her hand again. "Sorry, that's not the point. You're here to learn about your grandmother."

"Is it a coincidence you live next door to me?" Lenny asked. It was one of many questions swirling inside her and she wondered how many she'd be allowed to ask today.

"Do you really believe in coincidences? Of that sort, I mean?"

"No," Lenny replied.

"Didn't think so. You were always far too smart for that. And practical. Your house was never for sale to anyone but you. One of Susannah's art students was a real estate agent and Fay told us you'd been looking. We bought it, then sold it to you. We worked it out with Fay—we needed the best way to give it to you without you asking all the questions about why. So we had it offered to you, at exactly the price you could afford. We were already in this one. Even before you moved in, Susannah said she could picture you there; something about it walking straight out of the pages of a Tolkien novel."

Lenny smiled. It was exactly what she'd thought when she'd seen the Tree House.

"I thought she died. Back then, in the garage when I found her." Lenny felt uncomfortable with the memory. She wished she'd known earlier that her grandmother had lived. It was so much better knowing she got out of that car and carried on being Zanny. "So where is she? Zanny?"

"It's been far too long since I've heard anyone use that name for her," Maureen said. "And I'm very sorry, but Susannah died the year you moved next door. She was never the same after Tammy left us."

"She's gone?" Lenny asked, hoping she'd heard wrong.

"Yes, my love, she's gone." Maureen intertwined her fingers and fidgeted with one of her rings. "Susannah was incredibly glad to know you were doing so well. We were both very proud of you."

"Then why not come over and say that? Remind me of all the things I forgot." Lenny realized she sounded curt, but she'd lost the opportunity to see her grandmother ever again and she wanted to know why. She didn't like other people pulling strings like she was part of a puppet show.

Maureen closed her eyes and bobbed her head. "Susannah wasn't well. Some days she was amazing, and almost her old self. And then other days she'd slip in and out of rooms like she was already a ghost."

Lenny wasn't satisfied with the answer.

"I regret not pushing her to see you. And then I ended up doing the exact same thing. I took the easy path too and I thought I was doing the right thing. But perhaps I was just being selfish. Because I could see you and know you were the sort of kind soul who would look after an elderly neighbor's yard for no reason at all. And you rode happily into your driveway every day after work with a smile on your face. And I saw you pottering about on weekends—happy as Larry."

"Not everything is always as it seems," Lenny said.

"Quite right. But I didn't want to be responsible for shattering your contentment. To properly reintroduce myself to you would have meant reminding you of all the horrible things that happened. And so I was a coward and did nothing. Also, you shouldn't think poorly of the deliveryman," Maureen said, her cool fingers reaching over to grasp Lenny's.

"What do you mean?"

"I put that parcel over there myself. I'm seventy-eight years old and not so well anymore. I didn't want to finish life with the same regrets Susannah had. And as we all know, Mother Time waits for no one."

"Did you know Fergus?" Lenny asked.

"Yes. I did. I was the reason your parents met. And I'll never forgive myself for that," Maureen said, the regret dancing across her face.

"But you didn't know what he'd do."

"Of course not. But I should have. I can't believe I didn't . . . I left an abusive husband a long time ago. And you think you'd see it in others. But I didn't and your beautiful mother—well, she was the softest, kindest soul. And she fought so hard for her family." Maureen's eyes grew damp and she cleared her throat. "You know, this place, here"—Maureen gestured around the room—"has helped heal many women. We took them in, let them stay, helped them repair. Not so much now, but for many years before. I wish I'd seen it in him. Or on Tammy, but I didn't."

"What do you mean 'healed'?"

"They came to us broken and scared. At the hands of their partners, or husbands, or fathers, or someone else they were meant to be able to trust. We let them try to have the space and the air and time to repair."

"This was a refuge?" Lenny asked, wondering if she'd mistaken the meaning.

Maureen nodded. "Of sorts. And you met many of the women at the solstice gathering. They were just a handful of the beautiful souls who I've been lucky enough to share some time with."

"What do you mean when you say Mum fought so hard for us?" Lenny said. "She picked him, she *always* picked him."

Maureen's eyes dropped to her feet. "She'd made plans to leave. We didn't know until after the police investigation. Tammy had been in contact with a refuge and she made all the arrangements to go there with you and Malcolm. It was just a matter of when."

Lenny took the blow of this news with a sharp exhale. Fergus's words ran through her head on repeat like a record jumping; *you did this you did this you did this you did this.*

"It wasn't your fault." Maureen jolted the needle back on track.

Maureen looked down to her hands, cupped together in her lap and worrying at the tassels on the throw covering her knees.

"He banned us from coming—that should've been the red flag, but we took it as him disapproving of *our* relationship. He was so full of hate and I see that now. I thought it was just because . . . well, for other reasons." Maureen's voice was strained.

"That's why we never saw you?"

"Yes. Susannah would sneak over sometimes, but she was careful to time it right. And Tammy was so nervous Fergus would come home, it just made it untenable." Maureen swallowed hard. "We should've known. We let you down."

The tears Maureen had tried to stifle started to run down her face, catching in the lines like tiny canals.

"And I'll never forgive myself." Maureen's voice gave way to a sob.

"What for?" Lenny asked, sitting forward.

"I took that call. From you. The night before it all happened."

Lenny remembered hearing the croaky voice and hanging up.

"I didn't know, I didn't know it was you, or I would've . . ." Maureen held her hands to her chest and took a deep breath. "I would've come. We both would have been there."

"I know," Lenny said and reached for Maureen's hand.

"You were so little," Maureen said through tears.

They sat quietly while Maureen composed herself, not taking her hand from the warmth of Lenny's as she dabbed at her eyes with a well-used tissue. Maureen looked worn out.

Lenny squeezed her hand. "I didn't mean to upset you or tire you. Maybe, though, if you don't mind, I could come back and talk some more about Zanny?"

"I'd like that. Very much. I've been waiting to talk to you for a very long time."

"Is that why you painted me?" Lenny asked.

"What do you mean?" Maureen looked confused.

"The picture at your front door. Of me."

Maureen sighed and wiped her face again with the tissue. "Oh. It is and it's not. But I see what you mean."

Lenny crinkled her forehead, hoping for an explanation but not wanting to push.

"That's your mum—Susannah painted it. You look just like her. But perhaps you never knew that."

Lenny hadn't known, in the way no one knew what someone that close to them looked like in comparison to themselves. And the details of her mum were not as clear as they once might have been. Instead, she remembered only a rough outline. As if she'd been given the summary of a book, but the pages themselves were blank.

Lenny stood to leave. Maureen was tired and Lenny was almost as full of information as she could be for one day. There were many questions, but they had plenty more time.

Maureen pulled Lenny closer to her and Lenny didn't feel the need to pull back. "You don't have to do this alone, you know."

"Do what?" Lenny asked.

"Life," Maureen replied, as if it were the easiest concept in the world.

CHAPTER 41

Saturday, July 2

Lenny sat beneath her front patio, drinking tepid tea and reading *Piranesi*. She was wondering how many times the word "vestibule" could possibly be used in a book when Malcolm sprung up from her feet, alerting her to a visitor. Kirra was strolling down the driveway; she gave Lenny a warm, shy smile and a little wave.

The two women embraced, Lenny stifling the urge to cut the physical contact short. She wanted to show Kirra how well she was doing by accepting the hug. Eventually, Kirra pulled away and looked at Lenny as if she were assessing a crystal vase for damage.

"I didn't know whether to come . . ." Kirra said, her words tentative.

"I'm glad you did."

"We miss you at school." Kirra sat beside Lenny on the bench seat.

"I'm sure not everyone does. But it's a lovely sentiment."

"No, really, we do. The kids don't know what to do without you and your replacement has big shoes to fill."

"Only size eights," Lenny said.

"Oh, I just meant . . ."

"I know the expression." Lenny smiled.

Kirra's shoulders relaxed noticeably.

"What about Amy?" Lenny asked. "Bet she's glad I'm not around."

"Well, she wouldn't dare say a thing after Lora ripped right into her. I have never seen Lora like that. She. Was. Furious. It was great."

"I didn't want to get anyone in trouble—Amy was just letting off steam," Lenny said, although she was quietly delighted that Amy had been knocked down a peg or two.

"Lenny, could you be any nicer? She was a complete cow to you. You had *nothing* to do with her and Ned breaking up—she was just looking for someone to blame."

"So they broke up?" Lenny sighed. "I did spend time with Ned and she may have misconstrued this as something other than platonic. Perhaps I should have been more—"

"Stop, stop, stop." Kirra waved her hands. "I've spoken to Ned about it; he said they were never well suited. Not to mention, he didn't completely trust her. She's like those girls they fill the cast of *The Bachelor* with every season to cause a stir. Immature, pernickety, hot as hell, good for ratings."

"I've never watched it," Lenny said.

"You've seen the ads, right?"

"Yes," Lenny agreed.

"Then you've as good as seen it, not missing a heap other than voyeuristic reality show brilliance. We should watch it together at some point." Kirra grinned.

"Maybe Amy should try out for it," Lenny ventured.

"They'd cast her as the troublemaker. Every season needs one," Kirra said, before leaning forward conspiratorially. "They could have Ashleigh too. They'd be perfect."

They laughed; it was a nice feeling to be in on the joke.

"So, how are you?" Kirra asked.

"I'm okay," Lenny said. Kirra eyed her warily and she decided to be as transparent as she could manage. "Most of the time anyway. I think I am a work in progress."

"We all are. But I'm glad you're doing better," Kirra replied.

"I'm sorry I wasn't nicer to you," Lenny said.

"What do you mean? You were always nice."

"I embarrassed myself trying to be friends with women who barely managed to veil their contempt for me. I thought I needed to be one of the 'cool' girls, like I'm still at high school. And meanwhile, I had a friend right there in front of me."

"Wait a minute." Kirra looked shocked.

"What?" Lenny asked.

"You mean you don't think *I'm* one of the cool girls?" Kirra tilted her head in mock indignation.

"Oh yeah, you and me, about as cool as a hotplate."

"That's a really strange way of putting it. But if you say so," Kirra replied, erupting into giggles.

"It's good to clear that up," Lenny said.

"I think it's the pregnancy. It's given me clarity. The complete opposite of pregnant brain." Kirra patted her stomach.

"You're with child?"

"Yes, I am, if you're from *Downton Abbey*. I would say 'accidentally knocked up' but potato-pot*ah*to, you know. Anyway, we're rapt."

"Congratulations," Lenny said, unsure why they were discussing potatoes.

Kirra raised one finger like she'd just recalled something important. "And because of my rapidly expanding midriff, I brought this for you."

Kirra pulled some folded material out of her bag. She handed it to Lenny, who unfurled it: the dress Kirra had worn to the trivia night. It was gorgeous, colorful and so unlike anything Lenny owned.

"Oh, and this came for you at school," Kirra said, passing her an overstuffed yellow envelope. "I found Mrs. Finlay steaming it open over the kettle."

"What?" Lenny asked, surprised even Mrs. Finlay's nosiness stretched that far.

"Well, not literally. But you know what I mean."

Lenny didn't really know and checked the seal, running her finger over it and finding it still intact. It appeared Kirra had managed to stop Mrs. Finlay from getting into it.

She flipped it over and read the front. The mail hadn't brought her anything good of late. The name on this letter was handwritten and it had been sent to the school, but marked *Private and confidential*. That would certainly have piqued Mrs. Finlay's interest. *Helena Winters*, it said, in scratchy blue ink that made her stomach fizz.

"And I have a message from Lora," Kirra said, and Lenny's attention snapped back to her friend. "Your long service leave is approved. She said she looks forward to seeing you for term four . . . But only if you're ready."

Lenny really had thought she'd done her dash with her disappearing act and had avoided contacting Lora for that very reason. As long as she didn't hear otherwise, she could pretend she was just on a break. Not a long-term, unemployed, you'll-never-work-with-children-again break.

"So she's not firing me?"

"She said you might bring that up and her reply was 'Does she think I'd have kept bloody Greg Schwartz on for this long if I held that sort of power?' And she categorically does not want to fire you." Kirra grinned.

Lenny nodded. "That seems pretty clear then."

"I think so," Kirra said. "Oh, and she loved the barefoot dancing thing. It's now once a week across all year levels. Let the kids be at one with nature, that sort of thing. We are in the forest after all."

"Wow" was all Lenny could manage, pleased at this turn of events.

"Now back to the dress. I'm not suggesting your wardrobe could do with a spray of color, but it actually could. I thought possibly you may need it for a special occasion sometime soon. A first date or something."

"A first date?"

Kirra waggled her eyebrows. "With a handsome supermarket manager perhaps?"

"Why would you think Ned is interested in me?" Lenny asked.

"Why would you think he's not? He said he's asked you out multiple times," Kirra replied.

"He has *never* asked me out."

"He told me he has: over to see his memorabilia, some *Buffy* retro film night at the Cameo, a couple of other things he reeled off."

"They weren't dates though, he was just being polite because he knew we shared interests," Lenny said.

"I don't know what you think being asked out on a date looks like, but that's what it looks like to me every day of the week."

"Really?" Lenny had been entirely unaware this may have been Ned's intention. "How can you be sure?"

"I have a sixth sense for these things. But also, because he told me," said Kirra. "It's not high school; sometimes you just have to cut to the chase."

Lenny ran her hands over the cool fabric of the dress. It was a light cotton, a kaleidoscope of colors and designs, a bit like a rainbow. It was only mid-thigh length and she wasn't sure she'd have the confidence to wear it. And if she did, she'd have to shave above her knees.

"You've got good pins, you should get them out occasionally," Kirra said.

"Pins?"

"Legs," Kirra clarified.

"I'm not sure I'm ready."

"To get your legs out?" Kirra asked. "Sure, take your time with it."

"No, I mean Ned. It's just . . ." She trailed off.

"I get it. It's scary putting yourself out there. But keep in mind, you don't have to marry the guy. Don't call it a date, just think of it as hanging out with a friend."

Lenny paused, took it all in.

"And maybe, who knows, you'll be showing him more than just your pins?" Kirra bit her bottom lip and giggled.

Lenny felt a blush erupt over her cheeks. She'd never discussed such an intimate topic with anyone, not even the only man she'd ever slept with.

"Just have fun with it, is what I mean. It's just dating, it shouldn't be taken so seriously. Once again, think of it like *The Bachelor*." Kirra smiled. "I really prattle on, don't I?"

Lenny shook her head. "No, it's great. And thank you, for everything. You've been so lovely to me and I've kept you at arm's length. I am not sure I deserve your kindness."

"Well, it's what friends do. We point you in the right direction, occasionally get it wrong and then come back and laugh about it. We weather the storms."

Lenny couldn't help but smile. She had a friend and she didn't even make her up.

Lenny farewelled Kirra and brought her things inside. The temperature was dropping and she could do with a fresh pot of tea. Maybe even a sandwich. She forgot to have lunch sometimes now; without her school routine she didn't keep track as well as she used to.

Fay would be back soon; she'd slept at the Tree House every night since Kirra smashed through the window. It was fortuitous timing that Lenny's need for Fay had arisen just as Paige and Skye were placed with their own grandmother. Fay was Lenny's sentry, and while she hated to be a burden she did sleep much better knowing her mum was in the next room. The co-dependency was creeping in alarmingly easily.

Kirra's message from Lora had lifted a weight she didn't realize she was carrying. Applying for other jobs was not something she wanted to consider, and having to explain why she had been fired was a hurdle she couldn't imagine ever being able to get over. And it wasn't as if she could just take Selby South Primary off her résumé; it was the only place she'd ever taught.

Lenny looked forward to telling Fay; it was good news. Her job was safe and she had a proper friend. The kettle hummed away on its base behind her.

She picked up the hand-addressed envelope, feeling its lumps and bumps, trying to determine what exactly was contained within. Tearing the self-adhesive strip, she peered inside. Whatever it held was thickly bubble-wrapped.

She ripped into the plastic and felt a couple of air-filled spots pop under her fingertips. A sensation she usually enjoyed, but not today. Not once she saw what was inside.

Peanuts.

She dropped the envelope and they spilled out, skittering across the wooden benchtop.

She wasn't allergic. But she knew someone who was.

CHAPTER 42

March 22, 1999
Supreme Court of Victoria

"And what did you intend to do by giving your stepfather an allergic reaction?"

The barrister fired questions at her, calling her *Ms. Winters* and using his gold-colored pen like an orchestra baton. The questions continued relentlessly. But since lunch she'd noticed a piece of food lodged between the man's front teeth. It was distracting and oddly affirming; this stern, robotic man *was* human.

"I didn't," Lenny replied, keeping her answer short, just as she'd been instructed. She'd been told to answer the question and only *that* question. And definitely not to fill any silences. Lenny was never one to speak too much, so she didn't think it was too tall of an order.

Given her age, the courtroom was cleared of all *unnecessary people.* A "closed" court, although it still contained more people than Lenny was comfortable with. Fergus remained and so did the steely, penetrating glare he directed at her from the moment she took her seat. Apparently he was *necessary.*

"Well, he didn't do it to himself, did he, Ms. Winters?"

When he said "Ms.," it sounded like it ended in a z. His eyes were intense and not kind and she couldn't meet his gaze. She stared instead at the smattering of dandruff dusting his right shoulder. It worsened every time he used the gold pen to scratch his scalp.

"Ms. Winters, did you try to kill your stepfather?" he asked.

Stepfather: theater, father, pester, free, pest

"No," she replied.

"Did you want him to go away?"

"Yes," she answered.

"Was that why you triggered his allergies? Not so he'd die, necessarily, just so he'd go away. That's right, isn't it?"

"No, that's not right," she said. "He had an allergic reaction and I called the ambulance. I saved his life."

Too many words, Lenny. Just answer the question.

"And his medication, did you move it? Where did his EpiPen go?" the barrister asked, rolling his tongue along his top teeth, but failing to dislodge the food.

"I don't know." *Keep it simple.*

Fergus stared from his seat. She could feel his hatred burning into her.

You did this.

The man who sat at the opposite table to Fergus, the one who had told her to answer questions truthfully, stood up. "This is not a trial for Ms. Winters, Your Honor. I'd ask my learned friend not to continue accusing the witness."

"I'll rephrase, Your Honor," Gold Pen said, scratching his head and releasing yet another snowdrift.

Lenny said nothing.

"You hated him, didn't you, Helena?"

"Yes."

"Enough to want to see him dead?"

"Yes," she said, thankful to be able to tell the truth. One of her only truths that day.

A week or so later Zanny told her Fergus had been found guilty by the jury. Zanny told her with mascara-stained cheeks and in a voice that Lenny understood meant her grandmother was not happy, and certainly not sober. Lenny wasn't sure what to make of it, but knowing she didn't have to go back to court brought her a great sense of relief. She didn't like lying in front of all those people, and she hated seeing Fergus.

"It doesn't change anything," Zanny told her. "It won't bring them back."

The next day Lenny found Zanny in the front seat of the Fairmont and nothing was ever the same again.

CHAPTER 43

Wednesday, July 6, 2022

"The parole conditions are strict, but he isn't electronically monitored," said Wendy with a reassuring, kind smile. "That is the case for some parolees, but not him. Fergus is not allowed to speak to you, that's specified in his order. No contact whatsoever, even through a third party. But I'd imagine, after this much time, he's probably not interested, and of course he wouldn't know where to find you."

Wendy Dalton had a lot to say, which was good because Lenny did not feel much like talking about her stepfather being released. On her arrival at the Tree House, Wendy had apologized profusely for her unannounced Selby South visit. She attempted to sugarcoat the conversation—quite literally—with a box of éclairs from a bakery in Belgrave. Lenny didn't have the stomach for them, but hoped Wendy would leave them behind so perhaps she could have one later, once the visit was over.

It was times like these she appreciated Fay being there; she could pretend she was a child all over again and let her mum do the heavy lifting during the conversation. Fay was never short of things to say.

The arrival of the peanuts was Lenny's notification that Fergus had been released. She had cleaned them up, thrown them in the bin and done what she had excelled at for years: said nothing. Acknowledging the delivery of those little brown legumes to Fay or Wendy, or anyone else, would surely invite questions as to what they meant. And what they meant was that Lenny had told round-about lies—not complete lies, mind you, just almost-truths and the odd omission as necessary.

The three women sat at Lenny's dining table. Fay had packed the Scrabble set away and put it on the bookshelf, beneath *The Hobbit* collection, which held steady at thirty-six.

"I can assure you he's not living locally. His accommodation is north of the city; obviously I can't say where. He has been in a rela-tionship, apparently, with a woman he met while incarcerated and he's living with her."

This got Lenny's attention. "Does the woman know?" she asked. "What he did?"

"I'm not sure. Due to privacy, it's up to him to tell her or for her to find out of her own accord. What she knows, or does not know, is not information I'm privy to."

"Of course," Fay said, nodding in understanding.

"Well, that's bullshit—that woman is in danger."

"Helena," Fay snapped. She didn't tolerate swearing, even in ex-tenuating circumstances.

"I understand your frustration. It's been a long time though," Wendy said, "and plenty of work has been done on rehabilitation. That's part of the parole conditions."

"So that's it for him then, is it? Now he gets to live happily ever after. He's turned into Prince Charming. I'm sure prison really soft-ened him."

Wendy and Fay eyed Lenny carefully. This was unusually forth-right of her but she was a little sick of pussyfooting around. They could have just sent a letter notifying her of his release; she didn't have the energy to sit through this visit. And why would Lenny need or *want* to know that the man who murdered her mother and brother was now living with another woman but not be able to warn her. It made her skin itch, thinking this woman might be oblivious to his past; surely she was entitled to such information. Manipulation came easily to Fergus; he would weave a tale to convince her of what a hard-done-by victim of circumstance he was.

Manipulator: paramount, animator, alarm, riot, trap

Lenny drained her cup and ignored the éclairs, willing Wendy to leave. Her bare toes gripped the bottom rail of the kitchen stool like a bird on a perch.

Her mind wandered to what it would be like to be the sort of person who would track Fergus down, avenge her family and return to teaching and frozen quiches and beheading Maureen's agapanthus like nothing ever happened. It was thrilling to imagine. She would be a modern-day Robin Hood, disguised in gray bengaline slacks, the perfect camouflage.

The conversation continued without her joining in, and when it seemed clear Wendy was not leaving anytime soon, Lenny stood up and walked into her bedroom. She made no attempt to excuse herself; under the circumstances, she was likely to get away with what would usually be considered very rude behavior. She let the door click into place and lay on her bed. Malcolm was napping on his blanket pile and climbed up next to her. He pressed into her side and was back to sleep in moments. His ability to sleep when and wherever was incredible.

Before long, there was mumbling that sounded very much like goodbyes, and then the heavy clunk of her front door closing. Fay knocked quietly and walked into Lenny's room. She wondered if Fay was about to take her to task over her impoliteness; she and Robert had instilled better manners in her than that. Lenny didn't care what Wendy thought, but she didn't mean to embarrass Fay.

"I'm sorry," Lenny said.

"Don't be," Fay said. "Wendy's lovely, but she nearly talked my ear off and that's saying something."

Fay sat on the other side of Lenny's bed and leaned back onto the pillow. She made an audible sigh as her body settled into the mattress. She pulled down the hem of her offensively bright yellow Batman tee and nudged Lenny with her elbow.

"What are you thinking?" Fay asked.

"About Mum," Lenny said. "Other Mum, that is. Not you."

"Thanks for spelling it out, Lenny-girl."

Neither said anything for a moment.

"Want to tell me about her?" Fay asked.

"Yes. And no." Lenny paused. "I didn't think I remembered her face, which made me think I'd forgotten her."

"We're more than just a face, is that what you've realized?"

"Yes. Kind of. But it's still nice to picture her."

Fay waited. Both of them knew Lenny would fill the silence at some point; she just wanted to figure out a way to start.

"Her ears didn't fold over at the top. Same as mine." Lenny ran her index finger along the smooth top of her ear. "She always drank her coffee in the exact same mug, every day, every time. If it wasn't clean, she'd wash it and use it, even though the cupboard was full of other mugs. She hated oriental lilies; the smell gave her a headache. Mum would jump in puddles with Mal. She wore gumboots just so she could, but I never wanted to. I hated the gritty feeling if the water got inside my shoes. But Malcolm loved it. Sometimes, in my wardrobe, where Malcolm and I would hide, she left things there. She never said anything about it, like she wanted us to think it was magic. There were different books so I could tell new stories to Malcolm. Jelly beans once in a little Tupperware container, and a torch that projected animals onto the wall. We both loved that one.

Her laugh was brilliant, contagious. But it was a different laugh when Fergus was in the room; more polite, fake but not obviously so. Her proper laugh was the sort that hurt your stomach muscles and risked you wetting your pants."

"That's a lot of things," Fay said.

"Just little things."

"That's all we have though, isn't it, really? Just little, everyday, extraordinary, ordinary things," Fay replied.

"Extraordinary," Lenny whispered, mulling over the word and the difference a single space could make.

Extraordinary: narrator, torrid, toxin, next, dire, die

"And Fergus, I keep thinking about him," Lenny said.

"Of course you do. Why they think that man should be released is beyond me. But he won't come within whoopee of you. Why would he?"

Why wouldn't he?

She wasn't meant to care about Fergus anymore. He wasn't meant to wield this power.

"Fay, it was my fault they both died."

"Oh, no, no," Fay said and she turned to face Lenny, leaning on her elbow. "You mustn't let him get into your head. He said a lot of things back then, that's what abusers do. They shift blame, they manipulate. *You* saved his life. Because you're a kind, good human being."

Fay rolled onto her back and Lenny stared at the ceiling, contemplating how different everything could've been. It was the closest she'd come to telling the truth since it happened.

"I just wish that turn he had had polished him off properly," Fay said. "Then you wouldn't have gone through any of this."

And that was the thing, *it was meant to.*

CHAPTER 44

Fay dozed off on the couch in front of an SBS crime drama Lenny couldn't get into because reading subtitles always bothered her. For her it was either reading or watching, but not both. Instead, Lenny hooked Malcolm to his lead and left a note on the bench to let Fay know they'd be back soon. She needed the fresh air and Malcolm was due some exercise after all the attention Fay lavished on him. Her attention largely consisted of dog treats and leftovers.

It wasn't long into their walk when she spotted Jase; she should've known she'd come across him sooner or later. He was on the old rail trail again, green bag in hand and not looking any less grubby than the last time she'd seen him. He was, she was sure, wearing the same Holden baseball cap, which was unlikely to have ever seen a washing machine. His look gave the impression he was homeless, which she knew to be untrue, unless he'd been evicted. This time, though, his slovenly presentation empowered her. A man who could not wash was unlikely to have much clout. Or so she hoped.

Somewhere between the parole letter, her canine larceny, the tea theft, Amy's antics and the mail bag of peanuts, a pilot light had been lit. Seeing Jase again made it flare into something larger. It wasn't a burn-your-house-down sort of fire, more of a mid-range bonfire. Her feet marched firmly in the direction of the unwashed lout. She was not going to lurk in the shadows. She was getting on the front foot.

He didn't notice her until she was almost within his reach. He held a smoke in one hand, and the way his free hand hovered over his jeans gave her the impression she'd interrupted prior to, or directly following, him relieving himself.

"You—" he started but she cut him off.

"Yes. Me. I took your dog, that's right. But I didn't steal him, I liberated him from the swamp you call a home. You are not fit to own a pot plant, let alone a dog. You are not getting him back and I don't care what you have to say about that. He is not yours anymore, and if you want to take issue with it, *report it to the police.* But I don't think you will because of the evidence I have of you abusing him. You should've thought about that before you laid your boots into an innocent creature for all your street to see. If you come looking for him, I will call the police. If you ever approach me again, I will make hell rain down upon your disgusting hovel. Do you understand me?"

It was such a well-presented argument she wondered how he would be able to form any sort of a comeback. The delivery was so perfect, she wished for an audience just so someone else could see stuttering, stumbling, insecure Lenny Marks stick up for herself. Despite her feeling of triumph, she sensed her cheeks pinkening in the involuntary way they did.

"You bitch," he spat.

"That's all you've got?" She was incredulous. "Go on then, what are you going to do about it?"

The stench of him, now she was closer, was an overpowering mix of dirt and something pungent she couldn't place: earthy but with an acrid and distinct scent. Whatever its origin, it was consuming the air around them and made her take a step back. Jase had a lot less to say on this occasion; perhaps it was because he was alone, or maybe he no longer felt the drive to fight for ownership of a dog he had treated like the scum on his boots. He appeared almost as if he was in some sort of daze and she wondered if he was unwell. Was she accosting a man who actually needed medical intervention? Maybe he was having a heart episode, or some sort of seizure.

But Jase collected himself and took a step toward them. Malcolm, tense and angry, lurched at him, clearly not ready to take any more of what his former owner had to offer. Along with his lunge, Malcolm barked, and whether it was the noise or the movement, Jase was thrown off balance and fell to the ground.

Lenny's first reaction was to help him, but he didn't give her a chance, instead kicking out a leg in her direction and rolling onto his knees in an effort to stand up. As he did, the green bag spilled onto the ground in front of him.

While she hadn't been able to place the smell, Lenny had no trouble identifying that what Jase kept in his Woolworths bag was certainly not available at any Woolies she'd been to. The fresh cannabis was a brilliant emerald green and cascaded like giant illegal confetti. The watering can his friend had carried, their trips out along the remote part of the track—it all made sense.

Lenny, who rarely made eye contact with anyone, locked eyes with Jase. Now she knew he had secrets to keep and she felt the power that gave her over him. Jase's eyes were glazed and unable to hold her own.

Wasting no time, she snatched the shopping bag, still half full. "Leave the dog and me alone or I take this to the police," she said, voice unwavering, power surging through her.

He scrabbled in the dirt, trying to stand, but his movements were uncoordinated. It was almost unfair to take him on when he was so obviously stoned.

"I never liked that stupid dog anyway, so you can fuck off. But give me back the bag," he said from the ground.

"No," she said. "You don't get this back so *you* fuck off."

Swearing didn't roll easily off her tongue, but it felt quite authoritative to say this out loud. Jase seemed to be taking her seriously enough anyway. He didn't know her pulse was racing and her stomach churning.

Jase was climbing to his feet as she and Malcolm started walking away. She picked up the pace because although he may not have been on top of his game, she was not stupid enough to believe him to be harmless.

This time, though, she'd seen him for what he was and it wasn't much of anything.

Lenny wondered as they powered into the bush if she'd think the same of Fergus now. Maybe he wasn't a giant after all. But she realized, with some satisfaction and possibly because of the adrenaline coursing through her body, she didn't actually care what Fergus was like anymore.

As before, Lenny and Malcolm didn't return directly to the Tree House. She may have new-found bravado but she had no desire to lead Jase to her house. Still, she wasn't running scared. If he dared to follow them, she felt ready. They wove and cut across paths until they were in a place she'd never been before. It was only now that she'd put a considerable distance between herself and Jase that she realized the implications of carrying a bagful of freshly plucked marijuana over her shoulder. It was a pickle she had never considered finding herself in.

There was plenty of foliage around; she could hide the bag in the scrub, or under a log, but she was worried kids might come across it, or wildlife would eat it. Littering suddenly seemed more harmful than possession of drugs. She wasn't sure they even counted as drugs. She knew what weed was, but surely something needed to be done with it before it was ready to smoke or whatever Jase was planning. At the moment it was just plant cuttings and seemed no more illegal than her grevillea prunings. She would be careful with it nonetheless.

And she worried about what would happen if the police stopped her. Surely they'd arrest first, ask questions later. In fact, she thought that was exactly the way they did it. Although she was hardly Pablo Escobar.

A sports oval appeared mirage-like through the forest in front of her. A building was positioned on the far side and no one appeared to be around. Lenny made her way across the oval, knowing the clubhouse would help orient her. And she would find a bin to off-load her illegal goods.

Lenny steeled herself—this was not a crisis of any sort yet, just an adventure she hadn't planned on.

As she neared the building she noticed a car parked in a manner that obscured it from the other side of the oval. Its shining red panels stood out among the green surrounds and she worried about running into its occupants. But it would be fine: she was just a woman walking a dog; she would dispose of the Woolies bag and then ask for directions back to Main Street. Simple. And she'd be happy to be rid of it, too; the smell was really something else.

Malcolm pulled toward a drinking fountain with a dog bowl attached. The metal receptacle held only a small puddle of water, so Lenny turned the tap to fill it further and Malcolm lapped appreciatively.

As she waited for his noisy slurping to finish, she noticed a distinctive sticker on the rear of the red car. It was a Ford Festiva and now she'd spotted the sticker, she realized she'd seen the car a number of times before. The crown atop the girl figure with a generic stick dog beside her was a giveaway: the car was Amy's.

The front door of the clubhouse swung open and Lenny saw the logo on the door: Belgrave Heights Football and Netball Club, *Home of the Bulldogs*. It gave her a rough idea of where she was.

The door slammed and Amy hurried away from it, head down. Lenny decided it was a good thing; she could offer an apology so they could be on good terms by the time school went back. But something in the prep teacher's demeanor made her hesitate.

The clubhouse door opened again and a man came racing out. He was trying to pull his t-shirt over his head as he caught up to Amy. She unlocked her car, which gave a shrill beep as she did so.

"Babe, just wait. I didn't mean it like that," the man said.

"Well, what did you mean?" snapped Amy.

"I mean *now* is not a good time to leave. But *soon*. Soon it will be easier," he said, closing the distance between them and reaching for her hand.

Lenny felt like she'd stumbled into a daytime movie.

"It will never be easy. Ever. But if you love me like you say you do, it shouldn't take so much fucking around. You've been on the fence for months. Grow a pair," Amy spat back, crossing her arms over her chest.

Amy wore a slouchy green top and a pair of tight shorts that made her look like she'd just finished cheerleading practice. It was not, Lenny thought, shorts weather and she'd be quite cold.

"Oh my God, you're like a broken record," he said.

"Whatever, Kurt." Amy opened the door to her car.

It wasn't until Amy used his name that Lenny realized it was Kurt Thompson. Her high school tormentor and, no doubt, Amy's "friend" who told her all about teenage Lenny and her made-up stories.

"You're *so* mature," he replied as he rushed forward and grabbed Amy's arm. Lenny tensed, thinking he was going to strike her, but he just held on to her and pressed his body against hers.

Amy was looking at the ground as he nuzzled her neck, and Lenny thought if the prep teacher wanted to leave she could do so easily. But maybe that's what people had said about Tammy. Fergus hadn't chained her up; she *could* have left. She *should* have left. Did Amy need her help? Maybe this was a Robin Hood moment.

Lenny should've revelled in catching out two people who'd been so unkind to her, but she didn't feel that way at all. Instead she felt sorry for them: for Amy, who thought a bored husband would ever leave his wife and for allowing herself to be grinded against in a car park by way of an apology. And for Kurt, who was lost in the idea he was something more than he was.

Amy was giving in to Kurt. He put his hand either side of her face and leaned into her forehead, speaking to her in low murmurs. And then Amy glanced over and noticed Lenny, standing there watching the Kurt and Amy Show.

Voyeur: rove, very, your, rue, you

Kurt followed Amy's gaze and it took a moment for his brain to register Lenny. Perhaps, out of context, he couldn't place her. Maybe had she offered him a cigarette, he would've recognized her right away.

"Oh shit. This isn't what it looks like," Kurt said, releasing Amy and throwing his palms up like he was surrendering.

Lenny said nothing; she didn't have to. The pair were awash with guilt.

"What are you doing here?" Amy snapped.

"This is just . . ." Kurt said, but petered off. Whatever his excuse was, it would be underwhelming.

They stood in a three-way stare-off until Malcolm started shuffling around, clearly fed up with waiting. Lenny realized she wouldn't be able to dispose of Jase's cuttings now, not with an audience. She'd take the bag home and burn it in the incinerator. Having come this far with it, she felt confident she could get it to the

Tree House. Surely the police would have better things to do than stop a benign-looking schoolteacher for a drug search. It was one of the benefits of being invisible; they might not even see her.

"Can you point me toward Main Street?" Lenny asked.

"Lenny, *honestly*." Amy's voice had softened. "Are you going to tell anyone? You know I could lose my job if someone finds out I've been involved with a school parent."

Lenny registered the connection: Amy was Jaxon Thompson's teacher. Kurt's wife had seemed so pleasant at the parent–teacher evening; she didn't deserve this.

"Rules are there for a reason," Lenny said.

"Come on, be reasonable," Amy pleaded.

"I think you'll find I'm always very reasonable. Now, can you tell me which way is back to Main Street?" Lenny really didn't want to get involved in another of Kurt's affairs.

Amy pointed up the hill, shrugging in defeat. "First right onto Hodgson and you'll run straight into it."

"Thank you." Lenny turned to go. She wasn't planning to tell Kurt's wife, or Ned, or to post it on social media for all of Belgrave to see, but they didn't deserve that reassurance.

"Did you even like Ned?" Lenny asked, turning back; she suddenly felt very defensive of him. "Or was it just to make Kurt jealous?"

Amy shook her head. "It's none of your business."

Lenny started to leave, but Amy's next words made her look back.

"I was very fond of him," Amy mumbled. It was the sort of comment someone made about a recently deceased aunt they didn't know very well.

"Ned deserves better than that," Lenny said and gave Malcolm a nudge. They started walking in the direction Amy had indicated.

She had walked about twenty meters when Amy caught up to her.

"Please, Lenny. I know we haven't always seen eye to eye. But it would really suck if everyone found out about this. For me at work and for Kurt's family," she said.

Lenny considered her. She wasn't the glowing, gorgeous, effortless vision she'd always thought Amy was. She was something else, insecure perhaps, maybe even unhappy.

"Amy. I don't know that I particularly like you very much. But you should really like yourself better than this." She gestured over Amy's shoulder at Kurt.

Amy blanched and her face sagged with defeat.

"Look after yourself, Amy," Lenny said, and she and Malcolm made their way toward Hodgson Road.

CHAPTER 45

Wednesday, July 13

The Tree House was quiet when Lenny woke. She could always tell whether Fay was in the house; she was not a quiet woman and generally made her presence known. It seemed delightfully indulgent to be the sole occupant of her house and she climbed out from under her quilt to enjoy the solitude.

She showered at a hotter than necessary temperature and washed her hair, which was no longer a chin-length bob. It was making a southwardly dash to her shoulders, which she didn't mind because it meant she could easily tie it back and out of the way.

It seemed like a nice day to visit Maureen. She'd been going there semi-regularly. Maureen would answer any questions that sprung to mind and they'd sit by the fire or on the verandah and enjoy each other's company. Lenny felt herself fast falling into the pace of a retiree.

Dressed and with damp hair resting on her shoulders, Lenny walked Malcolm across the driveway to Maureen's. Lenny heard voices as she stepped over the agapanthus boundary, but thought nothing much of it, despite it being unusual to hear a male voice at Maureen's. Her guests were almost exclusively women.

And both voices were louder and brasher than she would expect of a pleasant conversation. She slowed down and changed her path, not wanting to walk where she could be easily seen. Instead, she kept to the camellias and relied on being hidden by the vines over the verandah that Maureen refused to let her cut back.

Malcolm was pressed firmly into her side, his ears raised, ready to follow her wherever she went.

Lenny inched forward, able to see a man through the wooden slats of the balustrade. Maureen stood in her doorway, clutching its frame. Whether this was to prevent the man from entering or because she needed the support, Lenny couldn't tell. But her face was incensed.

Lenny could hear that Maureen's words were fizzing with anger but she was unable to process them. She wondered how best to intervene.

The man's face flicked toward Lenny, not at her, just in her direction, as he wiped his nose between his thumb and forefinger and then continued to gesticulate wildly.

It was then the penny dropped, seeing the man front-on like that. And it was hardly a surprise it had taken her a moment to realize who he was. After all, she hadn't seen Fergus for twenty-five years.

CHAPTER 46

Once she realized it was Fergus, Lenny was unable to cease her advance. The pull was almost magnetic. She couldn't tell if it came from a need to protect Maureen or because there were things she wanted to say to her stepfather.

He was older now. But so was she. He was grayer and rounder than he'd once been, but he held his body in a way that still implied strength.

She dug for courage to speak up. To say *You are not allowed to be here.* Or *Are you looking for me?* Something that would be written in a script when the unlikely hero finally managed to confront the bad guy.

But his words stopped her short.

"I am your only son. You can't just write me out of your life. What sort of mother does that?"

"But I can, and I have," Maureen replied. "I'm not giving you anything. You don't deserve it."

Mother? Son?

"Is that why you changed your name? Because you're hiding away out here? Are you that ashamed of me, Mum?"

"I wasn't hiding," Maureen said firmly. "It was all just so public—what you did."

"What I did? What *I* did? It wasn't my fault." He was shouting, arms flailing wildly, and looked ready to strike out at Maureen. Lenny remembered this sort of anger spewing from him; he was past the point of being reasoned with.

Lenny gulped, wondering what she'd just walked in on. He wasn't here to find her. Fergus was here for Maureen, which was not to say that was any better. Her eyes shot back toward the Tree House; it was too far away now and she couldn't leave Maureen. Instead she forced herself to step out from the bushes.

Fergus noticed the movement straight away. He turned his whole body toward her, sizing her up from the top of the stairs. He tilted his head, the recognition apparent.

"Well, well, well." He smirked. "If you don't look the spit of Tammy."

"Lenny, you need to go home." Maureen sounded desperate. "Fergus, you can't be around her, you know that breaches your parole."

"Mum," he said, opening his hands up and facing his palms skywards. "*She* came here, I was visiting *my* mum. How was I to know?"

Fergus glanced innocently from Maureen to Lenny.

She felt reduced to eleven years old again, and how she wished she'd stayed home. Malcolm stayed firmly beside her.

Fergus walked down the steps, closing the distance between them. Once he was level with her she realized she didn't have to look up to him now; they were the same height. Lenny pushed her shoulders back, trying to grow just a little bit taller.

"Where'd you come from?" he asked, motioning to the empty driveway. "Guess you're nearby? Which is good—you can keep an eye on Mum. Wouldn't want something terrible to happen to her."

Hideaway: headway, ahead, away, hide

An ache shot through both her shins.

Say something, Lenny. You are not a child anymore.

"And look at your little guard dog. I hope he doesn't bite," Fergus said with a slow chuckle. "Best you keep him back, Helena. I would hate for him to be hurt."

Lenny wanted to take control like she'd done with Jase. She wanted to form words so she could say *The dog's not the one you should worry about*, but she knew her voice would shake even if she could manage it. And she was worried they were just empty words. Really, what was she going to do?

When Lenny didn't reply—couldn't reply—he continued.

"I came to tell Mum I was out. Figured she'd be in quite the state having not seen me for so long. Turns out she's been avoiding me on purpose. Can you believe it?" He gave an exaggerated shrug of his shoulders.

"You came here for money. Don't pretend this is anything other than that," Maureen said, stepping forward and gripping one of the verandah posts to steady herself.

"Prices have gone up in the past two decades. The world is a very different place and I'm just a bloke trying to find his feet." His voice was saccharine; he was always the hard-done-by one.

"Fergus," Maureen said, louder now, panicked. "You need to leave. I am calling the police; neither of us want you here."

She looked so frail and Lenny silently begged her to go back inside where she was safe.

Fergus put a hand to his chest, as if wounded. "You two are the last family I've got. And this is the welcome I get. You know I didn't get to see my son grow up. Someone fucked that up for me." His eyes pierced Lenny. She was surprised to find no drunken stench from him; instead he smelled like coffee. He'd moved so close she could've counted his eyelashes.

"Did you get my letter?" Fergus teased.

There was no escaping him. Fergus was suddenly everywhere. He knew where she worked, he knew she lived nearby *and* he was Maureen's son. Her world was closing in and it made her chest uncomfortably tight.

She met his eyes. The hateful eyes of the man who'd destroyed her family long before he took her mum and brother.

She didn't forgive him. Nor did she want to.

"So, what, you're a man-hating lesbian now too? Is that what my mum taught you?" The chapped skin of his lips danced in a smile, one offering no kindness.

"No," Lenny mouthed, sound coming out, but hardly. She adjusted herself, pulled her shoulders back and tried again. "No. I just hate you."

"Oh, she speaks." Fergus laughed. "Well done. You always were quiet. A bit of a strange one, actually. We had to convince other kids to be friends with you, you know."

"Go," Lenny said. "Before you can't."

Fergus cackled and clapped his hands together, giving no indication of being the slightest bit worried. He didn't know what she'd been doing for the last twenty-five years. There was a chance she was now proficient in martial arts, or held an extensive collection of handguns. But of course it was nothing to do with her, or Maureen. It was all about him. He was like a dog lifting his leg on every tree he passed to make sure it was still marked as his.

"Be careful, Helena," Fergus said. "You've got a lot to lose."

You did this.

I did it.

She bristled; his words still packed a punch.

Fergus moved back up the stairs to his mother.

"I'm not asking a lot," he told Maureen. "While I was inside, the house was taken by the bank; all my tools are gone, my car. You're sitting pretty here. I just need some start-up cash. And I know you took more than enough from Dad."

Lenny's eyes scanned the garden around her, searching for options, something to wield. She thought of tiny Bilbo being brave, although he'd had the ring to keep him hidden. But she might not get another chance. The opportunity was presenting itself and Gandalf was not coming to save her. She needed to channel the anger bubbling inside her. How did Fergus manage to make her feel so cowardly? And now he quite literally stood between her and someone she loved. Yet again. She wanted to yell the truth at him: *You killed them, Fergus! That was you, all you.* There was no point though.

He was a master of convincing people—himself included—to believe whatever he wanted. Even she'd believed the things he told her. *You did this.* He was an expert salesman and he was selling the family man, loving husband and doting father. The thought occurred to her that Fergus displayed many of the criteria on the Hare psychopathy checklist: superficial charm, manipulation, callousness, pathological lying. Liam Backman didn't come anywhere close to ticking as many boxes.

Manipulates: animal, pulsate, insult, menial, past, lies

This man was not reformed. He had no redeeming characteristics and never would. And now his unsuspecting new girlfriend was in danger because he'd manipulated his way into her life.

Save her, Lenny. Save them all.

It was still a choice. She had options; it was just a matter of picking the one she could live with. One seemed more appealing than any of the alternatives: no more Fergus. A world, a time and a place where he ceased to exist was better for everyone. Jail wasn't enough.

Your turn, Lenny.

A shovel sat against Maureen's house. The wooden handle had long cracks down the length of it from being outside for so long.

The shovel blade was rusted and she wondered if it would fall apart when any sort of force was applied. She could only try.

Malcolm had moved up the stairs and put himself closer to Maureen, his body taut and tense and ready to put up a fight. Only Lenny didn't want it to be up to Malcolm. She was meant to look after him. Fergus eyed the dog with a modicum of wariness, but didn't adjust his tone or volume. His self-control seemed no stronger than it had ever been. He reached into his jeans pocket and pulled out a folding knife. Fergus flicked it open and pointed it at Malcolm's black snout.

"Keep him away from me, Helena," he hissed, not bothering to turn to look at Lenny. He kept his eyes on Malcolm, maybe more worried about the dog than he wanted to let on.

It was more than she could stand. Last time she'd seen Fergus with a knife she hadn't been able to protect anyone.

While Fergus's back was still to her, she moved quickly to pick up the shovel. It would have to do. She watched Fergus closely, knowing that neither age nor time would have made him any less unpredictable.

Lenny moved toward the stairs. He was at the top of the steep wooden steps and far closer to Maureen than Lenny wanted him to be. Lenny felt very much at a disadvantage standing below them. Fergus checked for Lenny over his shoulder, saw she'd moved and spun about, throwing his arm out as he did so, making Maureen lose her footing and fall back onto the verandah. She cried out in pain and the dog shot in front of her, creating a barrier between mother and son.

"What are you playing at?" Fergus grunted.

Lenny held tight to the wooden handle, the weathered wood splintering into her palms. But it would only take one decent swing if she timed it right.

Fergus held the knife in front of him and didn't move down the stairs; he knew he had the better position. Lenny wondered how many prison scraps he'd been in. She'd been in a total of one fight in her entire life and lost that completely.

But there was no chance to consider her next move. There was a menacing bark from Malcolm, a flurry of movement from above her, and the next thing she knew her stepfather was falling toward her. Fergus's hands flailed and his body twisted and Lenny moved to the side; there was nothing else for her to do. He dropped hard and fast, only stopping when his head collided with a potted fuchsia at the base of the staircase. The sound of his skull cracking was sickening.

Lenny let the shovel clatter to the ground.

CHAPTER 47

Fergus lay unmoving on the path. His shoulders were rounded and his skin pallid; he was not the colossal giant he had been when Lenny was a child. Fergus Sullivan was insignificant and probably always had been.

Maureen held tight to her sturdy walking stick, the rubber-covered end of which had provided the perfect leverage for pushing Fergus. Although Lenny doubted this would be used as one of the features in marketing the mobility aid. Between that and Malcolm's well-timed aggression, they'd thrown Fergus completely off balance and he'd not had a chance to catch himself.

Malcolm nudged at Maureen's right leg and she leaned onto her stick, letting her body sag. The look on her face was a mix of determination and exhaustion. Lenny worried she was about to collapse, but instead Maureen made her way—relatively steadily—down the steps to her son. Lenny herself felt unable to move. Her limbs were having trouble catching up with her brain. She was running a list of options through her head, some sensible and some not: call an ambulance, run, administer first aid, hide.

Maureen knelt down beside Fergus, groaning as her knees rested on the unyielding concrete pavers. She felt his neck and paused, waiting to find a pulse. Lenny watched her try again, shifting her fingers and waiting to register a heartbeat.

The angle of Fergus's neck was uncomfortable to look at. The way in which he'd fallen and the stillness of him told Lenny all she needed to know. It was done.

Maureen looked solemnly at Lenny and shook her head. The elderly woman shifted, with some effort, from her knees to a seated position at the bottom of the steps.

"I will take full responsibility for this," Maureen said quickly. "You just need to get me the phone—I don't think I'll get there on my own."

"It's not your fault," Lenny said.

"I didn't have to do that, I could've called the police, or gone back inside." Maureen was breathless. "Helena, I think you should go home. Pretend you weren't here."

And be a coward again.

Fay had always told her there were choices, even if none of them seemed desirable.

Your turn, Lenny.

"No. I'm not going to do that," Lenny said.

"What have I done?" Maureen whispered, staring at Fergus. "I shouldn't have done that, I was just so angry."

Lenny wondered if this was what shock looked like. She needed to get Maureen inside so she could collect her own thoughts.

"It will be all right," Lenny said, with unexpected confidence. "I will sort this out, Maureen."

Lenny knew she should go inside and phone the police. That was the *right* thing to do. The police would arrive in a flurry of noise, lights and activity, and the day would become long and tiring. She thought back to the tiny cry her little brother had made and how she'd let him down. She didn't get to say goodbye; Fergus had made sure of it. Maybe they could tell the police they'd found her stepfather just lying there. They could say he probably fell (which wasn't exactly a lie). The decking did get slippery in the wet and he could've been drinking. Or she could say it was self-defense. He was there, threatening them both and he was going to hurt them. He did have a knife. Maybe the police would accept their story, but then again maybe they wouldn't. It was a gamble.

If she made that call, nothing would be the same.

There was a difference between what she should do and what she could do. Fergus was past saving now and calling the police wouldn't change that. Lenny could sense what was on the horizon and she knew if she phoned them now, she would wish to be back at this very moment in order to make a different decision. For the boy she couldn't save years ago, and for the woman she now could.

Choices.

There was really only ever one.

Lenny had always been levelheaded and methodical but applying these traits to disposing of her stepfather's body was something else altogether.

Calmly, she walked Maureen up the stairs and into the house. Although her neighbor wasn't obviously injured, she was shaking and unsteady and this worried Lenny. But before she could properly sort out Maureen, she had to deal with the most pressing of their problems. Fergus. She could only leave him lying in front of Maureen's house for so long.

Lenny made Maureen comfortable on the couch. She got her a glass of water and her book. Malcolm took up watchman position at Maureen's feet and Lenny stroked his head appreciatively.

"You're wonderful, Malcolm," she murmured, pressing her face against his fur.

"What do you need me to do?" Maureen asked.

"Nothing, just rest."

Maureen's eyes were teary. "You're not calling the police, are you?"

Lenny shook her head. "I'll move him for now, but later when it's dark I'll take him somewhere else."

Maureen looked relieved but confused, and Lenny wanted to stay with her and keep her company. But there was not the time. Nor was it appropriate to call any of Maureen's friends to pop over and sit with her. This was not something Lenny could burden anyone else with.

She spotted the array of glass bottles resting on the end of the kitchen bench and reconsidered the glass of water. Lenny poured Maureen a finger of whiskey and one for herself while she was at it. The warmth radiating through her torso as she drank it was immediate. When Lenny passed Maureen the glass, her neighbor grabbed hold of Lenny's hand and held it firmly in her own cold one.

"I'm sorry, Lenny."

"I'm sorry too, about Fergus. He's your son and it shouldn't have come to this. He shouldn't have put you in that position."

Maureen took a deep breath, tilting her head back and inhaling deeply. Tears were rolling down her cheeks.

Lenny rubbed her back. "I'll come back as soon as I can."

Maureen nodded, but said nothing. Lenny's confidence was reassuring, even to herself.

"I need to borrow some things," Lenny said, not waiting for a reply as she grabbed what she needed. She picked up Maureen's hat and jacket and started moving down the hall with the empty wheelchair.

As she stepped outside, her phone chimed with a message from Fay. Paige and Skye needed emergency accommodation and she couldn't get back that night; Fay hoped Lenny didn't mind. It was a relief knowing Fay wouldn't be showing up at any moment. She was glad to know those two girls had Fay's warm house to go to; she'd monopolized her time enough and it was Lenny's turn to act like an adult. Besides, she didn't think her newfound boldness had the wherewithal to undergo Fay's scrutiny. Had Lenny believed in fate, which she didn't, she may have been inclined to think it was smiling upon her in that moment. Her plan felt like Tetris pieces dropping into place.

All she had to do, for now, was find a place for Fergus until night fell. Lenny went to her carport, found a tarpaulin and laid it out next to his body. In his jacket pocket she found his keys, but nothing else. She rolled him onto the tarp and used it to lever him into a better position to get him into Maureen's wheelchair. The struggle was twofold: he was incredibly heavy, and she hated being this close to him. The feeling he would suddenly lurch out from the tarp kept her working at a frantic pace. Lenny wanted distance from him as quickly as possible.

After her fourth attempt to move him, she stopped, sank onto her haunches and breathed out in what felt very much like defeat.

"Don't give up now."

Even though she had her eyes closed, Lenny knew exactly who was behind her.

"You shouldn't see this," Lenny said to Young Helena, and pulled the tarp over Fergus to cover him.

"You see it, I see it. It doesn't matter," Young Helena told her. "But you have to finish what you started."

"I'm twenty-five years late."

"You did your best." Young Helena shrugged.

"Or maybe I'm no better than him? Look at what I'm doing."

"I don't think you really believe that."

And she was right: Lenny didn't feel bad about Fergus no longer being able to walk around and hurt people. She felt weak and cowardly because Maureen had done what she could not, and she felt pathetic for not being able to move him.

"Just get on with it," said her younger self.

So she did.

It was awkward and he was heavy, but she just had to find the right angle to shift him. Action and reaction; it wasn't impossible.

Finally, he was loaded in and covered up and she pushed the wheelchair into the dense bushes. Lenny left the jacket and hat beside him; she would use them later.

Before she walked away, she stopped and watched the blue plastic cover intently, lest Fergus move in the slightest. Surely it wasn't so easy to slay a dragon.

Maureen had barely moved when Lenny went in to check on her; she hoped it hadn't all been too much for her. She couldn't lose Maureen.

"I shouldn't have done that, should I?" her neighbor said, more to herself than Lenny.

"He was going to hurt us," Lenny said. "And he would've. He didn't care if you're an eleven-year-old girl or his eighty-year-old mother."

Mother. It was still a shock.

Maureen was tapping her fingers against each other, as if they were keeping time.

"You should tell her," Young Helena said. Lenny hadn't realized she was still there.

"Tell her what?" Lenny asked.

"Tell me what?" Maureen echoed, rightfully confused.

"About what we did to Fergus back then. That it wasn't an accident."

"It wasn't an accident," Lenny repeated.

"What wasn't?" Maureen asked.

Lenny looked from her younger self to her neighbor.

What would happen if she said it out loud? And what did it matter?

She would let it out and deal with the consequences.

"The allergic reaction. I did it to him on purpose, and then I lied about it. To the police, when I was at court, to Zanny. Everyone."

"Oh, darling. You've carried that all this time?"

Lenny nodded.

"You were trying to protect them?" Maureen asked.

"I wanted to kill him."

Death: hated, hate

Maureen didn't reply and Lenny wondered if she'd said too much. Never before had she uttered the real story out loud and now she was telling Fergus's mother. But it was out now, the truth still spilling from her.

"I crushed up peanuts and put them in his burger. Mum was out, I was in charge of dinner and I was so angry at him. I didn't know she was making plans to leave. I didn't know she even wanted to.

"I hid his medication. I still have it, stashed inside a teddy bear, of all things. To remind me what drove them away. Because that's what I thought did it: he convinced Mum I was evil, and it was a choice between him or me."

"And you thought she chose him?"

"Yes, I did. She could live without me, but not without him."

"All these years, you believed that?"

"Yes. Because that way, she could still exist. Pretty messed up, aren't I?"

"No, I don't think that at all. You were a little girl. And you fought for the ones you loved. You are very brave, Lenny Marks."

Maureen's tears were back and Lenny realized she was crying too.

"But I failed. It didn't work, so I knew we had to leave. I packed our bags and waited," Lenny sobbed. "I didn't know she'd bring him home so soon. And he knew what I'd done to him, that it was on purpose. And then he realized I wanted to leave, and I wouldn't just go on pretending nothing was happening anymore. And maybe he knew that Mum would go too. So he stopped us all."

The release of so much information made Lenny sweat.

"If I had just left everything alone, maybe Malcolm and Mum . . ." Lenny couldn't finish her sentence.

Maureen pressed her lips together and used a tissue from her sleeve to wipe her eyes.

"This is not on you, Lenny." Maureen spoke with unwavering certainty. "He was the adult and he made the decision to resort to violence. Nothing you did made it happen."

The two women sat side by side on the velour couch, wiping their tears. Lenny was so grateful that Maureen hadn't shown disappointment or disgust at what she'd revealed. Even so, Lenny wasn't entirely sure she wasn't at fault. There was still responsibility she had to take for the chain of events she'd set off with that peanut-laced burger.

You did this.

He was right, she had.

CHAPTER 48

It was just on dusk when she decided it was dark enough to shift Fergus. Ideally it would've been even later, but Lenny didn't think her anxiety could stand waiting any longer.

She left her phone on Maureen's bench and gave her strict instructions not to answer the door or the phone.

"If anyone asks later about where we were tonight, tell them we were out for a walk," Lenny told Maureen.

Maureen nodded sagely as Lenny hurried out the door.

Considerable thought had been put into Lenny's plans, and in her head at least, they had come together very neatly. A couple of hours earlier, she had taken Fergus's car keys on a walk of the surrounding streets. She knew he was innately lazy and wouldn't have walked far, and she was right. His beaten-up utility vehicle was parked just a couple of streets away, in Wattle Grove.

After leaving Maureen, she stepped out into the cover of darkness, stopping only to retrieve Jase's green shopping bag from behind the hot water system at the Tree House. She'd not yet got around to burning it, but now it seemed it could serve a better purpose.

Returning to Fergus, she took the tarp off him and held her breath until she was sure he hadn't moved. He was slumped forward, the back of his head a matted mess where he'd collided with the fuchsia, but he was otherwise in the same position Lenny had left him.

Draping her stepfather in Maureen's coat and pulling the black velvet cloche hat onto his head, Lenny wheeled him up her steep driveway and into the quiet court. It didn't take long to get him back to his car, and there was no traffic out and about. Of this she was very glad.

It was far easier getting him into the bed of the pickup from the chair than it would have been from off the ground. Lenny assumed the term "dead weight" came from just such a scenario. She made sure she moved as quickly and quietly in the dark as she could, agitated by the thought a passerby would stop to say hello, or worse, offer to help her out. They wouldn't know what they were walking into, and then she'd be well and truly done for. Unseen—at least to the best of her knowledge—she hooked down the truckbed canopy and snapped shut the tailgate. She tucked Jase's bag of weed under the driver's seat. The stench was dulled a little, but not completely gone.

Lenny hid Maureen's jacket, hat and wheelchair in the trees. She would collect them later, on her way back. Fergus was parked across the entrance to a fire trail, which was a parking infraction, but it also meant they weren't outside anyone's house. This minimized the potential of being watched through someone's front curtains. Beyond that, it was out of her control.

In the center console, Lenny found Fergus's phone. It was switched off and she left it that way. He'd been up to no good from the start: hiding his car, turning off his phone, bringing a knife. The notion of his rehabilitation was a joke.

Fergus's car was a mess. A haphazard filing system of receipts and mail was wedged between the windscreen and the dash. Sausage roll wrappers and half-finished bottles of Coke rolled around in the passenger footwell.

There was no moon yet that night, making a heavy black curtain for Lenny to play out one of the major scenes in *Lenny Marks Gets a Life*. She'd title it "The One Where Fergus Goes to Hell."

Lenny took the driver's seat, hoping luck would stay with her and she wouldn't encounter a booze bus or any other reason to stop. Fergus's baseball cap was on the passenger seat. It was as horrendously unwashed as Jase's, but it gave her an idea. She slipped the cap on and pulled her hair under it. Maybe in the dark and from a distance, she'd get away with being Fergus.

Placing her hands on the steering wheel made her recall Robert and his never-ending patience as they drove through the Lilydale industrial park all those years ago. Those two little L-plates, front and back, like yellow Scrabble tiles. The memory of his gentle voice coaching her was incredibly vivid as she started the—thankfully—automatic car. The muscle memory remained, making the twelve kilometers to Macquarie Park Lake relatively simple.

Once in the car park by the lake, Lenny switched off the headlights and sat in the dark, waiting to see if she could hear or see anyone. Back when Lenny's family had lived over the fence from this park, they would hear teenagers drinking in the wee hours and all sorts of noises. It was rarely empty of people. Even the dog walkers were there at all times of the day; shift workers or insomniacs, or people dumping bodies perhaps. But for now, it didn't appear anyone else was around, another Tetris piece sliding neatly into place. Her impetus had faded slightly on the drive and she leaned back against the headrest of the car and took slow, measured breaths. Some more courage was required to see out her plan.

Revenge: renege, veneer, venge, verge, even

That would be what she'd put on a motivational poster: *REVENGE*.

Revenge will set you free.

"Do we move him to the front?" Young Helena asked.

Lenny's head shot up in surprise. "I didn't know you were there."

"I'm always here," the girl replied. "You have to move him—it won't look right if he's in the back."

Neither would the gratuitous head wound, Lenny thought, wondering how noticeable it would be that he'd fallen and hit his head and not accidentally launched himself into Macquarie Park Lake. She was counting on the water making everything seem a little less obvious. Perhaps if she'd watched more *CSI* and less *Friends* she'd have been much better prepared.

Now was not the time to back out, but panic was rising fast.

What have I done?

What am I doing?

Onward: adorns, rowans, dorsa, drown

Finished: fiendish, fished, inside, fiend

"You know what Robert always said. A job half done . . ." Young Helena waited patiently for Lenny to compose herself. How was the younger her so much more stoic and determined? At what point in her life had she lost those traits?

Lenny steeled herself, moved to the back of the utility vehicle and slid Fergus forward enough so she could get him into a piggyback position and move him to the driver's side. She grunted under his weight, glad to not have an overweight stepfather. The blood he left behind was a problem; it was caught in the channels in the truckbed, not to mention Lenny was covered in it. She would have to burn her clothes when she got home, which was not too much of a problem. As for the car, she could only hope the water would wash away enough to make it look like he'd done this himself, intentionally or not.

Lenny took Fergus's phone and wallet and zipped them into her parka pocket. She had the perfect place for them.

"Ready?" Young Helena asked.

"Yes," Lenny said.

The car park was naturally slanted toward the lake. It was, actually, a terribly dangerous spot, although Lenny had never thought of it this way before. Before today, her memories of the park were all good. Ice-cream vans, pushing her brother on the swings and pretending the heavily treed area was the T. rex enclosure in *Jurassic Park*.

Lenny leaned into the pickup and turned the ignition. As she did so, she heard Fergus gurgle. She jumped back from him as if she'd been burned. But he hadn't moved. His head was still slumped, his eyes closed. There was no doubt, though, of what she'd just heard.

You did this.

The girl caught her eye. "What is it?"

"I think . . . he's not dead," Lenny told her.

Lenny put her hand to his neck and heard him make the noise again. There was a faint but steady pulse. Maureen, she realized like a slap in the face, wouldn't have registered such a weak heartbeat through her numb fingers.

Heartbeat: breathe, bather, threat, beat, hate

He was still with them.

"Fuck," whispered Lenny into the cold night air.

CHAPTER 49

Saturday, July 16
Three days later

Lenny was in Maureen's front yard when Ned arrived. She wore her gardening jeans and Blundstones and was washing out her wheelbarrow with the hose, as Cordelia motored down her driveway. She wasn't expecting Ned, but it had been a frantic seventy-two hours so there was a possibility she'd forgotten any plans.

He clambered out of his van and Lenny called his name across the driveways, waving to him through the trees. She was quite sure she'd done well enough for Maureen's front yard to withstand scrutiny from anyone popping over for a visit. That Fergus had been there, for the first and last time, should no longer be readily evident.

"You've been busy," he said, his boots crunching over the gravel driveway.

"I forgot you were coming," she said, turning the water off.

It occurred to her that she would've liked to be looking a little less utilitarian when she saw Ned again. She was covered in cement dust, nails ripped and caked with dirt, and her grubby hair was pulled back. A range of odors emanated from the heavy work she'd been doing: sunscreen, sweat and grit at the very least. She tried to recall putting deodorant on that morning but couldn't.

"That's because you didn't know I was coming. Sorry, you look busy. But I really wanted to see you. This looks great," he said, gesturing to Maureen's front yard. "Did you do all this?"

"Yes, I did," Lenny said, casting her eyes around.

The pavers had absorbed Fergus's blood like a sponge and it could not be erased with any combination of chemicals that Lenny tried. They needed a plan B, so Lenny had decided it was high time Maureen had a ramp installed to her front verandah. She wouldn't always be able to manage the stairs, and what better opportunity to start a new project than covering up a crime scene.

Lenny was pleased with her efforts and glad to find Ned complimentary of them. In the preceding days she had ripped up the old paving stones and disposed of them by breaking them into barely more than loose stones. These she scattered along the rail trail and the shoulder of the main road, getting rid of them a bit at a time. She wanted them hidden in plain sight and didn't have the trailer—or the license—for a trip to the dump, which would also seem out of character. She'd never disposed of her rubbish there previously, and stacking blood-soaked pavers until the October hard-rubbish collection was not a viable option.

"I was after a new project and Maureen needed this installed."

"So you felt inclined to help?" Ned said.

"Yes, I did."

"Inclined, Lenny, you were *inclined* to help." Ned chuckled. "And it's a ramp. Get it, on an incline."

She relaxed, dropping her shoulders as she realized he saw nothing at all out of place.

"Right, yes. Inclined. Both willing to help or an actual slope."

"I've been told I shouldn't make dad jokes until I'm a dad." Ned shrugged.

Lenny was never clear on what constituted a dad joke as opposed to just a normal one. "Is a dad joke just a joke that's not very good?" she asked.

"Oh, snap," he said. "That's actually exactly what it is."

Lenny laughed; it was easy to relax around Ned.

"So, you did this all by yourself?" he asked.

"Of course—it's not hard. Just like a big jigsaw, I guess."

"Yeah, but no one is likely to break their neck on a jigsaw, which is probably what would happen if I put it together."

"Well, you should engage a qualified person in that case," she replied.

The ramp was finished but she was still putting the final touches on the handrails. She'd picked out a lovely cherry-colored merbau wood to match the decking and ensured the angle was amenable to Maureen wheeling herself up and down.

"It's always nice to do something with your hands," she said, thinking of Fergus and inspecting her dirty palms and nails. She'd scrubbed them almost raw after getting back from Macquarie Park Lake, but they'd not felt properly clean since.

"True that. Up for a cuppa?" Ned asked, holding up a paper bag with the Bakers Delight logo on it. "I brought morning tea."

"Good idea," Lenny said, wiping her wet hands down the front of her jeans.

Lenny looked up to Maureen's deck and noticed her neighbor sitting on the patio, watching them.

"Would you like one?" Ned yelled out to Maureen; Lenny didn't think the two had officially met yet.

"No thanks, love, about to head in for a nap. You kids enjoy," Maureen called back.

"Maureen, this is Ned McKnight, of McKnight's General Store," Lenny called.

"I know who he is—you're not the only one to shop there, Lenny."

"Good morning, Ms. Simcock," Ned called.

"Not to mention, I've been hearing all about you lately," Maureen added mischievously.

Lenny pinkened and dipped her head. She gestured to the Tree House, indicating Ned should follow her home.

That Maureen was Fergus's mother shouldn't have shocked her as much as it did. Now she thought about it, she could have easily pieced it together, but she'd never had reason to. It had been the topic of more than one conversation in the days since Fergus had visited.

Maureen had told Lenny about the immense shame she felt for her role in introducing Fergus to Tammy. She'd tried to find a way to forgive him and had reached out multiple times while he was in prison, but he remained manipulative and overbearing, even in letters and phone calls. It was hard for her to concede that her only son was irredeemable. Maureen gave up in the end; he'd taken so much already and he was wearing her down.

Looking after Susannah had been Maureen's focus after Lenny was removed from them. Maureen wasn't deemed suitable to take on the guardianship, although she told Lenny she'd tried, more than once. She only stopped when the battle seemed to be doing more harm than good to Susannah, who felt endlessly guilty over what she'd done, letting down both her daughter and granddaughter. Maureen's application may have been on firmer footing if hers and Susannah's relationship was legally recognized. But it wasn't, and Susannah still needed help and they could both see how Robert and Fay loved Lenny. It didn't fix losing her, but it did serve to cool the burn it caused.

"Why didn't she want me there?" Lenny asked Maureen.

"Why on earth would you think we didn't want you there?"

"The day I arrived . . . I remember hearing her. She said she didn't want me," Lenny said, her stomach churning. It was the first time she'd ever said this out loud. "She'd been somewhere, decisions were made and she was disappointed. Or mad. Or something."

"What do you mean? What did you hear?"

Lenny thought back, remembering what she'd heard. "That the decision was made even though Zanny tried to tell them she didn't want me."

Maureen considered long and hard.

"The day you arrived, Susannah had been at court. That's why she was late."

"She was at court? I thought she was just caught up?" Lenny said, now unsure if the words she had heard years ago were accurate at all. Her memory could be so fickle.

"It was Fergus's first court appearance and she wanted to go there, advocate for you, Malcolm and your mum. She was angry because no one even noticed her, or told her what was happening. Fergus was one of so many people they had in court that day and it was all so clinical. She wanted to say her piece, stand up and tell the judge what he'd done. Now we know it doesn't work like that, but back then she was furious."

"I thought she had other places she wanted to be," Lenny said.

"She had to be in both places, that was the problem. That's why I was there, so you weren't alone." Maureen paused there before continuing. "I know I wasn't your actual grandmother, but I was Mal's and it was such a painful time. I don't think either Susannah or I were sure we were doing anything right. We just knew we needed to get you settled and fight for Tammy and Mal too."

Lenny tried to reconcile what she'd heard with what Maureen was telling her. Had she actually heard Zanny say she didn't want her?

Misremembered: remembered, redeemers, immersed, remedies, simmered

"I heard her say I should be at home with my mother," Lenny said. Those words were still as clear as if they'd been said yesterday.

"And that's absolutely right. You should've been. But it was no longer a possibility. Fergus stole that from you, from all of us." Maureen's voice turned husky with emotion.

"I thought she didn't want me."

"You *were* wanted," Maureen told her, emphatically.

And Lenny believed her.

CHAPTER 50

"Do you mind if I have a shower?" Lenny asked when they got inside. Her skin itched with the layers of dirt and she didn't want to spread the mess further around the Tree House.

"Of course not. I'll make some tea," Ned said, reaching for her kettle.

It was odd seeing him navigate her kitchen with ease and she watched him for a moment, feeling a weird mix of emotions, the strangest being that she actually liked having him there. He was particularly jubilant and she wondered if there was a cause for his elation. Although he was, in general, an upbeat sort of guy. He flicked the switch on the kettle and hummed something quietly as he spooned tea leaves.

He looked up and caught her gaze. He gave her a wink and carried on humming. Blushing, she ducked into the bathroom, embarrassed at being caught. She wasn't usually a fan of winking but Ned made it (almost) endearing.

As she waited for the shower to heat up, it occurred to her that perhaps his buoyant mood was because he and Amy were back together. It was absolutely none of her business if that was the case, yet she knew about Kurt and perhaps Ned did not. That sort of made it her business, although she really didn't want to be accused—yet again—of outing Kurt as adulterous. But Ned was more than entitled to know this if he'd recommenced his relationship with Amy. In fact, it was her duty as his friend to tell him.

She tested the water temperature and stepped into the hot, fast flow of her shower.

Perhaps Ned had been asked to come and check up on her. The thought was both infuriating and miserable. But maybe it was just all too convenient that he wanted to be her friend now. In thirty-eight years she'd never had so many people interested in being around her. Kirra had mentioned he liked her, but now that Kirra, Fay and Maureen all knew each other, she doubted the veracity of this. They all wanted her to feel better and maybe they'd engineered it.

Even Fergus had said *we had to convince other kids to be friends with you.*

She washed frantically and roughly, trying to scrub away the thoughts that felt preposterous *yet possible.* Ned's niceness seemed altruistic. Which was a clue in itself. There must be something in it for him—what other reason could there possibly be? She would ask him outright; he would have to tell her the truth then. No more being a passive part of her own life: if something was going to happen in it, good or bad, she would be the driver of it. And if Ned had been coerced or paid or whatever to make her feel better about herself with kind words and flattery, he could take his faux friendship elsewhere.

She finished her shower. Lenny was ready to embrace people in her space—figuratively of course; she didn't want to be too close physically—but only on the proviso they were there of their own volition and not because Maureen or Fay had put them up to it. Perhaps they meant well, but enough was enough. She was allowed to live her own life. And she was ready to do just that. *The One Where Lenny Gets a Life.*

She walked into the kitchen and found Ned arranging croissants on a plate.

"I would have got the coconut finger buns, but a kid before me got the last one and it's poor form for a grown man to jump a seven-year-old for his morning tea."

She laughed and then stopped herself, annoyed he was so effortlessly charismatic. The accusations she'd lined up to fire at him in the bathroom now seemed flimsy.

"Plus, there's cameras and stuff, I'd never get away with it." Ned smirked and pushed the plate toward her with a flourish.

"You'd be surprised what you can get away with," she said.

"Spoken like a character from *The Godfather*," he replied, raising an eyebrow.

Godfather: father, forged, death, hate, rage

"Speaking of which." She started tentatively, unsure how to frame her accusation. "You being here . . ."

"Oh, sorry about arriving unannounced—I'll call ahead next time," he said. "Which reminds me, I should really get your phone number."

"No, it's not that."

Faltering: altering, triangle, feign, frail, fear

"You good?" he asked.

Tell him about Kurt. Ask him who sent him.

"Why are you here?" she said finally, unable to meet his eyes. She fixed her gaze on the teapot on the counter, a plume of steam rising from the spout. He'd even made a proper pot of tea.

"For morning tea?" he said, unsure. "And a chat."

He was a brilliant actor.

"Do you want to be here?"

"Yes," he replied, eyes darting around as if there was a prank being played.

She wasn't explaining herself at all well. "What I mean is, did someone ask you to come and check on me?"

"Well, yeah. I guess, in a way," he said.

"Who?"

"Fay said I should pop by. But—"

She cut him off. "That makes sense."

Fay. Of course: always well-meaning, but misguided just the same.

She crossed her arms over her chest and felt like she was underdressed, or exposed somehow; uncomfortable in her own house.

"Have I done something wrong?" he asked.

"I don't need your pity, Ned. Whatever brings you here, you can cancel it, or call it off, or whatever you need to do. I'm fine on my own."

He looked perplexed, but she was resolute.

"It is true I don't always pick up on the subtleties," he said. "But I really do think I've missed something here. What am I canceling? And can you explain it to me while I eat a croissant?"

He wasn't balking, which was confusing. She thought she'd have him on the hop, that she would have the upper hand by knowing what the next scene might be in advance.

"Fay. She sent you here to make me feel better about myself. Made some sort of arrangement with you. A deal, a payment in kind, a favor owed or something?"

"No. I sent myself here because I like coming to see you. And because I wanted to tell you I've sold my game. Fay told me it would be fine if I stopped by. What do you think this is?" he said, indicating both of them. "You think I've been paid to come here?"

It did sound ridiculous.

Her conviction was fading fast. If Ned hadn't been asked to embark on this friendship, or whatever it was, did that mean he was there and spending time with her purely because he wanted to? She wasn't sure which idea was more preposterous.

"Lenny," Ned said, fixing her with a serious stare, "sometimes people are just nice. Like you are."

We had to convince other kids to be friends with you.

She pressed her eyes closed and wondered if she could just go back to being by herself. At least if she was alone she wouldn't have to rely on anyone else. She could go back to her routine. She did really like the smell of him though, or maybe that was the fresh pastries.

"I need to protect myself," she told him, eyes springing back open.

"We all do," he replied. She would've preferred reassurance but appreciated the honesty.

"Do you want me to go?" he asked.

"I want you to go if you don't want to be here," she said, and crossed her arms over her chest. She felt childish doing it but was too stubborn to drop them down again.

"Not everyone in life is going to let you down, you know," he said.

"It's safer to assume people will."

"It may be safer, but it's a shit way to live."

"Well, it's got me through fine this far."

"Are you sure it's as fine as you say?" he asked.

"Ned, I don't think I have to tell you, I am probably not the easiest person to be around. I've got a bit going on."

"Sure, but you're not the Lone Ranger there."

"No, but it's probably easier not to complicate things."

He paused, thinking. She wondered if he was about to pack up his croissants and leave. If she was honest with herself, which she was reluctant to be, she really wanted him to stay. She didn't want *Lenny Marks Gets a Life* to end up as a tragedy.

"Do you wish you could off-load Malcolm?" he asked.

"No," she answered quickly. "Why would I?"

"Because he's got problems. He has all this stuff that happened to him previously and probably will never forget it. I mean, he's probably more trouble than he's worth."

"That's an awful thing to say—none of that is his fault. I wouldn't change a thing about him."

"Exactly right," Ned said, leaning forward to take a large bite from his croissant. Pastry flaked down his shirt, but it didn't wipe the triumphant smile from his face. "You can't change your past, you can only accept someone as they come. I can sit here and tell you what a good guy I am, because I *actually am*. But I bet that's what every asshole in history has said. You decide for yourself, but if you think there's some sort of deal, bet, or weird setup that brings me here, just forget it. I mean, who does that? No one does that."

Words were just words, although they were some of the most important things in Lenny's existence. Fergus had all the words. He could convince her mum of anything, and routinely had: that his drinking wasn't a problem, that he only hit her because she made him, that Lenny tried to kill him.

People could be bad and they could hide it well. Like her.

But this was Ned. *Ned*. She tried to reassure herself of his kindness, his magnanimity, and how nice it felt to be in his company.

Magnanimity: maintain, inanity, taming, mating, mania

"And I've been practicing my Scrabble and I'd be really annoyed if I didn't get a go with you to see if I'm any good."

Lenny didn't reply, largely because she wasn't sure quite *what* to say outside of taking back the last five minutes of neurotic accusations.

"Or I can go," he said.

"Okay."

"Okay go? Or okay stay? You know a lot of words, don't scrimp on them now," he quipped.

"Stay. Play," she said, minimizing words and hoping he'd understand her attempt to lighten the mood.

He was very pleasant to look at. It suddenly felt very special to have him in her house, and she wanted to eke out their time for as long as possible. And then she recalled his earlier announcement. Ned moved to the dining table and slid open the Scrabble set.

"Ned, your game! You said you sold it, I'm so sorry I glossed over that."

He looked pleased she'd remembered and not at all disappointed it had taken her so long to ask. She felt guilty nonetheless.

"Doesn't matter. It's early days: they've made an offer; I've accepted. Contracts are to be drawn up and official stuff like that, so presumably the rug could be pulled out from under my smug feet at any moment."

"Surely they'd have to honor a commitment, even in its preliminary stages?" she replied.

"Yeah, well, there is that, I suppose. I'm just trying not to put the cart before the horse."

"And the game is the cart?" she asked, because she was unsure he'd chosen the correct proverb. "Or are you the cart?"

He paused while he worked it out. "The deal is the cart."

"Well, in any case, I'm pleased for you. I have no doubt your game is excellent and you've certainly put the hard work in. You really deserve this."

"And Dad is slowly getting his head around it. It's not bricks and mortar so he thinks it's unstable and irresponsible to bank my future on it. But honestly, Lenny, I would sooner gouge both my

eyes out than commit to a lifetime of suburban supermarket man-
agement."

"That's a little drastic," she said. "But let me know when the
time comes to move small, sharp objects from your reach."

He grunted a laugh while handing a tile rack to her and setting
his own up so it neatly aligned with the straight edge of the Scrabble board.

"Oh, and Dad also mentioned some 'mouthy little lady'—his
words, not mine—told him he needed to pull his head in."

"Oh." Lenny blushed. "That's not quite what I said."

"I knew it was you." He laughed. "And I appreciate it. Going
in to bat for me, that takes some guts. It was a good reminder, too.
Sometimes doing the easy thing isn't always the fun thing."

"I don't think that's quite the way the saying goes."

"No, it's not. But it applies here." Ned flashed his exceptionally
charming smile. "Seriously, thank you."

Feeling the need to be more congratulatory, Lenny stood and
walked around the table. She leaned down to wrap her arms around
Ned, in what was meant to be a celebratory embrace. But given the
way he was leaning onto the table and that she'd delivered the hug
without forewarning, it was altogether graceless and didn't have the
spontaneous warm vibe she'd hoped for. It could be safely described
as ungainly.

"Ah, well done," she said, releasing him as he tried to turn to
face her. She hurried to the kitchen bench.

Graceless: largesse, classer, resales, clears, lesser, grace

"I'll get something a little more special than tea," she said, turning her back to him so her embarrassment could subside.

Awkwardly: wayward, darkly, wary, wry

Taking a deep breath, she poured some of the remaining port
into tumblers and took them back to the table.

"I'm sorry, it's all I've got," she said as she sat down.

"It's perfect, it should warm the cockles." He clinked his glass against hers and took a sip.

"B," she announced, hoping to move on from her attempt at affection. She busily straightened her small wooden rack.

He selected his starting tile next.

"T. You're already ahead."

"Well, going first does give me a slight advantage, however, that is based on everything else being equal. And, well . . ." She stopped, realizing she was about to sound offensive.

"They're not," he finished. "I'm in the minor leagues, I know."

"Sorry." She blushed. "I've been doing this a long time."

"Teach me the ways, Grasshopper."

"Grasshopper?"

"David Carradine? *Kung Fu?*"

"I have no idea," Lenny admitted.

"Oh, then I have things to teach you too," he said, shooting her a smile she didn't want to read into, but sensed chapters behind.

She counted out her tiles and started to arrange them in alphabetical order, as she always did in the first instance. She quickly saw *besiege*, but decided to hold off on using all seven tiles this early in the game. She needed to give Ned a fighting chance.

He was murmuring as he picked his first seven letters, and she was surprised to hear the words he was humming. After he'd mentioned he used "She's Like the Wind" when overwhelmed, she'd listened to it on multiple occasions. It didn't have the same effect on her, but she did quite like the tune. Without wanting to be presumptuous, did hearing him sing it mean he was nervous in her company? She didn't think it was possible that someone could feel that way around Lenny Marks.

He pushed the tile bag back into the center of the table.

"You don't need to be nervous around me," she said, not daring to look at him. "Of all people."

He paused and she said no more, feeling she'd overstepped.

"I like you, Lenny," he said.

She couldn't help but look up at him then. "I feel the same about you, Ned."

"That's not the like I meant."

She felt the way she often did in Ned's presence, as if there were something wrong with her esophagus.

"I think I understand the implication." She considered that perhaps Amy was right: her intentions toward Ned weren't entirely platonic.

She placed *besiege* on the board, deciding it was best to be herself around him. She needed to practice being much more honest with the people in her life—to a certain extent anyway. Once the final "e" was done, she slid her hand across the table and let her little finger press up against his.

"I like you too," Lenny said.

CHAPTER 51

Friday, July 22

Ned was taking her on a date. "Date" was how he described it. It would never have been her choice of words. Far too bold and suggestive.

They were going to a small family-run winery on the outskirts of the Dandenongs that served tapas and, of course, wine. McKnight's stocked the family's wine in both stores and they had insisted Ned come and visit to try the wares. The idea of a lunch date was lovely despite it having her in conniptions for the two days since he'd mentioned it. She hadn't even been to Fay's house in Ringwood lately; the drive to Seville may as well have been to Irkutsk, Russia.

But maybe it was time.

It was time for a lot of things. Life had changed irrevocably since Fergus had turned up next door. And despite what had unfolded, Lenny felt buoyant. If Heather's claims had any real merit (and she still wasn't entirely sure) and there had been a blockage, it appeared to be gone.

She'd even agreed to see a psychologist. Lenny had announced it out of the blue, causing Fay to nearly fall off her stool. Despite the surprise, Fay didn't hesitate and immediately booked her an appointment lest she change her mind. Two visits later and she'd certainly not hated it.

Lenny got herself ready for Ned's arrival far too early. She was nervous and wanted to be prepared, slipping on Kirra's dress because it seemed like the perfect thing to wear. As she'd expected it was too short for her to feel comfortable, but after pairing it with black tights and her ankle boots she was actually quite pleased with how it all came together. It was hardly cutting-edge fashion, but it was a big day of color for Lenny Marks. The shift dress and her now shoulder-length hair (she was still planning to revert to her usual bob at her next Just Cuts appointment) gave her a look that was distinctly non-matronly. Almost, if she did say so herself, pretty.

She put on a *Friends* episode to calm herself down. It worked wonderfully, until she heard Cordelia arrive and then her butterflies turned into Atlas moths.

"Sorry I'm early, I just really wanted to see you," he said.

"That's fine, come in," she replied.

"Oh, wow. Look at you." He eyed her up and down.

"It's not too much?"

"It's the exact right amount of everything. You look great."

She smiled, relieved.

Malcolm came to greet Ned and sniffed eagerly at the hem of his pants.

"I'll bring Rosie for a visit next time, okay, buddy?" Ned spoke to Malcolm as if he expected a reply.

"Should we go now, or should I get you a drink of something?" Lenny felt fidgety and a little unsure of herself.

"No rush, we have some time. But there was something I wanted to do first." Ned approached Lenny until he was exceptionally close. She froze, thinking a spider was on her, or he was about to dust some of Malcolm's hair from her dress. Neither was the case.

"You hugged me the other day, but I wasn't prepared for it. Thought maybe we could have a redo?" he said.

"That would be nice," she said, not moving an inch. Thankfully Ned did the rest, pulling her into his chest. He felt warm and comfortable, like slipping on thick woolen socks. It was so incredibly simple yet intimate she shuddered.

"Are you okay?" he asked.

She nodded, still pulled in close to him and unable to form words to say she absolutely was okay, and not just in the way she used to mean it.

He leaned back and moved his face closer to hers, then closer again, giving her plenty of time to stop him if that was what she wanted. But she didn't want to. And then he kissed her. It made a warmth flood through her from her mouth to her thighs. It was like the rush of freewheeling her bike down a hill, but so much more than that. She didn't want him to let her go.

But then he did, pulling away and studying her, his arms loosely draped around her and a contented smile forming.

"You know, this line right here is one of my favorite things about your face." He brushed the tip of his index finger across the top of her lip. The soft touch of his skin on hers was thrilling. "And I got you something," he said, breaking their embrace.

He pulled a parcel wrapped in brown paper out of his jacket pocket and handed it to her. It was distinctly book-shaped.

"Saw this and I knew you had to have it."

"Thank you, you didn't need to get me anything," she said, stumbling over the gratitude—it never came naturally.

"No I didn't, you're right," he said. "Open it. You may already have this one, but I thought it was worth the gamble."

Lenny ripped back the corner of the brown paper to expose a cover she knew all too well. *The Hobbit.*

"I know you have a million, but I wanted to make it a million and one," he said proudly.

"Thirty-six actually. This is thirty-seven. I do have a similar copy, but"—she flicked open the book to the copyright page and her eyes scanned for the publication date—"I don't have this one."

Lenny loved that he understood thirty-six copies may not have been enough.

"It's perfect, I absolutely love it," she said and took it directly to the bookcase, wondering if she should rearrange them then and there or just add it into their current order. Her mind scrambled with the choices, a delightful predicament to be in.

"Hey, Len," Ned said, looking through the newly replaced glass door panel. "There's a cop car here."

CHAPTER 52

"Helena Winters?" asked the female police officer when Lenny opened the door. Although she was the first to speak, she stood farther back than her male counterpart.

Despite them not being in uniform it was clear they were police—and not only because of the blue and red lights on the car in the driveway. Their stance, demeanor and the bulge at their waists where their equipment sat concealed by heavy coats all screamed law enforcement.

"Not for a long time. It's Marks now," Lenny replied.

Her toes clenched and unclenched in her boots.

She'd expected this, but not with Ned in the house. And perhaps not this soon. It didn't seem like a good sign.

"Lenny?" Ned asked. "All good?"

Breathe, Lenny. You don't know what they're here for.

"I'm not sure. Police, I presume?" Lenny said, wanting the visitors to explain themselves.

Breathe, Lenny. You've lied before, you can do it again.

"Ah, yes," the woman said, and they both lifted their IDs from where they hung around their necks. It was an almost synchronized movement: lanyard up, forward, down.

"Detective Sergeant Rania Crew."

"John Wiltshire."

They spoke like they'd practiced their introductions.

"We're here about your stepfather," the female detective—Crew—said. "Can we come in?"

"If you have to." Lenny realized the question wasn't actually a question. "We have to leave soon. I don't have long."

"This is important, Ms. Winters," Detective Wiltshire said.

"Marks," Lenny replied and held the door open for them.

What do they know?

She didn't feel particularly hospitable and didn't want to make either detective too comfortable. Being overly accommodating might imply something like guilt. But then again, so might forced cheerfulness, not enough tears or lack of grief. This was not an easy situation to navigate, but she certainly wasn't about to offer them tea.

"What's happened?" Lenny asked once the four of them stood stiffly in the lounge room.

"Should I give you some time?" Ned asked.

"I don't know," Lenny said. "Does he need to go?"

"I don't know who he is," Crew replied. "But you can stay, if Ms. Marks is happy with that."

"Lenny, everyone calls me Lenny. Unless you're one of my students."

Ned sat on the couch and let Malcolm climb up beside him. Despite the circumstances, Lenny took the moment to appreciate how lovely it was seeing her dog and Ned getting along.

Lenny said nothing; if they were waiting for her to start the conversation, they hadn't counted on Lenny playing the silent game better than anyone.

Crew broke the ice. "Your stepfather was released from prison not long ago." *Breathe.*

"Have you spoken to him? Seen him?"

"No. I don't think so."

"You don't think so?" Crew replied quickly.

"I'm not sure I'd recognize him if I saw him, and I haven't spoken to anyone who has identified himself as Fergus Sullivan over the phone. But there's always the possibility, I suppose."

"That's an odd answer, Ms. Marks," Wiltshire said. Although Lenny knew he meant she just seemed odd in general. Which was fine; it actually made for pretty good cover.

"Do you know who he was living with?" Crew asked.

"No."

"Or where?"

"No."

"We have reason to believe he's been in Belgrave since being released."

Lenny waited and thought back to her long-ago appearance in court: only answer a question, don't elaborate, don't fill the silences.

"He appeared to hold quite a grudge toward you." Crew opened her folder. "Mind if I sit?"

Lenny nodded and sat opposite Detective Crew at the dining table. The detective pulled a pen from the folder. There were plenty of scrawled words already on the lined pages in front of her.

"Where were you, Ms. Marks, on the thirteenth of July?" Crew asked, a question unlikely to ever have been delivered without an accusation attached.

"Here, I'd imagine. I haven't gone far lately."

"We understand you've been off work?" Crew said, although she seemed to know the answer.

"Yes, I'm on long service leave."

Wiltshire spoke, still standing a distance away, despite there being room at the table for him to sit. "Makes it conveniently difficult to trace your movements."

"Or easier? I have barely left the house. I've been here or next door."

"And which neighbor is that you mean?" Crew asked, the pen making a pleasant scratching noise as it traveled across the paper.

Do they know it's Fergus's mum?

"Maureen. Over there." Lenny pointed at the house through the trees.

"Ah, Ms. Simcock, formerly Maureen Sullivan. Fergus's estranged mother," Wiltshire said. He wasn't taking notes, just watching her closely, arms folded across his chest.

"Yes, that's right."

What do they know?

"You knew that?" he questioned.

"Yes."

"Odd coincidence you ended up next door."

"No. It's not. My grandmother organized it that way." Lenny kept it succinct.

"Right, I see." The male detective did not seem convinced, but of what Lenny wasn't sure. Living next door to Maureen was just as she'd told them: not a coincidence, perfectly explainable and not at all illegal.

"Should I be worried? Might he come here?" Lenny asked, changing tack.

The detectives both assessed her. Lenny wished she wasn't in the bright shift dress; it could mislead them to assume she was an attention seeker.

"No. I wouldn't think so," Wiltshire said. "He's dead."

CHAPTER 53

Wednesday, July 13
At the lake

"We could call an ambulance. Or even just leave him here," Lenny said, brain scrambling. "Someone might find him."

"You *could* do that." Young Helena shrugged.

"He's not dead."

"He's not really alive though, is he?"

Now, if they did something to him it would be outright wrong. Before, while he was threatening them, it seemed justifiable. Self-defense.

He posed no threat whatsoever right now—but should she really be taking justice into her own hands?

Maybe she could just tell the police the truth, or part of it. Fergus had come to demand money from Maureen and wouldn't leave when asked. He'd had a knife with him and they were in danger. Only, what would she tell them: that he fell, or that he was pushed? And surely he would be in trouble for something—the threats, the knife, a parole breach maybe? But if not, what then? He said Lenny came to him. Her fault *again*. By not calling the police back at Maureen's when they could, it didn't look good for them. Now, with his pickup pointed directly at Macquarie Park Lake and no good reason for being there other than the obvious, Lenny was running out of viable options.

There was no easy return journey on this slippery slope.

Lenny's mind scrambled. She wanted to scream but instead buried her face in her hands, pushing her palms against her eye sockets.

Fergus made another noise, more definite this time. *More alive.* If they sought help now, he may have a chance. Or if they weren't going for help, they really needed to act soon. The longer they waited, the greater the chance of being seen.

Or at least, the greater the chance of Lenny being spotted, seeing as she'd been talking to a figment of her imagination. She supposed she'd have a good shot at an insanity defense, if it came to that.

She had a choice to make and she was running out of time.

Fergus in the world, or Fergus out of it.

And that was how the decision was made.

"A job half done is as good as none," Lenny said, knowing her foster father was unlikely to have had such a scenario as this in mind.

Young Helena nodded and Lenny leaned into the car, put her foot on the brake and clicked the car into drive. She lifted her foot and watched the truck make its way toward the lake. A slow movement at first, which became faster as it rolled downhill and into the water. It all happened slower than Lenny had imagined. She thought the vehicle would be sucked into the murky water like a vacuum. But it bobbed and floated and there was a moment of panic when she feared it wouldn't sink.

Mesmerized, Lenny watched the car, imagining Fergus appearing, spluttering, out of the water. But there was no such eruption. There was a gushing sound of water making room to pull the car in. Lenny pictured a snake slowly swallowing a small animal, sliding into oblivion.

It was done.

Lenny took Fergus's hat off her head and threw it toward the lake as if it were a Frisbee.

There was no shame or guilt. Instead, she felt lucid and wired. No one would think she was capable of this. She was the unlikely Ms. Marks, grade five teacher at Selby South Primary School. The woman whose most outrageous move, as far as anyone knew, was to down six wines at a suburban trivia night. She was a renowned truth-teller, honest to a fault. She was only conceivably deadly on a Scrabble board.

She would get away with this and the thought made her break out in a cold sweat.

CHAPTER 54

Friday, July 22

"He's dead?" Lenny repeated. That got Ned's attention; he looked like he wanted to come to her, but was unsure what the protocol was.

"Yep," Wiltshire said.

"Good," Lenny replied.

"Some might think that's a bit harsh, Ms. Marks."

"*Some* might not have had their family murdered by him," Lenny replied, meeting the stern detective's gaze. It took considerable effort not to break it first.

"Lenny." Detective Sergeant Crew interrupted the silence, perhaps remembering their good cop, bad cop roles. "We are just trying to iron out any concerns, follow his movements."

"Are you suggesting I'm a concern?" Lenny asked.

Crew almost looked apologetic. "Well, no. But we do have reason to believe he'd been in the local area. Quite a few times since his release, in fact."

"Why would he be here?" Lenny asked. The *quite a few times* caused genuine curiosity; had he been watching Maureen? Or her? Maybe it was no surprise to him to find her living close by after all.

"We don't know. We spoke to his partner—she was in the dark about what he did during the day. She was of the belief he went to work," the female detective explained. "But we can't find any proof he had a job."

"He was a good liar," Lenny said.

"People change though," Wiltshire chipped in.

"If you think so."

"Don't you?" he replied.

"Have you heard the tale of the frog and the scorpion?" Lenny asked, not recognizing the calmness of her own voice. Although if she had been wearing a heart-rate monitor, it would have exploded.

"Is it on Netflix?" Wiltshire asked, chuckling.

"No, I wouldn't think so. It's about certain instincts being irrepressible. Fergus can't help himself, it's in his nature to hurt others."

She didn't mention the scorpion drowned in the end; it sounded far too sinister given Fergus's fate and she reminded herself to be careful what she said.

Crew coughed and brought Lenny's attention back to her. "We'll have to prepare a brief for the coroner, so we'd like to get as much information as we can from the get-go."

"How did he die?" Lenny asked.

He drowned.

"His car was seen floating in Macquarie Park Lake by a dog walker. It appears he drowned. Do you know that park?"

"We used to live near there," Lenny said. "We went there often."

I never realized what a perfect place it was to dispose of a body until last week.

"Did he do it to himself?" Lenny asked.

"We don't know, hence the inquiries," said Wiltshire.

"It's possible he did," Crew said, shooting a look at Wiltshire. "But also it's possible it was an accident. He left home quite upset after a fight with his partner and was worried his parole was going to be revoked. He may have decided enough was enough."

"He was hitting her?" Lenny asked.

"What makes you say that?" Wiltshire replied quickly.

"Why else would he be worried about his parole being re-voked?" Lenny shot back just as quickly. Two could play that game.

"We can't divulge that," Wiltshire replied.

But they'd already told her enough.

"We found some of Mr. Sullivan's belongings at a house nearby. His phone and wallet. Do you know of any associates of his in Belgrave?" Crew asked.

"I haven't seen him for over twenty years. I don't know anything about him."

Lenny thought of the night by the lake. She'd jogged the entire way home, fueled by adrenaline and Young Helena keeping pace alongside her. It was nice to have her there, even if she was merely a projection of Lenny's mind. Perhaps it should have bothered her more, but given she'd just drowned her stepfather it seemed to pale into insignificance. They made one stop before going back to retrieve Maureen's wheelchair. Lenny returned to Jase's front yard, slipping through a gap in the fence as quietly as she'd done weeks earlier to liberate Malcolm. Only this time she was leaving something behind. She switched Fergus's phone on and dropped it, along with his wallet, inside the broken microwave on the front porch. She was glad to see the kennel sitting empty; perhaps Jase had decided caring for pets wasn't for him.

"This is a lot of the same book," Wiltshire said, running his fingers across her *Hobbit*s and removing one of the copies. He was knocking them out of alignment with his indelicate hands.

"Or just the right amount," Ned said.

Wiltshire shot Ned an indecipherable look.

Lenny was ready for them to leave and wondered how suspiciously they would view being hurried out the door.

"Where's your dog from?" Crew asked, as if something had come to mind.

Lenny hesitated. If they had Fergus's things that meant they'd been to Jase's house. Would he have told them about the strange woman who stole his dog, then his cannabis, and was possibly setting him up? Would it occur to him?

"He was a stray that wouldn't go away. Not microchipped, so I kept him."

Malcolm was on noticeboards all over Belgrave; maybe Crew had recognized him.

Lenny waited.

Don't fill the silence.

"My mum breeds Rotties, has done for years. I just thought he may have been one of hers." Crew smiled and shrugged.

Lenny wanted to hug the detective, who didn't appear to be investigating a suspicious death after all. It seemed she just needed to tick Lenny off her list and file her paperwork. A cold shudder washed over Lenny. Maybe Detective Sergeant Crew knew justice came in many different forms.

CHAPTER 55

Sunday, September 10

It was bitingly fresh when Lenny woke up in the Tree House. The night before, she and Ned had been out for dinner in Olinda to celebrate his contract signing. "Marauders of Titan" was in the hands of an international company and production would soon be underway. Ned was teaching her the rules, which were incredibly complicated, but she loved his enthusiasm and was slowly managing to get her head around it.

Lenny still preferred Scrabble.

She was comfortable where she was. In the Tree House, in her bed, with Ned beside her and Malcolm on his blanket pile. It was almost inconceivable how much had changed in such a short time.

Twelve weeks ago, she had pedalled out of Selby South Primary in a whirlwind of confusion, and now finally the days seemed easier. Fay put this down to the medication and counseling, but Lenny knew better. Everything had changed when Fergus's truck hit the lake. It had freed her.

The One Where Lenny Marks Gets Away with Murder.

The police hadn't been back and she didn't expect they would be. She was surprised at how little time and energy she gave that concern. She hadn't seen her younger self again either, not since returning from the lake, out of breath and completely wired. Young Helena had disappeared somewhere near Maureen's house and she wasn't sure if she'd see her again. Perhaps she'd served her purpose. Although Lenny suspected it might be that she just didn't need her anymore. It was liberating to know she could be strong when she had to be.

Ned stirred beside her, but didn't wake. It was a curious thing to have him there, in her bed, in her house. She hoped Fay wouldn't drop in early, which was an absurd thing to worry about, your mum catching you with a man in your bed in your late thirties. Fay would probably be thrilled and make them both a full English breakfast.

The skin around her lips felt tender from Ned's facial hair pressing against it. Ned was nothing like Damon Hughes in his university apartment. She'd had no idea what she'd been missing out on.

There was one thing still bothering her though, and she knew it was time to deal with it. Lenny quietly climbed out of bed.

She went to Errol, Malcolm's bear, but before that Lenny's, and her mother's prior to that. He wore a dapper three-piece green velvet suit and was missing an eye, an affliction of every well-loved teddy, or so it seemed. She squeezed Errol tight and felt the lump inside him.

Secrets: resects, crests, esters, recess, tree, sect

The remaining eye of the bear watched her passively. He had seen a lot, old Errol. Dust was embedded in his velvet-clad shoulders. It made a sneeze rise, but she sniffed it away. She flipped him over and felt down the seam in his back until she found the gap she knew was there. Digging into the stuffing she let her fingers grab hold of the cylinder and draw it out. The EpiPen. Still in the spot she'd hidden it on the long-ago Monday afternoon when she'd tried to kill her stepfather the first time.

At first she kept it so no one would accidentally stumble upon it. She didn't want Fergus to be proven right. That was before she wiped what had happened to her family from her mind. And then after the trial, when she'd compartmentalized things to survive, she'd kept it as punishment. Because she could never quite shake what she did.

You did this. Fergus Sullivan was right all along. She had caused it. She'd started it all. Whether it was their deaths or them leaving her, either way the result was the same and she was culpable.

Accountable: atonable, conceal, unable, alone, able

But she'd never admit it again and Maureen hadn't mentioned it since.

She wished she felt guiltier about what she'd done to Fergus, both by the lake and many years ago when she'd originally set out to rid him from their lives. Lenny couldn't bear to imagine how different life would be if she'd been successful the first time. And yet she didn't regret trying, she regretted failing. And those thoughts made her feel like a monster; it made her think she was a lot more like Fergus than she wanted to be.

It was why she had needed the almost-truths. The little lies and the omissions were what had made being Lenny Marks possible. By imagining her mum had walked away from her, Tammy could still exist. And by turning Malcolm into an imaginary friend, Lenny could survive the unthinkable.

She didn't believe in ghosts, but her neck prickled at the thought of her mum, brother and grandmother watching her. Did they know she'd finally done it? That twenty-five years later she finished what she'd set out to do in the kitchen that day? She hoped they knew.

If she could, she would hug little Helena Winters tight and take the pain and guilt from her. She didn't need to save anyone; she'd only been eleven. *Eleven*. She was meant to be reading books, skinning her knees. Her biggest concern should have been when she could get her ears pierced or if her bike tires were pumped up. She couldn't fix what Young Helena had gone through, but she could decide enough was enough. That she'd served her penance; it was time to move on, move forward, live her life.

Lenny pushed her face into Errol's fur, which smelled of dust and little else. She wiped her tears with one of the bear's paws.

She may not have *actually* been happy before, but now she understood certain things about that word so she could live inside it exactly as she pleased. Whether Lenny's life was confined to a suburb, or spanned the world, it was of no relevance. It was what filled her small, impossible, irrelevant space that was important. And she got to choose what she allowed in her tiny piece of real estate.

Which wasn't Fergus. He wasn't welcome there anymore.

Lenny realized she was shivering and wondered how long she'd sat there with Errol. The sun was properly up now and the day was beginning.

She looked at Errol and he eyed her back, with his one black, glossy button eye. He was good at keeping secrets, and so was she.

She held the EpiPen in her hands and turned it around and around. What she couldn't change, she would forget. What she couldn't forget, she would come to terms with.

You did this.

Yes, I did. And I'd do it again.

Lenny walked to the kitchen, threw the EpiPen in the rubbish bin and went back to bed, where she crawled into the space between Ned and Malcolm.

The One Where Lenny Marks Gets a Life. It was her favorite episode yet.

ACKNOWLEDGMENTS

This book was written and set during the COVID-19 pandemic. This is a time we will all remember with a range of emotions. I read to escape and so have not acknowledged that the pandemic is changing people's lives on a daily basis at this time. While Lenny Marks would've been a fan of the isolation, she would not have been going to work or trivia nights, and would not have been able to visit Fay. So, I decided to leave COVID-19 out of this book—which makes it historically incorrect but, as a work of fiction, probably just fine.

First and foremost, thank you to my book club, where I remembered how much I love reading, and in turn found out how much I love writing. They are an awesome bunch of ladies who will have been meeting monthly for about nine years by the time this book hits shelves. And I have no doubt they will not hold back in their reviews just because I'm the author. They are notoriously brutal, but have also become a little predictable. I imagine the following will occur: Bec won't have finished it; Lou without makeup will have a few choice swear words to say about it; Richo won't think there's enough crime in it; Megan will say "I told you so" because she did actually tell me to write a book a long time ago; Dee will score it 2.5 out of 5; Janine will be hilarious and drinking gin; Kush will be furious at Fergus; Lou with makeup will love the love in it; and Elaine . . . actually, I can never pick where Elaine's reviews will go. Anyway, you're a fantastic bunch of people who do not take my rules at all seriously. I really hope you like my book.

Book club was also my introduction to the glorious author Sally Hepworth, who is smart and clever and ever so generous with her time. She inadvertently issued me a challenge, which was "Just do it, then" in response to my mindless musings of "I'd love to write a book." Challenge accepted, Sally. Thank you to the wonderful Lisa Ireland. Knowing you and Sally has been wonderful and incredibly helpful. You are both excellent people, not to mention talented writers, who have bestowed many kindnesses upon me. What a duo to have in my corner.

Lenny's first readers: my mum Heather, Dee "Wifey" Burton, Alice "Oracle" Campbell, Lauren "Boombox" Savage, Louise Dewar, Megan MacInnes, Andria Richardson and Gary Mayne. Thank you all for being honest, but kind.

Thank you to my publisher, Beverley Cousins, for taking a chance on Lenny and me, even if you later "metaphorically bludgeoned" me. Honestly, I couldn't have been bludgeoned by a nicer person. Thank you also to Amanda Martin and Sonja Heijn, for making Lenny better than I could've on my own and for telling me where to put my semicolons. Thank you Bella Arnott-Hoare and Kelly Anne Jenkins, for letting me waffle when I came to meet you and for your support since. You didn't even laugh at me for having my top on backward.

To everyone else at Penguin Random House Australia, for making my book into an actual book—it's a dream come true, and I am still not sure how I got here.

To my agent Elaine Spencer at the Knight Agency: you are the reason Lenny Marks is traveling farther than I ever thought possible, and saying thank you is certainly not enough, but it's a start, so thank you!

To Sarah Grill and the team at St. Martin's Press, a bazillion (is that a real word?) thank-yous! I look forward to meeting you all in person one day so I can hug you all in a very un-Lenny-like manner. Thank you for taking my quirky heroine from a forest on the other side of the world and putting her in the hands of many readers. This is the stuff of author dreams.

I have a lovely bunch of friends and despite assuming people would laugh at me when I said I was writing a book, no one did. They were, in fact, incredibly supportive. I don't want to leave anyone out, but do have some special mentions: Mardi Wysman-Blunt for answering my questions about teachers, Brendan Nolan for talking about frogs and scorpions and making me more resilient to heckling, Colin Burton for your ridiculous love of board games (I'd never known what a meeple was before you came along) and Amy Bazely for lending the bitchy character your name (not based on *all* of your traits).

Mum and Dad—Heather and Keith—thanks for everything. You know, life and all that up until now. Dad was never much of a reader and very unlikely to have read this book. However, I do think he would've proudly owned a copy or three.

Thanks to Gary and our many children (really just four, but they do outnumber us) for making my life and days full. There's no one I'd prefer to be woken in the early hours by. I mean, preferably, no one would wake me at all. But if it has to be done it should be by one of you. I love your imaginations and questions.

A very special shout-out to CC's imaginary friend, baby chick, for inspiring a couple of the Malcolm moments in this book.

And thanks to you, reader, for picking up this book and making Lenny Marks part of your life. I hope you liked her.

Kerryn Mayne is an author, former wedding photographer, current police officer, and terrible (but enthusiastic) tennis player. When not at work attempting to solve crime, she is writing about it or preparing an endless stream of snacks for her four children. Kerryn lives in the bayside suburbs of Melbourne with her husband, children, and a highly suspect lovebird. She only owns eleven copies of *The Hobbit* (for now).